SEE CHARLIE RUN

SEE CHARLIE RUN

Brian Freemantle

BANTAM BOOKS
TORONTO · NEW YORK · LONDON · SYDNEY · AUCKLAND

SEE CHARLIE RUN
A Bantam Book / August 1987

Library of Congress Cataloging-in-Publication Data

Freemantle, Brian.
See Charlie run.

I. Title.
PR6056.R43S4   1987   823′.914   86-47963
ISBN 0-553-05213-6

Bantam Books are published by Bantam Books, Inc. Its trademark, consisting of the
words "Bantam Books" and the portrayal of a rooster, is Registered in U.S. Patent
and Trademark Office and in other countries. Marca Registrada. Bantam Books,
Inc., 666 Fifth Avenue, New York, New York 10103.

PRINTED IN THE UNITED STATES OF AMERICA

To Eve and Pete, with much love.

His flight was madness; when our actions do not
Our fears do make us traitors.

—William Shakespeare. *Macbeth*

Prologue

"A defection!" Her astonishment was complete.

"I can't go on like this," he said.

"I just didn't expect a defection."

"It will be difficult. But I can do it."

"What about the danger?" Her surprise became worry now.

"It would be worth it."

"There's no other way?"

He shook his head. "Not that would work completely."

"I'm scared," she admitted.

"There won't be any risk to you," he promised.

"Scared for you, I meant."

"I said I could do it."

"We'd lose everything, with just one mistake."

"I'll be very careful."

She lay very quietly beside him in the bed, her body still wet from their lovemaking, her head cradled against his chest. When she didn't speak for a long time, he said, "Well?"

"You know I'll do anything you want."

"I'll need your help," he said.

"I said I'd do anything."

"But there'll be no risk," he promised again.

She moved her head against his chest, a dismissive gesture at the reassurance. "I love you so much," she said.

"And I love you," he said.

"It *will* be worth it, won't it?" she said, with growing conviction.

"Worth everything," he said.

1

1

Charlie Muffin, who without conceit considered himself a master of survival, came carefully awake and wondered if he was going to survive this one. With his eyes determinedly closed and with the wiseness of an expert in such things refusing to shift his head, one way or the other, it was still awful: bloody awful. The pie, he decided. Bloody stupid to have eaten that plastic-wrapped meat pie out of that pub microwave just before the final drink. Had to be the pie. Nothing else it could be. Islay single malt didn't make anyone feel like this. Not him, anyway. Sodding pie. Probably hanging around for days in that display counter with shit-footed flies route marching all over it, left right, left right, let's give the silly bugger who buys this the worst hangover of his life. Not a hangover, though. Didn't suffer from hangovers. This was food poisoning: headaching, sweat-making, stomach-churning food poisoning. Sodding pub with the sodding pie deserved to be reported to the health authorities. Public menace, to old and young. Christ, he felt awful!

Charlie carefully opened his eyes, wincing protectively. The stab of pain impaled him against the pillow: been worse if the curtains hadn't been pulled against the half-light of seven-thirty. It was difficult to imagine anything worse, at that precise moment. There was something approaching it: he was dying for a pee. Couldn't blame that on the pie: at that moment he could have found good use for the dish, though. Probably how it had been used before he'd eaten out of it, the previous night. Experimentally Charlie moved his head from side to side, the slowest denial in the world. More arrows thudded painfully into his skull. More than likely it hadn't really been Islay malt! The doubt hardened in Charlie's pain-racked mind, developing conviction. A right little salmonella factory, in the basement of that pub: Sweeney Todd's pie shop on one side and bathtub whiskey on the other, brewing rotgut to be sold to unsuspecting and innocent blokes like himself.

Charlie moved with the slowness of someone testing broken limbs, easing his feet and then his legs over the bed edge and elbowing himself up into some resemblance of sitting, hunched forward over his knees. He blinked, testing the pain of the light, and saw that he was still wearing a sock on his left foot; blue, with a triangular pattern. And a hole, not on the big toe where it normally formed but in the middle. Charlie, who suffered from his feet and therefore devoted much attention to them, decided that his left foot wouldn't have been cold if his right one hadn't: must have forgotten to take it off, then. Funny place for a hole to be. Couldn't blame that on the pie, either. He moved his feet, rippling his toes; one of the few parts of his body that didn't hurt at the moment. They would, soon enough. Except that he wasn't using his feet much. Which was the problem, Charlie recognized. He was streetwise—the snide majority in the department thought "gutter-wise" more accurate—but wasn't being allowed out in the street. Bloody clerk, instead. So there'd been a defection and when a defection occurred it was necessary to review for damage assessment everything in which the traitorous bastard had ever been involved. But Charlie didn't go for all that crap about his being the most experienced man in the department, better able than most to spot the difficulties that a younger man might have missed. He was being pigeonholed, he decided: stuck in a fucking filing cabinet along with all those dust-smelling documents made out in triplicate and forgotten about. The snide majority found that easy to rationalize: consider it sensible even. Who better to know how a traitor operates than someone who'd been one? Except that he hadn't been, ever: just sacrificed the sacrificers. A lot of people still distrusted him for it, though. So what? They could all go to hell. Charlie stood, groaning: at the moment he knew what hell was like.

He made the bathroom, dealt with his most urgent need,

and then supported himself against the sink, grimacing at his image in the mirror. Little short of a medical miracle to look like he did and still be alive. He proceeded slowly, even when cleaning his teeth, knowing from long experience that any abrupt movement was dangerous. The hand-shake was such that he still knicked himself, shaving. He dabbed several times trying to stop the bleeding and finally stuck a piece of toilet paper over the cut. The bathwater ran cold and he realized the meter needed feeding and when he looked he didn't have the right coin. It didn't look like being a very good day.

Charlie returned to the bedroom, gathering his clothes. The shirt had been fresh yesterday, so it would do once more, and his other suit—the good one—was at the cleaners, so there was no problem of choice: have to get some leather put on the cuffs of this one, before the fray got too much worse. Last a bit longer, though. He was sure he had a blue tie but couldn't find it and reckoned the red one, with the blue stripe, was the next best thing. The shirt collar stuck up, like a flag of surrender. When he pushed it down, it gave up again, so he did as well. He stared around, looking for the missing sock, bending with difficulty beneath the bed and the two chairs without finding it. His vague search became a flare of immediate concern and he moved so quickly it hurt, jerking his head beneath the bed again and then gazing hurriedly around the room, sighing with relief when he located the Hush Puppies, one on top of the other just inside the door. Charlie regarded them with the devoted affection of someone who had succeeded in teaching a much-loved pet to roll over and die for its country. Charlie knew there were a lot of snipers within the department who believed his shoes had died, years ago, but they didn't understand, like they didn't understand a lot of things. It took a long time to mold shoes to the peculiarity of Charlie's feet and once it had been achieved they were lovingly retained, against the agony of replacement. He found another pair of socks which didn't really go with the suit but he didn't care, finished dressing, and then went uncertainly to the kitchen. There was acid in orange juice and Charlie didn't think his stomach could take it: certainly no breakfast. He drank two glasses of water with the eagerness of a Sahara survivor, looked at the contents of the sink, and resolved as firmly as he had the previous day to wash up as soon as he got home. Definitely do it this time.

The bus was crowded and he had to stand, every bump and hole in the road jarring through his head. He realized he wouldn't make it when the bus reached the Embankment. He got off heaving, supporting himself tight lipped and sweating against the river wall until the sickness passed. Sodding pie.

He felt slightly better for the short walk through St. James's Park, actually able to nod a greeting to the outside doorman and then the security officer who checked his documentation, according to the regulations, when he entered the building.

"Nice day," greeted the security officer.

"Needs to improve," said Charlie, with feeling.

Charlie's office—which from earlier experience he thought of as a cell—was at the back of the building, a functional rectangular room overlooking an anonymous rectangular courtyard despised even by scavenging Whitehall pigeons who normally didn't despise anything. Charlie didn't know the identity of anyone whose regulation net-curtained window faced his regulation net-curtained window and was confident none of them knew about him, either. The room was equipped with the required, civil service graded equipment: two five-drawer filing cabinets (central bar locking; color green), rubberized-topped metal-based desk (color green), rib-backed adjustable chair (color black), angle-poise desk lamp (sixty-watt bulb), wastepaper basket (metal), coatrack (five-armed), and carpet square (synthetic material, four feet by four feet) over a composite cork floor. If he were ever promoted, which Charlie doubted, the color scheme would be beige and the carpet square would increase to five feet by five feet. It would still be synthetic, though.

Apart from the curtained window, some natural light penetrated the room through the partition directly opposite his desk, which was fluted glass and enabled a distorted image of the neighboring occupant, Hubert Witherspoon. The man, whose name Charlie thought more fitting to a Noel Coward farce, was a university entrant who regarded Charlie as university entrants invariably seemed to do, as something unusual to be examined under a laboratory microscope. As Charlie slumped, relieved, into his chair, he was aware of the indistinct shape of the other man moving, to register his arrival.

There was the appearance of writing and Charlie wondered if Witherspoon was keeping some sort of log upon him: there were provisions in the regulations for one member of the department to monitor the activities and work ability of another, and Witherspoon was as regulation as the color-coded offices and the measurements of the carpet square. Sick though he still felt, Charlie flickered his fingers, in an obvious wave of greeting. Witherspoon didn't respond, but then he never did.

Sighing in discomfited awareness of the forthcoming concentration necessary, Charlie opened his desk drawer and took out the three files upon the defection he was analyzing, gazing down at the unopened folders. Jeremy Knott, the third secretary at the Bonn embassy who two months earlier had done a hop, skip, and a jump over the Berlin Wall, was, Charlie decided, a right pain in the ass. Picked out as a Foreign Office rising star, the bloody man had served in Brussels and Rome, been accorded access to far too much NATO tactical material, and, from all the evidence Charlie had so far assembled, leaked to his KGB-trained East German mistress enough secrets to give the other Alliance partners the shits for a month, if they found out. They wouldn't, of course. What London *would* be prepared to admit was enough to sour relations for a long time. Charlie opened the last file, recording the man's initial entrance into the diplomatic service and the academic and entry examinations record upon which the prospects for a glittering career had been based, and tried to ignore the on-off band of pain tightening around his head. He read steadily, looking up in sudden recognition and turning away to the rack of reference books behind him, taking out *Who's Who* and the *Diplomatic List*. It didn't take very long and Charlie sat back, smiling. It was only a hunch but Charlie was a man of hunches, a supreme professional who trusted an instinct honed from years of survival. It was certainly worth an investigation: and it would mean a report would have to be written with explanatory notes and that he could spend the rest of the day working on it, take a long lunch hour, and go home early. Maybe it wasn't turning out to be such a bad day, after all. Even the headache seemed to be easing. Hair of the dog at lunchtime, give the meat pies a miss, and by tonight he'd be back in as good a shape as he'd ever be.

Charlie went back to the files he had discarded as read and

assimilated, looking for the connection he wanted, but was vaguely aware of Witherspoon moving in the other office although he didn't realize the man was coming into his section until the door actually opened. Witherspoon stayed in the doorway, flax-haired, stripe-suited, school-tied, and faintly disapproving, looking down at Charlie.

"I took some messages for you, before you arrived."

"Thanks," said Charlie, ignoring the clearly implied criticism of his lateness.

"Accounts telephoned that you're four weeks behind with your expenses and that you're four hundred pounds overdrawn: they won't accept anymore withdrawals, not even if they're countersigned by the Director himself. . . ."

Witherspoon was enjoying himself, Charlie realized; the man actually looked like something out of a Noel Coward production. He said, "That all?"

"No," said the other man, confirming Charlie's impression. "The Director called himself, asking for you. I had to say you weren't in."

"Always essential to tell the truth," agreed Charlie.

"Said he wanted to see you, when you finally got here."

"So why'd you wait half an hour, before telling me?" The bastard, thought Charlie.

"Didn't see you arrive, not right away," said Witherspoon, easily. He came farther into the tiny office, staring intently at Charlie. "You've got a piece of toilet paper, stuck on your face!" he said.

"Disguise," said Charlie.

"Disguise?"

"I'm trying to become shit of the week," said Charlie. "Thought maybe there was a competition."

Witherspoon's own face tightened. He said, "There's something else. Security wants you. . . ." He looked pointedly at the disordered files on Charlie's desk. "Last night's patrol discovered restricted material in an unlocked drawer in your desk. They're red designation. Should have been returned to Records."

"Bet you can quote the regulation?" challenged Charlie.

"I can," said Witherspoon, a man devoid of humor. "It's 120/B."

"I'll try to remember that," promised Charlie.

"It's probably what the Director wants to see you about," said Witherspoon.

Charlie doubted it. General Sir Alistair Wilson was a professional interested in results, not books of rules. He said, "Looks like I might be in trouble."

"Which is entirely your own fault," lectured Witherspoon. "You know about expenses. Just like you know about red designation files."

"I'm a fool to myself," said Charlie, weighing the cliché.

"It's not a joke!"

Charlie remembered the previous day's shirt and fervently wished he'd had some advance warning of the Director's summons. It had to be seven months since he'd last met the man. He said, "Nothing is funny this morning."

Charlie used the internal, secure line and was told by General Sir Alistair Wilson's personal secretary to come up immediately, which meant it was priority and that they had probably been waiting. Charlie ascended the two floors burning with anger at Witherspoon's purposely delaying the message: sneaky little bastard. When he reached the outer office the woman said, "You're to go straight in," confirming Charlie's apprehension.

The Director was predictably up from his desk, propped against the radiator: the artificial leg fitted badly after the battlefield operation and it pained him to sit too long. He was a bonily thin man, with a large, hawkish nose, and when Charlie saw Wilson's concertina-creased, elbow-patched suit he felt more comfortable about his own shirt and tie. Wilson's appearance was in complete contrast to Peter Harkness. The deputy director was a small-featured, pink-faced man whose suits were always impeccably pressed, whose shirts were always hard collared, and whose hand-tooled brogues were always mirror-sheen polished. Before entering the service Harkness had trained as an accountant; if he'd had five pounds, Charlie would have bet Harkness was behind the expenses embargo.

"Sorry I'm late," apologized Charlie, at once.

"Some inquiry concerning the defector?" asked the Director, giving Charlie the immediate escape.

"Yes," said Charlie, gratefully. Sir Alistair Wilson was a good bloke, one of the few.

Harkness was sitting neatly in front of his superior's desk, knees and feet properly together, saucer in one hand, tea cup in the other. Charlie wondered if the man starched his underpants like he did his shirt collars: at least they stayed down. Harkness frowned up and said, "Are you all right? You don't look well."

"Ate something that didn't agree with me," said Charlie. He looked between the two men, going beyond the immediate impression of complete contrast. They were, he decided, a good combination. Wilson was a former Gkurha commander who specialized in jungle warfare and provided the entrepreneurial brilliance and Harkness kept the books and made sure they balanced.

"How's that inquiry going?" asked Wilson, easing himself into a more comfortable position in front of the window.

"Not too badly," said Charlie, immediately cautious. He'd been around too long to say it was practically over and get shifted prematurely from one rotten job to another rotten job.

"Could someone else take it over?"

Shit, thought Charlie. He said, still cautious, "Take a long change-over briefing. But it might just be possible." There was always the possibility, of course, that the job might be better and not worse: but that wasn't the way his luck usually ran.

"So it can be swapped?" insisted Harkness, determined on a positive answer.

"Yes," said Charlie, reluctantly.

The Director moved with stiff-legged awkwardness to the desk. Rose growing was the man's hobby and at one corner was a vase of Pascali. He looked briefly down at some papers laid out in readiness and then smiled up at Charlie. "It's good, Charlie; could be one of the best. But it won't be easy."

That was the trouble, thought Charlie: they never were. He said, "Another defector damage assessment?"

Wilson smiled, discerning the reason for the question. "It's a defection," he said. "But definitely not another office job. Asia."

The last vestiges of Charlie's headache lifted. Back on the streets: his proper place. Gutters too, if necessary. Whatever, as long as it was operational. He said, "Where?"

"Japan," said the Director.

"Worked Tokyo twice," said Charlie. "Went well both times."

"Let's hope it does this time," said Harkness. "It could be spectacular."

Wilson went back to his papers and said, with dictated formality, "Yuri Kozlov is an operative of Department Eight of Directorate S of the KGB's First Chief Directorate, currently attached to the Soviet embassy in Tokyo. For the past six months he has been negotiating with the Americans, to come over. They want us to share."

"Balls!" said Charlie, at once.

Both men looked up at him, surprised.

"Like you said," continued Charlie, "it could be spectacular. If Kozlov is genuine Department Eight then he's a killer, a trained assassin. He could give details of assassinations that have been carried out and not been detected as such; maybe some indication of future targets. He could detail the training and be used for incredible propaganda, publicly disclosing that the Soviets actually train and dispatch people to kill. To get someone like that, the CIA would think it was Christmas every day. They wouldn't let us or any other service within a million miles. And certainly not offer him, openly. It's wrong."

Wilson smiled again, at Charlie's objections. "I agree with you, absolutely: on the face of it, utter balls."

"Then I don't understand," said Charlie.

"The CIA don't want to share. I bet they're as mad as hell at the idea," continued Wilson. "But they haven't got any choice. From the caution he's showing, I think Kozlov is genuine. He's got a wife, Irena. Also KGB. And also stationed in Tokyo. The deal—Kozlov's deal—is that he'll go over to the Americans and the wife comes over to us."

"Why?" demanded Charlie, even more confused.

"He's openly told the Americans he doesn't expect them to keep the promises they're making, in their eagerness to get him over," took up Harkness. "The Americans have treated defectors badly in the past: milked them dry and then dumped them. And he knows it. Kozlov is taking out insurance, to see he gets everything. There's to be no complete reunion until they've got all they're asking for. Which would seem to be quite a lot. . . ." The neat man coughed, finishing his tea and placing it on the edge of the Director's desk. "If they both went across to the Americans," resumed Harkness, "they'd only be guaranteed one income. Kozlov is demanding separate payments and pension arrangements, his from the Americans, his wife's from us. . . ."

"Which we'll pay, of course: the lot," said the Director.

"They could be apart for years!" said Charlie.

"A further part of the deal," expanded the Director. "Conjugal visits, every month, on neutral territory, under our joint protection."

"I don't like it," said Charlie. "It doesn't feel right."

"Kozlov claims to have worked England," announced Wilson.

"Any trace?" demanded Charlie. Whatever the uncertainties, it was obviously something they had to go for: go all the way.

"Not under that name," said Wilson. "Doesn't mean it isn't true."

"We're going to share everything with the Americans: they tell us what Kozlov says and we tell them what Irena says?" asked Charlie.

"That's what the Americans are promising," said Harkness.

"They won't," insisted Charlie, at once. "They're getting the better part of the deal, with Kozlov himself. They'll just want us to get the woman out. From Kozlov we'll only get the scraps."

Wilson smiled, wolfishly. "Unless he tells us himself."

Charlie answered the smile. "We snatch him, once they're both across?"

"It depends," said Wilson. "I'd prefer to convince him it would be better for them both to come to us in the first place."

"The CIA will try to do the same," said Charlie.

"Of course they will," agreed Wilson. "I never thought it was going to be easy. That's why it's got to be you, Charlie. I want someone who can think dirtier. And quicker."

"Thanks for the character reference!" said Charlie.

"It's the game, Charlie," reminded Wilson. "And there's to be limited contact with the British embassy. . . ."

". . . To reduce any embarrassment if anything goes wrong?" anticipated Charlie. How many times had he heard that?

"It's the same game," said Wilson. "Embassy for communication, nothing else." He slid a photograph of a young-looking man toward Charlie. "Richard Cartright. Young fellow, third posting. We'll advise your arrival. . . ."

"I'll need some assistance," insisted Charlie.

"There'll be everything you want, once you've decided it's absolutely genuine," said Wilson. "Until then, you're on your own."

Charlie worked to rules—his rules, not anything written in triplicate in manuals marked Eyes Only—and an absolutely essential rule was to have someone to hold the shielding umbrella if the shit hit the fan. Which in his experience it nearly always did and this time looked inevitable. He said, "I quite understand about embassy embarrassment but I know someone in Asia on contract. . . ."

"Not Harry Lu," refused Harkness, at once. "He's on the suspect list."

"Why?"

"Auditors found he was charging for informants in the Communist Chinese office in Hong Kong who didn't exist," said Harkness.

Bloody accountant, Charlie thought again. He said, "Everyone does that."

Harkness winced at the admission. The deputy director said, "It makes him someone who has the potential for being bought. This operation has got to remain absolutely secure."

What about his security? wondered Charlie. He'd have to make his own arrangements. He said, "We've got the positive guarantee of cooperation from the Americans?"

Wilson looked briefly down at the papers in front of him. "The promise came from the CIA headquarters at Langley; the Director himself. Your liaison at the U.S. embassy in Tokyo is Art Fredericks."

Not a name Charlie knew. But then it had been a long time. He said, "Do they know it's going to be me?"

"I cabled them last night," said Wilson.

So all the inquiries about the progress of the Jeremy Knott defection were so much bullshit: nothing changed. Ever. He said, "No reaction?"

"Getting the Kozlovs out, where they're ours, is the only

consideration," said the Director. "What happened a long time ago is just that—history."

If Wilson believed that, then he believed in Father Christmas, the Tooth Fairy, and that the check was always in the mail, decided Charlie. He said, "You'll want me to go right away?"

"There's a direct flight tomorrow night. That gives you a day to hand over the other thing," said Harkness.

Remembering, Charlie said, "Jeremy Knott was at Cambridge: read history at Kings. Another undergraduate was Herbert Bell, who's now an under secretary here at the Foreign Office. They were both friends, at Cambridge; members of the debating society. I found a photograph of them, together. Bell was in Brussels, at the same time as Knott. And there was a six-months overlap in Rome."

"So?" asked Wilson.

"In the assessment survey afterward I found a statement from Bell that Jeremy Knott was only a casual acquaintance: that they had not met or had contact after Cambridge," said Charlie. "Foreign Office background reports record them occupying the same House at Cambridge, and Bell's father actually provided Knott with a character reference, for his Foreign Office entry."

"I can understand a permanent government official wanting to avoid the public embarrassment of known association with a traitor," said Harkness, reasonably.

"Bell had access to most of the NATO stuff that Knott was convicted of passing over," said Charlie. "I checked it. It smells wrong."

"You mean that Knott was just the conduit, who happened to get caught?" demanded Wilson. "And then kept quiet, to allow Bell to stay in place?"

Maybe the man didn't believe in Father Christmas and the Tooth Fairy, after all. Charlie said, "I mean I think it would be a good idea to put some surveillance on Bell; maybe channel something through him and keep a watch to see if it surfaces somewhere."

Wilson nodded the instruction to his deputy and said to Charlie, "Pass the files over to Witherspoon, to continue the assessment. . . ." He hesitated, briefly. "But don't tell him about the Knott and Bell connection. Let's see if he comes up with it."

The sort of thing he'd that morning suspected Witherspoon was doing to him, recalled Charlie. The snotty little prick deserved it. He said, "I'll do that. . . ." Charlie allowed just the right degree of pause and then went on, "I'm afraid there might be a problem making tomorrow night's plane."

"Why?" Wilson frowned.

"Seems accounts want my expenses brought up to date and won't advance me any more money until they are," said Charlie, intentionally avoiding Harkness's look. "And I'm going to need quite an advance, going to Japan. Expensive place."

The Director made an impatient gesture and said to Harkness, "For God's sake get it fixed, on my authority. Bloody men with adding machines!"

"It's regulations," tried Harkness.

"Bugger regulations!" said Wilson. "We haven't got time to waste, not now."

Charlie looked expressionlessly at the deputy director, registering the man's flush of anger. He'd *known* that Harkness had initiated the expenses purge. That would teach the prissy fart: and there was still that nitpicking security difficulty. Charlie said, "There could be another delay: there's some sort of security inquiry. I retained the files last night, so I could be sure of the connection between Knott and Bell. I know it was wrong, but I was only out for about thirty minutes, for a late supper."

"Nonsense to expect you to return them, while you were still working on them," judged Wilson, impatiently. To Harkness he said again, "Sort that out as well, will you?"

The color of Harkness's face deepened to match the desktop roses and Charlie decided that it was game, set, and match.

"Be careful in Japan, Charlie," warned Wilson. "I want the Kozlovs but I don't want it blowing up in my face."

I'm more interested in my face than in yours, thought Charlie. And nothing is going to blow up into it if I can help it. He said, "I have authority to abort?"

"Not without consultation," qualified Wilson. "And well done about the Knott defection."

Which, compared to what he was now having to do,

suddenly seemed an attractive assignment. Charlie said, "I'll need to be completely satisfied. I still don't like the feel of it."

"That's what I want you to be," insisted Wilson. "Completely satisfied."

The transfer order had come down from upstairs by the time Charlie had collected all the Knott files and carried them from one cell to the other, to pass the assessment over to Hubert Witherspoon. Pedantically Charlie had Witherspoon sign a receipt and Witherspoon said smugly, "On suspension?"

"Nope," said Charlie. "Reassigned."

The regulations—department, not personal—by which Witherspoon also ran his life prevented the man from making any sort of inquiry and for once Charlie was grateful for them, aware of Witherspoon's impotent irritation. Trying to increase it, Charlie added, "Feeling was that you could sort out the last bits and pieces of this: I've already submitted a provisional report."

"What am I expected to do?" asked Witherspoon, concerned.

"Find out what I missed," said Charlie.

"Anything I should particularly watch out for?" pressed the man.

Charlie hesitated and then said, "Yes. Be careful of the meat pies."

"The confounded man is intentionally insubordinate," protested Harkness. "You didn't believe that rubbish about slipping out for a late supper, did you?"

"Of course not," said the Director, who was standing against the radiator again. Through the window he saw the Ministry of Works gardeners working in St. James's Park rosebeds and made a mental note to stop on his way home to see what they were planting.

"And the accounts will be in a hopeless mess, by the time he gets back from the Far East," persisted Harkness.

"*If* he gets back from the Far East," qualified Wilson, turning back into the room.

"I'm not discounting the difficulties," said Harkness, detecting the criticism.

"I'm prepared to tolerate the insubordination and the

expenses fiddling and even some minimal security lapses," said Wilson. "This is Charlie's sort of job."

"Do you think he's actually done it?" demanded Harkness, obtusely.

"Done what?" said the Director.

"Invented informants, to pad his expenses?"

"Not for a moment," said Wilson. Harkness was an excellent deputy but there were irritations.

"They're a type, you know, he and that man Lu," said Harkness. He'd initiate an audit on Charlie Muffin, just in case.

"Harry Lu's a good freelance: deniable, too, if something goes wrong," said Wilson. "I don't really want to lose him, over a few pounds."

"It's more than a few pounds," argued Harkness, stiffly.

"Let's not do anything final, until after this is over," ordered Wilson.

"It's not just Charlie Muffin's insubordination that is intentional," said Harkness. "Everything about the man . . . the way he dresses . . . all that, is calculated to irritate, for no other reason than for his own amusement."

"I'm not sure that's the only reason," said Wilson.

"The Americans won't like it being him," insisted the deputy. "They won't have forgotten he brought their Director down as well as ours in that ridiculous retribution business."

"They'll accept him, to get Kozlov," said Wilson. He paused, then said, "Don't forget our predecessors planned to dump Charlie Muffin."

"I don't agree with the method but sometimes I think they had a point of view," said Harkness.

The secretary was waiting, when the deputy got back to his own office.

"Accounts want to speak to you," she said. "Charlie Muffin is indenting for a thousand pounds."

"Confounded man!" said Harkness, whose limit of outrage was restricted, because he never swore, considering obscenity a careless use of words and he was a man careless about nothing.

"I thought he is on the stop list," said the woman.

"*Was*," corrected the deputy, miserably. He'd definitely initiate an audit. And take another precaution. It was right that the embassy should be distanced but Charlie Muffin was unpredictable. It was necessary to warn Richard Cartright and have him monitor what the dreadful man did.

Jun Hayashi did not consider he had betrayed the failed revolution of the Japanese Red Army; rather, they had betrayed themselves, allowing the authorities to defeat them. Hayashi had not been defeated. Now it was a private revolution. He parked the Toyota coupe the Russian money had already provided and went—early as always—into Haneda Control Tower, the youngest supervisor there.

2

Art Fredericks disembarked from the train onto the miniscule platform, momentarily drawing back from the crush of people filing obediently in the direction of the first of the shrines in Kamakura, admiring Kozlov's choice and recognizing, reluctantly, that the Russian was a clever bastard. And recognizing, pleased, that he'd been cleverer.

Kozlov had chosen the location, which he had always done since establishing contact, and Kamakura was perfect. Wherever the Russian was—and Fredericks knew he would be watching from somewhere—the tiny station and the single exit from it enabled the man complete surveillances, to determine if Fredericks was alone or accompanied by minders: or worse, snatch squads. Fredericks joined the crush, thinking as he had a dozen times since coming to Japan that everything would have been a goddamned sight easier if he weren't a round-eye, so easily distinguishable from all the other tourists. By the same token, he accepted realistically, it should make Kozlov easier to identify. Fredericks didn't bother to search, knowing by now of Kozlov's expertise and that to try to locate him, wherever he was, would be pointless: another of Kozlov's insistences was that as well as selecting the meeting places he should always initiate the contact, never giving any indication where or how it might be. Clever bastard, thought Fredericks again, conscious of the attention from the Japanese immediately around him. Fredericks was a tall, heavy man fighting a losing battle to prevent the muscle of his college heavyweight boxing days turning to fat, but he knew, unoffended, that it was not his size which intrigued them. It was the hair. Not only was it tightly curled and thick on his head but thatched on his chest and obvious today because he wore an open sports shirt and matted, too, down from his arms, to cover the backs of his hands. His Japanese wasn't good enough to overhear if they were calling him monkey: he knew it was a frequently used word. One day, he thought, he would have to ask somebody why the Japanese never had any body hair.

The American went, according to the Russian's instructions, toward the Meigetsu-In temple. An expert himself, the CIA agent carried a camera and went into his tourist cover, stopping several times to photograph the foam of hydrangeas through which he had to climb to reach the building. He lingered at the main building and then stopped to photograph the smoldering fire upon which the students burned their wood-inscribed prayers for examination success, all the time alert for the approach. Which never came. Ten minutes had been the time limit.

As Fredericks turned and started to descend the long walkway, he saw Harry Fish at one of the side shrines. The other CIA man whom Fredericks had sent in advance, with the rest of the team, showed no recognition and neither, of course, did Fredericks.

The next designated spot was very close. Fredericks walked easily back toward the railway tracks, wondering if the whole business was going to be a waste of time. Langley was insisting he try and so he would, but Fredericks thought he'd reached a pretty sound judgment about the Russian on their three previous encounters and guessed Kozlov would tell him to go to hell. The American hoped that was the man's only reaction; Fredericks's feeling was that Kozlov was too valuable a catch to risk challenging the arrangements at this stage. The time to change everything was when they got the man across, when it would be too late for him to do anything about it. At this stage it was still possible for Kozlov to back away from the whole thing.

Fredericks entered the Enno-Ji temple, privately amused at his thoughts of Kozlov telling them to go to hell when he saw the ten kings of Hades grimacing down from their places. He hoped it wasn't an omen. He took more photographs, isolating

Hank Levine near a side door, apparently engrossed in an English-language guidebook about the temple. Fredericks bought a book of his own, to fill in the stipulated time limit, wondering if Kozlov would make him complete the entire route. It was possible. For the first time this was a meeting reqested by the Americans, not by the man himself. So Kozlov would be nervous, unsure of the reason and taking every precaution.

The American paused outside the second temple, looking at the guidebook he'd just bought. There was a map of the tourist spots just inside the cover and Fredericks decided that Daibutsu was too far away to walk. He had to return almost to the railway station to get a cab, and as he settled into the back he hoped he didn't have to make every point Kozlov had listed. At the entrance to the third spot the cabdriver said, "I wait?" and the American hesitated, momentarily, attracted by the thought of permanent transport. Reluctantly he shook his head.

Beyond the narrow entrance the Kotoku-In temple ballooned out, dominated by the enormous figure of the open-air Buddha, with its curious head-down stare. At least, reflected Fredericks, going into his routine, his parents in Little Rock were going to get quite a range of holiday pictures. In the tourist shop to the right, Jimmy Dale, who hadn't bothered with a camera of his own, was sifting through the professionally taken selection. Fredericks hoped that Kozlov's caution wouldn't prevent his making any sort of meeting at all. The guys were pretty pissed off losing this entire Saturday.

"Interesting, isn't it?"

Fredericks managed—just—to prevent the jump of surprise. He'd been tensed, waiting, and he'd still missed the goddamned man until he was right alongside. The irritation, at the thought of Kozlov's expertise being better than his own, dampened the satisfaction at the man's having kept the meeting. Falling into the role dictated by Kozlov, that of Western tourists getting into casual conversation over a point of interest, Fredericks said, "Yes. The position seems unusual."

This was the testing period, the time when both engaged in seemingly meaningless conversation while each checked that the other had kept to the understanding and come alone. Which was why Fredericks had moved the other guys in overnight, so they could get to the spots early and be in place when he arrived, not obviously follow him in. Although he appeared to be looking at the statue, Kozlov's attention was upon the narrow entrance. It was the only one there was and Fredericks realized why Kozlov had chosen this place in preference to all the others. Clever bastard, he thought once more.

Kozlov appeared to consult a reference book and said, "It wasn't originally created like that. There was a tidal wave, about a hundred years ago. It washed away the temple in which the figure was housed and forced its head forward, in that strange position. The people who worship him decided that he didn't want to live in an enclosed house; that's why he's permanently in the open. Why have you asked to meet?"

The circumstances meant that Kozlov had to be by himself, if the defection request was genuine. Which still had to be proved. Until which time he had to watch his own back. Dale had realized the contact and positioned himself perfectly, a roof support protectively behind him and the open square dominated by the Buddha set out in front. Covered then, thought Fredericks; there were a group of obvious Western tourists— fellow Americans, he guessed from their dress—filing in through the rear door to examine the hollow interior of the statue, but apart from that there were no Caucasians at all in the area. Maybe, decided Fredericks, there were certain advantages after all in being a round-eye in Asia. Kozlov was alone: it was an important point to make, when Washington made yet another of its demands for indicators whether or not Kozlov was for real. He said, "That's a cute story. There's something important for us to talk through."

"I don't know how they're going to interpret the next tidal wave or typhoon: this place seems to be right in the path of natural disasters," said the Russian. "You've got all the details of the British involvement?"

"No," said Fredericks, directly. There was no purpose in continuing the avoidance and the split-against-eavesdropping double talk, now that they were both sure. He was conscious of the Russian's abrupt head turn toward him.

"Why no?" demanded the man. "That was all that remained to be fixed, after our meetings. Why I agreed to come today, when I got the signal. Everything else had been discussed."

Kozlov's rising anger was as Fredericks had feared and warned it might be. After Kozlov's first approach their encounters had always been his decision, confirmed in the most simple—and therefore the safest—way. The Agency permanently maintained a room—323—in the Imperial Hotel, with its view of the palace: by some irony, Jimmy Dale, who was now guarding him against any unexpected eventuality, was the man who occupied it, to cover against any hotel-staff curiosity. If Kozlov wanted contact, he telephoned a supposed inquiry against the room number, giving the place. Every three days— purporting to be Dale—he called the hotel, checking messages. The American response, if they wanted a meeting, was for the message to be that a conference was necessary, as always leaving Kozlov to be the decider of where the meeting should be. Fredericks had invoked the system on the American part four days earlier, for the first time. The American said, "My people aren't happy about the British. You've no cause to distrust us. We'll keep every promise that we've made: on my life!"

Kozlov began to move, apparently wanting to view the Buddha from a different angle. Fredericks had to go as well, to keep up with him. Kozlov said viciously, "You're trying to trick me, like I always knew you would!"

"No!" said Fredericks, worried. "We're doing everything you asked. Hear me out."

The other man stopped, using the camera that he carried. "What is it?" he asked.

Inviting the other man's understanding, Fredericks said, "It's not me. It's headquarters. You know what headquarters are like."

"What do they want?"

"It's unnecessary—they feel it's unnecessary—to bring the British in. . . ." Fredericks saw the other man start to speak and said urgently, "Wait! Let me finish! You said you wanted five hundred thousand dollars, for yourself. We'll double it, to a million, which will give you what you'd get from the British, for Irena. We'll get you both out: new identities, protection, everything. You can choose whatever house you want, anywhere in America. . . ."

"We've talked through all this," dismissed Kozlov. "This is a ridiculous conversation."

"You've no *reason* to think we won't keep our undertaking," insisted Fredericks, desperately. "I've been told to offer you whatever guarantee you need."

Kozlov, who was a small, unobtrusive man of seemingly apparent calmness, said, "I've already set out the guarantees I need." He closed his camera, a positive movement. "It's over," he declared. "Finished."

"No!" protested Fredericks, yet again. He was hot with fear, knowing what would happen if he lost the man. They were a bunch of stupid bastards, back there at Langley: trying to impress one another with a lot of bullshit talk in comfortable conference rooms, we want this and we want that and we want this, ignoring the warnings he'd sent. And if it fucked up, because of how they wanted it done, it would be his fault and his butt, with a lot more bullshit talk about his incompetence and his inexperience and how they should have sent someone else, who could have done it their way. Fredericks said, "It was a sincere offer; *is* a sincere offer. But if you want it to stay the way it was, then fine."

"If it was fine my way, you wouldn't have tried to change," said Kozlov, unmollified.

Fredericks tried to subdue his apprehension, calling upon the other man's experience. "You know the way it is," he urged. "Wouldn't your people try to do the same, if someone from the CIA tried to split a crossing, say between Russia and Poland?"

"We control the Polish service," refused Kozlov, pedantically. "They'd do as they were told."

"You're aware of what I mean," persisted Fredericks. "We want you, Yuri. But we want the whole package, complete. Not divided, like this."

Kozlov smiled, a rare expression, and Fredericks felt a surge of relief. The Russian said, "I've made your headquarters nervous?"

Fredericks hesitated, unsure of the response the other man wanted. Then he said, "Yes. It's an unusual demand."

"It was meant to be," said the Russian. "I won't be cheated. Or tricked."

"Like I've said . . ." tried the American, but Kozlov talked across him.

". . . So don't bother saying it again," interrupted the Russian. "I accept that you were only doing what you were told to do by Washington. But that means you hadn't properly explained the situation, for them to understand how pointless it would be. It's my way or it's no way at all. You've known that from the beginning."

Kozlov was arrogant as well as clever, decided Fredericks. He said, "All right. Your way, entirely."

"What about the British?" demanded Kozlov.

"There's been some communication," qualified Fredericks. "No one has actually arrived yet."

"You delayed, to see what would happen today?" anticipated Kozlov.

Now Fredericks smiled. "Yes," he admitted. "I'm sorry."

"I believe it wasn't your fault," said Kozlov. "We suffer fools at Dzerzhinsky Square, too. It won't happen again?"

"No," promised Fredericks, hopefully. Damn Langley and empire builders, he thought.

"How much longer?" pressed Kozlov.

"I'll tell Langley today. Say it must be soon."

"Very soon," insisted the Russian. "It's easy for suspicion to arise in a Soviet embassy."

"You think something is wrong?" asked Fredericks, feeling new concern.

"Not yet: I'm sure of that. Irena is as alert as I am, so I'm confident we would have detected something, between us . . ." He smiled again. "I'm just a very cautious person; I was trained that way."

"I understand," assured Fredericks. "I'll make everything very clear."

"I want you to leave here first," said Kozlov.

"Of course."

"We'll maintain the same method of contact," said the Russian.

"Yes."

"Your people at Langley are stupid."

"Yes," agreed Fredericks, sincerely. "They're very stupid."

The American felt strangely self-conscious, going out of the temple with the Russian watching him. The feeling was soon overtaken by another, better sensation. Kozlov thought he controlled everything and that they jumped when he said jump, but Jim Dale was back there, watching everything the guy did. Which made him the cleverer of the two, decided Fredericks, satisfied.

The arrangement had been that each of the people guarding him returned to the U.S. embassy at Akasaka Toranomon directly after the failed meetings, to avoid any danger of identification from the possibly watching Kozlov, so Fish and Levine were back in Tokyo ahead of Fredericks. While they awaited the arrival of Dale—together with Winslow Elliott and Takeo Yamada, the two other CIA men whose wait at the other places set out but not used by the Russian had been pointless—Fredericks encoded Kozlov's reaction and transmitted it to Washington. He took a lot of trouble, wanting without making the criticism obvious for CIA headquarters fully to understand how near they had come to fouling up the whole thing by imagining remote control was possible. Fredericks waited in the code room for half an hour for their response. When it finally came it was limited to the briefly formal acknowledgment of receipt, and Fredericks knew he'd got the message home. Now they'd be scurrying around, each trying to dump on the other and avoid the responsibility for coming so close to disaster.

By the time he got back to the CIA section within the embassy, the other three men had returned and were waiting for him and Fredericks made no attempt to sanitize the account, as he had to Langley.

"Kozlov's right," said Levine, when the CIA supervisor finished the explanation. "Langley is stupid. Kozlov might appear calm, to you. But inwardly he'll be screwed up tighter than a spring; he can't be any other way. It'll only take the slightest thing to spook him."

"I've told them that," reminded Fredericks.

"What did they say?" asked Fish.

"Nothing."

They all knew, like Fredericks, what the silence meant and there were various smiles around the room.

"You know what I think," said Elliott, who was irritated at what he considered a wasted day. "I think we should snatch him. Arrange another meeting, like today, put extra men in everywhere and then jump him. Get some sort of knockout stuff from Technical Division, sedate him until we get him onto a military plane, and stop all this screwing about."

"What sort of dumb-assed idea is that!" erupted Fredericks, genuinely irritated but also venting some of his earlier anger upon the man. "That's kidnapping, for Christ's sake! We'd have Moscow going ape, Japan screaming, and Kozlov hostile without the wife he eventually wants with him. Why stop at Kozlov, if that's the way we're going to operate! Why not snatch Gorbachev and the entire fucking Politburo and run the Soviet Union from some cozy little safe house in Virginia!"

Elliott shifted under the ferocity of the attack, looking embarrassed. "It was an idea," he said, awkwardly.

"Dumb-assed," repeated Fredericks, dismissively. "Let's start behaving professionally." He looked to the men who had waited fruitlessly at the first two shrines. "Well?"

"No one was monitoring you," said Fish, "I'm sure of it."

"You were clean at the Enno-Ji temple, too," said Levine.

"Jim?" asked Fredericks.

The CIA agent who had monitored the actual encounter was a sandy-haired man newly posted from Washington. He nervously took off his glasses and said, "Squeaky clean. There was only one other group of Caucasians around the Buddha—"

"American?" interrupted Fredericks.

Dale nodded. "Made a point of checking, after you left. A Lions club, from Milwaukee. Throughout the entire time you were with Kozlov no one showed the slightest interest."

Fredericks was silent for several moments, remembering his assessment in the Buddha temple. "If he's by himself, it indicates he's genuine," he said, trying the opinion out on the others. "If it were some sort of trick, some entrapment embarrassment for instance, he'd be mob-handed: people identifying me, stuff like that."

"I'd say so," agreed Yamada, an American-born Japanese.

"Me too," said Fish.

"Still seems a lot of screwing around," said Elliott truculently.

Fredericks ignored the man, returning to Dale. "What happened after I left?"

"He checked, for surveillance," said the American, wanting to boast his recognition and avoidance. "Went right by me into the souvenir shop: actually bought a keyring. Then he went inside the Buddha. It's hollow, you know."

"Spare me the tourist crap," said Fredericks. "I heard it all from Kozlov when he was clearing his path. Sure he didn't spot you?"

"Positive," said Dale. "I told you I checked the Milwaukee group. Got into conversation with a couple of old guys and left the temple with them, like I was one of the party."

"Good deal," praised Fredericks.

"So we've got to work with the British?" said Yamada, introducing into the conversation what everyone had been avoiding.

"We've still to get the word from Langley," said Fredericks, cautiously. "But that's how it looks."

"But *him*!" protested Elliott, gesturing to the file that had been airfreighted overnight from Washington and lay on Fredericks's desk, a picture of Charlie Muffin uppermost.

"Him," confirmed Fredericks. "He's the person London nominated."

"Do you know what the son of a bitch did!" demanded Elliott.

"I know the stories, like everyone else," said Fredericks.

"He's a fucking Commie traitor!"

"There's an argument against that, sufficient for the British."

"I don't give a damn about what's sufficient for the British," argued Elliott, feeling on safe ground now and trying to recover from the previous mistake. "This thing is uncertain enough as it is, without his involvement."

"Could be useful, precisely because of that uncertainty," said Fredericks, evenly.

The tone of the supervisor's voice halted Elliott's outburst. He hesitated and then said, smiling, "We're going to use him?"

"We're still feeling out in the dark about Kozlov," reminded Fredericks. "More things can still go wrong than we can even guess at. The participation of someone like Charlie Muffin—a man who provably screwed the British and American services and got both Directors arrested by the Soviets in doing it— gives us a hell of an insurance policy, don't you think?"

Smiles from the other men in the room matched that of Elliott but it was the disgruntled man who spoke. "I *like* that," said Elliott. "I like that very much indeed."

"*Only* if something goes wrong with Kozlov?" pressed Levine, who knew as well the American side of the history.

"Let's get Kozlov in the bag," said Fredericks. "Once

we've achieved that and got the woman as well, we can think of settling things with Charlie Muffin."

"The British aren't going to keep the woman?" queried Dale, embarrassed the moment he spoke at showing his inexperience.

Elliott actually laughed, glad that finally the ridicule had shifted from him.

More kindly, Fredericks said, "Come on, Jim, what do you think! Do you really imagine we're going to let the Limeys—and more particularly a Limey who made one of our Directors prick of the month—get his hand in the cookie jar? Kozlov wants his particular cross-over deal and after this morning he'll get it. He'll get the British baby-sitting his wife and he'll get us, promising the keys to Fort Knox. And when we hit them, the British—but more importantly Charlie Muffin—will think World War Three has started in their own backyard."

"Which will serve the bastards right," said Yamada. "Can you believe the incredible arrogance, sending that man at all!"

"We'd have screwed them whoever their man was," reminded Fredericks. "Charlie Muffin just makes it that much sweeter."

"Me!" demanded Elliott, with sudden urgency. "When it happens, I want to be the one who fixes the son of a bitch: who teaches him a lesson!"

Fredericks recognized that Elliott was a worrying weakness, someone whose objective balance could not be trusted in a moment of absolute crisis. "We'll see," he said, avoiding any sort of commitment. "There's so much that's more important, initially, before we start concerning ourselves with side issues."

"I don't regard settling things with Charlie Muffin as a side issue," disputed Elliott, who saw retribution as the surest way to impress those gray-suited, anonymous men at Langley upon whom promotion always depended. "We lost a lot of face and a lot of people over that man. He can't be allowed to escape, not a second time."

"We'll see," reiterated Fredericks. He would have to take care that this man did not become a difficulty. There were already too many uncertainties as it was.

The Shiba Park is conveniently close to the Soviet embassy so the contact was arranged there. Although the meeting was flexible, for Irena's benefit, she was still later than the time they had estimated. Kozlov showed no impatience, either while he waited near the Tokyo Tower, with its added radio mast to make it taller (and therefore marginally better) than Paris's Eiffel Tower, of which it is an exact copy, or when she actually entered the recreation area. He did not approach her even then and she made no attempt to make directly for him, either. Instead she walked with apparent casualness along a perimeter pathway intentionally chosen to take her a long time to reach him, enabling Kozlov to seek any pursuit for which he knew she would already have checked, at least six times since leaving the Soviet enclave. Kozlov was actually against one of the struts of the tower, confident that he was completely concealed, because they had rehearsed and ensured that, too. It was a hot evening and the park was crowded—another advantage—but Kozlov was sure no one who came in after his wife was following her. Still he waited, not breaking the arranged pattern, remaining intent upon those behind her in case the followers—either American or fellow Russian—were as professional as he considered himself to be. It was unlikely but still possible. Still nothing. Waiting for Irena to complete the prepared route, Kozlov allowed himself a brief, satisfied smile. Today had been unsettling, a minor hiccup, but he was still absolutely in charge and in control of everything. It was a comforting feeling. It was going to work brilliantly, as he'd always planned that it should.

Irena showed no recognition when she reached the base of the tower, waiting for Kozlov's approach to signal they weren't under any observation, and positioning herself against a concealing strut as an added precaution. When he eventually approached she said, unsmiling, "Well?"

"You're clear," he said.

"I already knew that," she said, the confidence obvious. Irena Kozlov was an altogether big woman, prominent nosed, large featured, big busted, wide hipped, and much taller than her husband. She wore her hair strained back in a severe bun, and because of her size it was difficult for her to buy clothes in small-statured Japan. Those she had on today had been bought in Bonn during their first posting together, and worn in preference to anything Russian against the unlikely but still remote possibility of their being identified as coming from the Soviet Union.

"Was I monitored?" he said.

"Every time," confirmed Irena, who had been her husband's protector in the three meeting places at Kamakura that Art Fredericks had visited that day. "They weren't very impressive, any of them. I took photographs of all three and compared them for confirmation back at the embassy, against the picture files we have on the American diplomatic personnel. The man at Meigetsu-In is named Harry Fish, at Enno-Ji it was someone called Levine, and during the meeting it was Jimmy Dale. . . ." The woman paused. "We didn't have Dale positively identified as CIA, incidentally. So everything can be justified to Moscow quite properly. Is everything arranged?"

Kozlov shook his head, abbreviating the purpose of Fredericks's summons, looking not at his wife but beyond her, still checking the park.

"Today it was to be settled!" complained Irena, at once.

"I threatened to call everything off, to withdraw." Kozlov looked toward her. "Frightened the silly man to death."

"They are trying to trick us!" she insisted.

Kozlov shook his head again. "I was expecting it," he said. "It was something they had to attempt."

"Why didn't they take you seriously, from the beginning!"

"They do now," insisted Kozlov. "It's good they only put one man in each place, to protect Fredericks. I was nervous of a commando squad."

"There's been no warning, from Hayashi at the airport."

"They could have arrived by commercial airline, not necessarily military."

"You've briefed Hayashi?"

"Of course," he said. "Anything military, British or American."

"We always chose public places, to avoid a snatch," she reminded him.

"Did the man Dale take any photographs?"

"No," said Irena. "Pure surveillance. Not particularly good, either."

"He couldn't have identified you?"

"Don't be ridiculous!" she said, annoyed at the suggestion. "I tagged on to a party of Americans, as if I needed the translation. Dale actually spoke to two men, within a few feet of me."

"No one followed me out," said Kozlov. The statement was faintly questioning, because he had been alert.

"He left with me, while you were in the souvenir shop!"

Kozlov shook his head in disbelief and then, reminded, said, "I bought you a present. There'll be something better, later."

Irena took the keyring, smiling up at her husband for the first time. "There's a lot I want, when we get to the West."

"There won't be any more stupidity like today," promised Kozlov. "Fredericks was really frightened."

"I wonder if the British will be more professional," said the woman.

At that moment Charlie Muffin approached the bar in the departure lounge of London airport, eight hundred pounds in travelers' checks comfortably fat in his wallet and two hundred pounds in cash even more comfortably bulging his trouser pocket. There wasn't any Islay malt so he chose Glenlivet, peeling off the first of the notes that Harkness had failed to stop him from getting and knowing the drink would taste all the better because of it. And not just because of the thousand pounds. Aware of how the clerks gossiped—despite the supposed restriction of the Official Secrets Act—Charlie had allowed exactly twelve hours for the word to circulate before demanding a first-class ticket. And got it because the permanent mandarins had been too shit-scared to query the authority.

"Going far, sir?" asked the barman, the perpetually polite question.

"As far as I can go," said Charlie.

3

Adapting the When in Rome principle, Charlie took a Suntory whiskey from the room bar and carried it to the window, gazing out over Tokyo. He was high in the tower block of the New Otani and he decided it was a pretty good hotel: a vast, sprawling place with a concealing people-packed shopping complex and more entrances and exits than he'd so far had time to work out. Which he would, of course. First of the Charlie Muffin Survival Rules was always secure an escape route, before discovering what it was necessary to escape from. The early evening lights were coming on, and ironically using as a landmark the Tokyo Tower beneath which the Kozlovs had earlier met, Charlie worked out the positioning of the port and then, closer, the embassy section of the Japanese capital. Minimal use, Charlie remembered. Okay, so if it was important to protect the embassy it was important to protect himself. Doubly so. The CIA would have moved a bloody army in by now, tanks, rocket boosters, and all. Naïve then to expect him to operate without someone watching his back. On a suspect list for charging for nonexistent informants! Charlie snorted, in loud derision. Harry Lu was a damned good agent who'd worked Asia for twenty years as a contract freelance without even the scant protection of a Foreign Office or embassy: probably forgotten more about intelligence than Harkness had ever learned. Bloody daft, not to use him: too late to call Hong Kong now but he'd do it first thing tomorrow, to open up a line of communication. Be good to see Harry again: good drinker,

Harry Lu. Reminded, Charlie helped himself to another miniature bottle of local whiskey, coming to more immediate
considerations. Getting literally to know the ins and outs of the
hotel was the initial priority. See what the bars looked like,
maybe. Then an early night, for tomorrow's meeting with an
American named Art Fredericks: certainly didn't want to eat
again, after all that first-class grub on the plane. Charlie smiled
happily at the thought of Harkness's reaction. Served the
parsimonious bugger right.

Charlie took the elevator to explore the garden lounge area
on the main floor. It was packed with intense, never-say-no
Japanese exchanging business cards in place of handshakes,
anxious to sell a computer and a car to everyone in the world.
Charlie checked out the foyer and then returned to the
secondary elevators serving the shopping floors. He went down
to the ground level and wandered around, feigning interest in
the stores, and then did the same on the four remaining floors
before he got back to the main hotel area, recording the service
stairs and then the fire escape feeding each. A right little rabbit
warren, Charlie judged; it had been a good choice.

On the first walk-through reconnaissance Charlie had noted
the piano bar. A nightcap, he decided: perhaps two. It would,
after all, be the last time he could relax for he didn't know how
long. He was offered a seat at the bar but refused, preferring a
table with a better view of the room and more importantly the
door. He stayed with Suntory, which didn't compare in any way
with single malt but wasn't bad, looking casually around. There
were two Japanese girls seemingly by themselves at the bar and
a European sitting alone at a table. He caught the eye of the girl
at the table and smiled and she half-smiled back. A pleasant end
to a pleasant day? It was an attractive thought, but Charlie
decided against it. He couldn't afford any encumbrances. The
reflection led naturally to his reason for being there. What would
Irena Kozlov be like? he wondered. Not that he was considering
the Russian as he was considering the still hopefully smiling girl
a few tables away, of course. Never mixed business with
pleasure; well, not often, anyway. And definitely not this time.
Too much he still didn't understand or know and he didn't intend
to try to find it out between the sheets: keep the best friend
firmly zipped. He'd never brought a woman defector across
before. He wondered if he would this time; be satisfied, Wilson

had said. And Charlie was determined to be just that, as satisfied as he could possibly be before putting even a usually aching toe into the water. Hell of a catch, if it was genuine.

Predominantly because of his size, Charlie was particularly conscious of the man's entry into the bar, before he directly approached the table. He stood with hair-matted hands against the back of the empty chair and said, "Charlie Muffin?"

"Sorry," denied Charlie, instinctively protective. "You've got the wrong man."

"You may be right," said the man, heavily. "We checked you off the plane at Haneda, followed you here, saw you book into room ten fifteen, and covered you every step of the way while you cased the hotel. Which was the first remotely professional thing you did since arriving. . . ." Uninvited he sat with difficulty in the small chair and said, "I'm Art Fredericks."

Shit, thought Charlie. It *had* been unprofessional, not troubling to clear his path from the moment of arrival. Trying to recover, Charlie stared obviously around the crowded bar. Fredericks saw the look and smiled at the attempt. Nodding to the piano area, where a small bass, guitar, and drums group had replaced the single pianist who had been performing when Charlie first entered, the American said, "The music overlays any listening device. They always come on at eight; that's why I waited until now."

Shit again, thought Charlie. He said, "Very textbook."

"No," said Fredericks, disdaining the mockery. "Properly done—the way it should be. And always is."

"Glad to hear it," said Charlie, foundering and knowing it. "I wouldn't like to be involved in anything amateur."

"Neither would I," said Fredericks. "That's why I'm worried. So far I'm not very impressed."

A waiter hovered and Fredericks said, "Club soda, with ice." The man looked inquiringly at Charlie, who nodded for another whiskey. Charlie finished the one he had and said to the American, "You want to know something! I couldn't give a fuck whether I impress you or not. That's not what I'm here for."

"I know why you're here because I started all this," said Fredericks. "And if you screw up, then the whole thing becomes a disaster. So I *need* to be impressed."

"So do I," fought back Charlie. "I'm not yet convinced that

this is a big deal; is anything at all. So *I* need convincing, about a lot of things."

"I've had four meetings," said Fredericks. "It looks right to me. Every way."

Both men pulled back for the drinks to be served. When the waiter left, Charlie said, "You made any arrangement for me?"

Fredericks stopped with his glass halfway to his lips, frowning. "Arrangements for what?"

"To meet Kozlov. And the woman."

Fredericks put down the glass, without drinking. "It obviously hasn't been properly explained to you," he said, patiently. "Kozlov is ours. You're baby-sitting the woman."

Thank Christ the chance had come, thought Charlie. He said, "I thought I was getting a lecture on professionalism from a professional."

"What are you talking about?" demanded the American.

"Are you seriously suggesting that I go into this without seeing the man himself . . . assessing things for myself. Without seeing the woman, too . . . come on, sunshine!" Although the bar was dark, Charlie was aware of the pinpricks of color on the man's face, showing the anger. Charlie was glad he'd finally managed to unsettle the American.

"This is *our* show," insisted Fredericks. "He came to us. He stays with us. You get the woman. I'll tell you where and when."

"Bullshit," said Charlie.

"What's bullshit?"

"You. The operation. Everything," said Charlie. He sighed, drinking deeply from his glass. "Pity," he said. "I really enjoy Japan. Would have liked it to have lasted longer."

"You want to say something, why don't you say it straight out?" said Fredericks.

"Sure," said Charlie. "The British just withdrew."

Charlie spoke intent upon the other man, alert for the sign and he saw it. If there had been any other way of getting the Kozlovs out, Washington would not have approached London. So the fact that Fredericks was meeting him—within hours of arrival and trying to impose himself as the controller from the word go—meant not only that the British participation was essential but that the Americans were desperate for it.

"You haven't got the authority to withdraw," challenged Fredericks.

"I have," said Charlie. "And that's what I've just done." Dismissively, the action of someone bringing an encounter to a close with a gesture of politeness, Charlie said, "Would you like another drink? Maybe something stronger? I'm going to have the last one." As he turned to catch the waiter, Charlie saw that the smiling girl at the adjoining table was deeply in conversation with a blond-haired man who used his hands a lot when he spoke. Lucky bugger, Charlie thought: she looked like she might have been a goer.

"What do you want?" demanded Fredericks.

"I thought I told you," said Charlie. "I want to see Kozlov and satisfy myself. And then—myself, again not through you—I want to arrange a meeting with the woman and be satisfied about her, as well. And I want you and I to get together and go through everything you've done, from the very first moment of contact. And when I'm satisfied about that, we'll start making plans. . . ."

The waiter's return prevented Fredericks's immediate reaction, which was probably fortunate. This time he ordered whiskey—imported, not local—and when they were alone he said, "I know all about you: what you did. I don't buy that crap, your getting even, for being set up. You cost us a Director and your people a Director. In my book, that makes you a traitor. I don't know how—can't believe how—you managed to convince your own people you're loyal. You haven't impressed us. We think you should have stayed in jail and rotted there. . . ." The drinks came and the American had to stop. "I did everything I could to stop your coming," resumed Fredericks. "I don't want you to be a part of anything."

It was impressive bluster but Charlie guessed he'd won. He said, "You got a point?"

Fredericks's face stiffened as he realized his early advantage had gone. Striving to regain it, he leaned across the table toward Charlie and said, "You listen and you listen good. We've got a hell of a file on you so I know all about the act, too: the fuck-everybody-I'm-the-best routine. And I don't buy that, either. You're a jumped-up jerk and if you try anything clever—anything at all—it's going to be your ass. That's a personal promise. You understand?"

He's a big bastard, thought Charlie, letting the silence grow between them: probably thinks he could do it. Charlie said, "I'll be careful crossing roads."

Fredericks's face grew taut, at the open mockery. "Yes," he said, with soft-voiced sincerity: "You be very careful."

"Haven't we sidetracked a little?" It was good to be in control, Charlie thought. It had definitely been careless, earlier, though. He promised himself he wouldn't make another mistake like that: he couldn't afford to.

"What?" demanded Fredericks.

"You've got a contact procedure?"

"Of course."

"Use it, to set a meeting up for me. Alone."

Fredericks shifted, uncomfortable at Kozlov's reaction the last time. He said, "He expects the crossing details at the next meeting."

"Before anyone's met the woman!" jeered Charlie. "You just answered a question. The guy's not professional and the whole thing is a load of balls. No one in their right minds would move, at this stage. He should know that. So should you."

Fredericks was sweating, angry at being so easily exposed. He said, "He's frightened. Wants things to happen as quickly as possible."

"I'm frightened," said Charlie. "Too frightened to move things more quickly than they should be moved."

"He's very cautious, too," said the American. "I'm his contact. He won't make a rendezvous with anyone else."

"Meet him first, then," agreed Charlie. "Tell him the reason. I won't come in, to scare him away, until I get the signal from you."

Fredericks controlled any expression of satisfaction. It would mean that he would be present throughout the entire encounter: that the son of a bitch couldn't try anything smart. "You won't go ahead, without a meeting?" said Fredericks, as if the agreement were being forced reluctantly from him.

"Definitely not," said Charlie, positively.

"I'll do it," said Fredericks. "It'll take a day or two."

"So there'll be time for you fully to brief me on everything that's happened so far?" said Charlie.

Fredericks just succeeded in biting back the go-to-hell

refusal that came automatically to mind. "Sure," he said, instead.

Later, back at the tower block window and looking out over the now lit-up Tokyo, Charlie decided it hadn't been bad, after all. Not as good as it should have been, of course, but still not bad. He'd made a good enough recovery and recognized sufficiently early that Fredericks was overconfident and been able to use it against the man. There was always the danger that Fredericks would review everything that had been said and promised and realize the mistakes he'd made, but Charlie didn't think so. The American attitude at how he'd screwed their Director was inevitable, Charlie supposed. It had been another mistake of Fredericks's, making it as obvious as he had. It meant, reflected Charlie, that he'd had good early warning. Which was always a bonus.

"You were lucky, Charlie: bloody lucky," he said to his own flop-haired, loose-tied reflection. He hoped he stayed that way.

"I don't believe it!" exploded Levine, when Fredericks finished the account to the assembled CIA team. "What the hell does he think he's doing, running the operation!"

It hadn't been posed as that sort of question, but Fredericks paused before responding and then said, "Yes. I guess that's exactly what he thinks. Or wants to do."

"Tell him to go kiss ass," said Elliott. "This thing is going to fuck up and it's going to fuck up over Charlie Muffin."

"I'd have argued the same way as he did, in the same circumstances," said Yamada, more reasonably. "I wouldn't take second string in a British setup, not without trying to make some sort of independent assessment."

"From the sloppy way he behaved when he arrived today, I'm surprised he thought of it," said Levine.

"Sloppy is a good word," said Fish, who had been the airport surveillance. "I've seen bag women on Forty-second Street in better shape than he's in."

"Think he meant it, about pulling out?" asked Dale. "We'd be in bad shape if he did. Don't forget what Kozlov said."

Fredericks looked irritably at the man, not needing any reminder. "I think he meant it," he said. "What I don't know is if he's got the authority. Which is why I'm checking. Be great to slap the cocky bastard into line."

* * *

Harkness handed the Director the inquiry that had come from Langley and said, "That's directly contrary to what you insisted. There *had* to be communication between us, before he considered an abort. He hasn't even been in contact with our embassy. I've checked."

"I know what I said." Wilson smiled. That morning he'd brought some Anne Cocker floribunda from the garden in Hampshire. He took one of the roses from the vase on his desk, sniffing it reflectively. "Charlie's only been in Tokyo a matter of hours," he said. "That's not enough time for anyone to decide whether to abort or not. He's bargaining."

"He should have made contact," insisted Harkness.

"Maybe the circumstances didn't allow it," said Wilson.

"Shall I advise Langley he hasn't got the authority?"

"Good God, no!" said Wilson, hurriedly. "Tell them he has."

"But that's . . ."

". . . Backing our man in the field," finished Wilson.

"There are some other things I'd like to discuss with you," said Harkness, starting to open Charlie's accounts file he'd brought with him to the Director's office.

"Later," said Wilson. "Not now."

The deputy director decided he had been right in alerting Cartright.

4

Not having to pay for his own laundry was a perk of foreign travel. Charlie included for pressing the more creased of his two suits—the one that had been a giveaway bargain in the January sales and the green check in the trousers only slightly different from that in the jacket—and gave himself odds of six to four that Harkness would knock it off his expenses. Charlie was still pissed off, getting caught out the previous evening. Only temporary, he thought, a private promise to himself. He left unhurriedly, increasing his pace immediately outside, going at once to the lifts serving the shopping area. He managed to get himself into the corner with his back to the wall, enabling him to see everyone who entered after him. Three Asian men, a Caucasian couple, and a man by himself, Charlie noted. The single man disembarked on the first floor and two more Japanese got in after another couple, talking animatedly in what Charlie thought to be German but wasn't sure. The new arrivals filled the elevator, so the grouping stayed until it reached the ground floor. Charlie made as if to emerge, behind everyone else, but then mimed the pocket-patting charade of someone who had forgotten something and stepped back into the lift, to return to the hotel level. One of the Asians who had traveled down with him just managed to get back in with the freshly entering group. Gotcha! thought Charlie. Back at the hotel level, he went directly to the long, open-lounge–bordering corridor, toward the main exit, stopping abruptly to feign interest in the antique shop at the end. His pursuer was trapped in the middle of the walkway. The man still made the effort, halting like Charlie at one of the arcade shops. You're dead, cowboy, thought Charlie. He went farther on toward the main area, wondering if there was any more surveillance.

As the taxi went toward the Ginza, Charlie decided Tokyo was a city full up with people and tight-together houses. It was the uncertain time, sticky with rainy-season heat. Although it was dry at the moment, everyone carried condom-sheathed umbrellas that by an ingenuity of engineering bloomed into the real thing at the first shower.

Charlie sat with his money ready, isolating the Akasaka Mitsuke underground station as the car went beneath the elevated roadway and glad of the clog of traffic. He waited until the cab was practically alongside before stopping the driver, gesturing with supposed impatience at the traffic delay and thrusting notes into the man's hand. The impression of a full-up city was greater in the subway, and as well as the people noise there was the crickets-in-the-bushes clatter of the passenger counters at the barriers. He chose a train already at the platform, not trying to check for pursuit until he was actually on board. As the doors closed, Charlie thought that if he had one pound for every time he'd used tube trains to lose a tail he could afford his own personal chiropodist. Charlie knew it would be difficult for him to spot his follower in a crowded situation of many Japanese, which was why he'd taken particular care. The man in the lift had been wearing a gray suit, muted tie, and sport shirt, with neither hat, topcoat, nor spectacles. The mistake had been the shoes—a subject frequently on Charlie's mind—black and polished so highly they could have been made of some plastic material. Four men nearby matched the description, except for their footwear. Charlie moved slightly and found his man at the far end of the carriage. By studying the color-coding chart, Charlie worked out that he was on the Yurakucho line; when the train hissed into Aoyama-Itchome station he realized he was going the wrong way, with too many intermediary stops. Charlie did not immediately disembark at Omatesando, wanting as many people as possible to clear ahead of him. He slipped through the closing doors as the warning bell sounded, hurrying toward the sign for the Hanazomon line, but at the last moment switching to Toei Shinjuku. He was lucky with a waiting train again and ran on. He was sweating and his ribs hurt, from having to hurry. He looked around the carriage, intent upon the feet. There was one man again at the end of the carriage who qualified, but he got off at Akasaka and Charlie reckoned it was looking good. He made another delayed departure at Hibaya, caught the first train and got off at the next stop, at Ginza. He ran up the stairs, breath groaning from him, and plunged at once into the man-wide labyrinth of paths and alleys behind the main streets, stopping frequently now, openly seeking the pursuit. There wasn't any, but Charlie still wasn't satisfied. He kept twisting and turning, managing to reach the larger Miyukidori Street entirely by back alleys. He remained drawn back, until he saw an unoccupied, cruising taxi, emerging to hail it at the moment of passing.

Charlie gave the location of the British embassy and sat back gratefully, wet bodied and panting, against the upholstery. Maybe he was getting too old for all this Action Man stuff; then again, perhaps he should exercise with something heavier than a whiskey glass in his hand. He saw the driver was taking him the longer way, through Marunouchi and around the park, but didn't protest; after all the buggering about, he needed time to get his breath back.

Charlie went patiently through the identification procedure at the embassy and sat where he was told by the crisply efficient receptionist who didn't respond to his grin. Crabby old virgin, dismissed Charlie. Couldn't be many left: veritable museum piece.

Richard Cartright was a thin, well-tailored man whom Charlie estimated to be about thirty. There was an attempt at extra years with a thin mustache, which didn't work, and an obvious Eton tie, which always did. Charlie had tried it once but got caught out before lunch: during his early, inverted-snobbery days. Cartright gave an open-faced smile, offered his hand.

"I've been expecting you," said Cartright. "There's been some traffic." Charlie Muffin was certainly an odd-looking cove.

"Thought there might be," said Charlie.

He followed the younger man into the rear of the embassy, where the sectioned-off, secure intelligence area was kept at arm's if not pole's length by the rest of the diplomatic staff. Over the door to Cartright's office were some charm bells to ward off evil spirits and a bonsai arrangement of miniature trees on the window shelf. The furniture was better than London and the carpet was genuine, Charlie saw. He hoped the charm bells worked.

"Minimum involvement, I gather?" said Cartright, at once.

"For the usual reasons," said Charlie.

"Nasty then?"

The man should know better than to question, thought Charlie. "Could be," he said.

"Ready to do anything I can," offered Cartright.

"I'll remember that," said Charlie. "What was your guidance from London?"

Cartright indicated the prepared and waiting dossier. "Always necessary to obtain clearance."

Harkness, guessed Charlie. He said, "I want a blank British passport, picture slot and nameplace empty."

Cartright made a sucking noise, breathing in. "Means involving a recognized diplomatic department of the embassy," he said. "No one likes that. Why didn't you bring one from London?"

Because it didn't occur to me until I was on the plane and thinking of all the possible ways of getting her out, thought Charlie. "Couldn't do it for me as a favor, I suppose?"

Precisely the sort of thing Harkness had alerted him to report, realized Cartright. He didn't like spying on his own side. He said, "Not without London finding out. Have to be Foreign Office clearance. You know what they're like about official documents."

"Don't I just!" said Charlie. He wondered if that security complaint had been squashed or merely postponed.

"Sorry," said the Tokyo Resident.

"Not your fault," accepted Charlie. It was actually unfair to ask the man.

"Sensitive?" asked Cartright.

"What?" replied Charlie, intentionally misunderstanding.

"Whoever you're getting out?" Harkness's instructions were to test the other man. Dislike it as he might, Cartright saw himself as someone trying to establish a career, and if he was going to do that it required a ruthlessness beyond his upbringing scruples.

Nosy bugger or primed? wondered Charlie. In fairness, he supposed the passport request made it obvious. Still wrong;

wrong to ask and wrong to respond at any length. He said, "Could be."

Cartright noted the reservation and felt embarrassed. Trying to cover the awkwardness, he said, "I could ask London about a passport issue. Ambassador won't like it, I should warn you. He doesn't believe decent chaps read other chaps' mail and actually uses words like *rotter*. He'd have to be consulted, of course." If he did it that way he would have complied with the orders from London and still not betrayed a colleague.

"Do you know the American head of station?"

"Art Fredericks," identified Cartright, at once. "Met him a few times at embassy things . . . receptions, stuff like that."

"What's he like?"

"Huge man . . ." began Cartright, but Charlie said, "I meant as a person."

"Came here six months after me," started Cartright again, pausing momentarily for the calculation. "Just over three years then. Takes part in most of the sports events the U.S. embassy puts on. Word is that he's ambitious."

"What's the full CIA complement here?" asked Charlie.

"Three, including him," said Cartright, at once.

"Sure?"

"Positive. I like to know the competition, even if it's friendly."

"*Is* it friendly?" demanded Charlie.

"Amicable," said Cartright, in qualification. "Depends if they're asking or telling."

Charlie realized he was lucky that Cartright was so certain of the CIA staffing: it gave him a figure to work from, when it came to calculating the opposition he was facing. "What if they're telling?" pressed Charlie.

"Not easy," said Cartright, quickly again.

Which made the Kozlov operation like he imagined it to be, bloody difficult. He said, "Any other names, apart from Fredericks?"

"Harry Fish and Winslow Elliott," said Cartright. "Fish is a nice enough guy but Elliott seems upset he was too late to wear a six-gun and ride off into the Wild West sunset."

"So the Agency is the next best thing?" said Charlie. Like Cartright, Charlie liked knowing as much as he could about competition, friendly or otherwise.

"Something like that," said Cartright. "They going to be with you or against you?"

It was another intelligent if rather obvious question, after the passport request, but Charlie had the impression it was more than a surface query. He said, "At the moment, I'm not quite sure."

"Joint operation: something big, then?"

The persistence definitely showed the knowledge of some prebriefing, Charlie decided. Wilson or Harkness? Despite the attempt at fairness, Charlie reckoned the answer was obvious. If he could prove that, after the security classification, he'd have some ammunition in the battle against the polished and buffed asshole. "Too soon to judge yet," he said, generally. He wondered if Cartright would withhold messages and keep a time sheet on him.

"How about the traffic?" offered Cartright.

"Thanks," said Charlie, accepting the dossier.

The London transmissions were very brief, which was hardly surprising at this stage, just the original and strictly formal notification of his coming, the instruction that any local assistance had first to be cleared by either the Director or deputy, and a query whether or not he had reported in upon arrival. The messages about London authorization and the arrival query were both signed by Harkness. Charlie wondered where the second batch of messages were, briefing Cartright on what to do.

"That the lot?" asked Charlie.

"Everything," promised Cartright. "Were you expecting more?"

"Nothing separate, to you?" pressed Charlie. It would be wrong to let the other man think he was a prick, even if he'd been a bit of one last night. He'd also expected something about the empty boast to Fredericks that he had power to abort. Charlie accepted that if the American had checked and London reacted wrongly he'd be in the shit, right up to his neck. Fredericks's cleverness had gone beyond putting him under immediate surveillance; making the direct approach at the hotel had wrong-footed him into having to improvise.

"That's all there is," lied Cartright. Hurrying on in his discomfort, he said, "Do you want the code room?"

"Not yet," said Charlie. "You can tell them I've arrived, okay?"

Cartright looked doubtful. "I rather think they are expecting to hear from you," he said.

I bet they are, thought Charlie: Harkness first in line, bleating about authority. He needed something to fight back with, before the was any contact. He was pretty sure Cartright had been appointed watchdog and regretted it: the man seemed nice enough and Charlie wanted friends, not enemies. He said, "Things to do first. It's only a formality, after all. And you will check about the passport, won't you?"

"Certainly? Sure that's all?"

"There are telephones, in the code room?" Let him work that out.

"Of course."

Charlie recognized the standard design, trying to remember the first time he'd ever enclosed himself inside a secure capsule like this: certainly he'd been younger than Cartright. An inner, sealed chamber was supported by four metal struts he knew were tested weekly against electronic interception. The chamber was reached across a small walkway that lifted, separating it from the outer shell and isolating the occupant completely. The door had a system operated from the inside which displayed on the outer part a color-code designation, indicating the degree of sensitivity of the material being transmitted or received inside the sanctum, pink for the lowest through a varied rainbow to purple, the highest. Charlie itemized red, which was an exaggeration, and direct-dialed Hong Kong: Harry Lu's telephone would not be secure, of course, but the electronic gadgetry in the code room prevented any trace of source if the conversation was intercepted.

Harry Lu answered on the third ring, gruff-voiced from the sixty cigarettes a day. Charlie identified himself at once and then without pausing said, "You clear your end?"

"No," confirmed Lu, aware at once from the query that it was an official call. "You?"

"Yes," said Charlie, telling the other man he was in an embassy somewhere.

It was still difficult for Lu to contain himself. "Charlie! For Christ's sake, Charlie! I thought you were dead!"

"Almost was," said Charlie. "Very much like it at least."

"Somewhere local, Charlie?" asked Lu, guardedly.

"Nearby," said Charlie, with equal caution.

"Near enough for a meeting?"

"No."

"Pity, I'd have liked that. Talk over old times."

Charlie smiled at the cue: the man was bloody good. "Maybe new times as well," he said.

"Not a lot of contact with head office," warned Lu.

"Accountants are out to rule the world," guided Charlie.

"Always a problem," said Lu, understanding.

"Doing anything else?" probed Charlie.

"Things are very quiet," said Lu.

"Maybe possible to put something your way."

"I'd like that," said Lu. "Be good to meet, too."

"Not going anywhere?" asked Charlie, an important question. He wanted Lu instantly available if the need arose, as it might if he decided Kozlov's defection was genuine: certainly now he wasn't sure that he and Cartright held tickets for the same performance.

"Best time of the year in Hong Kong," said Lu. Still searching, the man said, "What's the weather like where you are?"

Charlie grinned at the most frequently asked question during any long-distance call, admiring again Lu's expertise. He said, "About the same as yours, I would think."

"We'll keep in touch then?"

"Definitely," said Charlie.

"Soon?"

"Difficult to say, at the moment," cautioned Charlie. "Lot of clients to meet."

"Hope it goes well," said Lu, playing the part.

"Me too," said Charlie. "Might be some sticking points over the contract."

"Contracts can sometimes be difficult."

"This one might be particularly so."

"Good luck then, Charlie."

Hong Kong wouldn't become part of China until 1997, and as a British possession it was certainly the best transit point in the area through which to smuggle something (or someone) Britain didn't want the world to know (or see) was happening. Alerting Harry Lu was wise insurance, then: and it would be bloody good to see and work with the man again. Maybe even sort out the nonsense of making a few quid on his expenses. He said, "We'll be in touch."

"I hope so, Charlie," said the other man. "I really hope so."

Charlie replaced the telephone, warmed by the contact. It was a comforting thought to have a consummate professional just down the road: well, practically, anyway. Other things were still uncertain. He had definitely expected some indication from London whether or not the Americans had called his bluff. And hadn't got it. So there was no alternative but to continue bluffing. If the Americans had caught him out, he'd discover it soon enough.

Fredericks answered at once and said, "I know this is a secure call."

Too anxious to recover, judged Charlie. He said, "You can train monkeys to watch embassies. What happened to your guy on the train this morning?"

"Aren't you the smartass!" said Fredericks.

"Thought it was proving time," said Charlie. If the chain were to be pulled, flushing him down the toilet, the hand had to be reaching up by now. So there was no further point in blowing bubbles at each other. He said, "So okay. Are we going to meet?"

The silence lasted for several moments and then Fredericks said, "Of course we have a meeting. I thought we decided that last night."

Charlie grinned at the blank wall in front of him. He'd demanded a review as well as an encounter with Kozlov and if Fredericks was agreeing to that then he was also agreeing to his seeing Kozlov. Things were on an upswing. Charlie said, "I'm glad things are working out," letting the sentence trail, so that "my way" was clearly implied.

"This afternoon?" suggested Fredericks, who got the point.

The response showed yet more anxiety, like coming to the hotel the previous night. Recognizing that it was bridge-building time, Charlie said, "Why don't I come down to see you at the embassy?"

"That'll be fine," said Fredericks, tightly.

Charlie signaled his emergence from the code room and Cartright was waiting when he lowered the walkway and went back into the main body of the embassy. "Always feel uncomfortable in these things: like I'm in one of those funny spy films where people have code names and kill each other," said Charlie.

"Sometimes it happens and it isn't in films," said Cartright.

"You know something?" said Charlie. "Until now it's been a great day. You just pissed all over it."

"Well?" demanded Wilson.

"It could have been luck," said Harkness, with insufficient thought.

"Luck had nothing to do with it," insisted the Director. "It was intelligent assessment from a damned good operator. . . ." He paused and said, "Disappointing that Witherspoon didn't establish any possible connection."

Witherspoon was a protégé of the deputy director, who ignored the remark. Instead he said, "How did we get such an immediate confession out of Knott?"

Wilson smiled and said, "Promise of an early parole review and a five-year reduction of the sentence."

"We're going to do that!" exclaimed Harkness, surprised at the concessions.

"Of course not," said Wilson, surprised in his own turn. "I wanted a confession in a hurry and that was the way to get it. The bastard will serve his full time, with no remission or parole consideration."

"What about Herbert Bell: he's dangerously in place."

"Don't want another espionage trial so soon upon the other one," said Wilson. "It would unsettle NATO more than they are at present: particularly the Americans. And I definitely don't want any uncertainty between us and Washington, no matter how peripheral, until this business in Japan is settled."

"We can't just leave him," protested Harkness. "He's been positively identified as a Soviet spy."

"I'm not going to leave him," said Wilson. "I'm going to use him. I'm going to make Herbert Bell a conduit for as much confusing misinformation to Moscow as I can possibly manage. And then, when we do arrest him, the Russians won't know what they can and what they can't trust, out of everything he's sent, for years."

"Let's hope Charlie Muffin is as lucky in Japan as he was on this thing," said the deputy.

"I keep telling you, it wasn't luck," insisted Wilson. "Charlie's better than most, for all his faults."

One day Charlie Muffin would make a mistake impossible to cover up or lie about, thought Harkness: a mistake he was determined to uncover and expose. Hopefully Cartright would provide it. Harkness wondered how long the Director's strange loyalty would last, after Charlie Muffin made the inevitable slip.

Kozlov concluded the arrangements with the rental agency and then went by himself to the apartment in Shinbashi, overlooking the Hamarikyu Garden and the sea beyond. Aware of the accommodation problems of Tokyo, Kozlov decided it was extremely good: a bedroom separate from a living area, a small kitchen, and—most important—a telephone. The Russian would have enjoyed staying longer but he was late and Hayashi was important.

Hayashi was waiting at the appointed railway-arch *yakitori* stall where it was habit for homegoing commuters to stop, for chicken and sake. He smiled anxiously when he saw the Russian and said, "The message said it was important."

"You *do* control the military section of the airport?"

"Yes," said Hayashi, at once. He'd ordered but wasn't eating.

"I must know of any U.S. or British arrivals," said Kozlov.

"I can guarantee it," promised Hayashi.

Beneath the table Kozlov handed the man his retainer: a bourgeois revolutionary, thought the Russian, contemptuously.

5

Charlie set himself the test as he left the embassy, guessing at
the black Mazda, and got the confirmation that it was the CIA
surveillance car when it pulled out at once and began following
his taxi. Charlie turned back inside his vehicle, shaking his head.
It was something he'd have to sort out with the American:
things were going to be difficult enough as it was, without
constant game-playing between them. Not this sort of elementary game-playing, anyway. He still needed positively to know
whether Fredericks had checked his abort authorization. The
man should have done so, if he was the professional that
Cartright suggested. And if the American believed he had the
power, then Charlie knew he possessed the lever which put him
slightly ahead in the forthcoming bargaining. About bloody time.
He tried to shrug off, literally, the irritation of the previous
night. He'd been caught with his pants down and his pride had
been hurt but it was stupid—and worse, a distraction—to go on
thinking about it. Keep it in mind, for when the opportunity
came. But in its rightful, second place, where the need to even
the score didn't intrude.

At the entrance to the compound he identified himself to
the Marine guard and then again to the receptionist in the main
vestibule. While the receptionist made a muffled telephone
confirmation a second Marine checked his identification, closely
comparing Charlie's photograph against the man in front of him,
obviously reluctant to allow him any farther into the embassy.

He'd worn a fresh shirt, too, thought Charlie. Indicating the photograph, he said, "I could have been in pictures. A star."

The soldier looked back, face unmoving. "You got any ID other than this?"

Miserable bugger, thought Charlie. "Afraid not," he said.

From behind the guard, the receptionist said, "Someone's coming. Will you wait?"

"There," said the unhappy Marine, pointing to a seating area near the door, where Charlie would have been directly in sight.

Charlie ignored it, going instead to the American Tourist Office information rack and leafing through the brochures. It had been a long time since he'd been to America: during the time he'd been on the run from his own people, after having set up the Directors. Which had been a silly thing to do, he thought, in rare self-recrimination. They had been prepared to sacrifice him at a Berlin border crossing and so they deserved the embarrassment of Soviet arrest and humiliating exchange. But he hadn't properly calculated the personal cost. And not just the running and the hiding; he could have managed that, because so much of his professional life had involved running and hiding. It was the other things. If he hadn't determined his own personal vengeance Edith wouldn't have been killed, in their retaliation hunt for him. So lonely, for so long. And then Natalia . . . Charlie snapped shut the unfocused brochure, closing out with it the reflections and the unaccustomed self-pity. His wife was dead and Natalia beyond reach and to think about either was another distraction he couldn't afford: he'd made his mistakes and they couldn't be undone and he had to live with them.

"You'd never get a visa."

Charlie turned, to the huge figure of Art Fredericks, putting the booklet back into the rack. "Got some good references."

"Soviet or British?"

Fuck you, thought Charlie. "Take your pick," he said.

Charlie walked deeper into the embassy alongside the CIA Resident, grinning at the Marine as he passed and thinking what an incongruous couple they must look; Charlie realized he scarcely reached the other man's shoulders. There was a further identity check from more Marines at the actual entrance to the intelligence section of the embassy and Fredericks signed his personal authority for Charlie's admission. Beyond the desk, the corridors were blank walled and the doorways contained no glass, so that the offices beyond were completely concealed. Charlie looked up expectantly, found the camera monitor, and winked.

Fredericks's office was large, because he was the CIA officer in charge, but it still didn't seem big enough for the man. Charlie guessed the enormous enveloping chair had been specially imported. There was the obligatory U.S. flag in the corner and the nameplate on the front of the desk, and behind, on a low cabinet, an array of sports pictures and pennants. Charlie identified the boxing prints and thought there was also a photograph of Fredericks in an American football uniform. It would, thought Charlie, have been a sight to see. On the desk itself was a family photograph of a pretty blond-haired woman and two blond-haired girls, faces of both dominated by freckles and a foundry's supply of steel that always seemed to go into American teeth braces.

"So we're going to work together?" said Charlie.

"That was always the plan."

"You're setting up the meeting for me, with Kozlov?"

Fredericks hesitated, glad he'd given the undertaking the previous night and was not being forced into an open capitulation or admission of how he'd tried to screw the scruffy son of a bitch. Harry Fish was right; the bag women on Forty-second Street were in better shape. He said, "I've started things off. Like I said, it'll take a while."

"You also said you thought Kozlov was genuine. Why?"

There was another pause from the American. He'd worked his butt off, regarding this as probably the most important case he was likely to encounter in a dozen years, and now this guy was coming in and expecting to be fed it all on a plate. "Everything he's said checks out."

Charlie sighed, conscious of the attitude. Openly to challenge would make things worse. He said, "Okay, let's start at the beginning. Anything known, in your records?"

Fredericks shook his head. "We've run the name—and his wife's—through every computer there is: ours, FBI, NSA, and military and navy. FBI have two Kozlovs, both who served in Washington at one time or another. One is now in the Soviet embassy in Ankara, the other in Paris. . . ."

"Photo comparisons, to make sure they're the same people?" interrupted Charlie.

"Of course we made photo checks!" said Fredericks, irritably. "The Kozlovs who are in Ankara and Paris are the guys who were in Washington. Neither of the wives' names were Irena, either. Kozlov's clean."

"Sure that's his real name?"

"We've no way of telling."

Charlie frowned openly at the evasion. "You want me to believe you haven't taken a photograph, during one of your four meetings!"

Fredericks smiled, in reluctant admission. He said, "Twice. We freighted the pictures back to Washington. He's not on any mug file we or any other agency have."

"Born?"

"Leningrad, 1940."

"Age seem right?"

"Yes."

"Anything unusual?"

"Unusual?" queried Fredericks.

The man knew what he meant, for Christ's sake! Charlie said, "Facial hair. Or lack of hair. Scars. A limp. Missing fingers. Jewelry. Odd-shaped rings. That kind of unusual."

Fredericks decided that Charlie's mind was sharper than his suit. He said, "No."

"No what?" pressed Charlie, determinedly.

"Nothing unusual whatsoever. No facial hair. He's not losing it up top, either. Full head. No scars or limps. Doesn't wear any jewelry at all, not even a ring," itemized the American.

"Full head?" isolated Charlie. "Do you mean he's got more than you'd expect, for a man of his age?"

"No, I don't think so."

"Color?"

"Lightish brown."

"Lightish brown? Or a tendency to grayness?"

Fredericks paused and then said, "I'm sorry. Would you like a coffee or a drink or something?"

"Nothing," said Charlie, refusing a deflecting interruption. "Genuine light brown or graying?"

Beneath the desk, Fredericks gripped and ungripped his

hands in frustration. Why this guy, of all people? "Genuine brown."

"You said light brown," reminded Charlie. "So what is it, light brown? Or brown?"

"What the hell is this, a fucking inquisition!" erupted the American, at last.

"If you like," agreed Charlie, unperturbed by the outburst. "You've already told me it's my ass. And it is. And I've already told you that I'm not risking it until I'm satisfied. Which I'm not . . . not by a long way. If I don't get it all, then we both get nothing. . . . " He hesitated, wondering if he should take the risk, and thought, shit, why not? He said, "London confirmed my authority to abort, didn't they?"

"Wouldn't you have checked?" said Fredericks, defensively.

"Of course I would. That's what I'm doing now," said Charlie. No doubt about it: General Sir Alistair Wilson was a bloody good man to have watching your back. Or ass, which seemed the buzzword.

"Light brown," capitulated the American. "His hair is definitely light brown, without any gray."

"Eyes?"

"Blue."

"Light blue or dark blue?"

"Dark blue."

"Spectacles?"

"Yes."

Charlie came forward slightly in his chair. "Don't you regard that as an unusual feature?"

"No," said Fredericks.

"Of course it is," disputed Charlie. "Heavy frame, light frame, metal frame, or frameless?"

"Heavy," replied Fredericks. There was very little he was going to be able to hold back, for themselves.

"Heavy what?"

"Plastic, I guess. Black."

"Thick lens?"

"Not particularly."

"So they could be false, some sort of minimal disguise?"

"It would be minimal, wouldn't it?"

"That's all it's got to be, in most cases," lectured Charlie.

"People, even trained people, respond to immediate impressions, not careful studies. Heavy black glasses are a feature and if they are missing when you expect them, the immediate impression might be that it's the wrong person . . . the sort of hair you've described can easily be tinted, to heighten the change. . . . " Charlie stopped, annoyed at an oversight of his own. "Is it parted?" he said.

"Yes," said Fredericks.

Charlie noted the hesitation. "Which side?" he said.

"Left," said the American. The hesitation was still there.

"You sure?"

"Yes," said Fredericks, doubtfully.

Charlie hoped the photographs were good: they were a bonus he shouldn't forget. He said, "And if Kozlov really needs glasses, then the opportunity for an appearance change is still there. He could use contact lenses and even alter the proper color of his eyes."

"Why!" demanded Fredericks, annoyed once more. "What's the point of debating disguise! The man isn't trying to hide from us."

The point was intentionally to cause an apparent side issue to lure the other man into disclosing everything there was to learn, but Charlie didn't tell him that. Instead he said, "I would have thought that if this thing goes ahead the possibility of disguise might be pretty important to you."

Fredericks swallowed, uncomfortable at the lapse. "Getting Kozlov out is our problem, not yours," he said, belligerently.

"How tall?" resumed Charlie.

"Five ten."

"Weight?"

"About one hundred sixty-eight pounds," said Fredericks.

Charlie, who had never adjusted to the American weighing system, made the quick mental calculation: twelve stone. He said, "So what's his appearance, average, heavy, or what?"

"Average."

"No gut?" said Charlie, instinctively breathing in. "It's possible, even though the weight is about right for the height."

Fredericks shook his head. "He's completely nondescript."

Charlie decided that it was the first time the other man had said anything to indicate that Kozlov might be genuine.

Fredericks, with his distinctive bulk, must find operational work difficult. But then, thought Charlie, in contradiction, he hadn't isolated the man during the arrival-day surveillance. Subjugate the irritation! he told himself. He said, "He admits to being Executive Action?"

"Yes," said Fredericks.

"Did you take him through it?"

"Through enough," said Fredericks.

Enough for you but not for me, thought Charlie. He said, "Tell me about it."

"It came out the first time," recalled Fredericks. "He always insists on stipulating the meeting places: sets out several so that we can't stake them out properly and then chooses the one at which to make the contact. . . ."

"So he can check and ensure he's not going to be jumped, either by you or his own people?" clarified Charlie.

"That's the reason he gives."

That was certainly professional, judged Charlie. "You were talking about the first meeting?" he encouraged.

"It was at Tsukuba, where the '85 Expo was held," resumed Fredericks. "Good choice. Crowded with people. He identified me. . . ."

"How?" came in Charlie. It was a genuine and important question but he also wanted to jolt the other man from the prepared, withholding delivery he suspected.

"Part of his proving himself," said Fredericks. "Claims to know every Agency man on station here. The instruction was that I should simply tour the various stands and the exhibition site and wait for an approach . . . it came in a revolving theater, in the Hitachi Pavilion. . . ."

"How?" broke in Charlie again. "How did that instruction come in the first place? How did the CIA learn Yuri Kozlov wanted to come across?"

Charlie Muffin was a bastard who didn't deserve to be readmitted into any intelligence environment. But Fredericks realized the man wasn't the jerk he'd accused him earlier of being. As he prepared to answer Fredericks thought again how much the defection was his personal operation and felt a fresh surge of annoyance at the degree of cooperation that was being surrendered. He said, "It was direct, to me. There was a reception, at the Swiss embassy. Low-key affair that the ambassador didn't even bother to attend. I only went for a drink. There was an anonymous note in my car, when I left."

"Wasn't the car locked?"

Fredericks smiled, in further grudging admiration at Charlie's attention to detail. "Yes," he said. "Kozlov seems to enjoy showing how good he is."

Don't we all, thought Charlie. He said, "Was the car alarmed?"

Fredericks nodded. "That too. He bypassed it. I checked with the guards. No one heard a thing."

"What did the note say?" demanded Charlie.

"Just that I was to go to the Expo site."

"No indication who it was from?"

"No."

"Not even Russian?"

"No."

"So why'd you go?" said Charlie.

"*Because* whoever it was who'd written it had got into a supposedly secure CIA car without anyone knowing about it," listed Fredericks. "Because whoever it was knew who I was; it was addressed to the CIA Resident. Because the word *Resident* was used, it had to be from someone who was in intelligence."

"All of which could have been setting you up."

"Wouldn't you have gone?"

"The note said something else," insisted Charlie. "It just didn't say, 'Go to the site of Expo '85.'"

Fredericks felt a renewed burst of anger at how easily the other man appeared to have backed him into a corner. "'I have killed and now I want freedom,'" recited Fredericks. "That's what it said."

"That the lot?" insisted Charlie.

"That was it," said Fredericks. "'I have killed and now I want freedom.' Expo site. Twenty-seventh . . ." He stopped and then added, "That indicated the date, February twenty-seventh. The Swiss reception was on the twenty-fourth."

It was coming, decided Charlie. Slowly—too slowly—but the snippets were there. Would there be enough, though, to build the sort of picture he wanted to see, to be satisfied? "Dramatic!" he said.

"Good enough to go," insisted Fredericks.

"So it wasn't *at* the first meeting you learned he was a killer?" questioned Charlie. "You knew from the note?"

"If you want to be picky," sneered Fredericks.

"I want to be picky," insisted Charlie. "So what happened in the Hitachi Pavilion?"

"I just wandered about," said Fredericks. "That first time he didn't set out a route, like he has done since."

More professionalism, recognized Charlie: the note could have been intercepted by someone other than Fredericks if Kozlov had been seen planting it, so the Russian would have needed as many escape routes as possible. He said, "Didn't you have backup?"

"Two guys," said Fredericks. "That was the first occasion we got some photographs."

"If Kozlov knows the identity of every Agency person, he would have identified them."

"He did," admitted Fredericks. "He said he was glad I was a cautious person and just that time he would allow it but in the future it had to be one for one. Like I said, he enjoys proving himself."

"Has it been?"

"Of course not."

"So you've endangered any crossing already?"

Despite the air-conditioning, Fredericks was conscious of the perspiration moving down his back, a physical irritation to match the other he was feeling at having to make a further concession. "He didn't tell me until the third meeting that he knew them all, and I'm not convinced he does anyway."

"You told me there have been four meetings," remembered Charlie. "Did you go to the fourth meeting by yourself?"

"I told them all to be careful."

"How about the guy you sent after me?" said Charlie. "Didn't you tell him to be careful?"

"Kiss my ass!" said Fredericks, in a fresh eruption of anger. "I'm not answerable to you!"

Charlie was as unperturbed as before, aware of how successful it had been to anger the man and juggle the interview. He wondered if Fredericks was aware of the importance of what he had just admitted. "Let's go back to the first meeting," he said, quietly.

Fredericks blinked again, assembling his disarrayed

thoughts, and said, "I said he was nondescript and he is. That time he was alongside me before I realized it and it's happened that way since. He thanked me for coming—"

"In English?"

"He speaks it very well . . ." resumed Fredericks. "It's an unusual theater. It revolves in front of various stages. I'd taken a seat and was just watching the show, thinking the whole thing was some sort of dumb hoax. And then there he was, suddenly beside me. Like I told you, he thanked me for coming. . . ."

"Just like that? 'Thank you for coming'?"

"Yes."

"No!" said Charlie.

"What the hell do you mean, no?"

"You said he knew your name?"

The American began feeling drained. He said, " 'Thank you for coming, Mr. Fredericks.' "

"Mr. Fredericks? Or Art Fredericks?"

"Does it matter, for Christ's sake!"

"Of course it matters," said Charlie. "Mr. Fredericks indicates some subservience: that he was uncertain. Art Fredericks would show that he was proving himself again. Haven't you ever carried out any in-depth debriefings?"

Fredericks hadn't but wished now that he had. "He used my first name. He said, 'Thanks for coming, Art. That is your name, isn't it? Art Fredericks?' "

"Exact words?"

"Exact words."

"What then?"

"I asked him what he wanted."

"How?"

"This is ridiculous!"

"How did you ask?" persisted Charlie.

"I said 'Okay, I've come here: what is it all about?' "

"You sure?"

"Of course I'm sure!"

"You'd gone to an exhibition after a mystery note in a locked car, wandered about for a long time, sat down in a theater believing you were wasting your time, and suddenly a man sits beside you and says, 'Thanks for coming, Art. That is your name, isn't it? Art Fredericks?' And you didn't ask him how he knew your name!"

"Of course I asked him!"

"Then?"

"Yes!"

"That wasn't what you said."

The drained feeling worsened. "I asked him how he knew my name and he said he knew all the names . . . that he knew the two who were with me that day. . . ."

"Did he?"

Fredericks nodded. "Yes."

"By name?"

"Yes."

"Which was?"

"That's not important."

"A sparrow you saw pissing in the next field is important. Who were they?"

"Harry Fish and Winslow Elliott."

Cartright was right, Charlie recognized. "Used them since?"

Fredericks paused. "They're experts!"

"You're not!" accused Charlie, wanting the man's anger again.

"There've been a lot of places to cover: five or six each time."

Got it! thought Charlie. If Fredericks conducted the meetings and had an extra man at each, that meant a minimum of six, against him. He would have expected more. "You asked him again how he knew?"

"Yes," said Fredericks. Maybe he'd let Elliott loose on this guy.

"And?"

"He said it was his job to know. Although his English was very good, like I said, I guessed from the accent he was Russian. I said what was his job and he said he was KGB. . . ."

"He said that!" demanded Charlie. "He said KGB?"

"Yes."

Charlie caught the doubt again and said, "You sure? Absolutely sure?"

"He used a Russian word and I said I didn't speak Russian and he said KGB," recalled Fredericks.

Charlie wondered whether to prompt the other man and decided against it. "You can't remember what it was?"

"I told you, I don't speak Russian."

He wouldn't give it to Fredericks, decided Charlie. The awkward bugger wasn't giving him anything without a struggle.

"Is it important?" asked Fredericks.

"We'll never know, will we?" avoided Charlie, easily. "What happened then?"

"I asked him straight away what he meant by having killed and wanting his freedom."

"And?"

"He said he was Executive Action. That he'd murdered and that he wanted to stop but they wouldn't let him, so he had to defect. . . ."

"Let's stop for a moment," said Charlie. "Is that what he called it, Executive Action?"

Fredericks was cautious now. "Not at once," he conceded, immediately. "I asked him what department he was attached to and he said the First Chief Directorate and then I repeated what department and he said another Russian word. . . ."

Charlie cut across, deciding he had to prompt this time. *"Taini otdel?"*

Fredericks remained cautious, frowning. "That sounds like it," he said. "I can't be sure but it sounds like it."

"It means secret division," said Charlie. "It's an expression they sometimes use. What happened then?"

"I told him again I didn't speak Russian, so he said Department V. I recognized that, but to be sure I said 'Executive Action' and he said yes."

"Who's he killed?"

"He won't say."

"He must have given some indication!"

"He point-blank refused," insisted the American.

"To a direct question: you asked?" demanded Charlie.

"Of course I damn well asked!" said Fredericks. "Told me the knowledge was his value and that he'd tell us everything . . . victims, reasons, dates and locations, Russian rationale, everything . . . once he was safely across and his wife was safe, too."

There was no way to discover if Fredericks was lying.

There was a pathway he could follow, from what the American had given away so far. He said, "Tell me about that; it's the reason I'm here, after all. Why this separate crossing business, with him and Irena?"

"He's frightened of being cheated . . . of being brought across, sucked dry of everything, and then dumped . . . prosecuted even," said Fredericks. "I told him we didn't operate that way: that we kept our word. But he said intelligence agencies were the same anywhere and that he wanted a guarantee."

That's what the Director had said, during the briefing, remembered Charlie. "He's right about one thing," said Charlie, pointedly and from personal experience. "Defectors are always traitors, to whichever side: they're usually shat on, once their usefulness is over. Did he explain how the splitting of the defections gave him protection?"

"He talked of going public, in England and America."

Autobiographies and lecture tours had made a few cross-overs rich, reflected Charlie. The thought continued, worryingly: lecture tours in America, not England. It was a remark to remember and pass on to London. He said, "The figure was five hundred thousand dollars?"

"We'd pay more," said Fredericks.

And had probably offered it, for the double package, guessed Charlie. Throwing out the lure, he said, "You just talked in generalities?"

"That's all," said Fredericks.

Too quick, judged Charlie. "No specifics?"

"No specifics."

Charlie decided to let Fredericks run awhile and believe he was getting away with the bullshit: there was plenty of time to open the trap and let the man fall in. He said, "How was he?"

"How was he?"

"Demeanor?"

Fredericks appeared to consider the question, sure he was snowing the bastard. "Strangely calm," he said. "It's been something very obvious, from that first occasion in the theater."

"And that doesn't strike you as unusual?"

Fredericks's caution returned. "I don't follow?"

"He wants to quit being a murderer: presumably sickened

and revulsed by it," challenged Charlie. "He wouldn't be calm, surely? Particularly with the additional tension of planning as complicated a defection as this?"

"He's a trained man," argued Fredericks.

"Who's going against that training," said Charlie. "Further cause to be nervous."

"He *is* nervous!" insisted the American. "I've told you about all the crap of separate meeting places and only he being the person able to make the contact."

"That's not nervousness," disputed Charlie. "That's trained, professional caution. The opposite of nervousness, in fact."

"I think you're making too much of it."

"I'm not making too much of anything," said Charlie. "I'm just trying to separate facts from impressions."

"You're getting all the facts," said Fredericks.

Almost time for the drop, thought Charlie. He said, "How long has he been here, in Tokyo?"

"He said he arrived in late '83. It checks out with the diplomatic registration at the Japanese Foreign Ministry," said Fredericks.

"Before that?"

"He talked of London. And Bonn," said Fredericks, intent for an obvious reaction from the Englishman.

There was none. Charlie remained quite unmoved and expressionless. He said, "What came from the checks of the diplomatic lists in both places?"

"Nothing," said Fredericks, disappointed. "No Kozlov listed in either place."

Inwardly Charlie was churning with excitement. If Koslov had been posted—and had killed—in London, then they and not the American *had* to have the man. And they would, Charlie determined. He determined something else, too. It had been right not to challenge the American until now. He said, "Is that it?"

"That's it," said Fredericks. There was even a look of satisfaction.

Charlie sighed, loudly, wanting the other man to hear. "Do you know what I think?" he said.

"What?"

"I think we should decide something, you and I," said Charlie. "I think I should stop regarding you as stupid and I certainly think you should stop regarding me as stupid. Which is what we're both doing at the moment. Like it not—and I don't like it any more than you do—we're going to have to work together on this. Those are my instructions from London and yours from Washington. . . ." He paused, for the point to register. Then he took up, "You told me he's genuine. You told me everything he said checks out . . . and you know what you've got so far, from what you've told me? You've got fuck-all: absolutely fuck-all. Nothing from what you've told me *could* check out, because there's no independent corroboration. No photographs, no confirmation of posting, just the name on a Japanese Foreign Ministry register: you don't even have proof that the man who's met you four times has the name of a few CIA agents and speaks in accented English really *is* Yuri Kozlov. . . ." Charlie stopped again. "Now you know and I know that isn't right. And you know and I know that a Boy Scouts group wouldn't accept him on what you've so far told me. And although it's sometimes debatable whether they actually succeed, the CIA try to do better than the Boy Scouts. So why don't you stop buggering about, imagining you're conning an idiot, and tell me how the man in the Hitachi roundabout theater proved he was genuine?"

Charlie was intent upon the other man, pleased at the obvious reaction. Fredericks shifted in the chair, appearing to find it constricting despite its size. Then he sighed, for a different reason from Charlie's earlier, and said, "On the second meeting, he gave us a name. It was one we didn't have: we checked it out and it was right."

Charlie shook his head. "No," he said. "That won't do."

"The name was Rodgers, William Rodgers," conceded the American. "Kozlov said he was an illegal, infiltrated into America from Canada five years ago. His real name is Anatoli Ogurtsov. He's settled in San Francisco: runs an import-export business there. Deep cover. We've liaised with the FBI, of course; it's their responsibility. They've so far identified four others that he's suborned. Silicon Valley stuff, all high-tech."

"You said it was a name you didn't have?" insisted Charlie.

"The FBI either," expanded Fredericks. "Rodgers—or

Ogurtsov—wasn't on any file. And he's been getting a lot of stuff out. It means we're able to block a damned great hole."

There was more, Charlie knew. He said, "Okay, so illegals are run through the First Chief Directorate. But they're trained by a completely closed-off directorate: just like Department V—Kozlov's supposed division—is closed off. Because they both have to be. There is *never* any liaison or link-up to prevent what's just happened, identification from someone who's become disaffected. So how come Yuri Kozlov knows that William Rodgers is really Anatoli Ogurtsov?"

The goddamned man really did want to know about sparrows pissing in adjoining fields, thought Fredericks. He said, "The routing. The major conduit for the high-tech stuff that Ogurtsov has been getting into the Soviet Union has been through here, Tokyo. It's been a known throughway for years."

"He told you that?" said Charlie. "That he discovered Ogurtsov's name because they were the onward shippers?"

"Irena's the source," said Fredericks. "She's the Control, apparently."

Bingo, jackpot, and all the other winning words, thought Charlie. If Irena Kozlov had masterminded technology espionage into the Soviet Union from America—and maybe elsewhere—since the couple's posting to Japan in 1983, she was a potentially bigger catch than her husband. Because she would know the identities of other illegals and other technology smugglers running operations, throughout the world. Who was it who had said this could be spectacular, Wilson or Harkness? Charlie couldn't remember. It had been a pretty accurate assessment, though. Charlie's mind ran on, objectively honest: if he'd been Fredericks, he'd have been as difficult and tried to hold as much back as he could. No, not *as* difficult; more so. He hoped he would have done better. Charlie said, "That's the sort of bait that catches the fish."

"The Kozlovs are the fish," said Fredericks. "Prize winners."

"Can the FBI bring Ogurtsov in without any suspicion coming back here?" asked Charlie.

"Easily," said Fredericks, confidently. "There are others, don't forget. All the evidence will be that the Bureau found out through crooked American businessmen out to make big bucks.

There'll be a plea-bargaining deal, lesser sentences for full confessions. All the usual stuff. Japan won't even enter into it."

"All nicely topped and tailed," accepted Charlie.

"Well?" asked Fredericks.

"I said the bait looked good," qualified Charlie. "I didn't guess at the fish. You did."

"You're the smartass!" challenged Fredericks. "Have you ever known a better cross-over offer?"

Charlie considered the question and then said, honestly, "No."

"So it's kosher?"

"I didn't say that," contradicted Charlie.

"For Christ's sake!" exploded Fredericks. "What does it take to convince you!"

"Not even Him," said Charlie, twisting the American's exasperation. "He should have fingered Judas as a double."

"What's that mean?"

"Nothing," evaded Charlie. "Just me smartassing." Why should he keep warning the Americans that things were not always as they seemed? Let them work it out, like he hoped to do.

Fredericks looked doubtful. Then he said, "That's it. You've got it all now."

Charlie had distrusted people who told him he had it all from the moment he'd been parted from the tit. What he did have was enough—well, almost enough—for the moment: more, in fact, than he'd expected to get. He wanted just one more thing. In passing, Charlie wondered if Fredericks would ever know how much he'd conceded; and apparently missed. He said, "The photographs?" and recognized at once from the expression on the American's face that Fredericks had hoped he would not make the request. Silly sod, thought Charlie; as if he'd overlook something as important as photographs.

"I said . . ." started Fredericks, but Charlie interrupted him yet again, aware of the advantages he'd finally secured and aware, too, that the time was for apparent impatience. "Don't!" warned Charlie. "Don't tell me that you sent everything for picture analyses to Washington and nothing is left here. Because I thought we'd agreed to stop being stupid towards each other, and if you told me that I'd say you were stupid to entrust something so important to a diplomatic pouch which might have been destroyed in an air crash or intercepted and opened during an airplane hijack. And if you said it was done by personal air courier I'd say you were mad to let go of one of the most importance pieces of material you've so far managed to obtain, since Kozlov's approach. And then I'd go on to say that I don't think you're that stupid. Any more than I'd hoped you wouldn't think I'd be stupid enough to believe it. . . ." Charlie grinned, accusingly. "Do you know what I think? I think that somewhere in a safe not very far away—maybe in this very room—you've not only got the negatives of every photograph you took of Kozlov but a whole interesting selection of prints, as well."

Fredericks made as if to speak but then shook his head, in self-refusal. Instead he moved slightly to his left and opened what appeared to be a panel where the desk drawers should be. Charlie couldn't properly see, from where he was sitting, but guessed it was a safe, floor-mounted. Unspeaking, the American offered four photographs to Charlie, who took them and said thanks. They wouldn't be all and they wouldn't be the best, Charlie knew: but at least he had four. He took his time, examining each. Fredericks's assessment of the Russian as nondescript was very apt: ten Kozlovs had a place in every bus queue there'd ever been.

"The right," insisted Charlie.

"What?"

"You said he parted his hair on the left. But you forgot the reversal effect of a photograph. It's the right."

"It's a deal: I won't regard you as a fool," said Fredericks.

"It's a deal: I won't treat you like one either," said Charlie. Which was altogether different from promising not to cheat and lie and do everything else he could to screw the other man, to come out on top. To achieve which it would, in fact, be stupid to consider Fredericks . . . well . . . stupid. Suddenly remembering, he added, "Stop having people follow me. It's ridiculous."

"I won't do it again," promised the American, again too easily. He said, "There's not a lot that we can do now until we get Kozlov's meeting arrangements?"

"No," agreed Charlie. Not much, sunshine, he thought.

Charlie extended the reflection, on the way back to the hotel from the U.S. embassy. He'd still have liked to know more. But then possibly, with the benefit of hindsight, so would the captain of the *Titanic*. What he had was sufficient and it would take a lot of assembly and assessment and he was glad there was going to be a gap before any possible meeting with the Russian. Thank God he'd contacted Harry Lu. He wondered what additional fall-out protection he could get together: sure as eggs were things that usually ended up all over his face he was going to need some.

He called Cartright at once and when they were connected he said, "I need to come into the embassy."

"You do," agreed Cartright. "There are messages."

"Problems?" asked Charlie.

"How do I know?" said Cartright.

He was able to confront Harkness now, Charlie decided. He said, "Tell them I'm coming."

Those sections of Soviet embassies occupied by the KGB—and by the *Glavnoye Razvedyvatelnoye Upravleniye* or GRU, the military branch of Russian intelligence—are internally the most restricted, without exception anywhere in the world forbidden to any ambassador or any supposedly genuine diplomatic staff. Intelligence personnel are an elite—as they are, indeed, within the Soviet Union—answerable to no one, beholden to no one. Except within their own rigidly enforced, rigidly observed confines, where KGB inform upon KGB and GRU inform upon GRU and each service informs upon the other. Ostensibly, for each service, there is a Rezident or chief, but so well is a tangled intricacy of suspicion constantly maintained that no Rezident knows whether he truly occupies the office or whether someone he considers his subordinate is in fact the real holder of the position, reporting upon him and monitoring his performance. The situation is further complicated by the official existence within each branch of the service in every embassy of a security officer, who is not responsible to the Rezident—and certainly not to the ambassador—reporting and monitoring as actively and as independently as everyone else.

The same-color jigsaw creates the maximum suspicion and uncertainty, and the Soviet Politburo remain convinced since

1953, when Nikita Krushchev innovated the system, that it has preserved their intelligence organizations against dissent and defection better than any other in the world. Statistics of known defections appear to support that confidence.

Boris Filiatov was officially the KGB Rezident in Tokyo but the security officer was a woman whose reputation was such that the majority of Tokyo-based Russian agents believed that Olga Balan was the bona fide Rezident, unencumbered by any unknown superior. Olga—whose job it was to know of these and other rumors—did nothing to discount them, because she enjoyed the respect and because it encouraged the informants to confide their secrets to her, which increased her reputation and revolved the wheel of rumor the full circle. The earned reputation for ruthless determination contrasted with Olga Balan's obvious and real femininity. She was taller than most Slavic women and she did not have the usual square-jawed features, either, but a soft, oval face and a cowl of blond hair: those who feared her complained that her very appearance made her all the more frightening, because it concealed the sort of person she really was. The stories positively identified two agents who had been sent to the number 27 gulag in the Potma complex upon her evidence of their enjoying too much the pleasures of the West and involving themselves in the black market, to guarantee some comforts back in Moscow against the time of their recall. Both were true. One had been her fiancé, for whom she had genuine affection and whom she had therefore warned several times to stop before filing her report. If she hadn't she knew someone else would have done so and she did not want to occupy a prison camp herself, either for failing properly to do her job or because of her known involvement with the man. Olga Balan regarded being a good Russian as more important than being a loyal fiancée and anyway toward the end she found the man sexually lacking.

Olga conducted everything to order and most of all the weekly meetings. Kozlov entered precisely on time, because such things were noted, exchanged the formalized greeting, and sat in the already arranged chair. Each KGB officer maintained a work log, which was required to be submitted the morning in advance of the afternoon encounter; his was open in front of the woman.

"Kamakura?" she said, looking up at him. She had deeply brown eyes.

"Yes," said Kozlov. "A day visit."

"Why?" She had an unnerving, staccato way of questioning.

"We are maintaining observation on CIA personnel attached to the American embassy here. A joint operation with my wife, approved by Moscow. I was following their Resident, Art Fredericks," said Kozlov, with formal accuracy. All interviews were recorded.

"It appears to be taking a long time."

"We isolated another one, at Kamakura. Jimmy Dale. We've confirmed it from their diplomatic list." He spoke intentionally in the plural.

"Your wife is Control for this operation?"

"She suggested it to Moscow," said Kozlov. "They approved."

"How is it worked?"

"The object is identification," said Kozlov. "I maintain observation on known CIA officers and through them discover others."

"You operate as a team?" persisted the woman.

"We do not remain all the time together," qualified Kozlov. "That would be dangerous."

"Why dangerous?"

"In the event of one of us being identified, leading to the other," said Kozlov.

"You suspect your identities are known to a Western intelligence agency!" The demand was peremptory.

"I consider separation a sensible precaution," said Kozlov, qualifying again.

"Any findings, from this surveillance?"

"I believe there is a buildup of CIA strength," said Kozlov.

"Why?" demanded the woman.

"I hope to find out," said Kozlov.

Fredericks sanitized his account to the other CIA operatives but even so it was clear that the Agency supervisor had conceded more than he wanted, in the encounter with Charlie Muffin.

"Was it right, to disclose Ogurtsov?" questioned Elliott.

"Do you think I'd have done it if it hadn't been necessary!"

said Fredericks, upset at the obvious criticism from the other men.

"He winked!" said Levine. "The bastard winked at the monitor!"

"Listen. And listen good," instructed Fredericks. "Don't let tricks like that upset you. Because that's what they are: nothing more than tricks."

"Why?" questioned Yamada.

"So we'll underestimate him," judged Fredericks. "And that would be a mistake. We all know what he did once. He's a tricky son of a bitch."

6

Charlie opened the first Suntory, closed the curtains against the intrusive glitter of the nighttime awakening of Tokyo, and sat at the desk facing the blank wall, paper and pen before him. As he set out the preparations, Charlie guessed Witherspoon would go apeshit at his writing down in insecure surroundings the conclusions of a secure briefing. It transgressed every regulation codified in the British intelligence system since Walsingham founded it after Queen Elizabeth I agreed it was a good idea if it singled out the bad guys in the black hats from the good guys, wearing the white ones, although not quite in those words. At least after four hundred years the principle remained the same. It was a pity, he reflected further, that the assholes who sat in paneled offices with the very pictures of Lord Walsingham and Queen Elizabeth I on the walls got their colors and images blurred and relied too much upon those old school ties when it came to judging Blunt and Cairngorm and Philby and Burgess and Maclean and all the others who'd made the service a bad joke as well as an object of suspicion among other intelligence organizations. Was he one of the others, minus that all-important school tie? Charlie asked himself. Certainly Fredericks thought so; which showed clearly enough the thinking within the American agency. Rubbish, of course: absolute rubbish. He'd never been a traitor—just vindictive—and proved his right to reentry in a Moscow operation that would have worked if Wilson had at the time completely trusted him. Not just a professional loss, either: personal, as well. Darling, wonderful Natalia, who had refused to come back with him . . .

Consciously, as he had before, Charlie closed his mind to the distraction, concentrating upon what he'd got from the meeting with Fredericks. Which had been a hell of a lot. Charlie wrote "Leningrad 1940" as a reminder for the major calculation he had to make, qualifying it at once by noting that he would be working from the birthdates which Kozlov provided, which might for any number of reasons be inaccurate. Against it he put 1983, which appeared to be a positive date because Fredericks insisted he'd checked Kozlov's arrival with the Japanese Foreign Ministry records. Forty-three years then from the time of the man's birth and his posting to Tokyo. In between which he'd worked in London and Bonn. And killed. Kozlov would not have been chosen for KGB training until high school or early university entry. Eighteen was the average, for initial entry. From his unsuccessful Moscow infiltration Charlie knew there were two years of aptitude tests and training before specialized selection in the Soviet service. Full instruction took two years. And in the case of Department V, from which men emerged assassins, there was a further year of psychological evaluation, to guard against breakdown and the sort of revulsion from which Kozlov appeared to be suffering. Charlie added up a total from his jottings, did a quick subtraction from the forty-three, and came out with a figure of twenty. There would not have been an immediate posting. Charlie reckoned he could afford to build in an extra year—maybe two—before Kozlov would have been judged safe for overseas service. Which gave him the date of 1963. Where? During the interview Fredericks had said London first, then Bonn. Was that the way Kozlov itemized the tours? Or the way Fredericks had translated them, because he was talking to an Englishman and London would have come more obviously to his mind? No way of knowing. Certainly not of checking with the American because it might show him the way. Thank God for computers, thought Charlie. He circled 1963 as the date from which London would have to start checking any suspicious deaths of political, trade union, or expatriate dissidents and then considered the way the search could be narrowed. Fredericks had been insistent, more than once, that Kozlov's name appeared on no diplomatic register or list in

England or West Germany. But Russians serving at the Soviet trade mission at London's Highgate or with international commercial organizations like the Wheat Council were not accredited diplomats and therefore did not appear on any such lists. Any more than they did in Germany. It was an unlikely oversight, but Charlie was well aware how rigidly requests relayed through headquarters from one overseas intelligence Residency to another overseas intelligence Residency were frequently interpreted; asked to check diplomatic lists, they checked only diplomatic lists, without spreading the inquiry further. Charlie wrote the unanswered questions on the page in front of him, listing identity first. Fredericks had twisted and turned and tried to avoid giving anything away. So had he been lying in insisting they hadn't found a trace of the man, anywhere? Or had they covered the trade outlets after all and maybe come up with some sort of cover posting in the United States, despite Fredericks's denial? Maybe even knew some-one he'd killed there? To his English and German checklist of trade missions Charlie added those in America and then made a further addition not just of the U.S. diplomatic list but of that of the United Nations in New York.

Charlie sat back, examining his graph of positive results from his meeting with Fredericks, beyond those which had been obvious to him at the time. With the bonus of the photographs, which he could wire to London from the embassy, it was pretty good: pretty damned good, in fact.

What about the not-so-positive intangibles? From the few indications that emerged from Fredericks, Kozlov *did* appear to operate in a way that Charlie would have expected a profession-al intelligence agent to conduct himself. Naming Fredericks's two guardians at the first meeting was professional and confidently indentifying Fredericks himself was further profes-sionalism. And more again, with the Russian, according to Fredericks, picking out the surveilling CIA men on the subse-quent meetings and actually warning Fredericks not to be accompanied anymore. Which Fredericks had ignored. Knowing the sort of training to which Kozlov had been subjected—and how comparatively easy it had been, once he'd started being professional himself, to isolate his own tail on the subway—Charlie decided it was inconceivable that Kozlov would not have picked out the Americans the last time. Yet the man maintained a further meeting, without apparent protest. Which didn't make sense. Anxious disregard? A possibility: Charlie knew from experience that nearing the moment of crossing, a defector's nerves were invariably piano-wire tight. But against that was another contradiction: Kozlov's calmness. Strangely calm, were Fredericks's actual words. A calm man—let alone a strangely calm, well-trained professional—did not behave with anxious disregard. Charlie annotated several question marks after that query.

Irena Kozlov shouldn't be ignored, either: not at all, in fact. Charlie's immediate impression of her importance, at the American's disclosure, hadn't been an exaggeration. Providing there was nothing he'd missed—and Charlie needed a lot more yet—the couple were the prize that Fredericks determined them to be. So why was she remaining the mystery woman? Professional caution or something else he didn't yet understand.

Charlie sat back, sighing. Why weren't things always easy to understand, like the plots in those spy books with hammer and sickle motifs and Kaleshnikov guns on the front cover?

Charlie ran the encounter with Fredericks once more through his mind, determined against any omission, wondering if the American would ever realize the mistakes he'd made. Charlie remained attentive going through the rambling lobby area, interested to see if Fredericks would ignore that afternoon's undertaking about surveillance, like he'd ignored it with Kozlov. When he passed the piano bar the girl of the previous night was entering; she smiled in recognition and Charlie smiled back. His greater duty was to Queen and country, Charlie decided, sadly. There was the minimal delay, for the cab to come up the ramp, and Charlie was glad of it, openly studying those who followed him from the hotel. No one seemed at all interested in him but that didn't mean much. There were lots of well-polished shoes. Charlie abandoned the exercise as he entered the car: tonight it didn't really matter.

The British embassy is outside the diplomatic enclave in which those of the other countries are clustered and as the vehicle began moving through Niban-Cho Charlie looked around, frowning to remember if it was the sex-and-sake district where Harry Lu had proved to him that the Japanese geisha was something of another sort of romance. It looked familiar but he wasn't sure. If Kozlov stalled on a meeting, maybe he'd be able to find out; be an interesting experience if he still had some of Fredericks's people in tow. The gardens and parkland of Chiyoda-Ku formed to his right, a mass of comparative blackness against the surrounding lights, and almost at once the car stopped at the embassy. Cartright hurried into the main vestibule within minutes of being summoned by the night duty clerk and Charlie said, "Good of you to stay on."

"Need any help in the code room?" asked the man.

"No thanks," said Charlie. Had it been a polite question or one from a man given an over-the-shoulder brief?

"London has reacted predictably, I'm afraid," said Cartright. "Can't really say I'm surprised."

Neither was Charlie, in absolute honesty. Cartright's office was antiseptically clean—there was actually a smell of some chemical cleanser—with the desk and cupboard tops clear and the filing baskets empty.

"Just like home," said Charlie. "Can I see the traffic?"

Cartright went through the ritual of opening a double-security key and combination safe and handed across the manila folder. Charlie saw it was marked "Confidential" and thought at this stage that was an exaggeration, like his color designation that morning in the code room. Cartright had set out the passport request very simply, not intruding any local objections, and Wilson's response was a one-line message demanding personal contact.

"Not exactly an outright refusal," qualified Charlie.

"Not approval, either," said the local man.

"Ever worked out of London?" asked Charlie.

"No."

"Try to avoid it," advised Charlie. "Full of wankers."

"Always treated me all right," said Cartright.

"Matter of personality, I guess," said Charlie.

"How's everything going?" queried Cartright, openly.

Definitely a too direct, entrapping question, gauged Charlie. "Who knows?" he said, as awkwardly as possible.

Cartright wondered what irregularities Harkness expected from this man: at the moment he was behaving and operating quite properly.

In the code room, with the door security slide showing red this time, Charlie sent London the notification of his presence with the request that they open up the photo-transmission line while he encoded his material. The response was immediate and Charlie worked concentratedly, breaking away from his hotel room notes only when one picture had been completed and needed replacing with another on the revolving drum. When the picture wiring was finished he opened up the separate transmission line and began sending his impressions of the encounter with Fredericks, checking as the message was relayed against his original reminders. At the end there was the formal acknowledgment from London and at once an instruction to stand by. While he waited, Charlie fed his notes through the shredder and then burned them: just like the hammer and sickle books, he thought again.

The telephone ring jarred, making Charlie jump. He picked up the red receiver, switched on the scrambling device which would distort his voice to anyone except the person at the other end whose telephone had the antidote scrambler, and said, "Hello?"

"You seem to have got quite a bit," said Wilson. The Director's voice was clear and unaffected by the electronic protection.

"It will mean a lot of work for the analysts," said Charlie.

"That's what they're employed for," said the Director. "The Americans are being helpful?"

"No," corrected Charlie at once. "Suspicious and difficult."

"So we shouldn't channel any of this checking officially through Langley?" said Wilson, just as quickly.

"Definitely not," said Charlie. "I don't want them to know what we're doing."

"Or the West Germans?"

"No."

"Able to reach any impression?" asked the Director.

"Not yet," replied Charlie. "As I said in the message, some things fit, others don't. It's still too early."

"Do you think you'll get your own meeting?"

"I warned the Americans I wouldn't continue without one: told them to make that clear to Kozlov, as well. . . ."

"I would have liked some warning about that," broke in the Director.

"Sorry," said Charlie. "There wasn't time." Thank God, Wilson would never know how Fredericks had scooped him up and blown him out in bubbles that first night. He added, "Thanks for backing me up."

"I wouldn't like it to happen too often: not without some prior contact."

"It won't," promised Charlie.

"Why a passport?"

"Giving myself options," said Charlie.

"I told you I'd send a squad in," reminded Wilson. "Rather have trained men with our own transport than any civilian aircraft."

Military preferences emerging, thought Charlie. He said, "Just covering eventualities. I don't like getting boxed in, with only one choice."

"Makes sense," conceded the Director. "But I want to keep the local embassy at a safe distance, apart from necessities. Passports are numbered: be easily traceable back to Tokyo if there were some sort of problem and it got into the wrong hands."

"Any meeting with Kozlov won't be immediate," pointed out Charlie. "There's a contact procedure, which causes delays. You could pouch one out from London."

"It would be better," accepted Wilson. "Foreign Office will raise hell, of course."

"Tell them I'll be careful."

"They wouldn't believe me."

"What about Cartright?" asked Charlie, directly.

"I don't understand the question."

"Any change of heart, about his involvement?"

"We discussed it before you left," said Wilson.

If Cartright did have a watching brief, it didn't come from the Director. Charlie said, "So Cartright is out?"

"Restricted to the barest minimum," confirmed the Director.

"I believe the Americans are heavy on the ground," said Charlie.

"If you confirm, you'll get all the help you want," insisted Wilson. "And don't you take any chances yourself."

"I never do," said Charlie, sincerely.

"Sometimes, Charlie, sometimes," disputed the Director.

"Don't forget the passport," said Charlie, anxious to move what he knew to be a London-recorded conversation beyond the point where the refusal might later prove to be a positive order.

"I won't," undertook Wilson, who was as anxious as Charlie to progress, not wanting to restrict the man either. "And pouch the original photographs of Kozlov from your end. The quality of those you've wired is good but the originals will be better."

"I'd like to get something, before I meet Kozlov," said Charlie.

"It's been a good start," praised Wilson. "And there's something else. Herbert Bell was positive. Well done."

"Brought him in?"

"Better as a conduit at the moment," said Wilson. "Do as well on this. But be careful."

"It's the same thing as not taking chances."

After breaking the London connection Charlie packaged and sealed the photographs that Fredericks had supplied and signaled his emergence to the waiting Cartright.

"London wants this in the diplomatic bag," he said.

"It'll go tonight," guaranteed Cartright. Pointedly, the man said, "No problems?"

"I asked London if there had been any change of heart about your involvement. Wilson forbade it," said Charlie. If the man was playing Sneaky Pete on Harkness's instruction, invoking the Director's authority might reduce his enthusiasm.

"Why did you do that?" asked Cartright.

"Thought maybe that things should be reclarified," said Charlie. He hoped Cartright got the message. He wondered if the man would attempt to open the sealed envelope of Kozlov's pictures, to see what was inside. That's what he would have done, in Cartright's position. He knew Harry Lu would have opened it, as well.

Kozlov thoroughly swept his car electronically for any listening devices with Irena watching but she was dissatisfied and insisted upon carrying out a second, independent check. When she was finally sure, they drove aimlessly around the streets of the darkened city, safely to talk about Irena's weekly encounter with Olga Balan.

"You satisfied her?" demanded Kozlov.

"I'm positive," said his wife, at once.

Kozlov glanced briefly across the vehicle at the woman. "We shouldn't be too confident," he warned.

"What's that supposed to mean!" she said.

"Just what it said."

"That *I* shouldn't be too confident!"

"Both of us," said Kozlov, avoiding the dispute.

"It was Kamakura, like you," said Irena. "She'd checked and it was obvious she didn't like it that the CIA identification had the approval of Moscow."

"What about Kamakura?"

"How we traveled," remembered the woman. "Whether I was aware of what you were doing all the time and whether you were aware of what I was doing."

"She believed you?"

"I told you—she was satisfied," insisted Irena.

"I think we should cover ourselves further," said the man.

"How?"

"Moscow knows how successful this apparent surveillance of the Americans has been. We should suggest extending the evaluation to the British."

"Why?"

"The Americans want to meet again," disclosed Kozlov. "I've said the day after tomorrow."

"So the British have been brought in!"

"It has to be that," agreed Kozlov. "I want to take every precaution. Suggesting identifying the British will give us the same explanation that's worked with the Americans."

"Nothing from Hayashi at the airport?"

"Not yet, but I'll tell him again what I want," Kozlov paused and said, "We know they'll try to cheat, so I've guarded against that, too."

"How?" she said.

"I've got our own 'safe' house," he said, Twisting the professional use of the word, Kozlov said, "It's going to keep you safe and it's going to keep me safe."

In the Rezidentura office at the Soviet embassy, Boris Filiatov rose to greet Olga Balan, smiling a greeting and offering vodka, which she refused, so he didn't take one either, because he was nervous of her reputation, like everyone else.

"You consider we have a problem?" he said. He was overly fat and greasy skinned, the sort of man who perspired under the shower.

"I do not like this operation that Irena Kozlov has initiated," announced the woman.

7

Identifying the man called Yuri Kozlov turned out to be remarkably—and in a truly literal sense comparatively—simple. And there was an irony in the fact that it was made so by the American pictures from which Washington appeared to have learned nothing. Britain's counterespionage service, MI-5, has since 1965 maintained current and past photofiles on all known Soviet personnel who have served in any capacity, either diplomatic or trade, in the country. In 1976, for speed analysis, the entire system was computerized under a system in which photographs can be compared not side by side but from physiognomy characteristics, and four years later it was updated with technological improvements which enable a thousand images an hour to be considered. General Sir Alistair Wilson, who in the 1950s Malaysian campaign led his Gurkha troops on horseback and wore a regimental sword, was a committed believer in—and user of—technology. While he was still considering the incoming cable from Charlie—before, even, they talked on the secure line—Wilson invoked the internal agency's technical help at Director-to-Director level but guided by Charlie restricted the picture comparison to Russians appointed to trade rather than diplomatic positions.

The computer recognition is not positive: it singles out similar or matching characteristics, requiring final identification to be made by visual examination. By mid-afternoon, London time, thirty possibilities had been eletronically pulled from MI-5's picture library, and by the time Wilson summoned his deputy to Earl Grey tea and digestive biscuits the photographs which Charlie wired only hours before lay beside three separate stock prints of a Russian attached to the Highgate Trade Center from 1976 until 1981.

"The name then," disclosed Wilson, consulting the accompanying files, "was Gordik: Ivan Gordik."

Harkness stood at the Director's side, staring down. Two of the London prints illustrated the man they knew to be Kozlov at what appeared to be reception-like functions. The other, obviously snatched by a concealed camera, showed him getting into a car. "It's the same man," Harkness said. "There can't be the slightest doubt."

"There isn't," said Wilson. "To be absolutely sure I've had our analysts confirm it. Gordik is Kozlov: or Kozlov is Gordik, whichever way you want it."

"What's the record say?" asked Harkness, going to his chair.

Wilson looked briefly up from the dossier, shaking his head. "Very little, factually: nothing, in fact. But what is there is fascinating, put against what we now have, in Japan."

"Proof?" demanded Harkness, coming forward in his chair in unaccustomed eagerness.

"No," disappointed Wilson. "Just supposition. Kozlov—we'll use that name, to avoid any confusion—was among a party of Russian trade representatives kept under surveillance in March 1980, during a visit to a technology fair at the exhibition center in Birmingham. The fair ended on March twenty-eighth. On the night of March twenty-eighth a car carrying the Permanent Under Secretary to the Board of Trade, his secretary, and the driver went out of control on the M-1. The severity of the crash was never explained; a police scientific engineer said he couldn't confirm that the accelerator was jammed, because of the damage, but that was his surmise. The brake drums were smashed, so it wasn't possible to establish if they failed, either. . . ."

"Were they killed?" asked Harkness.

"The Permanent Secretary and his secretary," said the Director. "The driver lost a leg. They hit one of the bridge supports: there was another car involved, a family going on holiday. A child died."

"Holy Mary!" said Harkness, a Catholic who went to Mass

twice on Sunday and usually extended the swearing ban to any open blasphemy.

"There's more," said Wilson. "The Secretary to the Board of Trade should have been in the same car: at the last moment he decided instead to go back early to his constituency, in Wales."

"Who was . . . ?"

"Harold McFairlane. He was opposing both in the House of Commons and in Cabinet a technology exchange program which would have allowed Russian engineers, as inspectors, access to some of our restricted factories with which the Soviets had placed orders," completed the Director.

"All very circumstantial and completely unprovable," judged Harkness.

"Very professional, in fact, if it were an assassination attempt," said Wilson, making a different judgment.

"That all?"

"MI-5 have five dossiers open on unexplained but suspicious deaths, during the period," said Wilson. "A division technician at the Fylingdales early-warning station in Yorkshire whose death was ascribed to a heart attack, two months after an annual medical passed him completely fit. Harry Albert, the anti-Communist president-elect of the Electricians' Union, who became ill shortly after returning from an official visit in Nigeria. Pathologists at the Hospital for Tropical Diseases couldn't identify what it was, after he died. Bill Paul was an American, based in London, who edited a right-wing magazine which the CIA funded, through a Delaware-incorporated charity foundation. His was straight murder, in his Islington home. There appeared to have been a burglary attempt. Inquest verdict was murder by a person or persons unknown. Valeri Solomatin was an exiled Ukrainian writer who'd been published by Paul's magazine. Solomatin, who was a strong swimmer, was found drowned on a fishing holiday, in Scotland. . . ." The Director looked up briefly from the recital. "And then there was McFairlane. There was open speculation of his being chosen party leader, which the way the election went would have meant prime minister. Happily married, no mistresses, no scandal, millionaire through family money, everything to live for. There was some discussion at the inquest about pressure of work, but it was no more than any other government minister: certainly not sufficient for a man with no history whatsoever of mental illness to contemplate suicide. And there was no note. . . ."

Wilson stopped, sipping the tea although it was cold now, looking questioningly across his desk at the other man.

"Kozlov couldn't have killed them all!" said Harkness.

"I'm not suggesting he did any of them," said Wilson. "I'm just recording an incident from Birmingham, where we know Kozlov was present, and five other cases when important people died in this country in questionable circumstances, also while Kozlov is known to have been here." He stopped, head to one side. "Just one would have been too many, surely?"

"How about West Germany? And America?" asked Harkness.

"Too soon," said Wilson. "And Charlie's right in not wanting us to go through any official channels, so it's going to take a bit longer. I don't want anyone else to get the name Gordik: that's the key."

"Let's hope it goes on unlocking doors," said Harkness, in unusual entry into metaphor. "What about the wife, Irena?"

"Nothing," said Wilson. "No record, under either name, while he was here."

"I find the technology association interesting," said Harkness, who had already read everything Charlie had sent from Tokyo. "The Birmingham trade fair was technology and McFairlane was technology and the Fylingdales technician and the trade unionist could be put under the same umbrella . . . and now Irena Kozlov is Control for a technology routing in Tokyo."

"It's the focus of most of Soviet intelligence," reminded Wilson.

"To find out precisely how much of a focus, which would seem to be possible if we got them across, would be incredible," said Harkness, distantly.

"I'm ahead of you," said the Director. "It was good from the moment of the American contact: to call it then potentially spectacular was really an exaggeration. Now it's not."

"You going to tell the Americans?"

The Director looked surprised. "Of course not!" he said. "Do you think they would have told us?"

"What if they've made an identification of their own?"

"Charlie wouldn't have got the photographs," said the Director, positively. "Kozlov is supposed to be theirs, don't forget: we get the wife. The Americans in Toyko would have jumped backwards through blazing hoops to deny the existence of any pictures if they'd proved useful. We got them in the hope we would make a connection and a greater hope we would share. Besides which—not that it's a factor which would affect the decision—Charlie says they aren't properly cooperating."

"This is big?" said Harkness. "Genuinely spectacular?"

The Director's expression was one of curiosity at the question. "Yes?" he said, doubtfully.

"'Heavy on the ground,'" quoted the deputy. "That's what the transcript of your conversation with Charlie says about the American presence. I know the intention was to wait until Charlie was completely sure, but don't you think we should start sending more people in? It would be a disaster if this went wrong because we relied too much and too long on Charlie Muffin."

"You haven't thought he was the right choice from the start, have you?" challenged Wilson, openly.

"I think there are other operatives who might have been more suitable," said Harkness, formally. "But that's not the consideration, not now. We need numbers."

Wilson paused, needlessly adjusting the vase of poppy-red Paprika roses on his desk to cover the hesitation. He said, "The timing has got to be just right. A circus could frighten Kozlov and his wife away. You've heard the tapes: I've promised Charlie help the moment he calls for it."

"Charlie Muffin is arrogant, always looking for a windmill to tilt at," said Harkness. "We plan to snatch. So will the Americans, obviously. Where will we be if the Americans move at the very moment of crossing, before each gets to the supposed safety of either America or England. And we're not ready or, worse, not in place? Charlie has done well enough. I think we should move, now. Certainly not wait."

Wilson, who was an objective man, recognized Harkness's argument to be the right one. He said, "Start assembling a squad. Not provably SAS because they'll have to be deniable. All sorts of logistic backup, too. Better liaise closely with the Foreign Office: we'll be overflying God knows how many countries and intruding into all sorts of air space. The routing will have to be over the most friendly countries and of course it's going to have to be a westerly route: I won't risk bringing her out over or through any American territory. We wouldn't last five minutes."

"The Americans have Clark Air Base and Subic Bay, in the Philippines," reminded Harkness. "That covers them in the west."

"And to the immediate north we have the Soviet Union," completed Wilson. "Geographically it's a mess."

"We'll need all the surprise time we can get," said Harkness.

"It's hardly necessary, but I'll warn Charlie," said the Director, more a personal reminder than a remark to Harkness. "Tell him about the incoming squad, too. . . ." He smiled across at the other man. "He has done well, hasn't he?"

"It would appear so," said Harkness, clearly reluctant.

"What's it going to take for you to trust Charlie Muffin?"

"A lot," conceded Harkness, who was disappointed at how little Cartright was providing from Tokyo.

Irena Kozlov smiled as she greeted Olga Balan but the other woman did not respond, so Irena knew the recall interview, which in itself was unusual, was being filmed as well as recorded.

"There are still things about the Kamakura outing that I find difficult," announced the security officer, at once.

"What?" asked Irena. There was a defiance about her attitude.

"The degree of separation from your husband."

"We traveled separately, for safety, and each protected the other at the various tourist spots," said Irena.

"You were always aware of where and what your husband was doing? As he was with you?"

Irena hesitated. The perspiration on her upper lip and forehead was a problem but because of the unseen cameras she knew it would be wrong to be seen wiping it, indicating nervousness. "Not all the time," she said, cautiously.

"How did you know they were going to be in one place at one time?" The question snapped out, like the closing of a sprung trap.

"We didn't," avoided Irena, easily. "It began as a surveillance of Fredericks. He led us to the others: my impression was that it was some sort of cultural outing."

Olga Balan looked doubtfully across her desk. "The idea of such an operation was yours?"

"Yes."

"Why?"

"I thought the identification of CIA personnel had a high priority," said Irena, refusing to be intimidated. Playing her ace, she said, "Moscow agreed with me. Comrade Filiatov, too."

Olga Balan colored, at the reminder of superior authority. She said, "Do you think everyone at the embassy has been identified now?"

"I'm not sure," said Irena. "I think it's possible, which is why I intend putting another proposal to Moscow."

"What!" demanded the security officer.

"That we should extend, to do the same with the British."

"I do not think that is a good idea," said the other woman.

"I have the right of direct approach to Moscow," said Irena, in direct confrontation.

Olga Balan accepted it as such. "I will oppose it," she announced.

"That is *your* right," said Irena. It was ridiculous the way people—grown men, even Filiatov—practically wet themselves at the thought of an encounter with this woman. Irena knew she was handling things quite correctly in opposing her; to show the slightest fear, at this stage, would be disastrous.

"Which I shall utilize to the full," said Olga Balan, matching the arrogant opposition.

"Is there anything further?" said Irena, wanting the end of the encounter to come from her.

"Have you ever made contact with a member of a Western intelligence organization?" asked the security officer, formally.

"What?" The question fortunately emerged as outrage, covering Irena's uncertainty. It was right not to show fear, but she was unsure that she had not overplayed her part.

"Made contact with a member of a Western intelligence organization?" repeated Olga Balan. There was a wearing-down relentlessness at the way she conducted an interrogation.

"Of course not!" said Irena. "The question is preposterous!"

"I shall also recommend to Moscow that this American surveillance is terminated," declared the other woman. "I consider enough has been achieved and that to continue any longer is pointless."

"There is a need to continue," insisted Irena.

An hour later, in the security of the Shinbashi apartment, Irena said, "Damn the woman! Cow!"

"There is a definite time limit now," accepted Kozlov.

"She's suspicious," agreed the woman. "I think Filiatov, too."

"It's her job to suspect," said Kozlov, soothingly. "We made the allowance, by getting Moscow to approve the surveillance. For headquarters to terminate would be an admission that they made a mistake in the first place. When have you ever known them to admit a mistake?"

Irena smiled a big-toothed smile at him. "I told her I was going to suggest isolating the intelligence officers in the British embassy."

"What did she say?"

"That she'd oppose it."

"Hayashi made contact while you were with her," announced Kozlov.

"Why did you wait to tell me?"

"Wanted it to be the good news, after the bad," said Kozlov. "London has filed a flight plan, for a military arrival."

"That's got to be it," she said.

"I only hope we can hold Olga Balan off long enough."

"Of course we can," said Irena, in impatient confidence. "Olga Balan is an irritation, nothing more. And Filiatov is a fool."

"I hope you're right," said Koslov.

"I'm always right," said the woman. She looked pointedly in the direction of the bedroom and said, "I like the illicit feeling of it here. Let's make love. A lot of love."

8

Charlie was as objective as Sir Alistair Wilson—perhaps more so where his personal safety was concerned—and recognized at once the need for the incoming commando squad. He just hoped they wouldn't start clumping about in their bloody great army boots and get in the way. Childish thought, he corrected himself at once. On the occasions he'd worked with the specialized military groups he'd found them shit-hot. It would still have been nice if Wilson had trusted him to blow the whistle, but that—like thinking too much about the first night—was a reaction of pride rather than professionalism. Charlie continued transcribing the message, alone in the locked and secure embassy code room, nodding gratefully when he read that Wilson was sending copies of the identifying photographs and the passport by diplomatic pouch and not with the arriving squad. The diplomatic mail was quicker and not subject to any Japanese customs search. The men were coming in on a military-passenger aircraft, officially described as a unit on its way to exercises in Australia and so they would have to go through all the usual entry formalities. Charlie's mind moved immediately to the practicalities. To come in wasn't the problem; it was leaving, with everything they wanted and no one getting in the way. Would it be possible to take Kozlov and his wife at the same time? That was the ideal and clearly a reason in the Director's mind for sending in commandos. But here in Tokyo, at the actual moment of crossing, was where the American protection would be at its height: more than likely with trained soldiers of their own, as well as their CIA circus. Every potential for disaster then, an attention-grabbing tug of war between the two groups, risking the intrusion of the Japanese or, worse, the Russians, ending up with neither of them getting whom or what they wanted. Security would be tight during the conjugal visits, of course, but they'd be competing then on their own ground—wherever that might be—without the possibility at least of Japanese or Russian involvement mucking everything up. Better to get one rather than neither and to try the dirty stuff later. By herself, Irena would be a good enough catch. And . . . Charlie sat back positively in his chair, stopping the run of thought. He was ahead of himself; too far ahead. London might be happy enough with the identification and it certainly gave him the sort of advantage he always liked to have, but there was a long way to go before the uncertainties were resolved in Charlie's mind.

He sent the formal acknowledgment of receipt, read Wilson's transcribed cable a second time, to memorize it, and then shredded and burned it.

Cartright was in the outer office, apparently working on some documents, when Charlie emerged. Charlie said, "There is quite a lot of stuff coming for me in the diplomatic bag."

"I'll warn Dispatch," said the Resident.

"It's important," stressed Charlie.

"Do you want it at the hotel?"

Charlie was about to say yes and then stopped, recognizing the pitfall; definitely a trick question. "Probably safer here," he said instead.

Cartright was hot with discomfort. He said, "I'll be glad when this is all over."

"So will I," said Charlie. "I usually am." Until three or four days after the return to London, boring desk work and poisonous meat pies, he thought.

Charlie remained observant on his return to the hotel, although accepting—objectively again—that so varied and so many nationalities gathered up in a complex this large made any proper sort of incoming surveillance check impossible. He gave up after half a dozen possibilities, because it didn't matter. He'd make a definite check tomorrow: Charlie knew he had to get Fredericks and his merry men off his back before things got serious. Definitely before he got into any sort of negotiation with Irena: *if* he got into negotiation with Irena. Still a long way to go: miles, in fact. Keeping things in their order of importance when he reached his room, he first removed his spread-apart Hush Puppies, flexing his toes and feet against the day's incarceration, and was looking toward the efficiently restocked refrigerator and bar when the telephone rang.

"Wondered what you were doing," said a voice he recognized to be that of Fredericks.

Not necessary to check surveillance tomorrow, Charlie accepted, knowing they'd covered his return to the hotel: Fredericks was an asshole. He said, "Exercising my feet."

"What!"

"Nothing important," said Charlie.

"Thought maybe we might eat?" invited Fredericks.

"With friends?" asked Charlie, immediately attentive.

"Not quite," said the American.

So there was something at least, Charlie thought. He said, "I'd like that."

"You enjoy Japanese food?"

"Very much." Harry Lu had been the teacher, Charlie remembered. Challenging at first, so they went beyond the raw fish of *sashimi* and because it was winter progressed to the *fugu*, Harry trying to put him off with stories of how many people died from eating the poisonous bits of the blowfish. He'd have to introduce Harry to meat pies.

"The Japanese eat early, you know? I thought we might."

Another hint, decided Charlie. He said, "Eating early suits me fine."

"I know a good *shabu-shabu* place near your hotel. That all right with you?"

"Shall I meet you there?"

"I'll pick you up," said Fredericks. "How about five minutes?"

"I'll be waiting," said Charlie. Fredericks had obviously been doing the same, maybe in the hotel itself; there was definitely some movement. Charlie felt a stir of anticipation. Reluctantly he encased his feet again, leaving the shoes unlaced until the last moment, looking toward the inviting refrigerator. Not time, he decided.

The American's summons from the lobby came precisely on time and the man was waiting when Charlie emerged from the elevator, smiling a greeting. Charlie nodded back, aware of the changed attitude.

"We'll take a cab," announced Fredericks, leading off toward the second set of elevators.

"Sure," said Charlie. Was that important?

Fredericks gave the address in Japanese and the taxi took a route away from the Ginza and Charlie was glad they weren't going somewhere overly touristy. He glanced through the back window, wondering how much protection Fredericks had around himself. By now, reflected Charlie, his own military squad would already be airborne.

In the cab, Fredericks played the guide and Charlie adopted the required role, nodding appreciatively at the identified landmarks, noting in passing that from the American's description Niban-Cho was the fun place he remembered from earlier trips and deciding, sadly, that it would have to remain one of fond memories.

The restaurant was formal. Charlie removed his shoes at the entrance and placed them traditionally correctly, with the heels against the step, toes pointing outward.

Fredericks watched and said, "You didn't tell me you knew Japan."

"There's a lot we haven't talked about," said Charlie, pointedly. He looked down at the discarded footwear and said, "Just imagine if they were stolen."

The American looked down in disbelief. "I shouldn't worry."

"It's taken a long time to get them like that," said Charlie.

"I believe you," said Fredericks.

They were shown to a discreet, two-only table with a recessed dip beneath, so they did not have to sit cross-legged, Japanese fashion. A smiling, bowing waitress placed the copper-protected charcoal cone on the table between them and then poured in the moat of water, to heat. Another smiling waitress brought the see-through Kobe beef and the sauces.

Indicating, Fredericks said, "This is *ponzu*. . . ."

". . . Which is vinegar-based," took up Charlie. "I prefer the sesame taste of *gomadare*."

"I didn't mean to patronize," apologized the American.

Charlie deftly used the chopsticks to hold a strip of beef in the water to boil, dipped it into the sauce, and said, as he ate,

"Good restaurant. I like it." Patronize as much as you like; that's what you're supposed to do, thought Charlie. When people were mocking and convincing themselves what a mess he was and imagining how superior they were the mistakes—their mistakes, to his benefit—were usually being made left, right, center, and backward. And the silly buggers never realized it. He said, "There's been some response?"

Instead of replying directly, Fredericks said, "What about the stuff I let you have?"

"Sent it all to London," said Charlie, apparently intent upon his meal. It would be wrong for him to stop being careful.

"And?" prompted Fredericks.

The American wasn't eating much, Charlie saw. He said, "Nothing, not yet. You couldn't expect anything this quickly, surely?"

"Kozlov talked of London: I hoped you guys might have had some record to which we didn't have access."

Sure you did, thought Charlie. "I'd hoped the same thing," he lied, easily. "So far, no luck."

The vegetables arrived. After the dish was deposited on the table Charlie said, gesturing with his chopsticks, "*Hakusai, shiitake, negi, yakidofu*, and *shungiku*."

"You've made your point and I said I was sorry, okay!"

I made it but you missed it, thought Charlie. The nonsense of picking out the food was to irritate the man, deflecting his concentration. These were the times Charlie enjoyed, producing words like conjurors pulled colored scarves out of hats, so quickly it was hard to see the trick.

"What about Germany?" tried Fredericks, in a persistence of his own.

Charlie dipped some cabbage into the water, deciding from the quality of the meat and vegetables that the soup it was making for the end would be excellent: Harry would have approved. He said, "Make some allowance, Art, for Christ's sake! If we can't turn up anything from our own records, what chance have we had so far to get anything out of Germany? We need time: you've *had* time: what have you come up with!"

"All right, all right!" said Fredericks. "I just wanted to know. . . ." He stopped, smiling. "And I *would* know, wouldn't I, Charlie? We've got a deal, haven't we?"

Consciously trying to continue the other man's distraction,

Charlie cooked and then wrapped some spring onions in chrysanthemum leaves and said, "I hope so. . . ." He allowed the pause. "I was thinking earlier that if we're not careful, you and I—and those we represent and who invariably overreact and fuck everything up—we're going to end up with nothing. . . . Try the combination, it's terrific."

Competing in the game they were playing, Fredericks identified the *hakusai* and employed his chopsticks as expertly as Charlie and said, "This is very good." Then, just as expertly, he wrapped the onions in the leaves and said, "The meeting's tonight."

Charlie gave a head-bowed nod to the waitress who came to skim the detritus off what would later become the soup, welcoming the interruption. He continued the ritual, cooking some fungus, and said, "How?"

"Street designations."

"Car pickup, then?"

"Could be something else, but I can't think of it. . . . I forgot to ask if you'd like something to drink?"

Fredericks was employing his own distraction ploy, decided Charlie. "Maybe a little sake," he accepted. "You gave a reason?"

"I said someone from Britain had arrived." Fredericks summoned the waitress and ordered the wine.

"You haven't ever met the wife?" asked Charlie, directly.

"No."

"Did you ask?"

"No," said Fredericks again.

"Why not?"

Both men waited while the wine and the tiny *choko* cups were delivered to their table. Then Fredericks said, "It hasn't got that far: I've let him make the running."

Charlie raised his cup to the other man, thinking how differently he would have conducted the negotiations. "Haven't you thought that Kozlov might be fronting for the woman?" It was a maverick question, thrown out to make ripples.

"Why should he be?" demanded the American.

"No reason," said Charlie. "Just seeking your thoughts." Shit, he thought: the idea had been to get Fredericks reminiscing from that first moment of contact, at the unimportant embassy meeting. Charlie had hoped he could pick up something. As smoothly—reasonably smoothly at least—as everything was going, Charlie couldn't lose the nagging feeling that there was a yawning gap that he'd failed to recognize and that if he did not realize where or what it was he was going to fall ass over apex into a great big hole.

"How quickly could you move?" asked the American.

"Whoa!" said Charlie, avoiding the question. "I haven't met either of them yet; heard what they have say. . . ." He drank more sake and said, "Being so far ahead, as you are, you must be ready?"

Now it was Fredericks who sidestepped. He said, "Kozlov won't move until he's seen you; is satisfied about his wife. So we haven't made any plans."

The man spoke looking directly at Charlie, who decided the American was as good a liar as he knew himself to be. He wondered if Fredericks had any source at Haneda airport from whom he could learn of the arrival of the commando unit: the man would see immediately through the Australian maneuvers cover story. He said, "What time?"

"Nine: the first place, that is."

The waitress cleaned the water for the last time and poured the stock into bowls for them.

Charlie said, "Same meeting arrangements as before?"

"This is really very good," praised Fredericks, sipping the soup. "He's set out six different places: all near enough to tourist hotels so we won't attract any unnecessary attention, hanging around."

From the number of meeting places Charlie decided he'd been right in his estimate of extra CIA men. "Very cautious," he said.

"I told you before, everything's professional."

If only you knew, thought Charlie. He said, "Have we far to go?"

"I chose this place because it was close," said the American.

Charlie raised his cup. "Here's to success."

"We're working together on this, okay? No tricks?"

"No tricks," agreed Charlie. At least not until I've decided what they're going to be, he thought. He wondered what Fredericks was planning.

Fredericks drank, belatedly, and said, "Here's to success."

At the exit Charlie said, "No one took my shoes."

"Let's hope it's our lucky night," said the American.

In another taxi, Charlie acknowledged the importance of the first cab: if Kozlov did intend a vehicle pickup, their own car would have been a burden. The drop-off was at the Diamond Hotel but after paying the fare Fredericks led him away from the entrance, toward the park. Charlie oriented himself, recognizing how close they were to the British embassy. Would the diplomatic bag have arrived by now?

"We'd better not stay together," warned Fredericks.

"Surely he knows the point of the meeting?"

"I don't want to spook him, straight off. I'll make the contact, then bring him to you."

Charlie gazed alertly around him. Was that Fredericks's only concern, unsettling the Russian? Or was there something he hadn't anticipated? "I'll be close," said Charlie, with no alternative.

Fredericks went ahead, stopping about ten yards away at the intersection with the main road. Charlie remained where he was, tensed for anything. He made out the entrance to the Hanzomon subway station and remembered the trail clearing of the first day: how close, he wondered, was the man in the shiny shoes tonight? Ten past, Charlie noted, checking his watch; he hadn't asked Fredericks what the waiting period was to be, which was an oversight. The American's movement, at quarter past, answered the unasked question.

"Marunouchi. The post office," said Fredericks, coming back to him.

"You put watchers in place?"

Fredericks's hesitation was just a few seconds too long. "No," said the American. "I didn't want to screw anything up."

Let's hope you haven't, thought Charlie. As the cab picked up the Shinjukudori highway Charlie said, testing, "What's after Marunouchi?"

"Why?" demanded the American, at once suspicious.

"Just curious," said Charlie. "Checking the expertise."

"A secondhand bookstore, near the Surugadai Hotel," said Fredericks. "District's called Jimbocho."

Charlie smiled and said, "He knows the business."

The American frowned across the cab. "How come?"

Charlie indicated the darkened Chiyoda-Ku to their left and

said, "That's the pivot. We're going around it to get to Marunouchi and then virtually continuing in the same circle to the hotel. Easy traveling. But more for him than for us. Means he can monitor and keep ahead of us all the time. The circle goes on, after Jimbocho, right?"

"The Yasukuni shrine," confirmed Fredericks.

He'd got two further meeting places, Charlie noted. He said, goading, "Be easy to isolate any surveillance."

Fredericks grunted, not bothering to respond. The separated wait by the post office was as fruitless as the first and there was difficulty this time in getting another taxi, so Fredericks was shifting impatiently by the time they set out for the third designated spot.

"It's pretty easy to get pissed off," complained the American.

"Prefer this to being trapped, through carelessness," said Charlie. "I was once, remember?"

The bookshop provided the best cover of all. It was crowded, like Japanese bookshops always are, and Charlie went in, to use the people for concealment while Fredericks remained outside, slightly to the right of the shopfront and its lights. Charlie wondered if Fredericks's protector was inside or outside the shop. Charlie was lucky with an English-language rack which gave him perfect observation of the waiting American. He pretended to browse, aware of the developing discomfort in his feet. If the runaround went its full course he'd be standing practically for three hours: it was going to be bloody agony.

No it wasn't!

Fredericks started moving before the anonymous, silver-colored Toyota came completely to a halt at the pavement edge. Charlie moved, too, as quickly as he felt it was safe to do so without attracting any sort of attention. The very brightness which enabled him perfectly to see Fredericks became an immediate disadvantage because it blurred his vision into the darkened Toyota, reducing the driver to a gray, indistinguishable mass. At the doorway he paused, holding to the arrangement he'd made with Fredericks, letting the American prepare Kozlov. Charlie was alert not just to the car but to everything around, nerves tuned for the first indication of anything wrong. The bookshop customers swirled around him and there were a lot of people on the pavements and everything appeared perfectly normal. Charlie didn't relax: in his bruised experience things always looked perfectly normal seconds before the steel-shod boot came up to catch him right in the balls. Come on! come on! thought Charlie, impatient now: things had actually moved remarkably quickly but he had the impression of having hung around too long. The passenger door of the silver car opened and Fredericks started to enter and Charlie shifted again. They were in Kozlov's hands but there was no planning for his being left behind: was he expected to wait here or move on, to the Yasukuni shrine? And what, after that, if Kozlov went on playing follow-my-leader?

Charlie decided he'd spent too much time in word games with Fredericks and not enough on the elementary who-does-what-and-where-and-how planning for this encounter. So he had the advantage of the London identification: apart from which, Charlie decided, in sudden frustration, he was still being held very much on the outside of this sodding affair. Tonight was when it stopped. Which meant not being left standing on the pavement like a runny-nosed kid who hadn't been invited to the party. Charlie's uncertain movement became positive and he was actually making toward the vehicle—prepared to run to it if Fredericks's door started to close in positive abandonment—when instead the American turned, looking for him.

"What the . . . !" began the man.

"If I'm in, I'm in," announced Charlie. And he was.

Winslow Elliott, who had been the bookshop observer, was at the pavement edge before the Russian's car properly entered the traffic stream. He stood momentarily uncertain and then hurried to his own car, congratulating himself on having parked it so conveniently close. He pulled out in pursuit, with the Toyota comfortably in view.

Still in the bookshop, Irena Kozlov watched the American take off, shaking her head at the obviousness of it. That hurried entry into Yuri's car of the man she assumed to be the Englishman had been too abrupt, as well. Useful, though. He'd hidden himself well and until he'd moved she'd had difficulty in isolating him. Which had, after all, been an additional—actually the main—reason for her monitoring the meeting place tonight. She hoped Yuri's encounter would be as successful.

* * *

Filiatov looked across his desk at Olga Balan, his apprehension obvious.

"You can't be serious!" he said.

"There is a pattern," insisted the woman. She nodded to the documentation she had assembled. "Everything is there. As a matter of courtesy I felt I should show you, before communicating directly with Moscow."

Filiatov swallowed, the sweat bubbled on his forehead. "It's a courtesy I appreciate. Very much indeed," he said. Maybe the rumors about Olga Balan's single-minded pursuit of personal success were misplaced.

9

An odd, almost embarrassed silence developed inside the car, each man awaiting the lead from someone else. It was the Russian who spoke. With barely a movement of his head toward Charlie in the rear, Kozlov said, "I appreciate your coming."

"Hardly likely we wouldn't," said Charlie. The man's English was very good, as Fredericks had said.

There was a small lift of the shoulders. "One can never be sure."

Charlie was conscious of Kozlov's eyes upon him, in the rear-view mirror, and also of the Russian's alertness to the traffic following and around him. Charlie said, "Always important, being sure."

Kozlov's mirrored attention was briefly concentrated and for a moment their gazes met and held. Although the impression was distorted by the lights of passing vehicles and street illuminations, Charlie saw clear, untroubled eyes—maybe blue, as Fredericks had reported—and an open, unlined face. Being a killer didn't seem a strain.

"Everything has been explained?" questioned the Russian.

Charlie saw that Kozlov had abandoned the circular route and was driving away from the center of the city. He said, "Yes. Which is why I am surprised."

"Surprised?" Kozlov's full attention was on Charlie.

"Why are we all together?" demanded Charlie. He saw Kozlov's half-smile as Fredericks turned in the seat in front and began, "What the . . . ?" but Charlie talked on: "I understood your wife was coming separately, to the British?"

"Now wait a minute," tried the American again, realizing what was happening. "We arranged . . ."

". . . Nothing beyond this introduction," stopped Charlie, maintaining the pressure. "From here on, British involvement is a matter between the two of us. America has no part."

A filter road came up on the right and Kozlov drove off Hongodori Avenue and abruptly took two more quick turns, until the traffic quieted about them. He pulled to the side of the road and said to Fredericks, "He's right. You must leave now."

"I think we should talk about it . . ." Fredericks tried to persist but Charlie overrode him yet again. He said, "Okay! Fine! You going to involve me in all the discussions and planning on your side?"

Although it was semidark inside the car, the American's look was obvious and Charlie thought, I don't like your guts either. The hesitation continued for a few moments and then Fredericks felt behind him, releasing the door catch.

"I'd like you in the front," Kozlov said to Charlie.

The effect of the transfer was to have Fredericks holding the door open for Charlie. Fredericks said, "Remember it's your ass."

As Kozlov drove off, leaving the American at the curbside, the Russian said, "I was worried, briefly."

"Worried?"

"I wasn't sure you were going to protest: that it might have been some sort of complicated double-cross, your pretending to be British but in reality working with them, so that they'd get myself and Irena together, with a trick."

Kozlov was good, thought Charlie. "It still could be," he said.

There was another brief smile from the man. Kozlov said, "I don't think so. I don't believe Fredericks is a good enough actor to feign the dislike he just showed."

Having proved himself once, Charlie continued, "I have nothing to do with the surveillances the Americans are imposing."

"I accept that," said Kozlov. "They're really quite silly. . . ." He looked fleetingly at Charlie. "Fredericks has already been picked up," he said. "Their car is about three vehicles behind."

"Why do you want to come across?" said Charlie, abruptly.

The intention was to off-balance the man into a flustered reply. It failed. Kozlov rejoined Hongodori but in the reverse direction, going back toward the heart of the city, and instead of replying, said, "You can get Irena out safely?"

"If I'm satisfied about everything," said Charlie, making his own refusal. "I want to know a lot more."

"Why?"

"My safety," said Charlie, honestly. "So why defect?"

"You are aware of my department?"

"Yes."

"I do not wish to continue any longer," said Kozlov, shortly.

Charlie thought back to the first night's meeting with Art Fredericks and the American's assessment that Kozlov was frightened; Charlie's initial impression wasn't of fear. He said, "Why not?" It was an interrogator's trick to keep the questions as short as possible, making the other person do all the talking.

Kozlov hesitated, as if unsure how to say it. "I have carried out too many operations. Soon I will get caught. I know I couldn't stand any sort of incarceration for a long time."

Charlie, who had endured imprisonment and at one time thought it would send him mad, recognized the fear at once and reversed just as quickly his earlier doubts. He found that explanation absolutely understandable. It also made other things understandable. The reference to Kozlov's strange calmness, for example: the man was calm—and superbly professional—because his trained nerve had not broken, which was the erroneous inference Charlie had reached. He said, "Your people will come after you."

There was another quick exchange of looks. "I know," said Kozlov. "I've pursued others myself. That's why everything has got to be right, from the beginning."

Charlie made a note to have Wilson check unexplained or unusual defector deaths beyond Valeri Solomatin, the exiled Ukrainian writer. He said, "Are you sure you can trust the Americans?"

"No," said Kozlov. "That's why you are involved."

"I did not mean immediately, here," expanded Charlie. "I meant later when . . ."

"I know exactly what you mean," interrupted Kozlov. "Just as I know you've got to make the effort and why I am not annoyed; indeed, it would have been something else that would have worried me if you hadn't attempted to cheat the Americans. Fredericks has tried to keep Irena and me together, at every meeting I've had with him. Says I can't trust you."

You can't, thought Charlie. He saw they were on the park-encircling highway again and decided the car was as secure a place as any, once the checks for surveillance had been carried out. Reminded, and not yet completely abandoning the persuasion, Charlie said, "They have monitored every meeting, despite your insisting they shouldn't."

"I told you I knew that," said the Russian.

"So why didn't you withdraw?" demanded Charlie, coming to another of his worries.

"Because it didn't please me to," said Kozlov. "Every meeting has been like that tonight, a series of places where they've no idea when or how I'll make the contact. Every time we've seen what they are doing and how they are doing it. If there had at any time been a concentration of people, indicating a kidnap attempt, then everything would have been off."

Charlie digested what the man said, filtering the important points. "'We,'" he quoted. "You said every time *we've* seen what they are doing. Has your wife been involved in the checks?"

"Fredericks needs protectors: so do I," said Kozlov.

"Tonight?"

"Particularly tonight. I wanted her to see what you looked like."

Charlie stirred, discomfited: yet further surveillance he hadn't identified. It was happening too bloody often. He forced his mind on to the more important points. Kozlov clearly expected a snatch: a further reason for not attempting one, here in Japan. Another impression came to him and he said, "If you've watched, like you say you have, for the four meetings, you must have a pretty good file on the CIA staff here?"

"Every one," confirmed Kozlov. "That's my cover, if there are any questions from my own people."

So Kozlov's hadn't been an empty boast to Fredericks. Charlie's mind stayed on the American. The man had been right about one thing: the Russian was professional in everything he seemed to say or do. Charlie glanced outside, realizing they had done one complete circle of the park.

Kozlov saw the look and said, "Yes, it's time to alter the route. I wasn't becoming careless."

"I didn't think you were," said Charlie, honestly.

Kozlov took the car off the circular road, going in the direction of the docks, and said, "You haven't told me officially how your people feel?"

"Of course we will accept you," said Charlie, at once.

"Irena," qualified Kozlov. "It's Irena you're taking."

"I still don't completely understand how you intend making this work," said Charlie.

"I am valuable, yes?" demanded Kozlov.

"Yes," agreed Charlie. If there was to be a slip—a mistake to show him things weren't right—it was most likely to come now.

"Irena too?"

"Yes," said Charlie again. Stick to one-word responses, let the other man talk, he thought.

"And you—and the Americans—plan to try to grab us for yourselves once we're safely out of Japan?" completed Kozlov. He looked across the car once more, smiling triumphantly.

Charlie realized that a lot—perhaps everything—hinged upon his answer. He hoped to Christ he was going to get it right. He said, "Yes, that is exactly what we'll try to do."

"Thank you," said Kozlov. "I'm glad you didn't lie: most people would have done. You're proving yourself to me as much as I am to you, don't forget."

There was a jump of satisfaction, but Charlie curbed it at once: another interrogation technique was trying to confuse a questioner with praise. Charlie thought, I'm not forgetting anything, my son. "I still don't understand," he persisted.

Kozlov nodded and Charlie didn't know whether the gesture was one of approval or something else. "So the Americans will guard and protect me, absolutely. And your people will guard and protect Irena absolutely."

Time to attempt some deflection of his own, Charlie decided. "From what?" he said.

"Broken promises," said Kozlov. "At the moment you and the Americans will give any undertaking, just to get us. I want to be confident they will be kept."

The rehearsed story, Charlie recognized. He said, "The only way to guarantee that, then, will be for you and Irena to live permanently apart? Once you're together, your guarantee goes."

"No," argued Kozlov. "Before we come together permanently we want the full arrangements made, for income and pensions and changes of identity. Houses, too, of course . . . and going public. Did Fredericks tell you of that insistence?"

"Yes," said Charlie. He'd led the Russian along perfectly, he decided. Time to spring the trap. "It won't work, though, will it?" he challenged. "You gave me the reason yourself, a few moments ago."

"What do you mean?" demanded Kozlov. He looked completely across the car, ignoring the road.

"You know your people will chase you: one of the conditions is to have your appearance altered, isn't it?" pressed Charlie.

"Yes," agreed Kozlov.

"So from the moment of your first lecture, you're an easy target," said Charlie. "Bad flaw there, isn't there, Yuri?"

"What lecture?" said the Russian.

"That's going public," said Charlie. "Where you guys make all the money."

"No," said Kozlov. "There is no flaw on my part. You've made assumptions and they're wrong. The flaw is yours."

"How?"

"I know completely my value as a defector," said Kozlov. "It's in the embarrassing disclosures that I can make, of what I've done for the Soviet Union," said Kozlov. "Before Irena and I are reunited I want a contractual agreement for my account to be published. . . ." Kozlov smiled again. "The money is to be additional to anything that is agreed to be paid to us by either yourselves or the Americans, of course."

"Of course," said Charlie. Greedy bastard, he thought. The reaction was largely personal irritation at his misconceptions. Thank Christ no one knew. Trying to press his point, he went on, "I wasn't talking about publishing a book . . ." but Kozlov refused him.

"I *was*," said the Russian. "And that's *all* I was talking about. I will not undertake any lecture tours; neither will Irena.

No personal publicity, either. Any meetings with publishers or writers will be before I undergo any appearance change. The same with Irena."

It was an explanation, decided Charlie. He felt uncomfortable with it. He said, "Separate book contracts, like separate defections?"

"Listing all the promises that are broken," confirmed Kozlov.

Charlie supposed it had some kind of rationale. He said, "Your wife is prepared to cooperate fully? She knows what's involved?"

"We've both considered it very fully."

"You're worried about getting caught," said Charlie. "What's her fear?"

"The same," said the other man at once. "If I am seized, she loses me. She is as worried at the possibility of an arrest as I am."

Time to move on, decided Charlie. "You used a word to describe yourself to Fredericks. He couldn't remember it," he prompted.

"*Cheka*," responded Kozlov at once.

Kozlov certainly wasn't an impostor. An impostor would not have known the abbreviation of Vecheka, the name of the first intelligence organizations formed after the Russian revolution and still how genuine KGB officers referred to themselves, as a term of pride.

"It must be fascinating in Dzerzhinsky Square knowing you're in the very place where your service began," persisted Charlie.

Kozlov laughed, openly. "You're much more skeptical than the Americans," he said.

The praise ploy again, thought Charlie. He stayed silent.

Spacing his delivery, Kozlov said, "Gorokhovaia Street, in Petrograd, was actually the first headquarters. It didn't move to Moscow until 1918. And even then not to where it is now: for two years it was at Bolshoi Lubyanka. . . ." He looked briefly at Charlie. "Right?"

"No!" said Charlie.

"But that . . . !" Kozlov began to protest and then stopped. "As a matter of fact it is, historically," he said. "But I see now. No part of my Chief Directorate is in Dzerzhinsky

Square. We're too big. Our building is on the Moscow ring road."

"What connects with Metrostroevskaya Street?" said Charlie.

Kozlov did not speak for several moments. Then he said, "I didn't know the British service was that well informed."

As before, Charlie remained silent, refusing to be drawn, and Kozlov said, after a further pause, "Turnaninski Pereulok."

"And?" urged Charlie.

"Yes," said Kozlov. "I received initial training there: rifle and pistol shooting, unarmed combat . . . it's the school."

"I want the other place," demanded Charlie.

"Kuchino," said the Russian, at once.

"What's the specialization?"

"Poisons. And drugs that dissipate in the body within minutes of being administered . . ." He looked again directly at Charlie. "You know Moscow too well."

Sometimes I wished I lived there, with Natalia again, thought Charlie. He said, "There was an operation once. It wasn't successful. I managed to get out." That was too much to have revealed at this stage; any stage, in fact. Wanting to cover the mistake, Charlie tried to off-balance again. He said, "Who was Harold McFairlane?"

And this time it worked. They were actually approaching the port now, able to see the anchored, lighted vessels. Kozlov took the bridge over the Sumidagawa River but turned away from the full dock complex, going inland: Charlie remembered that a lot of the waterside area was, in fact, islands where it would have been easy to become boxed in and trapped. Kozlov's throat was moving and there was a sudden, visible shake in the hands that held the wheel. "You have been extremely busy," he managed finally.

"It would seem that you were, too," said Charlie.

"Has it been an American identification?"

"You know I won't answer that," said Charlie. It was a careless demand anyway: Charlie felt a stir of anticipation.

"Tell me how close, at least?"

Charlie had no idea what the question meant. Using Kozlov's demand as the guide, Charlie said: "Very close."

"I *knew* it was wrong," said Kozlov. More than at any time

since the encounter began, Kozlov was reflective, deep inside his own mind.

What the fuck had been wrong! thought Charlie, desperately: this really was like being on the tightrope and watching the strands fray at the far end. He searched for a further way to urge the man on. Drawing upon his own experience, Charlie said, "They never listen to the people who have to do the job, do they?"

"I needed more time, after London. Bonn only gave me a month: it had to be messy," blundered Kozlov.

Enough, Charlie decided at once. He said, "There'll be a complete amnesty, of course. For McFairlane . . ." He allowed the pause. "And the rest."

"That's the most essential guarantee," said Kozlov. "I'll want that—so will Irena—before we'll agree to anything."

Charlie reckoned he had everything short of a written confession. He repeated, "You'll have every guarantee."

"How will you get Irena out?" demanded Kozlov.

Charlie paused. "Safely," he said. I hope, he thought.

There was another fleeting smile from Kozlov, the first in a long time. He said, "Yes. It is better I don't know."

"But there will have to be the closest coordination," warned Charlie. "Everything calculated to the minute, to leave at the same time."

"I don't need reminding of the disaster, if the timing is wrong," said the Russian. He paused. "If *anything* goes wrong."

"I need a photograph to recognize Irena," said Charlie.

"I expected you would," said Kozlov. He reached inside his jacket and handed Charlie an envelope.

"And to meet," continued Charlie. An idea was shaping in his mind; the commandos could be useful but for something different from what the Director imagined. Duck-and-weave time.

"Yes," said Kozlov. "There needs to be a meeting."

"How prepared are you?"

"Immediate. You?"

"Immediate," said Charlie. Which was a slight exaggeration because he had a hell of a lot to do. He said, "My planning with Irena can't be arranged through the Americans, naturally."

"Naturally," agreed Kozlov.

"Or through you," added Charlie.

"Don't be ridiculous!" said Kozlov.

"That's exactly what I am not being," said Charlie. "You're seeking protection by being separated?"

"From your two services," argued Kozlov.

"From each other," insisted Charlie.

Kozlov pulled the car to the side of the road and stopped and Charlie was glad: it seemed they had been driving for hours. Why did his feet still hurt, when he'd been sitting down for so long?

Kozlov said, "How can things be coordinated if Irena and I don't know when and how it's going to happen?"

Charlie's earlier reflection that any sort of grab would be impossible as well as stupid, here in Japan, hardened into a positive determination against the idea as the Russian talked. So now getting the woman safely out came down to a logistical exercise, to thwart the Americans attempting anything so foolish. He said, "You'll know when, of course. You'll have to. But not how. Irena comes with me, without any details. You go—however you choose—with the Americans."

"That's how I want it to be," said Kozlov.

"It's still your choice, don't forget," said Charlie. "It's still possible to change your mind, even now; both of you can come with me."

"Fredericks made one last try," remembered the Russian.

"So?"

"We stay separate," insisted Kozlov.

"Then the planning is separate."

"All right," accepted Kozlov, without a choice.

Charlie looked at the dashboard clock, trying to calculate the amount of time he needed: it was fortunate that the difference was so great between Tokyo and London. A lot of potential problems still remained. He wished he'd thought it out and synchronized the possible flight schedules. Caught by a sudden doubt, Charlie said, "She speaks English?"

"Perfectly," assured Kozlov.

"The bookshop tonight?" said Charlie. "Will just that one occasion be sufficient for her to recognize me?"

"I hope so."

"It must be more than hope!" insisted Charlie.

"She'll recognize you," guaranteed Kozlov. "Where?"

"There is a tourist bus which leaves the hotel at noon tomorrow: a city tour," set out Charlie. "Tell Irena to catch it."

"You will be on it?"

"I will make contact with her," qualified Charlie. "She must wait."

"All the arrangements will be settled then?"

Charlie did not reply at once. Then he said, "Everything. And at the same time you must contact Fredericks; don't forget the necessity to coordinate."

"I've thought about this for a long time," said Kozlov. "I'm not going to forget any necessity."

Detecting what he thought to be doubt, Charlie said, "Don't worry. I'll get her out safely."

"I've been very careful, preparing her," said Kozlov.

"I'll protect her," insisted Charlie.

"It is difficult for me to believe that after so long, everything will be settled by tomorrow," said Kozlov, distantly.

More positively than you imagine, thought Charlie. He said, "That's how close it is, now."

"It must be over soon," said Kozlov. "There are some difficulties at the embassy."

"What difficulties?"

"There is a security officer: it is obvious there is some suspicion developing."

"By tomorrow everything will be fixed," reassured Charlie.

"We haven't settled the terms," reminded Kozlov.

"How much?" asked Charlie. Would the man stick with the American demand or try to hype the price?

"I've asked Washington for five hundred thousand dollars," said Kozlov. "I'll want the same for Irena."

"Agreed," said Charlie, at once.

"Index-linked, to take account of your inflation," continued Kozlov. "That's what your civil servants get, isn't it?"

This was one for the lecture rooms! thought Charlie. He said, "I'll insist it's index-linked."

"And something else," went on Kozlov. "I want it pegged to a fixed exchange rate against the dollar."

"I'll arrange that also," said Charlie, using the immediate response to cover his reaction. That insistence could only mean that Kozlov ultimately intended to settle with his wife in

America: another important warning to pass on to London. He said, "Is that all?"

"Of course not," said Kozlov, just as quickly. "I want private health care for her: your National Health Service suffers delays."

Definitely one for the training manual, decided Charlie. "That's possible," he said. Kozlov had made an omission which confirmed Charlie's thoughts about their eventually living in America.

As if aware of those thoughts—and the doubt—Kozlov said, "A house in Britain, as well . . . something that we can choose, after the necessary appearance change."

An afterthought recovery? wondered Charlie. He said, "Where do you want the plastic surgery to be carried out?" A hospital situation provided the best opportunity for a grab.

"We'll arrange that later," avoided the Russian.

The hospital potential was certainly something he should pass on to London, determined Charlie. He said, "We'll meet every one of those conditions."

"And the amnesty?" reminded the Russian.

"A positive guarantee," assured Charlie. He saw Kozlov had brought the car back into the center of the city and that they were very close to his hotel. He said, "Is there anything else?"

Kozlov stopped the car and removed the heavy spectacles, polishing them reflectively. The Russian looked quite different without them, Charlie saw, remembering the first night's conversation with Fredericks: but he'd used them to drive for more than an hour, so there had to be a genuine need, beyond any minimal disguise. Kozlov said, "I can't think of anything. It just seems there should be more."

"That's always the impression," said Charlie. "Really, once the decision is made and the agreements reached, there isn't."

"You've brought people across before?"

"Yes," said Charlie.

"Always successfully?"

Charlie hesitated. "I've always got the subject safely across," he said.

Kozlov isolated the qualification at once. "But others have been caught? Hurt?"

"Not often," said Charlie.

"I don't want it to happen this time," said Kozlov.

"Meet Fredericks tomorrow," insisted Charlie.

"Noon," agreed Kozlov.

"And where's Irena to meet me?"

Kozlov smiled at the rehearsal. "On a tourist bus, from the New Otani. Noon as well."

There was a need to hurry the Russian on, before he began thinking too deeply about the arrangements. Charlie said, "We won't meet anymore, not until after the crossing. From now on, it must be exclusively between Irena and myself. I'll explain everything to her tomorrow."

"I understand," said Kozlov.

"The offer to both of you, to come with me, is still there," said Charlie. He knew it was a waste of time but he hoped it would further deflect the man.

"We've been through that," said Kozlov, dismissively.

Remembering Kozlov's own remark, Charlie said in repeated reassurance, "By this time tomorrow, everything will be settled." Kozlov looked more like a senior clerk than a killer, he thought.

"At last!" said Kozlov, the relief obvious.

It really did seem to be resolving itself very easily, thought Charlie: maybe too easily. He opened but held the door and said, "Next time we meet we'll laugh about it."

"I hope so," said Kozlov. "You can walk from here?"

"I need to think," answered Charlie, honestly. And hurry, he thought.

The lobby travel desk was still open and the clerk found in minutes a 6:00 P.M. flight from Osaka the following day, possible by catching the 3:00 P.M. Bullet train from Tokyo. Tight but feasible, decided Charlie, booking both. Luck seemed to be with him: he hoped it stayed that way. He guessed London wouldn't like the idea. Be careful, the Director had insisted: so he was simply obeying orders. It was ironic, Charlie thought, that he was using Hong Kong and wasn't going to see Harry Lu after all. Always return through the colony, he supposed: be a good way to celebrate, a few drinks with an old mate. London—or rather Harkness—wouldn't like that either, which was tough shit. Good reason for doing it, in fact. Reward, for a job well done.

When he called Fredericks, the American said, "Quite the operator!"

"You couldn't expect to get away with it!" said Charlie, impatiently.

"Well?"

"We need to meet," said Charlie.

"Tomorrow," said Fredericks.

"Tonight," insisted Charlie.

Only at the end of setting out his impressions of the meeting with Kozlov did Charlie remember the photograph of the woman. He took it from his pocket, frowning down.

Irena Kozlov looked just like an Alsatian wearing lipstick, he decided.

Olga Balan stretched up, easing the ache in her shoulders after the intense concentration, happy at last with the Kozlov report. She read it for the final time, collected all the sound and television tapes of the interviews, and sealed them all together in the package for Moscow. The supposition was overwhelming, she decided: absolutely overwhelming. She guessed Boris Filiatov would soon be filing his own, back-covering report; stupid, sweaty little man.

10

The package freighted in the diplomatic bag was waiting at the embassy and while that night's encoded message was being transmitted to London Charlie examined the contents. The promised blank passport was uppermost, directly above the three comparison photographs of Kozlov under his previous name. Charlie concentrated upon them, recognizing at once that Irena wasn't in the background of any of the reception-type pictures.

The security-cleared telephone sounded within minutes of the transmission ceasing and this time Charlie didn't jump.

"Sure about Bonn?" demanded the Director, at once.

"Within a month of McFairlane," repeated Charlie. "Kozlov called it messy. I'd go for an obvious killing."

"No idea who?"

"None," admitted Charlie.

"So what's the verdict?" demanded Wilson. "Is he genuine?"

"Everything seems to fit," said Charlie. So why didn't he feel completely happy? Infantile to expect the man to present a resumé stamped KGB, Charlie told himself; never been an operation yet when there weren't uncertainties.

The Director caught the doubt. "But?"

"But nothing," said Charlie. "We've obviously got to go for it."

"Sure you have to get her out this way?"

"I think it stands the best chance," said Charlie, surprised the question had taken so long.

"It leaves the woman exposed."

"She's supposed to be trained: it's not far. And Kozlov seems worried about someone in his own security section, so it's got to be quick."

"What about the Americans?"

"It's the Americans I'm most worried about," admitted Charlie. "Kozlov expects a grab. Told me himself."

"Did you try to persuade him?"

"He turned me down. Said the Americans had tried the same."

"Believe they're going to try for the woman?"

"I'd take bets," said Charlie. "That's why I want to do it this way."

"They're not going to like you," forecast the Director.

"Not a lot of people do."

"There is something further from this end," said Wilson. "Done some deeper checks, from your original message. Bill Paul was supposed to be unaware of the finance sourcing of that magazine: it came through two cutouts. Doesn't look now as if he was. Indications are that he was definitely CIA employed. The whole thing was Agency."

"An obvious KGB target then?"

"Looks like it." Returning to his immediate concern, Wilson said, "Don't you think you should allow yourself more time?"

"The quicker the better," insisted Charlie. "There's no reason for any delay."

"The group leader coming in is named Sampson," said the Director, "Anthony Sampson."

"When?"

"Midnight your time," said Wilson. "Briefing is to follow your instructions."

"I'll go out to the airport," said Charlie, the escape plan formalized in his mind.

"Sampson's been ten years in the service," said the Director. "A lieutenant: one of their best."

"Nothing should go wrong then," said Charlie and regretted it the moment he'd spoken.

* * *

Kozlov got to the apartment ahead of his wife, which surprised him. He stood waiting for her, gazing out the window over the darkened harbor, smiling at the thought of all the planning and preparation at last coming successfully together. And it was going to be successful, he knew. He turned, as he heard her key in the lock, and smiled wider as she entered.

"Everything is finalized," he announced, at once.

"What's he like?" she demanded.

Kozlov considered the demand and said, "I think he's good."

"Tell me the arrangements."

Kozlov did, in absolute detail, and then insisted, "Repeat it all to me."

"The tourist bus at noon," she recited.

"And you'll recognize him?" persisted the man, determined everything should be absolutely right.

"Easily," she said, condescendingly.

Kozlov nodded toward the telephone. "I'll be waiting, if anything goes wrong."

"It won't," said the woman.

"There's nothing we haven't guarded against," said Kozlov.

"Nothing," said Irena, in unusual agreement. "Are you sure it's to be a military plane?"

"According to Hayashi, it gets in around midnight," said the man. "It's the only way."

Irena laughed, an abrupt, unexpected sound. "I'd just love to see Olga Balan's face when it happens. Filiatov's, too."

Harkness offered the Director the results of the audit and said, "I felt you should see the figures right away."

"Thank you," said Wilson, not attempting to open the folder.

The deputy appeared disappointed. He said, "There can't be any doubt. Three of the supposed informants can't be traced: that alone is a discrepancy of fifteen hundred pounds. I've itemized the other amounts; it comes to a total of practically eighteen hundred pounds."

"Thank you," said the Director, again.

"It means that Charlie Muffin has embezzled on his expense account," said Harkness, as if he feared the Director misunderstood.

"Not until it's proven," said Wilson. "I think we should give the man an opportunity to explain himself, don't you?"

"I wouldn't suggest anything else," said the deputy. "That would be most unfair."

"Quite," said the Director. He offered the audit back, unopened. "Why not keep this somewhere safe, until this other business is settled. We'll look at it then."

11

By the time he reached the darkened American embassy, Charlie had fully prepared his approach to the CIA Resident. There were none of the delays of the earlier visit: the Marine guard expected him by name and when he reached the vestibule from the main guard post Fredericks was waiting. The man hadn't shaved and after a full day and so late into the night his face was black with beard.

They walked unspeaking through the insecure outer offices into Fredericks's memorabilia-festooned, electronically protected room and the moment they entered Charlie went into the performance.

"No tricks," he said.

"What?" Fredericks frowned.

"Tonight we agreed no tricks," reminded Charlie. "So I'm keeping my side of the bargain. Everything up front, from now on."

Fredericks looked uncertainly at him. "Like what?" he said.

"We think we've identified someone Kozlov killed; one of your guys," said Charlie.

Fredericks came forward in his chair, all animosity gone. "Who!"

"The name was Bill Paul," said Charlie. "Ran a right-wing magazine in London: CIA financed. My people have confirmed he was deep-cover Agency. He was murdered in London, in January 1980. No one was ever arrested . . ."

"Son of a bitch!" said the American. It was a remark to himself, not to Charlie.

"There was another unexplained death, connected with Paul," continued Charlie. "A Ukrainian dissident called Valeri Solomatin. He used to write for Paul. Drowned in a supposed fishing accident. Our counterintelligence didn't accept it was an accident. Happened about a year after Paul's death; March '81."

"Kozlov was based in London?"

Give a little to gain a lot, thought Charlie. He nodded and said, "The name was Gordik: he was attached to a trade mission."

"But we . . ." began Fredericks.

"Not on the diplomatic list," said Charlie.

"The bastard," said Fredericks, another self-addressed remark.

"What will your people do to him, after debriefing?" asked Charlie.

"Not my decision," reminded the American. "I've just got to make sure he gets there. After that it's out of my hands."

The likelihood of American retribution provided just the sort of pressure to threaten Kozlov and persuade him to dump the CIA to come over to them, realized Charlie; bloody nuisance he hadn't known the details before his meeting with the Russian. Time enough later. He said, "Soon things will be out of both our hands."

"Fixed the meeting?"

"I said everything up front, remember?" enticed Charlie.

Fredericks nodded.

"I meant it," said Charlie. "It's tomorrow. . . ." He paused and then said, "And I'm going to take her."

Fredericks's astonishment at the announcement was obvious. At once he said, "But that means . . ."

"He's coming to you, at the same time," stopped Charlie. "Everything can coordinate perfectly. You're ready, aren't you?"

Fredericks hesitated, trying to assemble his thoughts in the proper order. He said, "No problem."

"That's good," said Charlie, a remark for his own benefit.

"You didn't give me a time?" prompted the American.

"Noon," said Charlie.

"You tell Kozlov it was going to be then?"

"No," said Charlie. "Best neither of them know, until the actual moment. Less chance of a last-minute change of heart."

"He seem unsure to you then?" demanded Fredericks, concerned.

The very opposite, thought Charlie, remembering the Russian's demeanor. "Not at all," he said. "But things can change, when it comes to making the commitment."

Fredericks paused again, wondering whether to risk the direct question. Taking the chance, he said, "Getting her out right away?"

"Safest thing to do," said Charlie.

"We'll do the same," said the American, as if he were matching the openness.

"This time tomorrow she will be halfway to England and the safety of a base." Surely he couldn't miss that as a pointer!

"Sorry if I got out of line a few times," said Fredericks.

"We both did," said Charlie.

"Keyed up, I guess," continued the American.

Soon they'd be dancing cheek to cheek, thought Charlie. He said, "Usually happens. No hard feelings about tonight?"

"Of course not."

"I'd have tried the same thing myself," admitted Charlie. He thought once more how well Fredericks lied.

"What did you think of Kozlov?"

"No doubt at all that he's genuine KGB," said Charlie. Continuing the truthfulness, because there was no danger, he added, "Still can't reconcile that lack of nervousness."

"He's a killer," reminded the American. "Trained to control any emotions. It was a point you made."

"Perhaps you're right," said Charlie.

"Anything else we need to talk through?"

"Can't think of it," said Charlie.

Fredericks rose, extending his hand. "Glad everything worked out," he said.

The handshake was crushing but Charlie didn't react. He said, "It hasn't, not yet."

"It's going to," said Fredericks. "It's got the right feel."

Charlie wondered what the other man's attitude would be tomorrow. "Let's hope you're right," he said.

It was past one o'clock when Charlie got back to the hotel and his body ached with fatigue, one part predictably more than any other. His feet didn't just ache: they hurt, like buggery. But worth it, he told himself: he was ahead, where he liked being. Secure in his room, he looked again at the photograph of Irena Kozlov, carefully inserting it into the passport slot and sitting back, realizing he didn't have a name. Inexplicably he thought of Sir Alistair Wilson's hobby and decided upon Rose. Which left the surname. There was nothing wrong with the one his mother had, when she finally married with him in the congregation. Adams, he completed, staring still at the document. She didn't look like a Rose; definitely a dog, wearing lipstick.

"Well!" demanded Fredericks.

The assembled CIA agents looked at one another and then Levine said, "Seems to be a sudden change."

"We *did* make a deal," reminded Fredericks.

"Did you intend to keep to it?" asked Levine.

"No," admitted the supervisor.

"Which is why I'm surprised he appears to be doing so."

"You reckon it's a military plane?" asked Elliott.

Fredericks nodded. "It's got to be some sort of aircraft, to get her out anyway. Halfway back to base; that's what he said. Military planes land at bases."

"What about us?" asked Fish.

"A C-130 from the Philippines," said Fredericks.

"Where do we snatch the woman?" asked Yamada.

"The most important question," agreed Fredericks. "So okay, let's go through it and make sure we get it right. There'll only be one shot and I don't want to lose it. . . ."

"Guess Kozlov will insist on the usual runaround?" said Levine.

"We've certainly got to allow for it," agreed the supervisor. "It means we're going to be stretched." He looked at Dale. "You'll have to cover the hotel, as always." To Fish he said, "You drive for me. . . ."

"What about me?" asked Yamada.

"We'll need liaison, between us with Kozlov and the others with the woman," said Fredericks. "Once we get them both I want us out of this country so fast there'll be scorch marks. That's your job. . . ." He came to Elliott, remembering the determination to settle with the Englishman and deciding to give the man the opportunity. He said, "You and Hank get Charlie Muffin."

Elliott smiled at once and said, "You better believe it; I'll get Charlie Muffin."

Fredericks felt a flicker of doubt. "It must be right, like I said," he warned. "We've no idea what she looks like so we've got to wait until the contact is made. His moving with a woman will be our identification, so nothing before then. And still not too soon. I don't want her having the chance to run. Remember, she won't want to come with us."

Elliott raised his hand, a stopping gesture. "Don't worry," he said. "There won't be any mistakes."

"There hadn't better be," said Fredericks. "Remember, he's a sneaky son of a bitch."

"I'm sneakier," said Elliott.

It was very late and this part of the airport was deserted and Jun Hayashi was nervous, pulled deep into the shadows of a cargo shed. He was completely unaware of the Russian's approach, grunting his surprise when Kozlov appeared abruptly beside him.

"Well?" demanded Kozlov.

"Americans as well as the British," said the Japanese, nodding behind him. The aircraft were too far away in the darkness to locate.

"You've done well," said Kozlov, handing over the payment. "Very well indeed."

"Damned capitalists!" said Hayashi.

Kozlov was glad of the darkness, which hid his amused reaction to the outburst. "They'll be brought down," he said.

12

Charlie was up early, with a lot to do before noon. "Smooth as silk," he told himself, in the bathroom mirror. So why was he still unable to lose the feeling that any minute that steel-shod boot was going to catch him where it hurt the most. Kozlov was unquestionably genuine: no doubt about that, like he'd told Fredericks. Reason for the split defection made sense, too, because defectors *were* despised and frequently dumped, when their usefulness was exhausted. All the negotiations had been convoluted, but that made professional sense, also, because at any minute Kozlov could have pulled back. Okay, so he hadn't withdrawn when Fredericks maintained his warned-against surveillance, but that wasn't an important inconsistency. Neither was the fact that Irena had been kept out of it; professionalism again, because it minimized the danger. Nothing wrong then. So maybe it was a hundred and one percent genuine; maybe he was a suspicious old sod with thinning hair and painful feet and bloodshot eyes who'd spent so much time making two plus two equal five that he couldn't properly add up anything anymore. And yet he could still feel that incoming boot.

Mind held by his self-description, Charlie leaned forward in the mirror. Eyes weren't bloodshot—well, not much anyway—and the hair wasn't thinning; just looked that way because he'd slept awkwardly. Not in bad shape at all, really, providing he remembered to breathe in all the time and walk with his chin up, to lessen the jowl droop. He managed to shave without cutting himself and chose the freshly pressed suit and the tie that no longer showed the pie stain, smiling at his unusual reflection in the larger mirror. Posh enough for a wedding, he decided. The reflection ran on, soberingly; people dressed up for funerals, as well.

He picked up the passport, checking his entries of the previous night, pausing at the photograph of Irena Kozlov. Certainly no rose, he thought again. He searched for the descriptive word and came up with *formidable*. Irena Kozlov certainly looked a formidable woman. He guessed it would take a long time fully to debrief her, everything having to be done at her speed and pace. Charlie hoped he didn't get stuck with the task; he disliked being boxed up for weeks in guarded country houses, painstakingly stripping the facts from the invariable self-important fiction with which defectors always attempted to make themselves appear better catches than they were. Bad as damage assessments, when one of their own people went walkabout. The thought led naturally to Herbert Bell; better as a conduit, the Director had said. Charlie wondered what disinformation they were feeding the Russians through the Foreign Office traitor. Sir Alistair Wilson was a cunning old bugger: whatever it was, Charlie knew it would be confusingly good.

Charlie did not hurry through the long walkway to the main foyer and stood back for a couple of moments at the taxi rank, wanting at this stage to make it as easy as possible. He didn't check until the vehicle was down the ramp and into the immediately clogged streets, looking idly through the rear window. Difficult in conditions like this, with so many cars, but he put five pounds on the black Nissan with the central roof aerial: two men, neither Japanese. There'd be plenty of opportunity to make sure; Haneda was a bloody long way from the city. Of which he had not seen enough, Charlie decided. When Irena was safely away he'd definitely do the rounds in Niban-Cho: he liked the look-at-me neon with bars the size of cupboards and bills the size of wardrobes, especially when it was Harkness's money. Invite Cartright, maybe; give him indigestion, if he was Harkness's man.

Charlie guessed correctly about the Nissan. Levine, who was driving, said, "I guess the airport."

"Where the hell is the pickup!" said Elliott.

"Could be a dozen places." His partner's constant anger worried Levine.

"Noon, he told Fredericks," reminded Elliott. "He's given himself a lot of time."

"Suppose it would make sense to meet her *at* the airport?" said Levine.

"Not good for a snatch," said Elliott. "Too open."

"I wouldn't like it either," agreed the other American. "Damn all we can do about it."

"Shouldn't we close up a little?"

"Don't want to spook him," said the more controlled Levine. "It's got to be the surprise of his life."

"What there is left of it," said Elliott.

"The woman first," cautioned Levine. He wished Fredericks had paired him with someone else.

They joined the airport highway and Charlie made another check and decided he was right about the Nissan. He wondered what Washington's plans were, to get Kozlov out. It had to be an aircraft of some sort: and military, too. With their bases on Guam and in the Philippines, the Americans were better placed than London had been. Alas, thought Charlie, for the passing of the British Empire, gunships and natives everywhere who knew the words to "Rule Britannia."

The routing signs began to indicate the airport and Levine said, "No doubt about it."

"Going to be a bastard if the meeting is there," said Elliott, echoing the earlier concern.

"The woman first, then him," insisted Levine. "Let's not fuck up by getting the priorities wrong."

"Hate to miss the opportunity, after what he did," said Elliott.

"His losing her will be enough," said Levine.

"No it won't," said Elliott. "Not half enough."

In the car in front Charlie leaned forward, indicating to the driver he wanted the military transportation area in the cargo section and not any of the main civilian passenger terminals.

Levine saw the car's change of direction and said, "Shit! We'll be obvious, if we stay this near!"

Elliott tensed against the windscreen and Levine saw him reach down to unclip the restraining strap on his ankle holster. Levine eased the car back, edging himself behind the hopeful concealment of a food delivery truck. As he did so he saw the camouflaged markings on some of the parked aircraft they were approaching and said, "It checks out with what he told Fredericks: a military plane."

"Where's the goddamned woman!" demanded the other American.

Levine saw the taxi stop against the military terminal building and managed to get his car into a filter road and behind a cluster of single-story sheds.

"What now!" said Elliott.

"We watch and we wait," said Levine.

Charlie Muffin entered the control area for transiting foreign military personnel, gazing through a window onto the apron, trying to identify the British aircraft. He saw an air force rondel about five aircraft away from the main building.

Sampson responded within minutes to the tannoy paging, a stiffly upright, closely barbered, open-faced man, obviously military despite the civilian clothing.

"I was expecting to come to see you, sir," said Sampson. There was an eagerness to please about the man.

Charlie tried to remember the last time even a restaurant waiter had called him sir. He said, "There was a particular reason."

"A lot was explained to me in London," said Sampson. "When's it to be?"

"Today," said Charlie. "But not from here."

"I thought . . ."

"Too many interested observers," said Charlie. "I'm running hare to the hounds." It took him fifteen minutes to explain how Irena Kozlov was going to leave Japan, and when he finished Sampson said, "Providing she can go through with it, everything sounds remarkably simple. Very little for me to do, in fact."

"The best ways are always the simple ones," said Charlie. "And there'll be enough to do, from Hong Kong."

"How will I recognize her?"

Charlie produced the passport and the photograph from his travel bag and said, "Rose Adams."

Sampson studied the picture, without comment, and then said, "She will expect me to be waiting?"

"At the arrival barrier," said Charlie. "She'll have your

name. Just pick her up, transfer immediately to your own aircraft, and head for London. No stopover. Just go."

"What time does her plane get in?"

"Nine tonight," said Charlie. "Six o'clock departure from Osaka."

"I'll have a flight plan filed from here for two," said Sampson.

"That should be more than enough time," agreed Charlie.

"Sorry not to have been able to help more," said the man.

"You're doing everything that's necessary," said Charlie.

Charlie had held the taxi and as it left the airport complex and rejoined the multilaned highway back into the city, Levine said from the watching car, "Checking the escape route. Very professional."

"So we know it *is* going to be from here," said Elliott. "And how to stop it. We've got him, Hank: really got him! The woman, too."

"It's looking good," agreed Levine. "Very good indeed."

Charlie turned back into his seat, in the car in front. This had been the easy part: he hoped the dutifully following CIA men had been lulled into believing it was going to continue just as easily.

They had. On the outskirts of Tokyo, Levine—the more cautious of the two—argued that they should pass on to the others the departure arrangements they had confirmed for Irena Kozlov. And when Charlie's taxi pulled into the shopping arcade entrance leading directly into the tower block in which they knew his room to be, Elliott agreed they had time.

Which they didn't. Charlie went to the elevator, stayed in it until the first-floor stop, and then left, going quickly back down the fire escape stairs. It could still have gone wrong for him, but for Levine's second mistake. The American was actually on the lobby telephone to Yamada, the liaison man, when he saw Charlie hurry across the short space from the emergency exit into the corridor to the main exit. Levine slammed the receiver down and instead of following alone decided instead to go back to Elliott in the waiting car. The lapse allowed Charlie to get to the exit, feign a movement toward the waiting taxis to check there was no dark-colored Nissan carrying two non-Japanese, and then double around behind the loading tourist bus to lose himself among the boarding crowd. Done it! he congratulated himself: left them foundering.

The euphoria was very brief. He looked expectantly around the bus and then, abruptly, checked a second time. Irena Kozlov, whose picture he carried in the waiting passport, wasn't there.

Fredericks and Harry Fish were still at the American embassy, waiting for the meeting instructions with Kozlov, when the liaison message came through and Fredericks said, triumphantly, "We can't lose!"

"Doesn't look like it," agreed Fish.

The supervisor shook his head at the other man's caution. "We've got the bastard! There's no way he can get the woman out."

"Still can't make up my mind whether we shouldn't wait: it's going to be proof to Kozlov from the word go that we are cheating them," said Fish.

"So what the hell can they do about it!" demanded Fredericks. "Say no, they've changed their minds and want to go back! We've played footsie long enough with a guy who's killed one Agency man at least. Once he's aboard the plane, there's fuck-all protest he or the woman can make. And they know it. From then on, we dictate the game plan."

"You know Elliott intends to kill Charlie Muffin, don't you?" demanded Fish. "How do you think the British are going to react to that, losing an agent as well as a defector?"

"I don't give a fuck about how they feel," said Fredericks. "It was an intentional insult for London to assign the man in the first place. So everyone gets taught a lesson; so what!"

Fredericks saw personal promotion in this, realized the other American. "So let's hope nothing fouls up," said Fish.

"You worry too much," said Fredericks, confidently. He looked at his watch. "Kozlov should be making contact anytime now."

Kozlov let himself into the Shinbashi apartment and sighed, a release of tension. Seized by an abrupt thought, he lifted the receiver, to hear that the dial tone was there and that the instrument was functioning; the best-conceived plans could be wrecked by the most inconsequential of things, like suddenly out-of-order telephones. It purred reassuringly in his ear. He sighed again. Now that everything was so close, he was held by an overwhelming feeling of anticlimax. Ridiculous, he thought: far too soon to imagine that nothing could go wrong. He checked the time. The Americans would be expecting him to call soon now.

13

There was a shoving pressure from behind, pushing him farther into the bus, and Charlie moved, hollow stomached. He took a seat on the side farthest from the hotel entrance, instinctively hiding from any pursuit, spreading his shoulder bag across the adjoining place to prevent it from being taken. Don't panic, he thought; another Charlie Muffin Survival Rule. A mistake to expect her to be sitting there waiting. He'd chosen the tour bus because of the intermediary stops, knowingly adopting Kozlov's own pattern. More than possible she'd use it, like her husband. No alternative but to take the ride and hope to Christ she didn't string out her moment of boarding too long: there wasn't much flexibility. In fact, if she waited . . .

Irena Kozlov came unhurriedly onto the bus, ensuring she was the last, muttering what had to be an apology to the guide and making her way farther inside. She didn't look in Charlie's direction or take the available spot next to him, instead settling three seats in front and on the opposite side. Charlie felt the anxiety go from him, a physical release, annoyed at the quickness of his unneccessary concern.

The commentary began from the guide as the bus descended the now familiar ramp, the palaces to the left being individually indentified. Charlie closed his mind to the litany, concentrating upon Irena Kozlov. The first and most immediate impression was of her size: she was clearly visible above the high-back seats, dwarfing everyone around her. Quickly there followed an admiration for her expertise; she actually appeared to be listening, twisting and turning to the landmarks, covering herself brilliantly. Irena didn't make her move until the tour got to Shinjuhu Gyoen Garden and then still brilliantly because the garden was on the right-hand side of the bus, enabling her to pretend difficulty in seeing and to look obviously around for a better vantage point. Even the approach, when it came, was absolutely right: a polite inquiry if the seat was free and the smiled thanks when Charlie moved the place-keeping bag. She *was* big, he decided, pulling himself toward the window to allow more room: she was tight against him. She went through the charade of looking at the park, justifying her move, and entered into the necessary conversation by offering Charlie the map she carried, as if she were pointing out a place he couldn't locate on his own guide.

"I was worried, when you weren't on the bus," he said.

"I needed to be sure," she said.

"I lost them," he said.

"You didn't," she contradicted at once. "There are two. One is named Levine, the other Elliott."

Charlie curbed the impulse to swing around, to examine the other tourists. "Where!"

"Not here; following," she said. "It's a dark Nissan, blue I think."

Charlie realized he'd overlooked Kozlov's boast that they knew every CIA officer on station in Tokyo. He said, "I did not agree or plan it. They followed me to the airport."

"They were panicked at the hotel," said Irena. "They only located you aboard at the very last moment; I saw their reaction."

"No one on the bus?" insisted Charlie, using her knowledge.

"If there had been I wouldn't be here," she said.

Charlie swiveled in his seat. The Nissan was four vehicles behind. From where they were, the Americans wouldn't be able to see with whom he was sitting: it still meant he had to hurry, before the first stop. Charlie employed his own map, for the benefit of those in the bus whom the Americans might later question, apparently consulting her. Irena responded superbly, taking from within its folds the passport and dropping it into her own bag.

"Rose Adams," he said. "That's the name."

"Easy to remember," she said.

Charlie thought he detected an arrogance about the woman. He hoped it would translate into confidence; she was going to need a lot of that in the next few hours. He said, "That's why I chose it."

He entered into the performance with the map again and this time her reaction was more hesitant. Irena dropped the contents into the same bag as the passport and said, "What is that?"

"Your airline ticket," said Charlie. "At six o'clock tonight there's a Japanese Air Lines flight from Osaka to Hong Kong. . . ." Charlie glanced at his watch, glad once more that she had got on at the beginning of the tour. "You'll make it easily. There's a Bullet train at three: the reservation is with your airline ticket. . . ."

"But . . ." the woman started to protest and Charlie was immediately doubtful about the confidence, after all.

"But nothing," stopped Charlie, in turn. "Yuri is going to the Americans today?"

"Yes," she said.

"They're taking him out too," announced Charlie.

"I have not packed," groped the woman.

"Don't be ridiculous!" said Charlie. "You didn't think you were going to walk out of the Soviet embassy carrying a suitcase!"

"Small things. Personal. Mementos . . ." she tried.

Charlie shook his head. "It's over, Irena. New life for the old: No mementos, no nothing." It was astonishing, how often they asked.

"I thought we'd go from here, from Tokyo. A military plane."

"This way is better," insisted Charlie.

"You're coming with me?" she said.

Charlie shook his head. "The Americans haven't left me, from the moment I arrived. You know they're behind, now. That's how they expect to identify you, through me. Then snatch. Get the train, go to the airport, and catch the flight. You'll be met in Hong Kong by a man named Anthony Sampson. He knows your assumed name and what you look like. Just go with him."

"Where?"

"To England."

"I thought I would be escorted."

She meant protected: maybe the confidence was not so assured as he'd imagined. "You will be, from Hong Kong," he said. "A whole squad of men, all trained."

"When will I see Yuri again?"

"A month," said Charlie. "That's the agreed arrangement, isn't it?"

"I didn't expect . . ." she stopped, unhappy with the word, ". . . think," she picked up, "that it would be like this."

"It's important to do what no one expects, for it to succeed," said Charlie. "Didn't Yuri warn you that the Americans would try to cheat?"

"Yes," she said.

"That's what I am ensuring against," he said.

"Yuri will be protected?"

"The Americans are ready."

"Yuri didn't expect it to be as quick as this."

"The important thing—the only thing—is getting you both safely across," said Charlie.

"I know that," she said.

"And this is the way," he insisted.

"You're sure what the Americans intend?"

"Positive," said Charlie. It wasn't an exaggeration. Preparing the ground for later, he said, "I tried to explain to him he would be safer if both of you came across to us, in the first place."

"We talked about it: it was a trick," she said dismissively.

"I know what Yuri has done," said Charlie. "Don't you think it's naïve, expecting the Americans to take no action?"

"I will be his protection," she said. "That's how we planned it."

Charlie decided any further pressure would be wrong at this stage.

"I never imagined it would be like this: the moment I mean."

"It will be all right," insisted Charlie, encouraging now. "A train ride, a short flight, and you're safe. No one, apart from Sampson and myself, even knows the cover name."

She sniggered, a nervous reaction. "Rose Adams," she said. "It's . . . it's . . ."

Not big enough, thought Charlie, looking at her. "Easy to remember," he reminded. "And you will remember it; the name that took you out to a brand-new life." He wished it hadn't sounded like a commercial for soap powder or a laxative.

"Thank you," she said, suddenly. "It's a sensible arrangement: clever, too."

"And simple," Charlie said, as he'd agreed with Sampson. For an operation that in London had risked being one of the most difficult, it had, in the event, turned out to be one of the easiest. He said, "In the wallet, with the airline ticket, there is some money. You shouldn't need it. Just in case."

"You've been very thorough," she said.

"So were you and Yuri," said Charlie.

"It's very important nothing goes wrong."

"It won't!" said Charlie. "Trust me when I say it won't!"

"I could be in England by tomorrow?"

"There's quite a wide time difference, but yes," agreed Charlie.

"Will you be my case officer?"

The expertise was reasserting itself, over the nervousness, Charlie decided. He said, "I'm not sure. Maybe. Maybe not."

"You're normally operational then?" she decided, appearing to want to prove herself.

"I do all sorts of things," sidestepped Charlie. Tradecraft did not allow him to discuss his status or working life with her. Actually his was a pretty accurate self-description: a general dog's body.

"There won't be any misunderstandings about the conditions, if it's someone else?"

It was developing into a rapid recovery. He said, "Of course not!"

She seemed to become aware of the tour and said, "I need to get off at the first stop?"

"Yes," said Charlie at once. "Give yourself as much time as possible."

"I'm nervous," she admitted.

"I'd be worried if you weren't," said Charlie. "What else can you be? Everything is going to be all right."

"We spent months planning this. Now it's all happening so quickly."

"The way it's got to be done," insisted Charlie.

"Sampson will be waiting at the airport?"

"I guarantee it," said Charlie.

"There's nothing else?"

"All very simple," reiterated Charlie.

"It is," she agreed.

Charlie realized she was searching for words, not wanting to end the conversation. It was a symptom he knew, the reluctance to let go at the very moment of cutting adrift. It was fortunate the decision was being reached for her. He said, "We're getting into Shibuya-Ku: the first stop is there, at an Olympic memorial and a shrine." With so many shrines, the gods should be on their side.

Irena breathed in, preparing herself, as the coach pulled off the highway into the parking lot. Remembering, Charlie swiveled in his seat, seeing the Nissan follow. Conscious of his movement, the woman turned too. As the Americans got out of the vehicle, she said, "Elliott is the fatter one, with the receding hair. Levine is the one driving, wearing the patterned sports jacket."

"Get away from me," warned Charlie.

She moved at once, slotting herself in with the disembarking tourists. Charlie waited in his seat, letting everyone else get off ahead of him, managing further delay by carefully looping the strap of the travel bag across his shoulders before getting off. The guide shepherded them into some sort of order and Charlie saw that Elliott and Levine had attached themselves. Irena was at the far side and Charlie recognized again how good she was, remaining with the group until the best opportunity arose and not attracting attention to herself by immediately splitting away. Dutifully they filed toward the Meiji Jingu temple and Charlie moved nearer to the guide, attentive to the commentary, totally ignoring Irena Kozlov. The two Americans closed up, clearly oblivious to her as well, and Charlie felt the jump of satisfaction.

Irena made her break at the huge entrance gate and did it so well that for several moments Charlie himself wasn't aware she was no longer one of the party. Still outwardly the rubbernecking tourist, he was tightly alert to Elliott and Levine. Both stayed within feet of him and Charlie allowed the boast and thought, you've done it, my son: and come up smelling of violets. It was important for Charlie Muffin always to win: that's what made him so good. He looked obviously at his watch, aware the gesture would register with the two shadowing men. Twelve forty-five. Sampson would soon be airborne, Fredericks would be linking up with Kozlov, and Irena had more than enough time to catch her train. Frequent as they were, Charlie guessed she might even be able to get an earlier one. He tramped on, experiencing the first twinge of discomfort and accepting that his feet were going to give him hell, after all this walking: no one would ever fully know the things he did for Queen and country. There was the pause for picture-taking at the shrine and Charlie resisted the temptation to sit, adopting instead an eagerness he hoped the two Americans would discern, imagining an anticipated approach. He remembered that Kozlov had selected a shrine, the night of their meeting, and wondered if the two men had trodden any other tourist routes during the negotiations with the Russian. More than likely, he supposed.

The trek from the shrine to the Olympic youth center was a long one and Charlie's feet were throbbing by the time they reached it. Definitely a celebration tonight, he decided: few drinks at Niban-Cho, and then a complete contrast, a *ryotei* restaurant for Japanese haute cuisine: traditional, too, which was important. He could take his shoes off. He wished to Christ he could do that now. Charlie remained looking intently around him; Levine and Elliott were expectantly behind now, Elliott at one stage standing right next to him. Too late, my loves; too late, he thought.

Charlie returned gratefully to the bus, settling in the same seat as before, aware of Elliott in conversation at the steps with the guide and then of the American boarding the vehicle and establishing himself two rows behind, on the opposite side. Charlie made another obvious time check. One-twenty. Two o'clock, Sampson had estimated; they'd be preparing for takeoff. Sampson seemed the sort of man who'd always build in allowances for the unexpected: perhaps he'd already left. Charlie decided to move at the next stop: Elliott might learn of the now missing Irena by questioning other passengers. There was no reason, in fact, to delay the signal to London that everything had gone off perfectly: absolutely perfectly.

The stop was at the nature study park in Shirokanedai and Charlie made no attempt to conceal his departure from the

Americans, because it didn't matter anymore, separating away as the group began their tour and heading for the road. He ignored the car that Levine parked, looking for a taxi. The traffic was bad, the air shuddering with exhaust fumes: several passing Japanese wore smog masks, like doctors looking for a misplaced operating theater.

He was lucky with a cab, sitting forward on the seat, impatient now to get to the embassy and find out from Fredericks how everything had gone with Kozlov. Perhaps he'd extend that night's invitation to include the American. Kozlov would be gone and there was nothing to be gained by continuing the rivalry. As far as Fredericks was concerned, the episode had ended in a draw, one each.

At an intersection, the driver made a sudden turn and Charlie saw, relieved, that they were joining the major Sakura-dadori Avenue and that it was comparatively clear. It stayed that way up to and then beyond the Imperial Palace. It was fifteen minutes past two when the cab pulled up outside the British embassy.

The Americans were two cars behind and Elliott said positively, "It's gone wrong!"

"Nothing happened on that bus," insisted Levine.

"It was the only place and we missed it," said Elliott.

"I'm sure nothing happened," said Levine, who wasn't and who knew that Elliott didn't think so either.

"What now?" asked Elliott.

"We wait."

"Shouldn't we contact the others?"

Levine shook his head, determinedly. "I did that last time," he said, in admission. "We're not moving."

"Holy shit!" exploded Elliott. "The bastard screwed us!"

Inside the embassy, Charlie was conscious of an atmosphere as he waited in the foyer for Cartright to arrive and take him through the admission procedure. When the intelligence Resident reached him, Cartright said, "Sorry if I kept you, Charlie. Hell of a flap on at the moment."

"What?" asked Charlie.

"Had some military people through, on their way to some sort of exercise in Australia. Still not clear yet . . . only happened about half an hour ago. . . ."

"Tell me!" demanded Charlie, shouting.

"Seems to have blown up, on takeoff."

"Fuck!" said Charlie. Where was the perfect planning now? More important, where was Irena Kozlov?

By one o'clock there was still no contact from Kozlov with room 323 at the Imperial Hotel and Fredericks hurried down to the hotel foyer to use the telephones there, leaving the one Dale was manning unblocked. From then on, the panic rising, he called Yamada, maintaining liaison at the embassy every five minutes.

"Still nothing," insisted Yamada, at two-thirty. "Last time I heard from Levine was just before twelve, from the hotel. Said he had Charlie Muffin under wraps."

"No problems at all?"

"Airport and back, obviously just checking arrangements."

"But he hadn't met the woman!"

"No," said Yamada, suppressing the sigh. It had been the same conversation, every time.

"Kozlov hasn't shown," said Fredericks.

"You told me already."

"So where the hell is he?" said Fredericks, exasperated.

"Where the hell is everyone?" said Yamada. "What's happened?"

It was the question Charlie Muffin was asking himself, in the code room at the British embassy.

14

Charlie Muffin recognized it was a damage assessment in every definition of the phrase. And he didn't have a clue how to assess it. Which way—or where—to start, even. The first priority was salvage, to save what he had. And he still had—he hoped—Irena Kozlov. There was insufficient time to try to reach the woman before she caught the train to Osaka. He supposed he could wait and telephone Osaka airport: he knew the flight number and there'd be no risk, paging her by her new name. She'd been frightened, Charlie remembered: unwilling at the last moment to let go. Psychologically wrong, then, to attempt any interception and half-thought-out rearrangements which might panic her. Which left Hong Kong, where she expected to be met by a man named Anthony Sampson and a military aircraft. And wasn't going to encounter either. Thank God for insurance, thought Charlie, sighing with relief as Harry Lu replied on the second ring.

"Hoping to hear from you, Charlie!" greeted the man. His voice caught at the end and the sentence finished in a wheezing cough. "How's business?" he picked up.

"Problems," admitted Charlie, at once.

"Serious?" asked Lu.

"Danger to a whole contract," said Charlie. "Someone's intercepted some samples. Damaged a whole shipment."

"What can I do?" said Lu.

Praise be for true professionals, thought Charlie. He said,

"Got a salesperson coming in. Rose Adams. Expecting a buyer who won't be able to make it."

"Like me to pick her up instead?" anticipated the man.

"And keep her from any rival buyers," said Charlie. "Japan Air Lines flight 208."

"This salesperson, she know the name of the buyer?"

"Sampson," said Charlie. "Anthony Sampson."

"Met before?"

"No."

"She likely to be disappointed?"

"She was expecting an immediate onward transshipment," said Charlie. "Likely to be very unhappy."

"I understand," said Lu, who did. "Anyone else from the firm coming to sort it all out?"

"Getting there myself as soon as possible," announced Charlie. He paused and said, "Transportation still reliable, in Hong Kong?"

"Same service as before," assured the other man.

"I remember," said Charlie. "Apologize to her for me, will you? Make it very clear that she hasn't lost the business. . . ." He hesitated, then added, "Tell her everything here is fine." She'd need the assurance, confronted with the uncertainty of not being met by whom she expected.

"Will do," undertook Lu.

"There might be some other determined buyers," warned Charlie.

"Business is tough all over."

"This is very tough," insisted Charlie. He said, "It's good to be working with you again."

"Like it to happen more often," said Lu, making clear the expected return.

"I'll see it does," promised Charlie. Another undertaking not backed by authority, he realized. If Harry Lu stood in for him until he was able to get to Hong Kong, Charlie determined to oppose Harkness any way that was necessary to resolve the nonsense of fictitious expense claims and get Harry Lu back on a London retainer.

Charlie was connected as quickly to General Sir Alistair Wilson in London and, assured of a secure line, did not have to go through the confusing ambiguity of Hong Kong. The Director listened without any interruption until Charlie had clearly finished and said, "The Americans did that!"

"It couldn't have been anyone else," said Charlie. "I led them out this morning, intentionally to confuse."

"Bastards!" said Wilson. Continuing, his voice becoming strangely soft, the man said, "I don't like losing soldiers, Charlie. Don't like losing anyone but soldiers least of all."

"I didn't have any alternative bringing Harry Lu in," said Charlie. People had been prepared to lose him enough times.

"I accept that," said Wilson. "You be able to get there tonight?"

"Yes," assured Charlie.

"What about another squad, to Hong Kong?"

"Let's first make sure there's a reason for their flying out," said Charlie.

"You think you might have lost her?"

"I don't know enough to think anything at the moment," said Charlie.

"No proof, about the plane then?"

"There wouldn't be, would there?"

"Bastards," said Wilson again. There was a long pause and then he said, "Imagine being prepared to kill that many people, just to seal an escape route!"

"Maybe I didn't think dirty enough," conceded Charlie, recalling the other man's remark at the London briefing.

"I'll still go along with it," said Wilson, more to himself than to Charlie. "I'll wait until that first joint meeting, and I'll get Kozlov if it takes me a regiment to do it. Two regiments."

"Need I tell anyone here about the squad?"

"No," said the Director, at once. "There *is* to be a several-nations exercise in Australia, so the cover story stands. Sampson wasn't carrying anything to link him to you?"

"No," said Charlie, in turn. He hoped the man hadn't made any notes, after their meeting. He thought it unlikely.

"No risk then," said the Director.

"I'll need Cartright now," said Charlie.

"Whatever is necessary," agreed Wilson, at once. "And, Charlie—really be careful, understand?"

"I told you I always was," said Charlie.

"Don't forget how I feel about losing people, will you?"

"No," promised Charlie. "I won't forget."

* * *

Cartright drove and as they left the embassy Charlie identified the waiting Nissan and said, "The Director called them bastards."

"Still difficult to believe," said Cartright. The Nissan started to follow and the man added, "They'll know it's the airport."

"I want them to," said Charlie. He told the other man how he wanted them stopped and Cartright said, "Christ, you're going to begin a war."

"We've already got one," said Charlie. "They started it."

"There's nothing more I can do?" The satisfaction, at involvement at last, was obvious in Cartright's voice.

"We're not sure yet if Irena Kozlov is even in Hong Kong," said Charlie. "You got Harry Lu's number?"

Cartright nodded and said, "There was an instruction not to use him, you know?"

"It's been changed," said Charlie. "Everything's been changed."

Cartright looked across the car and said, "It was Harkness's order. I got another one, about you."

"I guessed," said Charlie.

"There was nothing to report," assured the man.

"Thanks for telling me," said Charlie.

"I didn't like the position it put me in."

"Harkness is a bloody old woman," said Charlie, with feeling.

They passed a road sign indicating the airport and Charlie said, "You'll have to be quick."

Cartright looked in his mirror and said, "They're quite a long way back."

"Got the names?"

"Levine and Elliott," recited Cartright.

There are security barriers and obstructions permanently in place at Haneda airport but there were additional precautions after the earlier plane explosion, extra personnel at each checkpoint, examining every car. As the search started on their vehicle, Charlie said, "This should hold them, which will help."

From where they sat the two men could still see the smoke-blackened hull of the British plane. The blaze that followed the explosion had been extinguished, but the wreckage still smoldered and fire engines and rescue vehicles remained grouped around it.

"Wilson was right," said Charlie, as they were waved on. "They are bastards, to do that."

"Good luck," said Cartright, automatically, as they parted at the airport entrance, Charlie for departures, Cartright heading for the telephone bank.

"Yeah," said Charlie, sourly.

Cartright stayed by the telephone after making the call, watching the car stop and identifying the Americans as they left it. Levine and Elliott hurried in and were halfway across the concourse toward the departure gates when the security men who also used the Nissan to isolate the two swooped in a coordinated, encircling movement. The Japanese had their guns unslung and the demands, in English and by name, for the two men to halt were amplified through bullhorns. Levine and Elliott jerked to a stop, bewildered, and momentarily Cartright thought Levine was going to try to run. There was another amplified shout and hesitantly both men obeyed, raising their arms in surrender.

Irena Kozlov emerged hesitantly from the arrivals section at Hong Kong, looking around her. At first she did not recognize the name Rose Adams written on the piece of card and when she did frowned up at the man holding it. She stopped completely, uncertain, then at last approached the man.

"Are you Anthony Sampson?" she said, curiously.

"Yes," lied Harry Lu, for expediency, hurrying her away as quickly as possible. He thought she was alone but it was always difficult to tell, in a place as crowded as an airport.

15

The Japanese Interior Ministry followed the strictest protocol, approaching the American embassy through their Foreign Ministry, which meant the involvement of the full U.S. diplomatic staff, including the ambassador. A career diplomat only five years away from retirement and a $200,000 a year consultancy as an expert in Asian affairs at a Georgetown research institute, the ambassador ordered immediate discussion with Washington. The initial hesitation from the CIA headquarters at Langley, simply to gain time and seek clarification from Fredericks in Tokyo, was misinterpreted as indicating guilt by the inquiring U.S. State Department. Anticipating a major crisis, State played politics, directing a second and independent inquiry to the White House, where the Chief of Staff had the same reaction as State and alerted the President. That led to a direct what-the-hell-is-going-on call from the President to the CIA Director, who made the same demand, in a signed cable, to Fredericks. As well as responding to that, Fredericks was subjected to detailed questioning from the still-doubtful ambassador and after that had to go out to Haneda personally to sign for the release of Levine and Elliott. It was midnight before he returned to the embassy and the waiting, remaining, CIA group.

"What!" erupted Harry Fish, before Fredericks completed the explanation.

"The British escape plane, sabotaged at the airport," elaborated Fredericks. "There was an anonymous call from within the airport itself, claiming Levine and Elliott were responsible."

"How were they identified?" demanded Yamada.

"The car," said the Resident. "Described in detail, right down to the registration plate. Even witnesses who remembered it around the military section this morning."

"Jesus Christ!" said Dale. "You satisfy everybody?"

"I've got them released, but the ambassador isn't convinced," said Fredericks. "Langley is demanding a fuller explanation in the diplomatic pouch, so they're clearly taking out insurance. . . . Would you believe the President himself is riding shotgun, insisting we prove ourselves squeaky clean! Only people not demanding explanations and assurances at the moment are the office cleaners!"

"Jesus!" said Dale, again.

"What did you tell Langley about Kozlov?" queried Fish.

"That he didn't show."

"Just that?" questioned Fish, doubtfully.

"What do you want me to do!" demanded Fredericks, venting the anger and frustrations of the evening. "Admit we've been completely suckered by a guy who's screwed the Agency once already; someone we were warned about!"

"Okay! Okay!" said the other American, retreating.

"All because of Charlie Muffin!" said Dale, disbelievingly.

"So now it's recovery time," said Fredericks, positively. "We've lost him and we've lost Kozlov and we've lost the woman. Right now, all of us together, we're not worth a bucket of spit."

"He'll be halfway back to England by now!" protested Yamada.

"He isn't," said Fredericks. "Hank got a positive make on him, from a Cathay Pacific ticket clerk at the airport. He caught a flight to Hong Kong, forty-five minutes after their arrest. . . ." The man looked at the desk clock. "Their own plane left two hours ago. . . ." He smiled an expression bereft of humor. "They want him," he said. "They want Charlie Muffin so bad you can feel it."

"Just Levine and Elliott?" queried Fish.

"All of us," insisted Fredericks. "We're going down tonight on that C-130 and we're to shake Hong Kong until all the fruit falls out of the trees."

"What if we get him?" said Dale.

"We've *got* to get him," insisted Fredericks. "And we will. We've checked the civil flights: there aren't any more tonight out to Europe, so he's stuck there until tomorrow. I've activated every informant and person-in-place we've ever used and said they can name their own price: earn their pension in a day. Levine and Elliott aren't moving from the airport until we get there. And our military can monitor any air force flight. Hong Kong is *sealed.*"

"Okay," corrected Dale. "*When* we get him. What then?"

"The Kozlovs first," ordered Fredericks. "I don't know how he did it, but I'm sure Charlie Muffin got the goddamned man and the woman to go over to him, together. We've got to get them back, through him."

"Then?" said Yamada.

"And then we blow him away," said Fredericks, simply. "That guy's made his last smartassed move. Ever."

Olga Balan used her own key to enter the Shinbashi apartment, stopped immediately inside the door by the look on Kozlov's face.

"Darling!" she said. "What is it!"

"She's still alive," said Kozlov.

"But the plane . . ." she said. "I heard the reports. . . ."

"She wasn't on it," said Kozlov. He was white with anger.

"How . . . ?" she stumbled.

Kozlov indicated the telephone. "She kept to the arrangement . . ." In his frustration, Kozlov punched one fist into the palm of the other. "It was the Englishman," he said. "It was all planned so perfectly and Charlie Muffin did something I hadn't expected. . . ."

"What are we going to do?"

"Find them," said Kozlov, simply. "And this time make sure she dies." He paused and said, "The Englishman, too: he's definitely got to be killed."

16

The vodka had been for a celebration, of their freedom, but they drank it now for a different reason, needing its support. Kozlov walked aimlessly about the apartment, glass in hand, movement necessary to ease his frustration.

"Everything was perfect!" he said again. "Everything!"

"Tell me from the beginning," said Olga, confused and trying to understand.

Kozlov halted by the window, gazing out over the gardens, still gripped by anger. Instead of replying directly, he said, "I should have *known*! I thought the photograph was to identify her: I should have guessed a passport!"

"From the beginning," prompted Olga again.

"Hayashi alerted me as soon as the military planes arrived," began Kozlov. "It was easy, that late at night, to get onto the apron: he knows the airport very well. The British aircraft was locked, of course, so I put the explosive into two different engine cowlings. Pressure activated . . ." He stopped, drinking deeply from his glass. "For the meeting I went through the usual routine: ran the Americans all over town, choosing the place. Then insisted that I be left alone, with the Englishman. . . ." Kozlov paused again, halted by a thought. "He *was* clever: knew things about the KGB that surprised me: somehow he had linked me with McFairlane. . . ." He shook his head. "I wasn't careful enough. I'd confused the Americans and I thought I'd confused him: didn't imagine anything could go wrong."

"He didn't query the separate crossings?" asked the woman.

"Of course he queried them," said Kozlov. "He seemed satisfied by what I said. We arranged how he was to contact Irena and afterward I took her through it . . . everything was going just as I'd planned!"

"How did you learn it had gone wrong?"

"After she left this morning I came here. Heard the news reports of the explosion and thought it had all worked . . ." He drank heavily again. "You know the precautions . . . this place and this telephone. . . ."

"This was supposed to be our place," she interrupted.

Kozlov was suddenly aware of her need. He crossed to her, cupped her face into his hands, and kissed her, gently. "It *is*," he said. "And it's going to be."

"Why did she have to know?"

Kozlov frowned at the question. "You know why! There *had* to be a telephone point between us, away from the embassy. An embassy link would have made her suspicious. Don't forget the British and the Americans intended trying to get us both; the Englishman openly admitted it to me! This was the failsafe, to stop the Americans' interfering. I told her I would not cross to Fredericks until I had heard positively from her. She was to tell the Americans, if they intercepted, that I wouldn't cross at all until they'd released her and let the arrangements remain as they were supposed to be. That way I could guarantee her being on the British aircraft. This place was the last part of the perfect murder."

"And she called?"

Kozlov nodded, adding more vodka to both their glasses. "I thought it was you! She actually guessed something, from my voice; asked me what was wrong!"

"What did you say?"

"Difficult to say anything, at first. Told her she was imagining it and that maybe I was nervous."

"Where was she?"

"Osaka airport. About to take off for Hong Kong."

"So why did you let her leave!" demanded Olga.

"There has to be provable contact with a foreign intelligence organization," insisted Kozlov. "All your interrogations were geared to show that, on the tapes and films and the involvement of Filiatov . . . bringing her back to Tokyo would have ruined it all."

"But what's to prevent her getting on the next flight to London, from Hong Kong!"

"Me," said Kozlov. For the first time he smiled. "She'll realize at once that something *has* gone wrong, because the plane isn't going to be there. She'll imagine some disaster here. . . ." He indicated the telephone. "She'll call," he said.

The woman shook her head, doubtfully. "I think you've taken a terrible risk."

"I didn't have any alternative," said Kozlov.

"Darling," said Olga, slowly. "Why not just let her go: you tricked her into defecting. Isn't that enough?"

Kozlov wondered if Olga would agree to what he wanted, to make things right. "You *know* it isn't enough," he said. "It's all part of the explanation, to satisfy Moscow. That we realized at the last moment what she was doing, establishing the contact: and that I proved my loyalty by stopping her, as she tried to defect. It can't work, any other way. The families of Russian defectors are always interrogated and always remain on the suspect list. In my case, it would be a hundred times worse. I'd be taken back to Moscow under arrest. . . ." Kozlov paused, for the most important fact to register. "It would mean the end of it, all that we've planned, so carefully and for so long . . . the end of us, darling."

Olga bit her lip, making a performance of sipping her drink to cover the closeness of tears. "Damn her!" she said. "Why couldn't the bloody woman have agreed to a divorce!"

"I told you what happened before," reminded Kozlov. "Before I came to England and we met. She said she'd never be a rejected woman . . . never be abandoned."

"I would have accepted things going on as they were," said Olga.

"I wouldn't," said Kozlov, positively. "I want to get rid of her completely. I want you as my wife, not a mistress from whom I can be parted by a whim of some posting, from Moscow, for either of us. Look how long it took us to get together again, here!" Kozlov put his drink aside and sat next to her and said, "I love you, my darling. Completely and absolutely. So no more half-measures. No more hiding from everyone in the embassy, frightened of a chance look or gesture being seen and interpreted."

"I'm frightened," conceded the woman. "I thought it was a brilliant idea and I know I went along with it but now it's . . ." She moved her hands in front of her, searching for the words. "Now I think it's impossible: that it can't succeed," she said.

"It can," said Kozlov, coaxingly. Was now the time to tell her what she had to do?

Before he could speak, she said, "Did she ever come here?"

Kozlov hesitated. Then he said, "She had to; she had to think it was for her protection. I told you that."

"Did you make love to her here?"

Kozlov's hesitation this time was longer. At last he said, "It was meaningless . . . nothing. . . ."

"Just something else that had to be done!"

"Olga!" he said, consciously trying to avoid a different irritation. "For fifteen years I lived with a woman able to find fault with everything, hidden reason in everything, and question everything. If I said it was day, she said it was night. Black was white and white was black. I could have lied just now. I could have said Irena never came here, only knew the telephone number, and that I didn't go to bed with her here. I didn't because I love you and don't intend ever lying to you. I brought her here and made love to her here because I thought it was necessary: because she had to believe and not, for once in her life, question."

"I'm sorry," said the woman. "I'm really sorry. . . ." She smiled and said, "This has got to be our place, from now on. Somewhere secret, which nobody else knows. Make love to me now . . ."

Kozlov felt out for her and she was coming to him when the telephone sounded stridently into the room. Each jerked away from the other, startled. Kozlov said, "I told you it would be all right."

He nodded, in unnecessary confirmation, when he heard Irena's voice and said, "Darling!"

Olga, softly, said, "Bitch."

The aircraft made its lower-than-the-hilltops approach to Hong Kong and then the sharp starboard turn as if it were going to land among the skyscrapers, instead settling on the water's-edge postage stamp that is Kai Tak airport. With only a travel bag, Charlie had no luggage collection delay, hurrying through the terminal and out into the melee of the taxi and rental-car area. It was markedly warmer than Tokyo, a heat blanket wrapping around him, and Charlie felt the perspiration form at once.

He pushed his way through the touts, passing the taxis and then the rental-car reservations, going to the very end of the line. It was a yellow Mercedes, the For Hire flag on the passenger side. The driver was uniformed, a black or maybe dark blue outfit, and wore a peaked cap. Charlie got into the rear, settling back as the driver maneuvered himself through the traffic crush and then out of the airport complex.

"Any company?" said Charlie.

"Not yet. But there's going to be."

"Good to see you again, Harry."

"Like I said," replied Lu. "It's been a long time."

17

Harry Lu lit an inevitable cigarette as the car dipped into the tunnel to Hong Kong island and said, "It's put a strain on my loyalty, Charlie. If it hadn't been you, I'd have sold out, after the way London's cut me off."

"Tell me about it," said Charlie. Fuck Harkness and his columns of figures. He hoped Lu was telling the complete truth, not just covering his back.

"The Americans have woken up everybody they've ever used. I've had three separate calls from people, asking if I know anything. Money no object."

Let Harkness argue that away, thought Charlie. He said, "I expected it."

"People are coming in, apparently."

"That too," said Charlie. He smiled at Lu's reflection in the mirror and said, "See you've still got Hong Kong buttoned up."

"Like to know what's going on; feel safe that way," said the other man.

"How is she?" asked Charlie.

"Edgy," said Lu. "Very edgy."

"What have you told her?"

"That there had to be a change of plan and that you're coming."

"Where is she?"

"Mandarin," said Lu. "That was before I heard what the Americans were doing. Warned her we'll be moving on; it's too high profile and obvious now."

"She knows there's a pursuit?"

"Of course not!"

Charlie registered the frown of the man in front of him and said, "Sorry. Silly question." The American reaction meant any civilian aircraft was impossible. Charlie wished he'd agreed to a military plane being dispatched; now there would be at least a day's delay in getting Irena Kozlov away.

Lu said, "Russian?"

"Yes," said Charlie.

"Any link with the plane explosion in Tokyo?"

"They all died," said Charlie.

"Who did it?"

"CIA," said Charlie.

"They must want her very badly?"

"They're going for the double," said Charlie. "They've already got the husband."

The Mercedes emerged onto Hong Kong into an immediate traffic clog. Charlie looked up at the jumbled skyline of uneven skyscrapers and thought Lu was right about moving from the Mandarin Hotel: the island was too easy to block off.

"London know I'm in?" asked Lu, from the front of the vehicle.

"The Director himself," assured Charlie.

"No objection?"

Charlie hesitated. "They had no choice, did they?" he said. Lu was too experienced to be bullshitted; would be offended, in fact.

"What's my problem there?"

Charlie told him, feeling embarrassed, and Lu said, "I was building up my get-out fund. My name is going to be on the list after 1997."

"I hadn't thought of that," admitted Charlie. Harry Lu had literally been born into espionage. His father had been a colonel in the Communist Chinese army whose spying for Britain was discovered in the last year of the Korean war. Ironically it was a British not a pursuing Chinese bullet that shattered his arm as he fled across the dividing line, and it was in the Seoul hospital that he met the British nurse he later married. In Hong Kong, Harry's father established himself as London's foremost China watcher and inculcated the craft into his son when he was still in his teens, to take over the operation when he died. Charlie said,

"You really think Beijing will still have the file open, after all these years?"

"Don't forget the Asian mentality: a thousand years is a speck in time," said Lu. Apart from his surname and an olive complexion, there was no indication of his parentage. He was actually fair-haired and European-featured. He said, "Beijing have had their cells operating here for years. They know all about me."

As the traffic jam cleared and they began moving again, Charlie said, "I would have thought your father was the target."

"Sins of the father," quoted Lu, glibly. "Over the years I provided as much—maybe more—on China as he did: he began during a war, that's all."

"Convinced it's going to be that bad, when China takes over?"

"People like me don't even have a proper passport: not officially anyway," said Lu. "We're second-class citizens, just promised consular protection."

"What are you going to do?"

There was a gap before Lu responded. Then he said, "Canada is taking people."

"Without proper passports?"

"Something's always available, at a price. Like everything else in Hong Kong," said the man.

"So why didn't you, Harry?"

"Sell you out?"

"You don't owe any loyalty to London," accepted Charlie. "And this goes beyond whatever there is between us."

Lu smiled, kindling another cigarette. "Never the fool, Charlie."

"It costs too much."

"I'm displaying a Chinese characteristic," admitted Lu. "I'm gambling."

Ahead, to the right, Charlie saw the Star ferry terminal and automatically registered another escape point from the island. Remembering the London remark of Sir Alistair Wilson, Charlie said, "What's the game?"

"Getting a proper passport and all the entry permits to settle in England," announced Lu. He risked a brief, backward smiling glance. "Would you believe I've got relatives in a part of

London called Cockfosters! What sort of place gets a name like Cockfosters!"

Charlie spread his hands in a gesture of helplessness, knowing of the other man's absolute attention from the front of the vehicle. "I can't guarantee anything: you know that!"

"Wilson could," said Lu confidently and at once. "And after tonight I'm owed, Charlie. I'm owed a lot."

"I'm not sure he could, either," said Charlie, doubtfully.

"You going to try to fix it for me, Charlie?"

Charlie sighed, momentarily closing his eyes. Hubert Witherspoon was probably at this moment in his safe and centrally heated six-foot-by-six-foot office, with its synthetic carpeting, completing his up-to-date expenses in triplicate and concerned with nothing more than memorizing the latest amendments to regulations. He said, "Of course I'll try."

The Mandarin was very close now and although the traffic was not particularly congested, Lu slowed the car. "I'd like something positive," he said.

"Or?" said Charlie, who realized the other man meant want, not like.

"It's nothing personal. You must understand that."

"I do understand it," assured Charlie. And he did. Harry Lu was talking about survival and in Harry's place he would have done the same.

"It's an opportunity I can't let go."

"You don't have to explain."

"I'm sorry, Charlie."

"You don't need to be."

"It's just that I'd much rather live in Cockfosters than Poughkeepsie or Peoria."

"I think I would, too," said Charlie. "You want an answer before I leave?" He intentionally did not say *can* leave, but there was no misunderstanding between them.

"That's what I'd like," said Lu, still avoiding the absolute insistence. Heightening the awareness between them, he said, "That's what I'd like best of all."

At the current state of the game, although game was the last way in which he regarded it, Charlie knew the CIA would offer Harry Lu a passport, guaranteed residency, and promise to change the U.S. Constitution so he could take a shot at the presidency in exchange for what he knew.

"Let's get the woman somewhere secure first," said Charlie. Lu's strength was knowing where she was anyway, so he wouldn't balk at that.

"Sure," agreed Lu, easily. He took the car into the narrow runway to the Mandarin Hotel, nodded familiarly to the doorman, and parked in front of a no-parking sign. The doorman didn't protest.

When they got out, it was the first time they had faced each other. Lu gave another of his hesitant smiles and said, "No hard feelings?"

"No hard feelings," assured Charlie. He remembered the last time he'd agreed to that had been to Fredericks and a few hours later a plane had blown up. He said, "Let's keep everything clean: you settle the bill and I'll get the woman."

"Why *is* it called Cockfosters?" asked Lu.

"Maybe a lot of cock-ups happened there sometimes, too," said Charlie, leading the way into the hotel.

General Sir Alistair Wilson held the message toward his deputy shaking his head in uncertainty. He said, "Why should the American Director—the Director himself, don't forget—initiate a cable to me to say there appears to be a delay with Kozlov's crossing and making it clear, in a roundabout way admittedly, that they had nothing to do with the explosion!"

"Distancing themselves?" suggested Harkness at once. "That's what we'd do."

Wilson nodded but immediately came in with the qualification. "At *division* level," he pointed out. "The Director himself would not risk later being exposed as a liar in a signed message. I certainly wouldn't."

"What then?"

"I just don't know," conceded Wilson. "Everything about their approach is wrong."

"Unless they're telling the truth," suggested Harkness.

"That's a novel idea," said Wilson, disbelievingly. "No contact with Cartright from Charlie?"

"Not as of an hour ago," said the deputy.

"I wish to hell I knew whether or not we had the woman," said Wilson.

As he spoke, eight thousand miles away in Hong Kong,

Irena Kozlov opened the door to Charlie Muffin and said, "It's all gone wrong, hasn't it?"

"Not yet," said Charlie. But almost, he thought.

It would have been ludicrous to regard the approach from Olga Balan as anything like friendship but Boris Filiatov looked upon it as a gesture of cooperation at least. And certainly, from the material she had made available, there was strong circumstantial evidence that Irena Kozlov had orchestrated the American surveillance for a personal advantage. His immediate—and lasting—reaction was nothing as facile as a concern for any damage to the State: Boris Filiatov's concern was for Boris Filiatov. And he was well aware that other material was available from which it could be construed that he had supported the operation. Which he had, knowing of Moscow's approval and always quick to jump onto a safely rolling bandwagon: a bandwagon, he reflected bitterly, showing all the signs of running away down a very rocky road to an appalling disaster. Filiatov recognized at once that he had to disassociate himself: it didn't matter if the suspicions about the woman were later shown unfounded; the only consideration now was to get out before Moscow discovered what was happening, realized its own culpability, and moved to apportion the blame.

Filiatov sighed, replacing the telephone that had remained unanswered in four earlier attempts to contact Olga Balan. He intended his approach to appear reciprocal, a courtesy returned for a courtesy given, but in reality he was desperately anxious to know if the woman had already dispatched her reports to Dzerzhinsky Square.

The movements of all Soviet personnel attached to overseas embassies are strictly monitored, travel logs existing to record every exit from or reentry to the diplomatic compound against the reasons for those journeys. Filiatov checked the duty clerk, frowning at there being no listing against the security officer's name to account for her absence. Of all people, Filiatov supposed, Olga Balan could risk scorning regulations, but he hadn't been aware of her doing so ever before.

Filiatov decided to wait. But not for long: he'd already decided he couldn't wait long.

18

The silence lasted a long time, building into a division between them—a barrier neither had known before—Olga Balan all the while staring fixedly at him, wanting Kozlov to say more. When he didn't, the woman said, "This isn't how it was planned; how *we* planned it."

"You said then that you'd do anything I wanted," reminded Kozlov. He hadn't expected her to agree at once.

"Not kill her."

"You've been trained."

Olga shook her head, a positive denial. "For the State. This is different."

Kozlov indicated the just-replaced telephone on which he'd burned with discomfort assuring his wife he loved her with Olga looking at him stone-faced. "I told you what she said: that they're moving her on, but she doesn't know where. That telephone is our only link. So it *can't* be me, not now. I've *got* to stay here."

Olga stood abruptly, breaking the tension between them. She looked at her empty glass and the nearby bottle, then appeared to change her mind, going instead to the window. Tokyo was quiet outside, so late, a lot of the neon illumination temporarily resting and the streets briefly empty, until another day. With her back to him, she said, "You'd already decided it had to be me, before she called, hadn't you?"

Kozlov swallowed, glad she wasn't able to see. He was

surprised she'd guessed. He said, "Think of another way! Anything!"

Still not looking at him, Olga said hopefully, "Maybe Moscow wouldn't recall you if we just let her go?"

"You prepared the tapes . . . conducted the interviews and sent them to Moscow and involved Filiatov . . ." reminded Kozlov. "Do you really believe that!"

She turned back into the room. There were only sidelights on, so it was difficult to see if she was near tears but he thought she was. She said, "We're trapped, aren't we?"

"With a way out!" he said, urgently.

"How long!" she demanded, suddenly angry. "How long before Irena becomes suspicious at your still being here in this apartment or Moscow starts demanding answers or Filiatov does something; we've prepared him, don't forget!"

"You can do it," coaxed Kozlov. "It could all be over this time tomorrow. So there's no risk of anything from Moscow or Filiatov. Irena either. You'd even be doing your job, as far as Moscow is concerned."

"You never told me about the other time," she said, ignoring the assurance with another abrupt change of direction.

"Other time?"

"You said in Moscow Irena told you she'd never be a rejected woman. Why did she say that?"

Kozlov poured himself more vodka, not wanting the drink but needing the break from her demanding stare. "There was a woman. A choreographer at the Bolshoi. I told Irena I wanted a divorce. That's when she said it."

"So what happened?" The anger was obvious again.

"It was just before I came to London: met you. Irena stayed in Moscow, as you know. Used all the power she had in Dzerzhinsky Square—which was a lot—to hurt her. I didn't know, of course. Didn't discover it until I went back, between London and Bonn. . . ."

"You tried to see her again . . . this other woman?"

"Valentina," supplied Kozlov.

"You tried to see Valentina after our affair had already started . . . when you were telling me that you loved me!"

Kozlov brought his eyes to hers, knowing the suspicion and wanting to convince her. "No!" he said. "Not like that. Irena boasted what she'd done: 'taken care of your whore,' she said.

She actually arranged criticism of the choreography in Pravda and Tass. Valentina had been dismissed, by the time I got back to Moscow. Unsatisfactory had been registered in her workbook and you know that makes her unemployable."

"You met her again?"

Kozlov shook his head. "I think she went back to her home, to Kiev. I couldn't find out, not definitely. I'd have had to inquire through Irena's directorate and she would have learned about it: made it even more difficult for Valentina."

"So you never saw her again?"

"No," said Kozlov.

"And don't know what happened to her?"

"No," said the man, once more.

There was a long hesitation and then Olga said, "Do you still love her?"

Kozlov shook his head. "I feel responsible."

"Would it be as easy, to get over me?"

"I didn't say it was easy."

"It sounds that way."

"Darling!" Kozlov stood, holding out his arms. She refused to come to him and he dropped them, feeling foolish. Instead he went to her, reached out a second time, and took her shoulders, bringing her face close to his. "I love *you*," he said. "No one else. That's all I can say . . . no better way—other way—to make you believe me."

It was several moments before she replied and when she said, "I believe you," there was doubt.

"Will you do it?"

Another long pause. Then she said, "There's no other resolve, is there?"

"No," he said, positively.

"I'm not sure I can."

"Trapped," he said, coaxing some more. "Your words."

Olga started crying, making no sound but with tears moving across her face. "I'm so scared," she said, brokenvoiced. "So very scared."

"You can do it!" he encouraged again.

"I have to, don't I?"

Kozlov didn't reply, knowing it would be wrong at that second in time to say anything.

"Just Irena," insisted Olga. "Not him."

"Just Irena," agreed Kozlov.

"Over by this time tomorrow?"

"Everything," he assured her.

"You do love me, don't you?"

"Don't doubt me. Ever."

There was another period when her eyes searched his face and she said, "I won't," and this time there wasn't any doubt.

They left Levine at the airport, with two of the crew of the C-130 controlling the surveillance of the military section, and Elliott accompanied the rest of the arriving CIA group to the Peninsula Hotel on the mainland Kowloon side.

Elliott was already established as the contact point for the colony's CIA informants and at Fredericks's urging he went individually through everything that had been assembled.

"Definite airport arrival?" pressed the CIA supervisor.

"Three separate confirmations, from Langley's stock photographs," confirmed the man.

"Cars?" seized Fredericks, picking the most important point.

Elliott shook his head, the reluctance obvious. "Ground staff and immigration. Nothing outside."

"Son of a bitch!" said Fredericks, vehemently.

"Just a matter of time," said Elliott. "We're running checks on all the taxis and courtesy buses and rental cars."

"We haven't *got* time!" said Fredericks, exasperated. "This thing is on a very short fuse."

Elliott looked around the assembled group. "Now we're all here," he said, "we can start spreading out. There are a lot of hotels but we've got informants in a lot of them so it isn't really such a difficult task."

"I'd like to believe that!" said Dale, entering into the conversation to ease the pressure on a colleague.

"I don't care how difficult it is!" reminded Fredericks. "I want it done and I want it done completely and I want it done now!"

Elliott and Dale actually exchanged looks, their faces open but with no need of expression to convey their feeling at the burr-under-the-saddle attitude that was so obvious from their supervisor.

Elliott said, "It really is just a matter of time. An itty-bitty matter of time."

Fredericks's face suddenly opened, more a grimace than a smile. "Right!" he said. "The cork's in the bottle."

19

Irena Kozlov stood in the middle of the room, legs slightly parted, hands on her hips in a physically intimidating attitude, questions bursting from her in a machine-gun staccato. "Why blow up the plane?" was the most repeated demand, along with others. Like who—and how—caused the explosion and had they been caught and what he was going to do now to get her out? And how?

Charlie Muffin confronted her feeling like a one-armed juggler trying to keep twenty colored balls in the air at the same time, with his good arm strapped behind his back. And blindfolded as well. He attempted to concentrate completely upon the strident woman and to relegate the distraction of Harry Lu to the solve-it-later part of his mind, but it wasn't easy because what Harry Lu wanted was so inextricably linked with Irena anyway. As everything was. Charlie lied, repeatedly, insisting that the delay was only temporary and that soon—within hours, which was a further conscious lie—there would be another plane to take her safely to England.

"How can you say that, after what happened in Tokyo!" The challenge was immediate, puncturing the attempted assurance.

"Because this time we'll be more careful," said Charlie.

"So you were careless!"

Charlie sighed: she was sandpaper abrasive. He said, "It was something we didn't foresee." He was determinedly as

165

forceful as she, refusing to be browbeaten by her hands-on-hips attitude.

"Yuri expected some trickery but not this," admitted Irena. She hesitated, hands dropping to her sides, lowering herself into a chair. She hesitated and said with sudden and unusual quietness, as if realizing it for the first time, "I could have been killed."

"They wouldn't have sabotaged the plane if you'd been aboard," said Charlie. "They'd have snatched you."

"The man who met me at the airport!" said the woman, the sudden alarm obvious. "He's safe?"

I wish I knew anymore, thought Charlie. He said, "Quite safe. A friend."

"He said we have to keep moving."

"The Americans are chasing," announced Charlie. It was a harbor-view room, the black stretch of the waterway between them and Kowloon and the New Territories beyond. Charlie looked briefly across at the mainland, wondering how long it would take Fredericks and the other CIA agents to arrive. From the chair upon which she was sitting, Charlie was conscious of Irena moving as if she were going to make a response at once, but abruptly she shook her head. Instead she said, "So you don't know what's happened to Yuri?"

Charlie hesitated, unsure of the best reply, and decided that there was only one. "No," he said. "There's no contact between myself and the Americans, not anymore."

"How are the meetings between Yuri and I going to be arranged?"

"Through London and Washington," avoided Charlie, easily. Wilson was probably already mobilizing the squad to grab Kozlov on that first occasion. It was an operation in which he would like to be involved.

"You said hours, before we can leave?" queried Irena.

"I hope so," said Charlie.

She appeared not to notice the qualification. Unexpectedly, she said, "I do not feel well: I don't think I can travel immediately."

"What!" Charlie was off-balanced by the announcement: more colored balls had been thrown into the juggling act. He looked intently at the woman. Pale, maybe, but that was all.

Certainly her attitude since he'd entered the room gave no indication of her being unwell. The opposite, in fact.

"I need to rest before moving on," Irena said.

She was going to get the opportunity whether she wanted it or not, but the insistence unsettled Charlie. Minutes earlier she'd appeared anxious to get out as soon as possible, which was why he had lied. The strain had to be enormous; maybe she wasn't as strong as she appeared. He said, "There'll be time enough to rest."

"A day at least: I need a day."

"A day," agreed Charlie, because it suited him.

"Are you confident we can evade the Americans?"

"Yes," said Charlie, who wasn't. There was a desperate need to reach Wilson, in London; a desperate need to do so much. Up and down went the colored balls, a blur of impressions, nothing focusing.

"Where are we going now?"

Charlie hesitated, looking across at the mainland again. Certainly they had to get off Hong Kong island, so Kowloon was the obvious choice: a lot of small, no-questions-asked places there. "The Americans have woken up everybody"—Harry's warning, on the way from the airport. So was Kowloon too obvious, like here at the Mandarin? Or safe enough? Before he could reply to the woman's question there was a sound at the door. Irena jumped, nervously, and as he opened it to Harry Lu, Charlie decided the man had taken a long time simply to settle a less-than-one-night occupancy bill.

"All set," announced Lu.

For whom and for what? wondered Charlie. Pointedly, he said, "Where have you been?"

Lu looked directly at him, recognizing the suspicion. "Making calls, Charlie."

"To whom?"

"Don't, Charlie! There isn't any reason," urged the other man.

Irena, a professional, detected the atmosphere and said, "What's the problem?"

Both men ignored her. Charlie said, "I wouldn't like there to be, Harry."

"I'm trusting you," reminded the man. "It's got to go both ways."

Lu was right, Charlie accepted: and he didn't have any alternative anyway. Charlie never liked operating without at least one alternative. Preferably more. He repeated, "To whom?"

Lu didn't reply at once, conscious of Charlie's refusal to come to meet him on the assurance. Then he said, "People: people very anxious to know where you are. . . ."

The man finished speaking by turning to include Irena, who said at once, "Something else has gone wrong, hasn't it? Tell me!"

"Nothing else has gone wrong!" said Charlie, urgently, trying to quell the woman's obvious and rising anxiety.

"So what is it between you?" persisted the woman.

"A misunderstanding," said Charlie. It had been stupid, allowing the exchange in front of her. Trying to rebuild a bridge with Lu, Charlie added, "My fault."

Lu gave no response and Charlie decided the apology had come too late. The annoyance flushed through him, anger at his own stupidity: things were bad enough without his making additional contributions to the fuck-up. "My mistake," he said again, directly and to the man alone this time.

"We've got a deal?" asked Lu.

"Yes," agreed Charlie, who still hadn't considered how to achieve—even if he *could* achieve—what Lu demanded.

"Then I'll keep my side of it," undertook the man.

"Freelance!" identified Irena, showing further expertise. Accusingly, to Charlie, she said, "You involved a freelance!"

"I involved the best man," insisted Charlie. The whole bloody conversation was getting out of hand.

Uncertain doubt was obvious in Irena's look. She said, "Yuri thought you were good," in a voice indicating that she didn't agree with the assessment.

Irritated with the dispute—and not knowing how to continue it without further unsettling the woman—Charlie turned back to Lu and said, "So what do these people say?"

"The Americans have arrived. In force. Military, too."

Charlie recalled his reflection on the journey from the airport: it looked as if a military as well as a civilian aircraft departure was going to be difficult, without some sort of pitched battle. He said, "Where are they?"

"I don't know: not yet." Lu smiled, fleetingly, and said, "I will, of course."

"Hope you find them before they find us," said Charlie, sincerely. He gestured around the hotel room and said, "Where, after this?"

Lu nodded across the waterway, toward the mainland. "It's got to be Kowloon, hasn't it?"

Obvious, thought Charlie again. He said, "What about Macao?"

Lu frowned. Surprise? Or annoyance at a change to an already-conceived arrangement? wondered Charlie.

"It's small," argued Lu.

"That's the problem: everywhere's small and easily covered," said Charlie. "But it's an alternative, isn't it?"

"I suppose so," said Lu, still reluctant.

"We'll make it Macao," decided Charlie. To the woman, he said, "Let's go."

At the doorway she stopped, looking directly at him. She said, "You lied. Everything *has* gone wrong. I know it has."

Olga Balan used an Australian passport—describing her as a single woman named Hebditch—and landed in Hong Kong on the gritty-eyed dawn-arrival flight which was the first available and which had originated in Hawaii, with a Tokyo stopover. Not that it would have been possible for her to have slept, had she tried. She knew she was right in telling Yuri they were trapped. They *were* trapped and she *felt* trapped. Unless she killed Irena. Why couldn't Yuri have understood when she said she was frightened! But then how could he know? No one knew. Only her.

20

Charlie fought against the light-headedness of fatigue, trying to calculate the last time he'd properly slept and abandoning the exercise because it was an intrusion and there were enough intrusions already. At least Irena Kozlov was safely resting now. He hoped. Like he hoped so much else.

It was omens time and certainly luck had been following them with the hydrofoil. They'd managed to catch the last one to the Portuguese colony, changed the harbor cab for another once they reached the tiny township, and used a third to cross the sweeping bridge over the Pearl River to the Hyatt. Where he'd spent exactly five minutes in his own room, after settling Irena, before moving again. Not strictly true. There'd been the further fifteen minutes in the bar with Harry, trying to restore things between them and drinking the scotch he'd needed at the time but now wished he hadn't had, because it was contributing to his tiredness. Had he buggered things up, with Harry? Certainly with the suspicion in front of Irena, but alone, in the bar, the man had appeared to relax: actually showed photographs of his Chinese wife, whose name translated to Dawn Rising, and their child, a five-year-old girl called Open Flower. Not just relaxing, Charlie accepted. It had been necessary for the man to introduce his family, so there would be no mistakes about the entry documents required. Wrong to read too much into it then.

Charlie sighed, staring through the water-flecked windows of the early morning return hydrofoil at the land chips of the outlying islands, haloed in a permanent haze-made rainbow. Wrong, as well, to dwell too long upon it. Harry had made his ultimatum clear enough so it was ridiculous for either of them to imagine their relationship remaining as it had been, no matter how many different ways Harry said it was nothing personal and Charlie assured him there were no hard feelings. If Harry blew the whistle on him to the Americans it was going to be very personal indeed and his feelings were going to be hard, fucking hard. And they both knew it.

There were other far more immediate considerations. Like keeping ahead of a mob-handed CIA squad now backed by some sort of military presence on a colony all too easily sealed. And placating a nervously demanding woman who knew very well things had gone disastrously wrong, despite the lies he tried to make sound convincing. And most important of all, at this moment, conning his way into one of the most secret spy installations maintained by Britain.

The hydrofoil edged alongside the pier from which he'd left, just a few hours earlier, and Charlie slotted himself into the main body of departing passengers, instinctively using them as cover. He ignored the waiting taxis, walking instead toward the clustered-together Connaught Center and Chartered Bank and the Landmark complex, giant trees that man made. Tiredness carried the usual ache from his feet into his legs and Charlie envied the people around him who'd slept the previous night. Further to clear his trail he detoured off the main highway several times, moving through side alleys where he could be more aware of people around him; outside several shops incense sticks burned from tiny holders, to fend off evil spirits, and Charlie hoped the protection extended to passers-by who needed it, like he did.

He waited until Exchange Square, with its fresh skyscrapers, before hailing a cab. Once more he was cautious, isolating Repulse Bay for the first leg, settling back against the seat and momentarily closing his eyes against the growing sun glare as the vehicle began its climb over Victoria Peak. Almost at once he felt the sink of sleep and blinked awake, fighting it off, knowing he'd feel worse if he relaxed and had to start functioning again after only an hour.

How easy would it be to get into the Composite Signals Station? Something else he should have fixed with the Director before severing contact in Tokyo: just like he should have agreed to the dispatch of some sort of military aircraft. Charlie shifted, moving against the recurring drowsiness but also in irritation, worried at the things he had overlooked. If you lose your touch, my boy, your balls are going to end up on a hook, he told himself.

The car started its descent from the high spine of the island, edging down to sea level on the back-upon-itself road, and after one of the curves Charlie caught the first sight of the orange-roofed villas of Repulse Bay and thought it looked like a part of the French Riviera that had been put down for a moment and then forgotten.

He paid the cab off by the beach and walked slowly farther into the tiny settlement while the taxi reversed and then set off for the return trip. It was more difficult than he'd thought it would be to get another car and when he finally managed it and gave the address at Chung Hom Kok he was aware of the driver's examination, in the mirror. To be expected, Charlie supposed. The Composite Signals base is an electronic intelligence-gathering installation with equipment sufficiently powerful for Britain to listen to radio and telephone communication as far away as Beijing and to both the Soviet naval headquarters at Vladivostok and the Russian rocket complex in Sakhalin Island. Charlie wondered what would happen to it after 1997: it would certainly be on a spy-category list even greater than any upon which Harry Lu's name appeared. Moscow was probably shitting itself, aware of how the Chinese could use the ready-made and well-functioning station. He hoped to Christ he could use it too.

He came forward in his seat, as the car approached. There were a lot of angled radio dishes, and Nissan-hut hedgehogs of bristling radio antennae, but like most secret installations Charlie had ever visited, it still looked like a temporary army barracks, ready for a war. Which perhaps it was. Alert, Charlie saw the camera monitor maneuver to their arrival, to record the car—and its license number—before he even alighted, and as he walked toward the gatehouse Charlie registered the inner protection of wire which he guessed was electrified and the further array of cameras beyond that focused upon him and guessed the perimeter would be sensor-seeded, to detect any entry which got past either.

Self-rehearsed, Charlie asked for the guard commandant and when the man—sparse-haired, sun-worship brown, and in a tropical uniform so uncreased Charlie expected the starch to crack with each movement—came curiously across the quadrangle, Charlie asked for the duty officer. For identification he provided his Foreign Office registry number, as well as his name. It was obvious that the registry number meant something to the man, who withdrew without asking any questions: seconds after he disappeared into what appeared to be the main administrative building at the end of the entry road Charlie heard the muffled ring of a telephone in the gatehouse complex and soon after that three more uniformed gatehouse attendants appeared to support their original colleague and Charlie accepted that he was under guard. Which was fine with him and he wished he had more of it. He smiled at them. No one responded but at least there wasn't the disdain of the American embassy reception in Tokyo.

Charlie had hoped to get through the gatehouse area, but the crackling-uniformed officer returned with another man who also wore a tropical suit but this one bagged and was actually dirty at the cuffs and lapel edges, the shirt rumpled beneath. Charlie thought he looked the sort of bloke to suffer the morning-after ravages of bad meat pies, but perhaps that was too much to expect.

The telephone call Charlie had detected had gone further than Charlie had imagined because at the approach of the two men one of the additional guards opened a side door, gesturing Charlie into what he saw, when he got inside, to be an interview room. With the obvious limit on talking, Charlie passingly thought an interview room was an unnecessary luxury.

The crumpled man came in alone and did not attempt to identify himself. Instead he gestured with the paper upon which the commandant had recorded the registry number and demanded, "Where did you get this?"

"It's mine," insisted Charlie. Before the man could speak, Charlie added his department categorization, its clearance level, the communication code to London, with its standby alternative, and the demand code for the Director. "You'll need to take a note, so I'll repeat them more slowly," he finished. He'd just disclosed enough for a ten-year sentence under the Official Secrets Act, Charlie realized; maybe not as much as ten years.

He'd only got fourteen for screwing two intelligence Directors. Certainly five, then; and perhaps this time not the way out he'd been offered before.

There was a barely discernible relaxation in the man's attitude. He said, "What do you want?"

"Communication," said Charlie, simply. "Believe you're good at it here."

"Don't be ridiculous!" rejected the man, at once.

"Ask London," said Charlie. When the man remained impassive, Charlie added, "Please!"

The duty officer looked toward the door behind which Charlie knew the four guards would still be waiting. Charlie extended his hands, palm upward, and said urgently, "You have a facsimile machine here: take a full set of fingerprints and check them out with London, in addition to what I've already given you."

"You seem to be in a great hurry," said the man, still doubtful.

"A hell of a hurry," agreed Charlie. "An emergency. Call London . . ." He hesitated and added again, "Please." It had always been a difficult word for him.

"It's not the purpose or function of this facility," said the man, adamantly.

"I said it was an emergency!"

"I heard what you said."

Charlie felt the sweat bubble burst, and then find its way down his back. He nodded toward the door. "Effectively I'm under arrest, even though I haven't penetrated any part of this establishment. You can do with me what you like. I'm no danger, to you or anything that you're doing here. All I want is secure liaison with London. . . ." The indication this time was to the paper upon which the man had made his notes. "You know that's not bullshit."

"I know that if it's genuine you've broken a lot of regulations."

Dear God spare me from another Witherspoon, thought Charlie. He said, "Which I know. Like I said, an emergency . . ." The thought came suddenly and Charlie said, "You'll have to make contact with London anyway now, won't you?"

"I'll need a passport as well as fingerprints," said the man.

"You can have whatever you want," said Charlie, relieved.

There was a delay, bringing the inkpad and paper, and when the man finally left the room Charlie experimentally tried the door and found it to be locked. He smiled, appreciatively; not offended. He'd risked—and endangered—everything by coming here like this. He closed his eyes, in brief contemplation rather than prayer: just one wrong word, the smallest misconception, and he'd be down the drain without even touching the sides. He was becoming accustomed to the perpetual apprehension.

It was a full hour before the man returned, an hour when, despite attempts not to, Charlie kept lapsing into a half-sleep, slumped awkwardly in a stiffly upright chair in the oppressively hot room. He dreamed but consciously, all the time part of him aware of what was happening, confronting a mental mirror of disjointed images: exploding planes and threatening Americans and an emotionless Russian and a big woman whose voice was too loud and who spoke with her hands on her hips, and more threats from a Chinese who looked like a European this time. Then the voices and the faces and the threats got further confused, coming from the wrong faces with the wrong voices, and that aware part of him, the part that knew it was a dream anyway, tried to get everything back together, in their right compartments, properly to understand what was really happening and that same, conscious reasoning part of his mind told him he'd come back to the major difficulty and that he still didn't understand properly what was really happening, not at all.

He heard the turn of the key and managed to rouse himself to avoid the duty officer's realizing how close he was to exhaustion; fully awake Charlie knew he'd been right to fight against the collapse in the taxi on the way here. Now he felt bloody awful and some of the images still overlaid one another, more confused than they should have been.

"You're to come," announced the man.

Not that his knowing mattered, apart from pride, but Charlie managed to conceal the relief from the other man. The guards were outside and formed up into some sort of loose escort, restricting him precisely to where he was to go. It was to the main building and down a central corridor: politely Charlie indicated no interest in things that were not supposed to concern him but there was an impression of sterility. There were no festooned notice boards or indications of occupancy and, like the CIA Residency at the American embassy, none of the doors he passed showed any designation.

The communications chamber was not suspended, like those to which he was accustomed at embassies throughout the world, and it was far larger than he expected. There were telex and facsimile and phototransmission and radio and secure telephone equipment Charlie knew how to operate but there were two separate banks of what appeared to be radio apparatus that he did not recognize and which he accepted he'd be incapable of using. In addition there were six television sets, separated in booths with an individual chair before each.

"Do you need any assistance?" asked the unnamed duty officer.

"I think I can manage," said Charlie. "And thanks."

"There's going to be trouble over this," predicted the man.

"It seems to happen," said Charlie.

"You're to wait for London to come through."

"I understand."

"We'll be right outside. . . ." The duty officer paused and then added heavily, "All of us."

The call came, on a red telephone in the second bank, minutes after the man quit the room. At once Sir Alistair Wilson said critically, "The only thing you didn't provide was the color of your underwear."

"After what's happened, it might have been embarrassing," said Charlie.

"Have you got the woman?"

"Yes."

There was a discernible sigh of relief, and the Director said, "Thank Christ for that."

"But there are problems," deflated Charlie. Again, as in Tokyo, Wilson let him talk uninterrupted and Charlie was surprised how quickly he was able to set out the overlapping and conflicting difficulties: something so complicated should have taken longer.

The Director didn't waste time with comment. The moment Charlie finished, Wilson said, "Harry Lu needs resolving first."

"I don't really blame him, in the circumstances," said Charlie. He owed the man that at least, from their past friendship.

"Him, his wife, and his child?"

"English residency," confirmed Charlie.

"You really believe he'd do it?"

"To get to America instead of England, as a second choice, sure he would," said Charlie. "Wouldn't you?"

"Yes," agreed Wilson, at once.

"Is it possible?" asked Charlie.

"It'll have to be made possible," determined Wilson.

"I can tell him it's fixed then?"

There was a hesitation from London and then the Director said, "Yes, you can tell him it's fixed."

"He'll want more than a promise."

"Everything will be available, at the High Commission."

"Which leaves the Americans," said Charlie, moving on.

"Who insist they haven't got Kozlov," said Wilson. Now it was Charlie's turn to listen without interruption as the other man recounted the exchanges at Director level. Wilson did so in complete detail, even setting out the inconclusive analysis he and Harkness had attempted, afterward.

"Nothing about this makes any sense at all," said Charlie.

"We've got the woman," reminded the Director. "That's the one positive fact. And we've got to keep her."

"U.S. military, with transport as well as CIA," said Charlie.

"We'll send another military pickup, right away."

"The Americans will go for her," forecast Charlie. "That's why they're here!"

This time the pause was longer than any before. Finally Wilson said, "Hong Kong is too diplomatically sensitive, with the Chinese takeover so close, for a major incident."

"What about a naval boat: get her away at sea and transfer her later on, somewhere where the Americans couldn't interfere?" suggested Charlie.

"There soon won't be a department of the British government you haven't involved in this!" said the Director.

"You plan to give her up then?"

"Of course I don't intend to give her up!" said Wilson. "A ship is a possibility: I'll check if there are any in the area."

"Anything more from Tokyo, on the plane explosion?"

"Forensic reports will take days," said the Director. "So I think Cartright should come down to you: we can monitor the Tokyo investigation through the Air attaché."

"I think he should come down, too," said Charlie. "And more people this time on the military aircraft."

"There'll be enough," said Wilson. "This time there'll be more than enough."

"We might have to move from Macao," warned Charlie. "There should be an established contact point."

"Harry Lu?"

"How about through the station here?"

Wilson detected the doubt and said, "You unsure about Lu now?"

"He's well known in the colony," avoided Charlie. "There could be an intercept: I'm just minimizing risk."

"Composite Signals is way beyond my jurisdiction," said Wilson. "There's going to be a hell of a row as it is."

"I've been told," said Charlie. "It's still the most secure."

"I'll try to fix it," sighed Wilson.

"And the documents for Lu and his family?"

"I'm hardly likely to forget, am I!"

When Charlie emerged, the escort and the duty officer were waiting, as the man had promised. Charlie grinned and said, "Thanks again. We might be cooperating further."

"There'll need to be specific instruction from London," said the man, at once.

"Of course," said Charlie. He wondered if rules-and-regulation men like the duty clerk and Witherspoon screwed by numbered decree and then thought, no; they probably don't screw at all.

"Entry documents for a man on the suspect list!" Harkness's usually pink face was deep red now, flushed with outrage.

"We don't have any alternative."

"It's blackmail!"

"Yes," agreed the Director, evenly. "That's exactly what it is."

"Muffin was specifically precluded from involving the man."

"He didn't have any alternative either."

"It's going to take months, placating the Foreign Office and the electronic surveillance division and clearing up the mess that the confounded man has caused," insisted the deputy.

"Charlie's got Irena Kozlov," pointed out Wilson. "That's what he was sent out to do."

"There'll need to be a lot of explanation, when he gets back."

"He's got to get back yet."

Harkness put his head to one side, in sudden thought. "The Foreign Office could always rescind Lu's entry permission, once we got Irena Kozlov here, couldn't they?"

"I suppose so, if someone could show proper cause why he shouldn't be allowed to stay," agreed the Director.

21

The planning meeting was convened, naturally, in Fredericks's
suite, everyone there except Jim Dale, who drew the first shift
monitoring the commerical flights out of Kai Tak airport. In
addition to the CIA men, Fredericks brought in the Special
Forces colonel commanding the army group which had been
brought in on the C-130, a hard-bodied, stiffly upright man
named Jamieson who appeared vaguely uncomfortable in the
tropical civilian clothes and looked out of place in them anyway.

"Well?"

The CIA supervisor directed the question to Winslow
Elliott, the liaison with the local informants and stringers and
the man coordinating the ongoing check of hotels.

Elliott shook his head. "Nothing, so far. We're still
checking out Kowloon. . . ." He looked needlessly at his
watch. "Should be starting on the island anytime."

"The bastard can't just have disappeared: it's not possible
in a place as small as this!" protested Fredericks. "What about
cars; he must have used a vehicle!"

"Nothing there either," said Elliott. "Still checking, obviously." He was as anxious as the supervisor to nail Charlie
Muffin but he didn't like the way Fredericks appeared to be
panicking.

"There should have been something by now!" said Fredericks.

"We've only just started," reminded the reasonable Takeo

Yamada, who was also concerned at their controller's knee-jerk attitude.

"Time we don't have!" insisted Fredericks, mouthing the much repeated injunction. He guessed he had three days before Langley began burning his ass: four at the outside. To the Green Beret colonel, he said, "What about leaving a minimum out at the airport and bringing in your guys, so we can section up the goddamned place grid-fashion?"

Jamieson made a doubtful rocking gesture with his hands. "I know Hong Kong; R and R'd here a lot, from 'Nam. It's not built that way. Cover all the obvious hotels more quickly than you are at the moment, maybe, but what if he's holed up with her in some apartment? Don't forget to the Chinese we're *gweilos*—white ghosts or devils, not people they should help. House-to-house stuff is never going to work."

"We've got to do more than just sit around and wait!"

"The airport is the place and we've got that blocked," said Jamieson, positively.

Fredericks looked around at the assembled men and smiled, an expression that surprised them. "What's the one edge we've got? Small, but still an edge?" The smile stayed, at the shoulder-shrugs and head-shakings. "Numbers," announced the huge man. "We've got numbers and Charlie Muffin is by himself. So what's he got to do?"

"Call in local help," accepted Levine.

"Right!" said Fredericks. To Elliott, the liaison man, he said, "Get back to everyone: some of them will double anyway, probably for the British. Get the names of anyone who deals exclusively for them . . . of *anyone* who's ever done anything for London."

"It could be a shortcut," agreed Harry Fish, speaking for the first time.

"You got a better idea!" demanded Fredericks, truculently.

The CIA man flushed at the unnecessary attack. He said, "And when we get the names?"

"Whatever it takes," said Fredericks. "Money, pressure, whatever . . ."

"Do you mean actually move against a guy, if we think he knows something?" demanded Yamada. He didn't intend getting his balls in a bind in some later inquiry because of an instruction as vague as that.

"If we come up with a guy who just maybe knows something then I'll personally stoke the fire and turn the spit until we find out what it is," said Fredericks positively.

It only took an hour to get Harry Lu's name and it linked with a coincidence. At the same time Elliott's hotel checks extended across the harbor to begin on Hong Kong island, and the Mandarin doorman identified Charlie Muffin positively and at once from the CIA file pictures. There very briefly, the doorman said; he didn't know the woman with whom the man left but Harry Lu was a local businessman, into a lot of things, including a car-hire firm. Actually parked his Mercedes against the no-parking sign. Harry Lu did things like that; tipped well, too. The doorman smiled, pleased the American took the hint.

"Here we go!" said Fredericks, triumphantly, when he heard the news. "What do we know?"

"He's a breed," said Elliott, who was given to American Western expressions. "Chinese father, English mother. Got a Chinese wife and a kid. Never worked for anyone else but the British."

"The family gives us a pressure point," judged Fredericks. "We get to Harry Lu and we get to Charlie Muffin and the woman. . . ." To the Special Forces colonel, he said, "We can just leave the plane crew out at the airport. Bring all your guys in."

"You planning to snatch?"

"You bet your ass," said the supervisor.

"Thank you," said Lu. He sounded sincere.

"I'm glad it was possible," said Charlie. Believing he was finally able to relax, if only briefly, Charlie had slept in the taxi on the return over the Peak and on the hydrofoil crossing back to Macao, but he still felt thick-headed. The whiskey was probably a mistake, but there'd been so many what did one more matter? Through the bay window of the ground-floor Hyatt bar he could see the leisurely arc of the bridge, linking the tiny peninsula with the town on the other side of the river, which was fouled thickly with the sediment brought down from the Chinese mainland. Deep yellow: definitely not pearl. He guessed the other Chinese tributary had got in first with the name, so pearl was the best alternative they could manage. They should have put more thought into it.

"I didn't think it was going to be," said Lu, in a hesitantly shy admission.

"Wait until you get everything from the High Commission," warned Charlie. Never believe the check is in the post, he thought.

"Wilson wouldn't have lied," said Lu, confidently. "It would have been stupid."

"Yes, it would have been," agreed Charlie.

Lu took the picture of his wife from his pocket, for his benefit rather than for Charlie's this time. Looking down at it, Lu said, "She'll be very relieved."

"To get out of Hong Kong?" said Charlie.

Lu looked up at him. "More than that," he said. "She has always been frightened, by what I do."

"She knew?" asked Charlie, surprised.

"Not everything: a lot, though."

"It's best they don't."

"Doesn't Edith?"

Charlie had forgotten Lu's training secondment to London and the pub crawls around the city bars and the late-at-night Indian or Chinese meals—all that had been available—where she'd tolerated their drunkenness and stayed sober herself, to drive them home. Harry Lu had been one of the few people in the business to whom he'd ever introduced her. He said, "Edith's dead."

"Oh," said the other man. He stopped short of the empty, automatic regret. Nor did he ask the question, leaving Charlie to explain if he wanted to.

"You never heard what happened?"

"To Edith, no," said Lu. "For a long time, whenever I asked about you, I was stonewalled, like you didn't exist."

Charlie examined his empty glass, uncertain, and then thought, why not? He gestured to the waiter for refills and said, "They tried to dump me. I beat them, instead. Caused a lot of grief. Edith got caught in the crossfire. Literally."

Lu's reaction was alertly professional. "So what are you doing here operating like nothing has happened?"

Charlie started the replenished drink, appreciating the man's ability and regretting the distance that had grown between them, despite the efforts each was making now. He said, "I suppose the word is rehabilitation. I was in a special position to do something and prove myself. The job didn't work out, but they don't seem to doubt my loyalty anymore." At least the Director didn't, Charlie thought. It was too involved—and didn't matter anyway—to explain his being a decoy for a jailbreak with another man he—but more importantly Moscow—believed to be a genuine spy. Or how, in Moscow, he'd screwed the man into gulag imprisonment, only to discover when it was too late and he was back in London that the poor sod was someone Wilson had trained for years to infiltrate the Russian service. He decided, too, against telling the man about Natalia, for whom he'd come close to chucking everything and staying in Moscow.

Refusing to lose his point, Lu said, "But Edith knew?"

"Yes," said Charlie. Edith was different from anyone else.

"Didn't she worry?"

"All the time," admitted Charlie.

"That's how it is with me. Why I'll be glad to quit."

Charlie looked intently at the other man, held by another fear, that Harry Lu had lost his nerve. There was no outward indication, no obvious apprehension, but the admission was worrying: he didn't want the man collapsing on him, not now. He said encouragingly, "You're going to get your papers: everything's going to be all right."

"I should tell her," said Lu.

"Time enough later," urged Charlie. "Let's get this thing over, first."

Charlie's concern registered, for the first time. Lu said, "She's safe." He offered the photograph and said, "Did I show you this one?"

Politely Charlie took the print. It was different from the earlier picture. This one showed the woman in a strictly formal pose, porcelain-faced, jet-black hair dressed high on her head, her wide-belted *cheong-sam* reaching the ground. The child called Open Flower was at her side, a miniature replica. Charlie said, "Don't endanger her—either of them—with knowledge."

Now it was Lu's turn to show concern. "They wouldn't move against them!"

"Why not?" demanded Charlie, in brutal honesty. He was surprised, at the man's thinking otherwise; perhaps it was time that Harry Lu did get out.

"I should see they're all right."

"Not personally," insisted Charlie, at once. He'd be glad when Cartright got here: better still when the army team arrived.

"Call at least," insisted the man.

"Don't say where we are."

"Don't be ridiculous!" said the man.

He'd deserved that, accepted Charlie. "Maybe you should call," he agreed.

Charlie ordered another drink, able from where he sat to watch the man go to the telephone bank. Had he exaggerated, about a risk to Lu's family? Maybe. Then again, maybe not. Had he been asked two weeks ago, he would have disdained the likelihood of six men being killed to block an escape route. Mind focused, he went again over the conversation with Wilson, trying—and failing—to reconcile the American denial of involvement. How much longer, before things started to make sense? He concentrated on the whiskey he held before him, in both hands, and decided it would be a long time if he went on drinking like this. In a moment he had to confront Irena Kozlov, who had the benefit of a night's sleep. He smiled up, at Lu's return.

"Everything's fine," said the man, whose apartment was in Wanchai, off the road leading to the Happy Valley racecourse. As Lu spoke, Fredericks, Levine, and Fish were arriving outside, spreading out at once to establish a triangular surveillance pattern.

And in her seaview room at the Macao Hyatt, five floors above where the two men sat, Irena Kozlov replaced the receiver after the conversation with her husband in the Tokyo apartment, warmed by the contact. It was wonderful, after the difficulties they'd had, to know that he loved her so much now: so determined to protect her against any trickery that he'd refused to go across to the Americans until she was beyond the risk of any interception. She smiled, remembering the assurance; relax, you're safe, he'd said.

"Darling Yuri," she said, aloud. "Darling Yuri."

22

To inculcate a mentality which enables a sane person to kill in dispassionate cold blood requires a prolonged period of specialized psychological indoctrination: indeed the KGB relegates the practical instruction, the unarmed-combat and weapon-handling expertise and knowledge of debilitating drugs and poisons, to the very end of any training course. And without its being considered in any way an absurd contradiction, that indoctrination makes a case for the moral acceptability of the act in dictated circumstances while supporting the forbidden criminality of wanton, needless murder.

The Russian instruction—refined and perfected since the maniacal, mass slaughter days of Stalin and of people like Genrikh Yagoda, a trained pharmacist who once ran the forerunner to the KGB and enjoyed experimenting upon prisoners in Lubyanka—is regarded as the best by other intelligence agencies which employ assassins.

A predominant reason making it superior to others is that Soviet psychologists are able fully to capitalize on an attitude inherent and peculiar to Russians: a practically mystical love of country. The persistent theme throughout the lectures and debates, therefore, is that there is a positive duty to eliminate enemies of the State: to kill, for one's country, is justified. It makes murder logical. Usually.

Olga Balan was a dedicated Party member, an absolutely committed and loyal officer of the KGB, but someone unable, no matter how hard she tried—and she tried very hard, spurred by that dedication and commitment—to forget her parents' adherence to the Russian Orthodox faith and its inherited effect upon her. When she entered the service, she worried that the stigma of their belief would mitigate against her: maybe even prevent her from being accepted in the first place. That it didn't only indicated an oversight in the background checks Olga knew were always carried out, and for a long time after her enlistment she existed in constant apprehension of the damaging fact emerging to destroy her. Over the years, that fear diminished but the memories of the childhood church visits and the before-meal prayers and the learned-by-rote scriptures would not go away. Now those recollections stayed as an irritation, a dull but nevertheless nagging problem, like an aching tooth no dentistry could relieve. As someone who embraced communism completely she had no religion, of course. And had succeeded, as her KGB career progressed, in subjugating the dichotomy in almost everything. The exception was to kill.

Olga underwent her psychological indoctrination at a complex known as Balashikha, east of the Moscow ring road, just off Gofkosvkoye Schosse. At first there was positive revulsion—an absolute rejection of the justification thesis—so much so she expected her dismissal from the course, which would have meant her automatic ejection from the service. But then the escape occurred to her. Olga realized she was being trained in the theory, not the actual practice for entry into the ultimately secret Department 8 of Directorate S of the First Chief Directorate: she could pretend.

She easily and unworriedly passed with commendations the assessments and the later, practical training and in her reference file in Dzerzhinsky Square she was listed as someone able—and capable—of killing. But only in theory. Until now: now it was no longer pretense. Now it was real: frighteningly real.

That very psychological indoctrination compounded her difficulty, beyond any childhood religious prohibitions. Enemy of the State was always the requirement, for the necessary justification. Was Irena Kozlov that? By defecting, she was, according to strict definition, but Olga could not accept the easy way out. Irena Kozlov had been tricked into crossing: so the formula didn't fit.

Olga sat hunched at an outside table of the hotel at the

beginning of the bridge, on the Macao side, the long-forgotten coffee cold in front of her, mind suddenly blocked by the reflection, confronting at last something that she had been avoiding for too long.

Why didn't Yuri suffer any agonized guilt?

Olga supposed that for his specialized department Yuri's indoctrination had been much more exhaustive than hers but she knew one thing—the basic justification—remained the same. Which meant Yuri was calculatingly—dear God, how calculating!—prepared to murder, without any excuse. Her reasoning became jumbled, trying to hold different thoughts at the same time, irritated at mentally invoking a God in which she didn't believe and at the uncertainty she suddenly felt, facing up at last to the numbing callousness in someone she loved so much. Did she have the right to think like this? Hadn't she known—but refused to recognize—all along that Irena Kozlov was being manipulated toward her own murder? Of course she had. *"You know I'll do anything you want."* Her own words— the long-ago undertaking after a night of lovemaking when he'd first proposed the idea—echoed in her mind, as if she could actually hear herself saying them. She'd known then what it meant and she'd conducted the entrapment interviews knowing what it meant. The only change to all the unobjected planning was that until twenty-four hours earlier it was going to be Yuri and not she who carried out the act. So she was as culpable and as callous as he was: worse than him, even, someone prepared to be involved in murder providing it wasn't she who had to pull the trigger or detonate the bomb.

Olga squeezed her eyes tightly against the tears of complete honesty, worried at attracting attention from the few people about her. She *had* to do it! She had to stop hiding behind mixed-up thoughts about half-forgotten religion she didn't profess and mixed-up thoughts about a morality she didn't have: to seek out Irena Kozlov in the hotel she could clearly see across the other side of the river and pull the trigger of the special plastic assassin weapon that did not show up on airport security monitors, the Technical Division's invention that employed compressed air to fire the killing, poison-impregnated plastic bullets. Dear God—damn the readiness of the plea!— how much she hoped she could do it!

Calling upon the theory so well taught at Balashikha, Olga

decided it wasn't going to be easy, irrespective of her personal anxieties. From where she sat, the hotel appeared to dominate the far side of the bridge: anything or anyone crossing it would all the time be fully visible, like someone going over a drawbridge to a medieval castle. And Olga reckoned from the antipathy existing between them in Tokyo that Irena Kozlov was probably more likely to identify her than any other member of the Soviet embassy.

Which was only one of the difficulties. The Englishman, Charlie Muffin, had already proved his cleverness getting Irena safely away from Japan. Professional, Yuri had called the man, in reluctant admiration. Definitely someone who couldn't be underestimated. And what backup did the man have?

Olga sighed, thinking back to the training and its most basic precept: never move before a complete and thorough reconnaissance to learn everything possible about the target's surroundings and only move when you were sure of avoiding arrest or detection after the act. She would not be able to do any of that, Olga accepted: the possibility of Irena's spotting her was too great and without reconnaissance she couldn't properly plan the killing and without a proper plan she couldn't devise a guaranteed escape.

Oh dear God! she thought, too consumed by apprehension to care any longer at invoking the deity. She was numbed with fear, a physical sensation like the tingling which happened bumping the sensitive part in the elbow, and there was another actual feeling, a welling sickness deep in her stomach, so real that she began to perspire, frightened she was going to vomit.

Olga stood, hurriedly, spilling coins onto the table to pay for the coffee and starting off away from the bridge into the township. As she walked she told herself she was utilizing her tradecraft, losing herself in the jumble of streets instead of crossing directly to pursue Irena Kozlov from the hotel where a waiter or another guest might have remembered her later during any police inquiry. But she forced herself to admit the other, more important reason. She was delaying what she had to do, by any means she could find.

She crossed the colonial square beneath the unfocused statues of Portuguese founders and plunged into the winding, haphazard alleyways beyond. Like Hong Kong, that other nearby relic of colonialism, Macao was being returned to Beijing and everywhere had the atmosphere of soon-to-leave neglect, like a house allowed to run into disrepair because its owners were about to move somewhere better. The warrens were crowded with stalls and people and noise and smells and bustle and she let herself be jostled along by the tide, a piece of willing flotsam. Still going in the wrong direction.

There were cabs on the wider cross streets. She let two, empty, pass her and only tentatively hailed the next but the driver was alert, jerking into the pavement, careless of upsetting both the pedallo driver and the tourists in his rickshaw, which shuddered to a halt against the pavement with obscenity screaming louder than brakes.

Olga closed her eyes once more, against the scene this time, as if she did not want to see herself set off. Everything was an effort yet she looked again. The car was just crossing the statued square: through a gap between the squared buildings Olga could see the yellow-stained river but not the bridge or the hotel beyond. No reconnaissance, no plan, no reconnaissance, no plan: the flaws repeated themselves in her mind and she frowned, trying to recall a familiar imagery, and realized it was like the litanies she'd learned as a child in incense-filled churches with head-bowed parents, bribed with sweetmeats into obedience. The taxi went around the centerpiece directly in front of the bridge and then began its climb toward the far side and she saw, with the benefit of some elevation, that there *were* buildings beyond the hotel. She leaned forward, changing the address, gesturing to go past the Hyatt to the further cluster, the relief popping inside her. She would be far less conspicuous to anyone in the foyer arriving on foot than by car.

The additional buildings appeared to be some sort of apartment complex. Olga paid off the taxi. She waited until the car was actually on the bridge before going with reluctant slowness toward the hotel. She remained in the shadows of the last group of buildings, seeking further protection safely to make her entry. Almost at once she was aware of the tourist bus crossing the bridge over which she had just come and she smiled at the good fortune. Olga didn't supposedly believe in superstition any more than in religion but she crossed her fingers and pressed them tight together, hoping the luck would last. She was aware for the first time how much her hands were sweating and instinctively pushed them down the sides of her skirt, to dry them. The wetness came back, immediately.

She timed her move with the confused disembarkation of a group she decided were German, letting herself be carried into the hotel as she had allowed herself earlier to be jostled through the alleys of Macao. Directly inside, she eased away, anxious not to be challenged by any tour leader. The reception area faced her, the elevators to her right. The ground area stretched away even farther to the right, and Olga saw a magazine kiosk and moved toward it, eager for any excuse to orient herself further. The move put her in the corner of the building, from which she could see the foyer completely to her left now, with the lounge and bar directly in front. There appeared to be a coffeeshop alongside the lounge and another larger dining area to the far side of the main bar. She bought two English-language magazines—*Newsweek* and *Cosmopolitan*—for their protection and went cautiously into the lounge, intent on everyone around her, looking for the face of Irena Kozlov, briefly relieved at not locating the woman but not relaxing for a moment. There were no hideaway nooks or banquettes: the best was a table beside which some long-fingered plant emerged limp-wristed from an ornate tub and Olga moved as quickly as she felt she safely could toward it.

She did not know what she wanted when the waiter approached, just subduing the spurt of panic because to panic over something so inconsequential would have been ridiculous. She chose vodka, adding tonic as an afterthought, realizing she still hadn't decided how to go about what she had to do and that she might need the excuse to remain there for a long time.

Olga moved the chair back slightly, better to gain the concealment of the plant, and held the *Cosmopolitan* in readiness, for further concealment, if Irena suddenly appeared. She was appallingly exposed, Olga recognized, professionally: transgressing just about every instruction and lesson she'd ever learned. And badly placed, in addition. The lounge in which she sat was in an awkward part of the L-shaped floor design. At least half the immediate foyer area and the elevators from which Irena might emerge were virtually hidden from her view. And sitting where she was—minimally concealed—it was impossible to see beyond the bar, into the formal dining room. From either direction, Irena Kozlov could be upon her in seconds. The awareness brought a fresh burst of nerves and Olga had to grip one hand over the other to quiet the shaking.

She sipped her drink, hoping it would help, striving to bring some rationale into her thinking. So she was here, in the hotel where Yuri three hours before had assured her Irena was hiding. Now what? She had to carry out some sort of survey— one more detailed than she had so far—but sitting for hours in a bar lounge wasn't going to get done what she had to do: another way of hiding, in fact, like walking farther into Macao than any precaution required. Room 525, Yuri had said. Was that the way: stop hiding behind sagging potted plants, go to the room with the special gun prepared for the moment Irena answered the door, and fire, just once? All that was necessary, with the ricin capsule in the bullet tip, according to Yuri. One wound, anywhere, and the poison would kill her. What if it wasn't Irena who came to the door? Panicked stupidity to expect her to be the one. There could be other people, an enclosing guard: so she could shoot her way in with the advantage of surprise, maybe take out one or two others but that was the maximum because the air pressure quickly dissipated from the gun designed for the assassination of unsuspecting, unguarded victims. Which left her empty-handed, facing the rest of the protectors, and possibly with Irena safely bundled into another, unreachable room. Stupidity, she thought once more. The inner chant came again: *no reconnaissance, no plan, no reconnaissance, no plan.* . . . What then? She didn't know, Olga acknowledged, in a further sink of despair. She was sitting there with an assassin's gun in the bag tightly held in front of her, intent to murder, but without the slightest idea how to go about it. Not *wanting* to go about it . . . Olga stifled the mental drift, bringing herself rigidly upright, as if a proper physical attitude would strengthen her weakening, inner resolve. She had to *find* a way: find a way to kill Irena and get back to Tokyo and Yuri and the life she knew they were going to have together.

In her room above, Irena Kozlov frowned at Charlie Muffin and said, in now familiar demand, "When?"

"Not today," said Charlie. "I thought you wanted to rest."

"Tomorrow?" she said, ignoring the reminder.

"Tomorrow," promised Charlie. With luck and a following wind, he thought: awkward bitch.

Relax, you're safe: Yuri's assurance. Irena said, "I don't want to stay cooped up here that long. Can't we go out?"

The summons from Boris Filiatov was waiting when Kozlov arrived at the embassy and Kozlov felt the flicker of unease: he'd forgotten momentarily how Olga had involved the Rezident and wished he'd had time to prepare. He actually considered delaying, to prepare a story, but he was already late and decided against it, not wanting to exacerbate any problem.

"I have had difficulty locating you: and your wife." The challenge came without any preliminaries, as soon as Kozlov entered the office.

"The surveillance upon the Americans. And the British," said Kozlov, cautiously. "It's recorded in the log."

"I know what's recorded in the log," said the Rezident. "It appears to have become a lengthy operation."

"Moscow considers it important," said Kozlov, falling back on the rehearsed defense. Filiatov didn't appear impressed.

"Where is your wife?" asked the Rezident.

"She made her own log entry," said Kozlov, uncomfortably.

"Where do *you* believe her to be?"

"Conducting surveillance upon the British."

"Where?"

Kozlov shrugged, needing time. Seeking safety, Kozlov said, "My wife and I are working separately . . . like the log says. I have remained with the American surveillance . . . my wife has transferred to the British observation. I do not know her specific whereabouts in the city." He would have liked it to have sounded better but maybe the vague uncertainty was more convincing.

"You've not discussed the British operation in detail, then?"

"No," said Kozlov, restricting his answer. He would have to be very careful: the doubts of the stupid, fat slob were obvious.

Throwing out a lure, in the hope of discovering what she might already have transmitted to Moscow, Filiatov said, "Have you discussed these operations with Comrade Balan?"

"Orders do not allow me to discuss elsewhere any conversation I might have had with Comrade Balan," said Kozlov, formally.

Filiatov's face went taut. He said, "Comrade Balan also appears absent from the embassy."

"I am unaware of anything involving Comrade Balan's movements," said Kozlov, still formal. That might be difficult to explain later, but it was safer than trying to improvise.

"From today surveillance will be suspended, upon both the Americans and the British," said Filiatov. It was a positive decision he could make, without committing himself too far if Olga Balan's doubts proved unfounded.

Kozlov was about to acquiesce, because it didn't matter any longer, but then realized it would be a mistake. "It had the direct approval of Moscow," he said, the other familiar defense.

"I have the power, as Rezident," announced Filiatov.

Pompous fool, thought Kozlov: the fact that Filiatov was prepared to invoke the authority showed how well Olga had sown the seeds. He said, "As you wish."

"And I would like the fullest report on what's been achieved," insisted Filiatov.

Which meant that so far the man hadn't communicated with Moscow, gauged Kozlov: nor would he, until he had the file, because Filiatov was a man who used bureaucracy like protective armor. "It will take me some time," said Kozlov, seeing the way of holding the other man off from becoming an additional difficulty.

"As soon as possible," insisted Filiatov.

Hurry, Olga, hurry, thought Kozlov.

"It's only circumstantial," insisted Harkness.

"Dovetails with everything Charlie said," argued the Director, reading from the account that had arrived from Germany. "Messy . . . in Bonn . . . and the date's right. . . ." He looked up. "Harry Bales, one of the toughest hawks in the American Senate, touring NATO installations and making a lot of waves about increasing troop strengths to confront the Warsaw Pact. That dovetails, too."

"I think it's circumstantial," repeated the deputy.

"I think Charlie's working well," said Wilson.

23

Charlie considered the inevitable delays—for any aircraft to arrive and for Cartright to get from Toyko, and for Wilson to discover if there was a British naval vessel in the vicinity—and accepted that someone as seemingly impatient and difficult as Irena Kozlov was going to get very pissed-off indeed, like he was. Which made a monotony-breaking outing not a bad idea for all of them. It took an hour for Harry Lu to carry out the precautionary checks. Lu extended the checks to the High Commission, who confirmed London's instructions to issue his entry documents. Three of the calls confirmed the CIA concentration on people working exclusively for the British.

"It was the obvious short-cut," pointed out Lu, objectively. "We knew they were doing it, before you arrived."

"Did you speak to your wife?"

"She hasn't noticed anything unusual."

"She wouldn't if they were good, would she?"

"My not being around is going to provide the confirmation," said Lu. "Why don't I get back to Hong Kong; play the innocent?"

And get hold of those immigration documents, thought Charlie. He didn't criticize the man for his eagerness. If Lu returned to Hong Kong it would put him by himself. But Cartright would be arriving sometime that day and being by himself was something he was accustomed to anyway. Providing Lu played his part convincingly, the man could actually send the Americans on enough wild goose chases to stock a dozen

Christmas larders. And now that he had his entry permission, there was no cause to doubt Lu's loyalty. Charlie said, "Any indication of their looking here, in Macao?"

Lu shook his head, "Just Hong Kong, at the moment."

"How sure are you?"

"As sure as I can be: I trust my sources."

Back in the colony, Lu would be able to monitor the Americans' movements far better than he was doing here, thought Charlie, recognizing another advantage to the man's return. He said, "Think you could carry it off?"

"No problem," said Lu.

Too quick, judged Charlie: understandably the man was thinking more of getting out to the safety of England than he was about what it would be like to confront the Americans. He said, "It is. If they think you know something—get the slightest suspicion—they'll put your prick through the mangle. Maybe literally."

"I can do it," insisted Lu.

"It could be useful," conceded Charlie, in final agreement, setting out how he wanted the Americans watched and misled.

"I can do that, too," assured the other man.

"Just be careful," urged Charlie.

"The balance has changed now, hasn't it?" said Lu.

"What?" Charlie frowned.

"I said when you arrived that you owed me: I guess now that I owe you."

"I'm glad it worked out," said Charlie, vaguely discomfited by the man's gratitude. Surprised, too: he hoped it was all as clear-cut as it appeared.

Furthering the discomfort, Lu extended his hand and said, "Thanks, Charlie: you're a friend."

Trying to lighten the mood, Charlie said, "It's the last station on the Piccadilly line."

Now it was Lu's turn to be confused. "What?"

"Cockfosters." Charlie grinned. "The stop after Oak-wood."

Lu smiled back and said, "Visit us there?"

"All the time," promised Charlie. He hesitated, considering the shoulder bag containing the material the Director had freighted from London, and decided it was safer carried than left lying about in a hotel room. He picked it up and said to Lu, "Come on. Let's give Irena the deluxe tour."

In the bar below, Olga Balan finished the second drink and shifted in her seat, disconcerted at the limited view of the lobby, and decided to risk checking with reception that Irena was actually in room 525 and not out of the hotel. Olga paid, gathered the unneeded protective magazines, and was halfway back toward the desk when she saw them emerge from the elevator bank and the magazines ceased being unneeded after all.

There was a line of taxis, so Olga let one go, to create a buffer over that solitary, easily identifying bridge, tensed forward on the seat to keep their car in sight. Only two protectors, which surprised her; one a shambles of a man, the other sallow-skinned, more aware of his surroundings: Irena in between, not actually dwarfing the two men but still noticeably big, just—but only just—deferring to their guidance. Olga's worries at the practicality of what she had to do began to ease away, confidence coming from the actual physical movement. She was undetected and stalking her quarry and crossing away from that impossible-to-operate peninsula. And Irena Kozlov was visible not more than twenty yards ahead. There was still the morality but she felt it was becoming something she could lock away in the private safe of her mind, the strong—or was it weak?—room to which only she had the key, to open or close as she decided.

Where were they heading? Back to Hong Kong? The barnyard of a man had a shoulder bag but no one else carried cases so that scarcely constituted luggage. And they had not paused at any cashier's desk, after that so-near confrontation close to the elevators, to pay a bill. She hoped it was a return at least, to the colony. The pierhead had been jostled on her arrival, a melee of a place, ideal for the sort of . . . her mind blocked, refusing to go on . . . for what she had to do.

In the vehicle in front, Lu was playing the tourist guide to the aloofly unimpressed Irena, talking of the Floating Casino where the Chinese indulged their passion for fan-tan and provided the multimillion-dollar-a-year income for Stanley Ho, who ran it, and the other betting outlets like the greyhound races and the trotting track and even the grand prix around the closed-off, tortuous roads every November, where the odds were more important than the invariable accidents, on the number of which bets were also taken.

It relieved Charlie, who tried to remain alert to everything about him, realizing the impossibility of any practical trail-clearing once they entered the enclosed, street-on-top-of-alley-on-top-of-street part of the town and hoping Harry Lu's informants had got it right about Macao being safe. They stopped near the genuine day-to-day street market, not any tourist creation, and as Irena got from the car she said, "It smells."

"So does Moscow," said Charlie, who remembered that it did.

Olga was alert for the stop lights and managed to direct her driver actually into a side street, so that she was able to get out completely concealed. She returned to the corner cautiously, unsure if they would be walking toward or away from her, smiling when she reached it. It was Irena's height, rather than that of the two men, which provided the marker: they were moving unhurriedly, sightseeing, their backs to her. She eased her way into the street, glad of the crowded market. She was trembling, willing the shaking to stop.

Irena halted at an open-fronted shop, fingering a Members Only windbreaker suspended from an outside rail, and said to Charlie, "What is this price, in rubles?"

Charlie grimaced at the conversion, making the most approximate of calculations, and said, "About fifteen."

She looked at him disbelievingly and said, "In Russia it would be four times that, on the black market."

"It's a fake, counterfeit," said Lu, patiently. "That's the business here. And in Hong Kong."

"The authorities do not stop it?" she demanded.

"Are the militia having a lot of success against the black market in Russia?" asked Charlie, pointedly. Maybe she had to be indulged but he did not see that they had to put up with patronizing, party line crap: Irena was going to have to make a lot of adjustments.

Olga risked getting closer, only four or five people separating her although one, a woman, was surrounded by a family, which increased the protection. Olga slipped her hand into the bag, feeling for the special pistol, her perspiration making the grip greasy. The compressed air had to be primed and she pumped the lever to make it operate, keeping on until the resistance was such that it wouldn't depress any more. Inexperienced and with slipping fingers, she was unsure whether she had prepared it sufficiently: she tried to push the lever down another time but it wouldn't move.

At the road junction ahead Lu indicated first left, then right, and said, "That way to the casino, on the river, that way to Saint Paul's church and the fort."

Charlie, whose feet dictated that tours were for tourists, never for him, said, "Which is nearest?"

"The church and the fort."

"The church and the fort," Charlie decided. For all the interest that Irena was showing, they might just as well have stayed at the hotel and watched incomprehensible Chinese television, piped in from Hong Kong. Time soon to stop for a drink, thank Christ.

Olga stopped, at their pause. It had to be now, somehow: there wouldn't be another opportunity so good. The shaking wouldn't stop and the sickness had come back: she swallowed, again and again, fighting the need to retch, and the perspiration worsened, leaking from her. The gun was silent, any faint discharge hiss certain to be lost in the babble of the street hawkers: all she had to do was get slightly nearer—not more than a yard or two—and fire. It doesn't matter where you hit, Yuri had said: the poison will do the rest. Just fire, then lose herself momentarily in one of the open-fronted, labyrinthine stalls, and then melt away, in the confusion. Easy. Now, then. She pressed forward, through the separating people, getting to the edge of the squabbling, gabbling family. Irena Kozlov appeared magnified, bigger than she really was. Small things registered, as if they were important. Olga could see how the faint wind had ruffled the other woman's hair, creating a gap at the back. The suit had a pink flower motif on a brown background, some sort of woolen cloth and too well made to have been bought in the Soviet Union, and the handbag looked foreign, too, well thumbed to the point of blackness in places but still good leather, like her shoes. The left heel was badly worn, needing repair. Close enough now; she couldn't miss. Olga turned her own handbag, its length hiding the weapon, easing it up so the muzzle was unimpeded, wet finger around the trigger.

They moved.

It wasn't abrupt but it appeared to be, to Olga. They'd been waiting for a break in the congested traffic and Lu saw it and walked through, leading the woman forward: one moment Irena had been no more than five feet away, the next twisting through the traffic block and the chance had gone. Olga sagged against the corner stall, oblivious to the immediate bargaining approach from the salesman, whom she vaguely saw to be a child, maybe twelve or thirteen years old. She backed away, shaking her head in refusal.

The steps leading up to the facade of Saint Paul's were shallow but there were a lot of them and Charlie looked dolefully at the huge castle alongside that they still had to tour and wished now he'd gone to the casino. This whole expedition was definitely a bloody big mistake.

Trying to avoid the castle, he said to Lu, "What time you going back?"

"There's a hydrofoil at three," said the other man.

"Back where?" intruded Irena, at once.

"Hong Kong," said Charlie. "He's got things to arrange."

"For me?"

"Naturally."

"For tomorrow?"

Charlie hesitated, momentarily forgetting his hotel-room lie. "Right," he said, remembering and repeating it. "Tomorrow." He had things to do, as well: link up with Cartright and contact the signals station, to discover what the Director had arranged. Most definitely too much to tramp around a bloody great castle he just knew would smell of a lot of quick pees and have walls covered with "John loves Jane" graffiti records stretching back practically to the time when the Portuguese fought off a Dutch takeover from its battlements.

There were protective stalls at the beginning of the steps but the huge walkway was entirely open, with no cover whatsoever, and Olga realized the other woman only needed to turn, to gain a view from the top of the promontory to identify her.

There weren't even enough tourists to give her cover, just an occasional straggler, groups of no more than two or three. She got behind the biggest party, five but not together, just coincidentally ascending at the same time, tensed against a new but actual collapse this time. Irena and the two men were at the entrance now but their figures were blurred and Olga blinked against the sudden surge of faintness. Mustn't collapse: fall down so that she would be discovered. Too close to fail.

"There's nothing here!" protested Irena. She stood just inside but to the left of the enormous front wall of the church, all that remained apart from the flagstoned floor through which weeds and even flowers were tufted.

"It got sacked, then fell down over the years," said Lu, almost apologetically. He gestured toward the solitary remaining facade. "It's still quite a monument: very old."

He'd been right about the graffiti, Charlie saw: there was even a John and Jane who'd left their mark. At least, with so much openness, there wasn't any urine smell. He agreed with Irena. There didn't seem a lot of purpose in bothering to preserve just one wall: God—as well as Kilroy—had been here but hadn't stayed.

They were farther away than they had been on the street corner below but still very obvious, from where Olga hid, tight against the slight snag of masonry that had once been the continuing right-hand wall from the surviving front. She squeezed in there from the front, without having to go through the only entrance, and was glad she hadn't tried because they were just to one side and she would again have been immediately visible, to Irena. But not here. Here she was absolutely concealed, the stone against which she was pressing her head for its coolness in front, tangled undergrowth and stunted trees at her back, shielding her perfectly from the castle. Olga took the primed pistol from its encompassing bag and laid it against the stonework, which formed a solid, unmoving support practically in line with her eye. Olga scrubbed her hands dry against a handkerchief this time, blinking again, completely to clear her vision. Suddenly she was cold, no longer worried by the perspiration, and her eyes were focused, too. The impression of enlarged detail came once more, of them all: Irena in that pink patterned suit and the scruffy man with a shoulder bag and those strange, spread-apart shoes and the neater one, European but sallow-skinned, who appeared to be doing most of the talking. Olga crouched slightly, sighting. Only Irena now, filling her vision, in the very center of the V-piece, big, very big, big enough to hit: anywhere, it didn't matter providing she was hit. There was no slack in the trigger, tight at once against her finger, and Olga blinked for the last time, surprised now the moment had come how calm she felt, knowing she could do it.

And she did.

At which precise moment Harry Lu said, "We might as well go," and turned, cupping Irena's elbow, putting himself directly into the line of fire.

He said, "Oh!" more in surprise than in pain and because there had been no sound of a shot neither the woman nor Charlie immediately realized what had happened. Lu slumped, falling against her, and Irena said, "What the . . . !" and Charlie became aware of the man falling and a lifetime's expertise and experience made the reaction split-second instinctive.

Charlie actually managed to catch him, taking the weight to bring him down against the wall. As he did so Charlie saw the wound, the hole where Lu's eye had been but wasn't anymore.

Charlie's physical response was quite separate from his immediate thoughts.

Before Lu finally reached the ground Charlie was searching for the heartbeat, wrist first, then against the chest, confirming that there was none, but he was thinking of an excited man with a wife and a kid in a party frock planning a life in a place with a stupid name like Cockfosters and how they'd got drunk together when Edith had been alive and that Harry Lu had been a professional and there weren't a lot of those, not real professionals. And then he promised himself there would be the balance and that he would see to it himself and then that lifetime of expertise and experience refused any more personal reaction, because if he were to balance the books he had to be alive to do it.

Surprisingly little blood but a bullet, obviously. But no detonation. Special then: professional. Not intended for Lu, though. Charlie snatched Irena down, reducing her as a target and also to cover the dead man from the smattering of sightseers who remained in the false-fronted church, all oblivious to what had happened. Closer, Irena saw the wound and knew the man was dead and she said, "Oh," too, a throat-tight exclamation, frightened.

Charlie couldn't tell from which direction the shot had come but he spread himself, going away from the man he couldn't help better to protect the woman, searching both sides for the vantage point where the assassin would be, seeing nothing. The instinct ran on, the reasoning unwinding in his mind. A professional killer who missed would try again, because he was a professional, and they were exposed like lined-up ducks at a funfair.

Charlie felt forward, gently despite the need to hurry, tilting Harry Lu's head against the stonework to hide the gaping wound, making him a man sleeping or maybe drunk, resting.

Irena began, "I don't . . ." but Charlie said, "Shut up. Later."

He kept her close to the wall until the door, hesitated, and then bustled her through and down the wide steps, hurrying but not running, which would have attracted attention. Still lined-up ducks, but going more quickly at least; the muscles were tight, across his back and legs, tensed for the impact from a bullet that made no sound. Near the bottom he turned, one professional alert and searching for another, in automatic reaction. Nothing.

They plunged into the narrow lanes, protective but dangerous too because among the very people who provided the shield could be the man using them in the same way, to cloak his next attempt. Charlie thrust himself into the path of the cab, forcing it to stop, physically pushing Irena ahead of him and stumbling in after her, careless that the urgency might later be remembered, when the police inquiries began. He demanded the pierhead and sat back beside her, looking through the rear window for any obvious signs of pursuit but not seeing any.

"Me?" said Irena. She was tightly controlled, another professional after all, but the fear was there, like it had been in the exclamation at the church.

"I don't know," said Charlie honestly, because he didn't. When the fuck was something going to make sense!

"Where are we going?"

Something else he didn't know. Charlie said, "Kowloon." It was the only place they hadn't been: he didn't bother to consider whether it would be safe or not, because nowhere was safe. Charlie emerged tight-muscled again from the protection of the car: there were a lot of people at the ferry terminal but it was not as jam-packed as the Macao alleys. Charlie hurried Irena through, arm around her back, guiding and hopefully protective, maneuvering always to maintain space around them. He made her stand in front of him—minimizing her as a target—at the ticket kiosk and aboard the hovercraft managed to get her into a bulkhead seat at the rear, so no one could sit behind, with himself blocking her from the left.

And as the craft throbbed back from the moorings, to become airborne, Charlie looked around the crowded cabin and decided that if the killer had got aboard with them, all the attempted precautions wouldn't be worth a bugger and they were dead.

But Olga Balan wasn't aboard. She was back down in the alleys, walking without direction or awareness, knowing that she'd failed and knowing, too, that she couldn't try again. There'd been the opportunity, when they'd crouched over the body: she'd actually tried to aim again, squinting down the barrel and fixing Irena Kozlov in the sights, but she couldn't pull the trigger that second time. Or when they'd fled down the steps, the steps she'd later stumbled down herself, waiting for the shouted discovery which never came. She tried to focus her mind, decide what to do. Get away, she supposed, before the authorities sealed the colony: put a search-check on the ferries maybe. Dump the incriminating weapon. Contact Yuri. Tell him she'd failed. That they were trapped, still trapped. More than ever now.

Fredericks and the CIA team spread the word about Harry Lu throughout their informants and sources and the word came back within an hour of the body being found, on Macao.

"Right person, wrong place," said Elliott, when Fredericks announced the wrapping up of the now pointless Wanchai surveillance.

Assembled back at the Peninsula Hotel, Fredericks said, "The way I see it, Charlie Muffin hasn't got Kozlov. His own people have. The Soviets somehow stopped him but missed the woman, when they blew the plane. Now they're chasing."

"Makes her the only prize left," judged Hank Levine.

"Which we're still going to have," said Fredericks.

"There's something from the airport," disclosed Jamieson, the Special Forces colonel who'd been awaiting their return. "There's a British military flight, on its way from London."

"The prize we're still going to have," repeated Fredericks.

24

Charlie's first thought was to go for one of the book-by-the-hour short-time whorehouse hotels in central Kowloon, among the clothes-festooned tenements, but then he realized how easily two round-eyes could be located in such complete Chinese surroundings and so he came closer—but not too close—to the waterfront and took a room in The Asia, which dollar-a-day vacationing students shared with working girls. There were still clothes-festooned tenements and cooking smells from outside streets zig-zagged with neon and inside rooms where some people really were on a dollar a day. There was a perpetual rustle and stir of noise, too, from outside again but competing against quick-breathed bed sounds from rooms around them and a farther-away competition, from transistor radios. Their room was at the back of the hotel, kept in a permanent half-light from the overshadowing buildings. The netted curtains against the window were gray with dirt and the bed covering was gray, as well, and probably from the same cause, although it was difficult to be sure even from the additional illumination of the single bedside lamp with its lopsided shade. The lamp was on a table containing the only drawers and when Charlie opened the plywood wardrobe a solitary but bent metal hanger clattered at him. Light in the adjoining bathroom was better. There was a tide-mark of blackness at the water level of the lavatory and several more, at varying heights, around the bath, the bottom of which had completely lost its enamel and was uniformly black. When Charlie put the light on, three fatly contented cockroaches made for the safety of the skirting board but unhurriedly, more confident of their permanence of occupation than he was. Just the sort of place where Harkness would expect him to stay, thought Charlie.

"We are occupying the same room?"

Charlie turned back from the bathroom, at Irena's question, and said, "Do you want to be alone then, after today!"

She seemed to have difficulty in replying, the demanding confidence still not recovered. Instead she said, "Who tried to kill me?"

"I told you before I didn't know," reminded Charlie. "I'm still unsure." There was so much to think about, maybe reconsider. He could find—just, and then certainly not justify— a rationale in the Americans blocking an escape route by destroying the plane, but today didn't have any logic. Irena Kozlov wasn't any advantage to them dead, and if he and Harry had been the targets of a professional CIA kill and snatch operation—and the weapon had most definitely been professional—why was he still alive and why hadn't Irena Kozlov been taken? He *had* been a sitting duck, incapable of any effective resistance. And it would have been obvious to anyone after their first week of basic intelligence training. So if not the Americans, then who? There was only one obvious answer—an answer supported by the use of the special assassins' gun that fired without noise—but against that were the same arguments as before. If the Russians had somehow found them there would have been a squad and a squad of trained experts would not have let them get three feet from today's ambush. Why the hell was the world full of questions without answers?

"That man, the one who was killed; you said he was a friend of yours?" she asked.

"Yes," said Charlie, reminded. "He was." Poor Harry, he thought: he wouldn't after all be taking a family with tinkling names to settle in Cockfosters, the next stop after Oakwood.

"I am sorry someone has died, because of me."

Charlie looked intently at the woman, surprised by the expression of regret and the continued humility, neither of which seemed in character. "So am I," he said. Wilson didn't like soldiers getting killed and Charlie didn't like his mates—even mates who'd made him temporarily suspicious—getting killed.

"What are we going to do?" It was a little-girl question from someone who wasn't a little girl.

Charlie moved closer to her but then didn't know what to do because Irena Kozlov wasn't the sort of woman to reach out to and offer some reassurance through physical contact. He did anyway and she further surprised him by responding, reaching out to take his hand. "We're going to get out," he said, wishing he believed it himself and hoping she did. Already rehearsed from his earlier reflections, Charlie went on, "They tried to kill us but we got away, so we must have lost them. Otherwise they would have tried again. So we're safe."

She looked back at him uncertainly, but didn't openly challenge him. She said, "It's got to be the Americans, hasn't it?"

Charlie caught the doubt in her mind, wondering if the fear of her own people in pursuit had brought about the changed attitude. While he preferred it to her earlier demeanor, Charlie decided it would be better if she only had the fear from one source. He said, "Yes, it's the Americans."

"They'll lose," she announced.

"Lose?" queried Charlie. Her hands were very soft.

"When I tell Yuri. He explained how you tried to persuade him to have both of us come to you, like the Americans. When I tell him what's happened, he'll abandon them and come to you. We both will."

"That will be good," said Charlie. Something to pass on to Wilson. In fact, there was a lot to discuss with the Director and he had to stop Cartright—initially anyway—from mistakenly crossing to Macao.

"Thank you, for looking after me like you have," said Irena.

What would a dark-haired woman whose name meant Dawn Rising feel about the way he'd looked after her husband, thought Charlie, suddenly. The entry documents were waiting at the High Commission; something else he shouldn't forget. He squeezed her hands in attempted reassurance and said, "It's going to work out just fine."

"I hope Yuri is all right, now."

"Don't worry," urged Charlie. How was he going to manage all that had to be done? It would take at least three hours, there and back, getting first to Hong Kong island and then across to the signals station and he couldn't leave Irena

Kozlov alone, not now. And he couldn't take her with him, either: apart from the risk of their being reidentified during the journey, it was inconceivable to take a KGB agent—albeit a defecting one—anywhere near an installation with the security classification that existed at Chung Hom Kok. It looked like rule-breaking time again.

It took a long time for him to be connected with the duty officer: Charlie sat perched on the bed edge, aware how hard it was, wondering if the bathroom cockroaches had any friends between the covers. When the man came onto the line, Charlie dictated his Foreign Office number, conscious of the intake of breath from the other end at the breach of security, and hurried on, stopping any protest or reaction, giving the hotel and the room and insisting Cartright be directed there the moment he made contact.

Able finally to speak, the man began, "London will . . ." but Charlie put the receiver down before he could continue: he bet London—Harkness—would complete the threat, whatever it was.

Irena was at the window, staring out at the dark, inner courtyard, properly standing to one side so that she would not be openly visible. There seemed more than a difference in the way she was behaving; she appeared physically smaller, weighed down by what had happened—and was happening. She'd probably be wishing she'd never defected and if she was she would be thinking there was no going back.

"Are you hungry?"

Irena turned, without coming away from the window. "Would it mean going out?"

"Only immediately outside; I saw some places, in the same road as we are."

"No."

"Tell me, if you change your mind."

"We just left him, sitting there!" she burst out.

"He was dead: we couldn't do anything."

"Was he married?"

"Yes."

"Children?"

"A girl."

She shuddered. "What will happen to them?"

"I'll see to it."

Some sort of emotion moved through her again and Irena said, "It's awful, this business, isn't it?"

The disillusionment that brought about the defection? wondered Charlie; it seemed a strange reaction from someone knowingly married to a killer. Coaxing, he said, "Is that what Yuri thinks?"

"He says not—that it's imprisonment he's frightened of— but I know it is."

Charlie didn't want to lose the momentum, but he had to make the briefest of pauses, correctly to phrase the question. He said, "He's worked a lot, then?"

Now Irena hesitated, not lost in any reverie but very aware of what she was being asked. "A lot," she said, not offering any more.

A mistake to push in that direction, decided Charlie. He said, "Did you find it difficult?"

Irena considered the question and said positively, "No, not at all."

"Where were you, before Tokyo?"

She moved finally, coming farther into the room. "Is this the start, the debriefing?"

"No," said Charlie.

"Acceptance interview?"

"It's a little late for that, isn't it?"

Irena smiled, big-toothed. "Far too late. What then?"

"Obvious, professional interest."

The woman examined him curiously, as if she didn't fully believe him, and said, "Bonn. It was the first posting Yuri and I had together; he was in London by himself."

An attempted deflection, gauged Charlie. "And you stayed behind in Moscow, throughout the time he was in England?"

The smile came again. "No," she said. "For part of the time but then I worked supposedly as a secretary at the Soviet consulate in San Francisco."

Which monitors the American high-tech industry to the south, in Silicon Valley, thought Charlie. There was a deter- mined and recognizable pattern, from the places where Irena Kozlov had worked: Silicon Valley, the technology crucible of the West, from there to West Germany, the major European smuggling conduit, and then to Japan, the major Asian route to the Soviet Union. The complete cell-building, spy-suborning tour, in fact: Moscow would unquestionably and immediately order her killed, to prevent what she knew from being passed on. At once came the stumbling block question: so why hadn't it been done? Knowing that all defectors try to elevate their importance—and wanting to prod Irena's previous boastfulness—Charlie said, "You must be highly regarded."

She sat on the bed, the only place available but at the bottom, away from him, and said, "Yes, I am." The boastfulness he'd expected wasn't there.

Remembering the fears that prompted their split defection, Charlie said, "You will be well treated, in England. I can promise you that."

"I'm afraid it might be a problem," she said.

"There's bound to be uncertainty, a period of adjustment . . ." began Charlie, but she talked across him.

"Not that," she said. "I know what will be expected of me . . . the cooperation. I think that's what I will find difficult. . . ." The smile came once more, a sad expression this time. "I'm well aware of what I've done but I still regard myself as a loyal Russian. Does that surprise you?"

"Utterly," admitted Charlie. Weren't there enough ambiguities, without this!

"I did it because of Yuri," disclosed Irena. "It was he who wanted to come over, not me."

More guidance for Wilson; or rather for the debriefer who would eventually handle Irena, if he managed to get her out. It meant the woman would have to be treated quite differently from how they might have envisioned: not as someone hostile but certainly as someone who would be reluctant to impart what she knew. Charlie thought back to his earlier reflection about how defectors usually embroidered, to enhance their value; Irena Kozlov was going to be the reverse. One reflection prompted another: now he definitely hoped he wasn't going to be the unlucky sod appointed her case officer. Get her out first, Charlie reminded himself, soberly. Unable to think of anything better, he said again, "Believe me, things will be fine."

"I'd like to think so," she said. "So much has happened, so quickly, that I'm not finding it easy."

Neither am I, love; neither am I, thought Charlie. He was spared the search for further, echoing assurances by Cartright's knock, a hard sound, just once. Irena started up from the bed and went to the wall by the window again, the farthest point from the door. She remained there after the Tokyo Resident identified himself and was admitted by Charlie, who said to her, "It's okay."

Cartright offered his hand, which she took hesitantly, and then the man looked doubtfully around the room.

"It's what the brochures call unchanged," said Charlie.

"What's happened?"

Charlie gave an edited account in front of the woman, avoiding any reference to Chung Hom Kok or the pressure Harry Lu had imposed, for the cooperation that cost the man his life. Throughout, Cartright stood nodding and when Charlie finished he said, "I never knew Harry Lu."

"He was all right," said Charlie. It didn't seem much of an epitaph for someone who'd worked his balls off for the service since he'd literally been a kid. Charlie was glad Cartright didn't waste time asking questions to which he didn't have answers.

Cartright looked at the woman, recognizing the difficulty of full conversation in front of her. "London wants to talk. Urgently," was all he allowed himself.

Charlie wanted to talk to them, but not yet: postponing confrontations seemed to be a growing habit, he thought, remembering his initial reluctance in Tokyo. He said, "More important things to do first. We've got to stay clean, as far as local law is concerned. We ran out on the Hyatt, in Macao, and that's going to show up when the investigation starts and puts Harry there, as well. I want you to go back and settle the account: just ours, of course. There was no obvious contact between Harry and us—only in our rooms—and I don't want any connection established. Cash, no traceable credit cards."

"They'll still have names, from registration records."

"Along with a hundred others," said Charlie. "They won't mean a thing as long as there's nothing suspicious like skipping out on a bill."

Cartright nodded and said, "London was very insistent."

"I'll let them know you passed the message on," promised Charlie.

Cartright looked uncertain, but didn't press the argument. "What after Macao?" he said.

Christ knows, thought Charlie. He said, "Back here. And be careful. There've been enough casualties."

After Cartright left, Irena said, "He seems very young."

"I always think that about policemen, in the street. Must be age," said Charlie. He'd meant it as a remark against himself but it didn't come out as he intended. She didn't seem offended. He wondered how old she was: late thirties perhaps, forty at the most.

"Thank you, for what you've done."

"You already thanked me," reminded Charlie.

"I mean you don't have to go on, looking after me so closely. I'm feeling much better now. I'll be all right."

Was she worried about both of them sharing the same room? She hadn't seemed to mind the reference to age and Charlie wondered if she'd be upset by the assurance that the last thing he had in mind was making any sort of sexual approach: the handholding had been part of the job, nothing else. He said, "I wasn't strictly honest with you, that first night at the Mandarin, when you asked me if everything had gone wrong and I said no. *Everything* hadn't gone wrong: but too much had. It still is going wrong. And like I say, I don't know why. I've got to get you safely to England and I *am* going to do it. And after what happened today I've decided that means not leaving you alone, for a moment."

"He said London wanted you, urgently."

"They want you, more urgently," said Charlie. "Cartright won't be long. When it's not me, it'll be him."

In fact he took longer than Charlie expected, so that it was already genuinely dark by the time the man got back to the Kowloon hotel: the single lamp was like a match in a coal mine.

"Any problems?" asked Charlie. There were enough, surely.

"None at all," said Cartright. He handed Charlie the hotel receipt and said, "London will want this."

Harkness really had the poor bugger trained, thought Charlie. He said, "Too late to speak to them now."

"The time difference is in our favor," disputed Cartright.

"I meant too late from this end," said Charlie, still avoiding any mention of Chung Hom Kok: avoiding London, too. To Irena he said, "Sure you're feeling better?"

"Positive," she said at once, brightly.

"Good," said Charlie. "Then we can go out to eat."

They went to the restaurant Charlie had already identified,

just across the road from the hotel. It was bare-floored and the tables were Formica-topped and Charlie recognized a Chinese restaurant that Chinese used and decided they'd scored, which they had. It was Szechwan: Charlie had Governor's Chicken and Cartright chose Ma-Pa Do Fu. Irena only picked at her fish, the brightness no longer there. Any normal conversation was practically impossible, although Cartright tried and Charlie did his best, and there were still long periods of echoing silence between them. But then, reflected Charlie, it was hardly a social event. They went directly back to the hotel, where Cartright had a room on the floor above theirs. At the door to their room, Irena stopped and said, "I really don't think this is necessary."

"I do," insisted Charlie. He opened the door and went in, refusing a corridor argument.

Irena followed and said, "Richard's room is just one floor up."

Cartright stood uncertainly at the door, looking between the two of them, unsure what—if any—contribution to make.

"Irena," said Charlie, with forced patience. "I'm sharing your room, not your bed. An airplane you should have been on was blown out of the sky and this morning someone I liked a lot was killed, not more than a foot from where you stood. . . ." If it made her frightened, so what: frightened she was more malleable. He picked up, "I told you this afternoon I was going to keep you safe; and that means my staying in your room, so let's cut the shit. In shit, I'm an expert."

She looked down at herself, smoothing her hands over her pink-patterned suit. "I don't have anything to change into."

Charlie sighed: on top of everything else, he had to get the KGB's original Vestal Virgin. He'd been sure there weren't any. He said, "I'll stay outside, while you get into bed."

In the corridor it was the first time Charlie and Cartright had been alone. Cartright said at once, "The Americans insist they haven't got her husband. A navy ship isn't possible: there isn't one for a thousand miles. So it's got to be a plane again; the troop leader's name is Clarke. Due early tomorrow morning: there wasn't a definite time, when I spoke to the signals station. And London is as mad as hell about that, incidentally: about a lot of things."

"You know the American expression SNAFU?" asked Charlie, wearily.

"No," said Cartright.

"Situation normal: all fucked up."

"This is serious, Charlie."

"It was serious when Harry Lu got a bullet in his eye."

"Sorry," said Cartright. He looked at the closed door and said, "She's not easy, is she?"

"Easier than she was," assured Charlie.

"Why don't I spell you, during the night?"

There wasn't any point in going absolutely without sleep, Charlie thought: he'd done enough of that. "Thanks," he accepted. He knocked on the door and said, "You ready?"

Irena was lying with the gray covers up to her chin and Charlie wondered again about companions for the bathroom roaches. He put his hand against his ribs and said, "You really shouldn't worry. Rape always gives me a stitch, in my side. Just here."

"Where are you going to be?"

It was a good question, in a shitty room like this. Charlie perched at the bottom on the bed, on the side opposite to her and with his back uncomfortably against the metal bed edge. "This far away."

Irena smiled, an expression difficult to define, and said, "I suppose I could spare a pillow."

Charlie wasn't at all sure he wanted one, from a bed like that, but he said "Thanks" and she maneuvered one from beneath the sheets still managing to keep herself covered. He made a support for his back and tried to get comfortable.

"I want the light left on," she said.

Usually the request was made in different circumstances, thought Charlie. He said, "Richard is relieving me, incidentally. Don't panic at someone else coming into the room."

She turned heavily onto her side, away from the light, bringing the covers farther up so that he could not see her face. Charlie gazed around the decayed room and then at his watch: Christ, it wasn't even ten! Should have brought a bottle back from the restaurant: the rice wine had been good, like the food. Pity Irena hadn't enjoyed it. Her breathing seemed heavier, but Charlie didn't think she was really asleep. Maybe a good idea he hadn't brought any wine back. Better that he sat there, boringly sober, and started all over again, from that moment in Wilson's office if necessary, and ran everything over just one more time, trying to find the key that would unlock all the doors so far remaining steadfastly shut in his face. Irena shifted, a settling movement, and Charlie eased slightly away, giving her room. It ruckled his jacket, awkwardly. He went away farther, actually from the bed, taking the jacket off and hoping she didn't look over her tented barrier and start yelling rape: in a place like this, there wouldn't be a translation for the word, in any known language. As he did so Charlie detected in an inside pocket the Hyatt bill that Cartright had given him earlier: like Cartright had said, Harkness would want it, to make his tidy sums add up in their tidy columns. He took it out, glancing without interest at the total and then stopping, looking closer, at first unsure in the dull light. Charlie stayed unmoving for a long time, although bringing his eyes up quite quickly from the no longer necessary bill. Then, quietly now, not wanting to disturb her yet, he went to the always-carried shoulder bag containing the material the Director had freighted from London, looking not for that but for the other bill he'd sent Harry Lu to pay that first night in Hong Kong: he remembered using the same phrase then—about keeping things clean—that he had today to Cartright. It was in the side pocket, still in the special departure envelope that the Mandarin always gave. The initial check only took Charlie seconds, but after so many mistakes and wrong turns—and with at last something which might at least lead him part way out of the maze—he determined to be sure, so he went right up to the bedside, directly beneath the light.

Fuck me, he thought. And then, that they had. He went back to the base with its supportive pillow and said, "Irena!"

She didn't respond at once and so Charlie said again, "Irena! You're not asleep: I know you're not asleep."

She came over the bedclothes, looking at him. "What?"

"I think we've got things to talk about."

Irena pushed the coverings down still farther, although remaining completely concealed. "What?" she asked again.

"Everything," said Charlie. "Everything you've got to tell me."

Olga didn't know—couldn't remember—how long the aimless wandering had gone on, through the alleys and then the wider streets of Macao. The floating casino was a positive recollection, the beginning of the gradual recovery, because she'd dropped the gun into the water there, tensed against the splash between the boat and the jetty that had sounded to her like the explosion that guns usually made when they were fired but appeared to be heard by nobody else. And where the second fear had immediately come, that it wouldn't sink, because it was plastic and light and floated initially on the surface while people jostled past behind her, eyes only for the fan-tan tables: and then water seeped into the barrel and filled it and it gurgled down and still no one had seen. She supposed she must have taken a taxi to the ferry, but she couldn't remember: her concentration had been on the terminal itself, apprehensive of thronged police and person-by-person checks which never occurred because when she arrived the departures proceeded quite normally, without any interruption. The crossing to Kowloon was gone, too—not completely, but almost—and it was not until she finally regained the mainland that any positive recollection and cohesion started to formulate, in her mind. She knew she had to get off the streets and she took a hotel which smelled and where babies cried, comparatively close to the Kowloon arrival jetty. And then she knew she had to speak to Yuri in Tokyo, at the Shinbashi apartment where he would be waiting according to their strictly timetabled schedule to hear that everything had gone as they'd hurriedly planned and that Irena was dead and that they were secure, forever. Which they weren't: couldn't be, not now. Because she'd failed. Olga actually felt out toward the telephone, several times, never once able to lift the receiver. Finally—instead—she let herself go sideways, against a counterpane that smelled like everything else.

"Oh God," she said, uttering the forbidden word for the first time. "Oh, dear God what am I going to do?"

There was a bizarre irony in that Olga Balan and the CIA group led by Art Fredericks—each of whom was pursuing Irena Kozlov for different reasons—were both at that moment just over a mile from The Asia, where the woman sat upright against the bedhead, still covered but confronting Charlie Muffin.

"I'm waiting," said Charlie.

25

Irena drew her feet up, creating a more positive barrier, the bedclothes still protective, staring at him but not saying anything, and Charlie refused to prompt with a positive question, just staring back. The hotel sighed and breathed around them but in the room there was a silence noisy between them.

After a long time, Charlie said, "Well?"

"I don't know what you mean . . . what you want."

"Look at the hotel bills," said Charlie, pointing to where they lay, between them.

To pick them up Irena had to reach over the covers and from the straps Charlie saw she still wore her bra. The woman made as if to study them but Charlie knew it wasn't necessary for her. He didn't know enough to ask probing questions, although he was giving the impression he did; the leads had to come from her. He said, "That really wasn't very clever, was it? Careless, in fact."

"I still don't know what you mean . . . what I'm supposed to have done wrong."

"Look again," urged Charlie, trying sarcasm. "It's marked with a T, on both accounts. Stands for telephone. The second symbol—still on both accounts—indicates long distance. You're supposed to be running, Irena: hiding where no one can find you. And all the time you're making long distance telephone calls. . . ." Charlie stopped, intentionally. He—or perhaps the

British service—was being set up but he couldn't work out how, so she had to provide the way to let him understand.

She smiled, an obviously open expression, and it surprised him although Charlie didn't think it showed. She said, "Is that all?"

"You tell me," persisted Charlie. Come on, come on!

"It was all part of the caution," she said, "The way Yuri devised to stop anyone tricking us. You. Or the Americans."

"Yuri!" He had the impression of a very small corner of a very dark curtain being lifted. But not enough.

"You know how careful Yuri was: how he always knew the Americans would try to cheat; you, too, if you could." The woman sat now with her arms comfortably wrapped around her knees, relaxed. "He never planned to go across, not at the same time as me. Always he was going to wait, until he knew I was safe . . . that way he could have forced the Americans to release me: keep to the bargain. . . ." The smile came again, rehearsed, like the words sounded. "He loves me, you see. . . ."

Charlie sat absolutely unmoving, needing to consider it all, analyze it properly: he would have liked hours—days—but he knew he didn't have either, just a few minutes to think it through and get it right, after so long. And he *had* been right, that first day in the Director's office, when he'd said it didn't make sense: right, too, in the continuous feeling of uncertainty. Which was still there. Bits of the puzzle were beginning to fit together but there were still some pieces missing. The biggest piece was *why*? Charlie remembered a man named Sampson who called him sir and Harry Lu without an eye and wanted to shout and make demands from the woman but instead, rigidly controlled, he actually managed to smile back at her, encouraging, and said, "Tell me about it, Irena. Tell me how it worked."

"Very simply," she said. "We couldn't liaise through the embassy, of course. Too dangerous. So he took an apartment, a safe house. The telephone there . . ." She stopped, nodding toward the hotel accounts with the long distance calls. "That was the contact point. . . ."

Charlie didn't want to interrupt the flow, but he needed to get the sequence right so he risked it. He said, "The day we first met, on the bus: when the Americans were following? You spoke to Yuri then?"

She nodded. "That was the arrangement: I've just told you."

"Where from, that day?"

"The airport. Osaka."

Charlie remembered something else from the tourist bus ride. He said, "A military plane!"

"What?"

"That same day on the bus: when I told you about Osaka you said you thought we'd go out from Tokyo and then you said, 'A military plane.' Why? Why specifically a military and not a commercial plane?"

For a moment Irena looked uncertain and then she shrugged and said, "We had a source, at the airport. We knew about your people coming in. The Americans, too."

"When?" demanded Charlie. "When did you know?"

"The night before."

The idea came to Charlie and it irritated him because it was stupid and so he dismissed it. Trying to make the question seem as casual as it could be, in the circumstances, Charlie said, "How was Yuri, when you spoke to him that time? From Osaka?"

Irena shrugged and said, "He was . . ." and then she stopped, both the gesture and the sentence.

"Was what?" pressed Charlie.

"Nothing," she said.

"Was what?" repeated Charlie.

"I thought he sounded strange: asked him about it. He said there was nothing wrong but perhaps he was nervous," remembered the woman.

"He didn't say anything about the plane blowing up?"

"Not then."

"When?"

"Hong Kong," said Irena. "Harry took me to the Mandarin when the plane wasn't there and I called. . . ." She felt out, touching the hotel bill. ". . . And Yuri told me what had happened. . . ." She paused and said, "I've told you about the bills now. Is this really necessary?"

Instead of answering, Charlie said, angrily, "And I missed it!"

"Missed what?"

"When I got to the Mandarin you asked a lot of questions

but you kept on about blowing the plane up," reminded Charlie. "And I already knew Harry hadn't told you, because I asked him. And I hadn't, either. Shit!" Would Harry still be alive, if he'd been more alert? Maybe, like his wife would still be alive if he'd been more alert, all those years ago.

"Does it matter?"

Charlie opened his mouth to reply but managed to halt the anger once more. Instead he said, "Go on. Tell me what Yuri said, when you spoke to him from Hong Kong."

"That the destruction of the plane showed how necessary it was, to maintain the arrangement . . . that it showed what the Americans were prepared to do. . . ."

"Moving!" interrupted Charlie again. "You knew we were moving on because Harry had already told you. Did you tell Yuri?"

"Of course," said Irena, grimacing as if it were another unnecessary question.

"What did he say to that?"

"That we had to go on being careful . . . that he would go on refusing to make any contact with the Americans until he knew I was safe. . . ." Irena stopped again and said, in head-lowered recollection, "And he called me darling."

Was the earlier idea so stupid? wondered Charlie. Maybe but then maybe not. It was still something difficult to believe. He said, "How was he going to know that: that you were safe?"

"The same way."

"You were to keep telling him where you were?"

She nodded and then said, "The last time from the airport."

"So you called from the Hyatt?"

She gave another smile and said, "There it is, on the bill."

Poor bitch, thought Charlie: poor, stupid bitch, hearing what she wanted to hear, believing what she wanted to believe. He suddenly remembered the momentary brightness, just before they went out to eat, when she might have imagined she was to be left alone; and then the absurd modesty of getting into bed that night, which he didn't think now had been modesty at all. He said, "What about from here! Have you called to tell him you're here?"

"I haven't been able to, have I?"

Charlie covered the sigh of relief, convinced he was right but recognizing at the same time it was all surmise. Unless there was something more she still hadn't told him. "How many calls?"

She blinked at the demand. "I don't . . ."

"From the time you met me, how many calls, to Yuri in Tokyo?" insisted Charlie.

Irena hesitated, head bent again as she enumerated in her mind. "Osaka . . ." she said, slowly. Then, gathering conviction, "The Mandarin . . ." She looked up, satisfied. "And from Macao . . ."

"Three!" persisted Charlie. "Only three!"

"Yes!" she said, her demand matching his. "I've told you all there is! I want to go to sleep now: I'm tired."

"No!" refused Charlie.

"What do you mean, no?"

"You don't believe it, do you, Irena? Not after what happened today?"

"You're not making sense."

"A lot hasn't, until now," said Charlie. Bringing in the recall again—the recall upon which he'd always relied so heavily but which this time had failed, too often—Charlie quoted, " 'It's got to be the Americans, hasn't it'?"

She looked steadily at him, pretending not to remember, refusing to speak.

Relentlessly Charlie went on, "Your words, Irena. Today. But it hasn't got to be the Americans, has it? We know—both know—what the Americans want; you, alive. Not in the wreckage of an aircraft or dead against the wall of a church that no longer exists. *That's* what doesn't make sense—never has—their trying to kill you."

"You told me they blew up the plane!" she fought back.

"It seemed the only logical conclusion, then," admitted Charlie. "It doesn't now, not any longer."

"Who then!"

"You tell me," said Charlie. "Who else but the Americans?"

"You're talking nonsense!"

"What exactly am I saying that's nonsense?" said Charlie.

She shook her head, eyes downcast again.

"What exactly am I saying that's nonsense, Irena?"

Still she refused to speak.

"Today was a professional attempt," continued Charlie. "Special gun: we both know that. Like we both know that Harry wasn't the real target: that you were. Who's the professional, trying to kill you, Irena?"

The woman came up, in furious anger. "Not Yuri!" she screamed, and Charlie was glad it was the sort of hotel it was. "He *loves* me," Irena raged on. "I keep *telling* you that. . . ." Her mind snagged on another thought, one she snatched at. More quietly, reasoning with an unarguable point, she said, "And it couldn't have been Yuri, could it? How could he be in Tokyo, talking to me, and be in Macao, as well?"

Charlie didn't know but wished he did. He was sure he wasn't wrong, not any longer. He said, "If it had been the Americans, they would have grabbed you, wouldn't they!"

Refusing the logic of one question, Irena clung to the irrefutable logic of her own, a drowning person saved by a passing raft. "So would the Russians! Today wasn't the Russians and it *wasn't* Yuri!"

"Who then?" said Charlie. It was like a race on a fairground carousel, one bolted-down horse never able to catch up with the bolted-down horse in front: and now the music and the ride were slowing because he couldn't think of any more questions to ask or any different ways of phrasing those he'd already put to her.

"I don't know," said Irena, impatiently. "How could I know?"

"You're not sure, though, are you: you weren't when you asked about it being the Americans this afternoon?" It was a bad, repetitive point and it was obvious, to Charlie as he asked it and to Irena, who disdained it.

"I'm tired," she said again, the defensive anger gone. "You know about the calls now: what they were for. I want to go to sleep."

She actually moved, to go back beneath the covers. Not wanting to lose the momentum, Charlie thrust into the shoulder bag, snatching out the photographs of Yuri Kozlov that had been sent to him from London and throwing them to her, on top of the hotel bills. He said, "He's set you up . . . you know he has!"

The insistence was no better than the previous question because it was an accusation Charlie couldn't support, but the effect was different this time and it wasn't from anything Charlie said. Irena was staring down at the prints, her throat working and then she whimpered, a mewing sound without any shape at first but then it formed into a word—"No!"—moaned over and over again. She let the photographs drop and the covers, too, sitting in front of him brassiered but huge-breasted, tears abruptly starting and then coursing down her face. She didn't try to wipe them or her nose, either, when that began to run. Charlie saw she had a yellow pimple, about to pop, on her left shoulder.

Charlie didn't know what to do, to discover what had caused the collapse. He got up from where he was and tried to pull the covers up for her but sitting as she was it wasn't possible without her holding them and she didn't try, so they fell down again. Instead he picked up the photographs, searching for what he'd missed and to what she'd reacted, seeing nothing.

Charlie reached out, to touch her shoulder, to comfort her, but then pulled back. He said, "Irena? What is it, Irena?"

Her voice was too choked for him to hear the word, at first, so he said again, "Irena. Tell me, Irena."

Then he heard the word, although immediately he didn't understand what it meant.

"Her!"

He looked at the disordered photographs, but not at Kozlov, remembering something else, the first-sight reflection about the woman in the background and then the later realization that it was not Irena.

"Who is she, Irena?"

The woman sobbed on, not answering for a long time, and when she did speak it was still muffled, so Charlie had to bend closer.

"Balan. Olga Balan."

Charlie let her cry on, to take her own time, knowing it—whatever *it* was—was coming now and he did reach out to her, edging onto the bed and putting his arm around her. Irena came to him, wanting the comfort, and there was another long period when she didn't—couldn't—speak. When she did, the words were halting and stumbled and Charlie had to strain forward, to make sense of what she said. Irena told him who Olga Balan was and about her reputation at the embassy and then, unprompted, she talked at first unintelligibly but later in a way that Charlie could comprehend of someone called Valentina who was or had been—he wasn't sure—a choreographer at the Bolshoi with whom Yuri had had an affair and for whom he had asked her for a divorce and of her refusal. And then why.

"Don't you think I know what I am!" she said, coherent now but the sob still in her voice. "I *know* the size I am: that people look at me. And I know that I intimidate and I try not to and then I realize it's happening and that I haven't noticed it and I try harder and it happens again. And I did try, with Yuri. I tried so hard! I stood in front of mirrors and I actually practiced with my arms, how *not* to be overpowering: trying to appear smaller! Can you believe that! And I thought—attempted to think— before I said or did anything when we were alone, so that it didn't seem that I was trying to dominate, which I know I do because I can't help it. . . ." She looked down at herself, shrugging the clothes up to cover her breasts and Charlie knew why when she said, "I did anything he asked . . . anything . . . even though some things I didn't like . . . tried so hard. Always." She turned her head, to look up at Charlie. "You know why I said no, when he asked for a divorce? I knew he didn't love me, before that: maybe never had . . . I was an easy way for him to get into the service . . . always outranked him. . . ." Irena stopped, realizing she had gone away from her point. ". . . Knew I couldn't marry again, that's why; that nobody would ask me. Didn't want to be alone: so frightened, of being quite alone. Wanted so much to keep him . . . tried so hard . . . anything he wanted . . . he said it would be a new life, in the West . . . anything . . ." She started to cry again and Charlie held her and thought, poor bitch, again, but this time with real pity.

"How do you know she's involved?" he said. Despite the sympathy, he had to know everything.

"I *knew* there was someone else, in London," insisted Irena. "I could tell; women can. Actually asked him. He said no: that he'd forgotten Valentina, too. And when Olga was posted to Tokyo and established the reputation I told you about I asked him if he'd heard of her anywhere else and he said he hadn't: that he'd never met her before, either. . . ." She sighed, a shuddering movement, and said, "She was part of it, of course . . . there were interviews and I know what she was doing now . . . all the questions of growing suspicion. . . ." Her voice gagged, with fresh emotion, and she couldn't speak again for several moments. Then she said, "How they cheated me . . . ! Made me perform, like some animal and all the time they were cheating me!"

There was still a lot Charlie didn't understand: that perhaps she didn't know either, so she wouldn't be able to tell him. But there was enough. There were bridges to rebuild, with the Americans. Who didn't have Yuri Kozlov and weren't going to get him. And who still wanted Irena, like . . . like whom? When he'd shouted at Irena that Kozlov had set her up he'd done it to shock her into some reaction, without properly considering the words, but could that be what the man had really done, set out on some convoluted private scheme to get rid of a wife who had refused him a divorce? The other nonsense—what he now accepted as nonsense—of creating supposed separate crossings fitted the scenario, putting him and the Americans in squabbling rivalry, concentrating more on their own interests than on the defection itself. And what happened today fitted, too: it explained why there hadn't been a squad of grab-back Russians at the Macao church. Except why hadn't there been more than one shot, from that special gun? And who fired it anyway, if Yuri was still in Tokyo, maintaining the fragile link with . . . Charlie's mind stopped at the reflection, looking down at the now quiet woman. There was still an occasional shoulder-shuddering sob but she was more fully against his shoulder now, face turned into him, and Charlie thought she might have drifted into some sort of exhausted, uneven sleep.

"Irena," he said, softly. "Irena."

She stirred, looking up to him. Her eyes were very red. "What?"

"The Tokyo number, at the apartment? Will Yuri be there, still?"

She made an uncertain movement. "I do not know. How could I?"

Vague thoughts—too vague and too disjointed to be called an idea—began to filter through Charlie's mind. Intermingled with them was the Director's remark about losing soldiers and the image of Harry Lu and a very positive realization, that whether or not Yuri Kozlov had set his wife up, the man had certainly set *him* up, and Charlie disliked being made prick of this or any other month even more than he disliked trying to break in a new pair of Hush Puppies. He pulled the photographs toward him, gazing at the beautiful woman whom Irena had identified as the embassy's KGB security officer, feeling sorry again for Irena slumped against him; it really was unfair competition. As the thoughts began to harden, Charlie decided he would need an example, to convince Yuri Kozlov. Olga Balan? She was obvious but even more obvious was a better advantage that could be gained, if she and Kozlov were working privately together.

"Who's the Rezident, in Tokyo?" he asked Irena.

The woman came away from him again, not immediately answering. Then she said, "Why?"

"There's a reason for wanting to know."

"Filiatov," she said hesitantly. "Boris Filiatov."

"Is there an arrangement, for contacting Yuri?"

"It had to be evening, Tokyo time. During the day he had to be at the embassy, to avoid anyone becoming suspicious . . ." Irena's voice trailed. "That is what he said: I don't know anymore whether that was the truth. . . ."

"That much could have been," said Charlie. Initially, Charlie realized, he would be playing a poker hand with a lot of the card faces up. But then he felt he couldn't lose—because he still had Irena—even if Yuri Kozlov called his bluff. Charlie—who'd financed his army National Service with a permanent poker game when he wasn't organizing his Berlin black market in motorpool gas—didn't just want to win a hand. He wanted the whole, overbargained pot. And he was going to gamble like hell, to get it. Didn't like to be a prick.

A sound came at the door and Charlie was momentarily as startled as Irena, forgetting Cartright's promise to relieve him during the night. The other man came curiously into the room, frowning at Irena's obvious distress and the disheveled, littered bed and at Charlie, who realized for the first time that there was a large wet patch on the front of his shirt, where she'd cried against him.

"It's been Truth or Consequences time," said Charlie, obscurely. "I know a lot of the truth now. . . ."

Irena came in, before he could finish. "And I know what the consequence is," she finished. And started to cry again.

Misunderstanding the cause of the woman's distress, Cartright said, "I think I've come up with another way of getting out."

All in all it was turning out to be a pretty productive night, thought Charlie.

Sir Alistair Wilson stumped into the office and Harkness knew at once how angry the Director was and thought that although it had taken long enough, it had finally happened. He remembered wondering—although not precisely when—how long Wilson's loyalty would last, once Charlie Muffin was positively caught out. He'd never imagined—hoped—it was going to be quite so complete as this: despise the man as he did, Harkness had still believed Charlie Muffin possessed more native cunning than to make quite so many mistakes.

"Bad?" prompted the deputy.

"Bloody awful," said Wilson. "A full session of the Intelligence Committee. Actually chaired by the Prime Minister. Foreign Secretary moaning about the issuing of passports and entry documents, Army Minister insisting upon an inquiry into the plane crash, and electronic intelligence demanding what right we've got to use their facilities like a public telephone box. And I had to sit and take it because I know bugger-all about what's going on: not even *if* anything is going on."

"I warned you about the confounded man's arrogance: the insubordination," reminded Harkness.

Wilson ignored the direct invitation. "Where *is* the bloody man!" he said, getting up from his desk to find more comfort for the stiff leg.

"I briefed Cartright very fully," said Harkness.

"It had better be a good explanation!" said Wilson. "It had better be the best explanation that Charlie Muffin has ever given, for anything he's ever done in his awkward, bloody life."

26

Which it was, although not at first. The news of Harry Lu's killing stopped the Director's tirade and before Wilson could recover, to continue the furious demands, Charlie talked hurriedly on, setting out what he knew—and even exaggerating into what he thought he knew—from his confrontation with Irena, anxious because of Wilson's obvious attitude to justify all the short-cuts. There was no immediate reaction when he stopped speaking and Charlie briefly thought that, despite the electronic expertise of the signals station to which he had crossed on the first available ferry from the mainland, the connection had been broken. Then Wilson said, obviously unconvinced, "You telling me you believe that!"

"It fits all the inconsistencies and uncertainties better than anything else."

"It's preposterous!"

"Why?"

Again there was a long pause from London. Eventually Wilson said, less sure of his own assessment, "It *has* to be preposterous."

"Explain it another way?" invited Charlie.

"Good God!" said the Director. Then, with gradual conviction, he said, "It would have been very effective, wouldn't it? Had she been aboard the plane we would have had the embarrassment of explaining the presence of someone attached to the Soviet embassy traveling in a British military aircraft and the Russians would have had the internal warning they like so much to any other would-be defectors."

"And Yuri Kozlov, who appears to spend a lot of time waving his dick in the air, would have been home free with Olga Balan," finished Charlie.

There was another pause and then the Director said, "Except that you stopped it, if indeed that were the way it was supposed to happen. Which doesn't matter anymore, now that you've discovered the telephone contact and blocked it. We're still ahead, Charlie. Well done."

Umbrella up just in time to keep off the nasty-smelling brown stuff, thought Charlie. He said, "I haven't finished."

"Getting—and keeping—Irena Kozlov is enough," said Wilson.

"I can do better than that," insisted Charlie.

"Like what?"

It took a long time for Charlie to explain, setting out what he considered had developed into a practical, feasible idea during the remainder of the previous night. When he finished, Wilson said, "You could never carry that off, not completely."

"You've wrapped up Herbert Bell?" asked Charlie, at once. Everything depended on their known spy still being in place.

"No," said Wilson, at once.

"So we could use him as the conduit?"

"Yes."

"Then it could succeed in stages, couldn't it?" pressed Charlie. "Every stage that comes off is a benefit: if it goes wrong, it goes wrong. We don't—we can't—suffer."

"It's very clever," conceded Wilson, reluctantly. "Ingenious."

"Soldiers died," reminded Charlie, adding to the pressure. "Harry Lu, too. Someone I liked."

"Someone could suffer," disputed Wilson. "You."

"Not now," said Charlie. "Not now that I think I know what's happening."

"Have you got a name?"

"Boris Filiatov," listed Charlie. "He's the Rezident: that alone makes it worthwhile."

"What's he supposed to have done?"

"It doesn't matter," said Charlie. "Anything you like."

"It would be marvelous, if it all came off," said Wilson, reflectively.

"I think it can," said Charlie. "Just like I think we can get Cartright and the woman out."

"How?"

Charlie told the Director, who said at once, "Whose idea was that?"

"Cartright's," said Charlie, who refused to take other people's credit like he refused to be responsible for their mistakes. "I suppose it was obvious why it didn't occur to Harry Lu but I should have thought of it."

"When will you know?"

"They're seeing if it's possible now."

"What about Commander Clarke?"

"I left the military until we'd talked," said Charlie. "I wanted your agreement, first."

"You're right, I suppose; about losing nothing."

"So I can go ahead?"

There was the now familiar pause. "Boris Filiatov?" he said.

"That's the name."

"I'll do it today."

"Make it good," urged Charlie. "I want it to happen quickly."

"You think Irena's a worthwhile catch?"

"Tremendous."

"Something for the Americans," said Wilson, moving on. "Bonn looks like an American senator. The name was William Bales: ascribed at the time as an assassination carried out by the Baader Meinhoff gang. It was a shotgun. Messy, like Kozlov admitted."

"Doesn't that add to what I've already said?" seized Charlie. "Kozlov could never have risked that coming out." He decided it was something more for him than the Americans, at the moment.

"I'm prepared to go along, Charlie," said Wilson, in final capitulation. "Prove to me you're right."

"I intend to," said Charlie. The reason for that determination recurred to him and he went on, "There was a difficulty about Lu's entry permission?"

"The Foreign Office didn't like it."

"But they haven't withdrawn it?"

"Isn't that an academic question now?"

"There's still the wife and a child. A girl."

"I don't know, Charlie," said the Director, cautiously. "It's outside the existing laws."

"So's getting a funny sort of bullet in the head."

"There'll be hell to pay, when they find out."

"Harry was working for us when he was killed." Fucking Whitehall mandarins, thought Charlie: why was the world full of regulation-governed assholes?

"It won't be so bad, if you can bring everything off."

Charlie accepted the further demand, on top of all the others. By the time he succeeded or failed, Harry's wife and kid could be in England: he'd find a way of arguing from there, if he had to. Charlie said, "I'll bring it off," and remembered Harkness and the stupid accounts: he'd have to clear that off Harry's records to prevent the man from doing something bloody awkward.

The Director said, "You think Irena will cooperate now?"

"More than ever now," assured Charlie. "She believes she's been abandoned and sees cooperating as some way of getting retribution: all we'll have to do is keep irritating the nerve."

"Kozlov's quite a bastard, isn't he?"

It was a crowded honors list, thought Charlie. He said, determinedly, "I'd like to get him."

"Good luck," said the Director.

He was getting it, decided Charlie: and about time. For several moments Charlie sat unmoving in the communications room, conscious of what he had to do and how essential it was to get it all in the right sequence. Which meant the Americans first. Harry Lu's family after that. Cartright's idea remained an uncertainty, so Charlie decided he couldn't fit that into any scheme, not yet. Then Kozlov. Charlie felt a stir of anticipation, in no personal doubt that the Russian had completely sucked him up and blown him out in bubbles. Now it was book-balancing time: in a way, thought Charlie, he and Harkness were very much alike. Charlie just sought different results.

The first part was easy. While he was waiting for the

British troop commander to be brought to the telephone at the airport, Charlie reflected where he should establish the meeting and decided upon the Mandarin again: he deserved a bit of comfort after the Kowloon hotel and there might still exist the need to draw the Americans off if Cartright hadn't been successful. Clarke came onto the line and called him sir at once and Charlie remembered Sampson and decided he liked working with special troop units. Charlie stipulated the Mandarin and made the man repeat the message and Clarke said, "Would you like me to be there?"

Charlie thought over the offer, wondering about the need for protection. Then he remembered that if Cartright's route wasn't possible they would need the military plane and everyone attached to it and reluctantly said, "Better you stay there."

Clarke queried liaison procedure and with continuing reluctance Charlie decided against giving the soldier the Kowloon address, maintaining the security of one-way contact against any American military interception or surveillance.

The first-day escorts and the unkempt duty clerk were at their posts outside the communications room when Charlie emerged and Charlie supposed a lot of the now-put-aside complaints had emanated from the man. He grinned and said, "That's all for now. But I'll be back later. . . ." Charlie allowed the pause and said, "You know my name; shouldn't I know yours?" setting himself the personal wager on the man's reaction.

The signals official actually went red with indignation and said, "You know perfectly well the answer to that! And I'll need further authority from London."

Won a fiver, decided Charlie: he'd pay himself out of Harkness's expenses advance, which was actually getting pretty low. About time he asked for more. He said, cheerfully, "You've got all day to get it. Shan't be back until this evening."

Charlie savored the trip back over the Peak, enjoying it more than on the first occasion and knowing the reason went far beyond his no longer being exhausted. He wasn't behind anymore, unable to see what was going on because of other people's dust being kicked up in his face. Now he was in front, throwing up the obscuring dirt: he wondered if he was going to be able to create a sufficient fog to confuse everybody. What he'd told Wilson was true—they couldn't really lose—but winning completely would be far better. Always was.

Charlie paid the car off at the beginning of Wanchai, wanting to see Harry Lu's apartment free from any observation. It wasn't easy, to be satisfied: the district was most similar to Kowloon, that part of the island where the Chinese lived and worked and ate, a one-on-top-of-the-other jumble of homes and shops and food stalls and restaurants, the lot finished off with the inevitable Christmas cake decoration of colored neon. For a while Charlie maintained his own observation and then remembered his sequenced time schedule and thrust into the entrance to the second- and third-floor apartments, through the door alongside the open-fronted duck stall. The stairs held the smells of the shops below and echoed with the noise, too. On the first landing, Charlie saw that a corridor ran the length of several of the blocks, guessed that each would be served by a separate stairway as well as perhaps some elevators, and recognized that Harry had chosen a place to live with careful, professional care. It would be difficult to the point of impossibility to get trapped here.

Charlie's luck held. Lu's wife responded at once to his knock, regarding him expressionlessly from the doorway. She was very pretty—more attractive than she had appeared in the photographs that Harry had proudly shown him—the black hair shorter than it had been in the picture and her deeply black eyes more obvious. She wore a floor-sweeping dress, in mourning white, and beyond Charlie could see incense sticks smoking in front of a small shrine.

"I am a friend of Harry's. Charlie Muffin. He may have mentioned me?"

"No," she said at once.

Professional in everything, thought Charlie. He said, "I would like to talk with you. There are things to say."

She waited, appearing to consider whether to let him into the apartment, and then stood aside, almost in resignation. The interior belied the exterior approach. The floors were of some white stone that Charlie actually thought could have been marble and the furniture was very modern, chrome and black leather. On a low table near the veranda window was a large and clearly powerful radio, not a transmitting device but a receiver upon which Harry could easily have listened to ordinary broadcasts from the Chinese mainland. There was a picture of the child, proud in Western school uniform, alone on a small bordering table and closer Charlie could see that there was a photograph of Harry on the smoldering shrine.

"I am very sorry," began Charlie.

"You know what happened?" she demanded at once.

"No," denied Charlie, just as quickly, feeling no embarrassment at the necessary lie. "I heard."

"I do not think anybody will ever be punished," said the woman. "The Portuguese are not concerned about the death of someone the Chinese didn't like. Neither are the authorities here. Both seem glad he's dead."

It was probably true, thought Charlie. Poor Harry, mourned by no one except a beautiful woman whose name meant Dawn Rising and a little girl whose name he couldn't even remember. Not being able to recall the translation that Harry gave him embarrassed Charlie more than the earlier, direct lie. He said, "I expect somebody will be punished," which meant something to him but which he realized would sound like an empty platitude to her.

She confirmed his impression by the disinterest of her shrug. "What are they, these things that have to be said?"

"I spoke to Harry, shortly before he died," said Charlie. "He told me how much he wanted to go to England . . . why it was necessary."

"They dispensed with him, too. Maybe they're glad he's dead." Her voice was leaden with bitterness.

"No," said Charlie. "That's not so; neither's true."

"How do you know?"

"I want you to come with me, now, to the High Commission," said Charlie, ignoring the question. "There are documents there: the documents to get you and . . ." he searched again for the name and failed, ". . . and the baby into England."

For the first time the lassitude drained from the woman, some animation reaching her face, but she still had the caution of someone expecting to be betrayed. "To live in England!"

"Yes," said Charlie, still not knowing how he could guarantee that. He went on, "Britain hadn't dispensed with him."

She became further relaxed. "You are from London?"

Charlie hesitated, then said, "Yes."

"You said you were a friend?"

"I worked with Harry in the past."

"Why didn't he mention your name?"

"It wouldn't have been right. Did he tell you the names of other people he worked with?"

She nodded her head, in slow agreement to the point he made. "Not *with*," she accepted. "Sometimes he told me the people he was working against."

There was the sound of a distant bell in Charlie's head. He said, "Working against here? Or in London?"

"He was very upset at how he was treated," she said, avoiding the straight answer.

"Who treated him badly?" persisted Charlie.

"One particular man called Harkness."

"How?" asked Charlie.

"Harry had to review his work: account for what he'd done," explained the Chinese woman, unknowingly using the accurate word.

Charlie isolated the accuracy, seeing a bargaining point. He said, "Harry had to write reports?"

"Very many, going back over years."

"These reports," tempted Charlie. "How many were there? Copies, I mean? Just one? Or more than one?"

Indignation settled on her increasingly mobile face. "You've said what sort of man he was; how properly he operated! Just one, of course!"

Shit! thought Charlie. Was she clever enough to bluff, if she had to? He said, "I was not suggesting criticism of Harry. There was a reason for my asking."

"What reason?" she asked.

"Later," avoided Charlie. "You can come now?"

"At once?"

She seemed uncertain, then she nodded. She said, "The police, when they came: they said I was to tell them if anyone approached me."

"I see," said Charlie.

"Am I to tell them about you?"

Charlie's impression had been of a mourning woman

erecting barriers behind which to hide her grief but now he wasn't so sure. He said, "It would not be wise."

She nodded and said, "I understand. But the papers I am to get—they are for permanent residency?"

Now it was Charlie who understood; just as he understood she would not have any difficulty bluffing if the need arose. He said confidently, "Yes. Permanent residency."

"Then we should go," she said, eager now.

The visa section of the High Commission was crowded, as they always seem to be in embassies and consulates everywhere, so Charlie demanded to see a counselor, glad he had accompanied her; there were Chinese sitting around on benches with the attitude of people who had been waiting for a long time. He wondered if all were those being pushed aside with the dismissive description of British Overseas Citizens, effectively making them stateless. It was an opinion easy to reach from the official High Commission attitude which began as one of impatience and only changed when Charlie demanded, with matching brusqueness, that the unwilling clerk check the degree of authorization from London. And then the change was quite dramatic: what Charlie anticipated would be a protracted formality was completed in under an hour, so quickly that the woman was suspicious.

She looked between the entry stamps in her passport, to Charlie and then back again, and said, "Permanent?"

"If anyone officially approaches you from the department, in England, tell them about the report that Harry was asked to prepare," said Charlie.

"That is not clear to me."

"It doesn't have to be," said Charlie. "Just talk about the report. And insist that a copy was kept."

"It *is* clear," said the woman, in immediate correction. "Won't that be dangerous?"

"You know how Harry contacted the department? The numbers?"

"Yes," she said.

"Contact me the same way if it happens." Charlie realized he was rapidly getting into some sort of guardianship relationship, but he felt very sorry for her. Angry, too: for his own brief attitude toward the man but more positively for the way

London—but more definitely Harkness—had behaved. Charlie suddenly got the recollection and said, "It's Open Flower, isn't it; the translation of your daughter's name?"

She frowned at the abrupt switch in the conversation. Unused to making the translation, she said, "Yes, I suppose it is."

"Harry told me."

"Was it bad?" she demanded, suddenly.

Charlie hesitated, then decided he couldn't lie and bugger how he was supposed to reply. "No," he said.

"I must know the truth."

"That is the truth."

"He would never talk about it . . . the possibility of it happening," she remembered. "Whenever I tried to discuss it, he always said it couldn't happen."

It shouldn't have, thought Charlie. He said, "It was the truth about being a friend, too."

"I thought there weren't supposed to be any, among you people."

"There aren't," admitted Charlie. He was glad he had remained within the building: there was something he'd overlooked.

"What do I have to do now?"

"Nothing," said Charlie. "You can go to England as soon as you like. Providing the police do not object."

"I can't imagine their bothering, from the way they've behaved so far," she said. "And thank you, for being Harry's friend. My friend, too. I was rude today. I'm sorry."

"It's forgotten," promised Charlie.

"Will we see you, in London?"

Why not, thought Charlie. He said, "You've got the number."

Charlie stood in the foyer, watching her go out into the skyscraper area, glad there had been no hitch: his luck really was holding. Definitely with the business about Harkness and the report: prissy bugger was going to regret that.

Charlie had to ask directions for the reference library, where the assistance was much more immediately courteous than it had been in the more public section. It took him only fifteen minutes to get the names he wanted from the out-of-date but retained diplomatic registers, including those from an old guide to the official Chinese news agency through which Beijing—when it had been called Peking—had maintained representation before the 1997 agreement with London.

It was still only mid-afternoon when Charlie got back to Kowloon and he was happy that his time schedule was being maintained. It stayed that way when he got back to the hotel to find Cartright and Irena already there, waiting for him.

"No problem," announced Cartright at once, actually producing his passport as if he feared Charlie would not believe him. "Entry visas into China. We can train to Canton, fly from there up to the capital, and then transfer at Beijing directly onto a London flight. I've checked: Pakistan Airways has a service."

And the intercepting Americans could sit around at Kai Tak airport until hell froze over, wondering how they'd got away from Hong Kong, thought Charlie. He said, "The Director knows it's your suggestion."

"That was good of you," said Cartright.

"It was a bloody clever idea," said Charlie, who wished it had occurred to him. He looked at the subdued Irena and said, "You okay?"

"I've heard more sensible questions."

She'd been right in her self-assessment the previous night, thought Charlie: she couldn't stop being aggressive if she tried. He said, "You really can be in London by this time tomorrow. I think I promised you that: it seems a long time ago."

"To what kind of life?" she said.

"Better than you'd get if you went back to Moscow."

She looked away at the rebuke, swallowing, and Charlie wished he hadn't come back at her so hard. She had every right to her self-pity: she'd been dumped into what was going to be a pretty shitty existence and to remind her she was alive—just—wasn't much compensation, not yet.

"No point in our hanging around?" said Cartright.

"None," agreed Charlie. "I want you as far away from here as possible before I even get in the same room as Fredericks."

"What's going to happen to Yuri?"

Charlie turned back at the woman's question. "That's what I'm going to discuss with the Americans."

"Can you get him across?"

"I don't know: I hope so."

"Tell them . . . tell the Americans . . . that I'll make everything available," said Irena. "All that he's ever done, against their people. He's done a lot, you know? Killing, I mean."

"I think I do know some of it. And I'll tell them," said Charlie, who had no intention of doing so. Hell, fury, and woman scorned, thought Charlie. And the play was *The Mourning Bride*, too.

"I want him to suffer," said the woman, turning venomously quiet.

"Seems quite a lot of people do," said Charlie. It was almost possible to feel sorry for the poor bugger: almost, but not quite.

"Run it by me again!" insisted Art Fredericks.

"I still don't believe it either," said Jamieson. "Their group commander, a guy called Clarke, wanders across the apron, says good morning like some jerk out of a B-movie, and then asks me to set up a meeting between you and Charlie Muffin. The Mandarin, he says. If you don't show up, he'll take it you're not interested."

"Son of a bitch!" exploded Elliott.

"It's another crappy decoy," suggested Levine. "Drawing us all across to the island while they sneak her out through the airport."

"That's the most obvious," agreed Fredericks. To the Special Forces colonel he said, "I want everybody ready and waiting."

"We've been ready and waiting for days," said Jamieson, always annoyed at how the CIA imagined command.

"What about the rest of us?" asked Fish.

"We'll all go," decided Fredericks, at once. He looked at Fish and Dale and said, "I think he's got a make on everyone except you two. So you stay in the foyer, for any pursuit. This time we're not going to lose the bastard."

"I think we should stop pissing into the wind," said Elliott. "We get him, we keep him. We squeeze him by the balls, his heart and mind will follow."

"I heard the same philosophy in Vietnam, too," said

Fredericks. "But maybe you're right. Maybe we've got to make him tell us where she is."

"I want to do it!" demanded Elliott, predictably.

"Don't move, until I give the word," insisted Fredericks.

In the Shinbashi apartment in Tokyo, Yuri Kozlov stared in frightened disbelief at the telephone upon which he had finally—at last—spoken to the jabbering Olga Balan, trying to comprehend everything she had said. Before he could, it rang again.

27

"It's me this time, Yuri. Not Irena."

Charlie knew the initial seconds were vital, the time he hooked Kozlov into completing the missing parts or lost him, from one wrong word, a misplaced nuance even.

Before Kozlov could respond, Charlie said, "She told me how you kept in contact: told me a lot, in fact."

In the apartment with its view of the park, the receiver slipped in Kozlov's hand, so that he had to use both hands to hold it. He strained to clear his mind of the conversation with Olga—"I killed someone . . . can't do it . . .I just can't"—to concentrate upon the Englishman, to pick his way through the words like a lost man in a minefield. Told him a lot, the Englishman said; she must have, to have given away the telephone number. The Russian strained further, to wipe his voice of the surprised reaction literally soaking through him, and said, "How is she?"

Good response, judged Charlie: didn't appear concerned and the seemingly innocuous question put the onus on him, to disclose more. Charlie said, "Very well, considering." First tighten the line, then loosen it.

"Considering what?" If she'd told him a lot, where was it? Kozlov felt the vaguest flicker of recovery at the clutch-at-straw thought that the other man didn't know as much as he had indicated.

"All that's happened," said Charlie. The man was still doing well: let the line stay loose for the moment.

"What has happened? She's all right, isn't she?" The confidence was growing, the apparent concern well pitched.

Run too fast and that hook is going to embed itself, asshole, thought Charlie. He said, "You don't know what happened?"

"No! Tell me!" The concern remained perfect and alone in the apartment Kozlov took one hand from the receiver, no longer needing the extra support.

"But she's all right." Almost time, thought Charlie.

"Tell me what happened! Let me speak to her!"

"Irena didn't know that Olga Balan was in London with you: came as a hell of a shock."

Kozlov swayed, bringing the hand up again to prevent the telephone from falling, eyes closed, trying to think how she could have known: then he remembered the Englishman's apparent knowledge during the Tokyo car ride. He said, "There is a file?"

"Extensive," said Charlie. Time to wind in, he thought. He said, "Lot of names. I told you we knew about McFairlane. Then there is a trade union official named Harry Albert and an editor called Bill Paul and Valeri Solomatin, who used to write for him. . . ." Charlie allowed the pause. "There's even an American senator, William Bales. Officially that's blamed on the Baader Meinhoff group, did you know that?" To continue the fishing analogy, Charlie realized what he'd just done to the man was to throw a grenade in the water sufficient to stun a whole shoal. And he hadn't finished, yet. "And now, of course, we've added Olga's name."

"She wasn't involved in any of that!" blurted the Russian, instinctively defensive but worse—far worse—unthinking.

"Just this?" risked Charlie: the moment he could win or fail.

"That's all," said Kozlov.

Won! thought Charlie, triumphantly. He moved quickly, not wanting the other man to realize the admission. He said, "You can't speak to Irena: she's not here anymore. But then, you didn't really want to, did you?"

"What do you want?" demanded Kozlov, professional to professional, accepting that the other man was—temporarily at least but only temporarily—in control. Temporarily again, Kozlov was unable to separate what Irena could have told the man from what the British appeared to have discovered from their own investigations. Whatever it was, Charlie Muffin knew a lot; too much.

"Several things," said Charlie. It was almost too soon but he felt a burn of contentment at finally understanding—completely—what the hell had been going on. He still had to win, though.

"Like what?"

"There's more to talk about first," refused Charlie. It would be a mistake for him to get too complacent, too soon. He had to keep Kozlov constantly off balance and permanently acknowledging who was leading and who was following, horse before cart, carrot before stick.

"What else to talk about?" There was obvious apprehension in Kozlov's voice.

"How about Boris Filiatov? Let's talk about him."

"Filiatov!" said Kozlov. He felt as if his mind were enveloped by fog, too thick to penetrate. He so desperately wanted to anticipate the Englishman but every time he thought he saw a way, the direction changed.

"It's unfortunate, about Filiatov."

"You're talking riddles," Kozlov openly complained.

"That's what Filiatov is going to imagine: riddles," said Charlie. "He isn't going to understand his arrest or what he is accused of, and because he won't be able to understand any of it—because he hasn't done anything, has he?—his interrogation will be a disaster: a disaster for him, that is. Because Dzerzhinsky Square will *know* it's true."

"What!" shouted the befuddled Kozlov, exasperated.

"That he's an enemy of the State: someone to be punished."

The awareness—at least Kozlov thought it was awareness—came at last. And desperately Kozlov tried to fight back, conscious of how much he had lost in the exchanges so far. "You're too confident!" he said, half-confident himself. "So you've got a double—a source—who's proven himself to Moscow: but by telling me, I know he's controlled by London."

"So fucking what!" Charlie felt able now openly to jeer, determined utterly to subjugate Kozlov into knowing just how powerless he was to do anything, anything at all, to control his own future. Charlie got no satisfaction from the bullying, just the mental imagery of Harry Lu, dead, against the wall of an equally dead church. He said, "How are you going to tell Moscow you know, Yuri? Going to mention my name, Charlie Muffin? Let them know our connection. That wouldn't make you very popular: they know that name. Believe me, they know that name." Charlie stopped short of telling the other man why, knowing that before they brought Yuri in for the scopolamine-induced questioning and the electrodes to the testes if the truth drug didn't work and a straight pummeling kick in the ass if he still stuck out, they would offer the man forgiveness and rehabilitation, by blowing him away. Deciding—like the survivor he was—upon the need for insurance, Charlie added, "You know what that would do? That would convince them you're an enemy of the State, just like Boris Filiatov. Poor bastard."

"Go on," said Kozlov, dully, beaten again.

"He's a hell of a source, the man we've got," said Charlie, intentionally patronizing. "And he's not a double. He's your man and Moscow believes everything he tells them. If he said Gorbachev was a paid-up member of the British Conservative Party, your people would investigate it. . . ." Charlie hoped he wasn't going too far. He took up, "You understand what I'm saying, Yuri?"

"Tell me," said the Russian.

"That's it," said Charlie, unable to imagine a better response from the other man. After the grenade came the bomb, not atomic but devastating enough: he hoped. Charlie said, "That's all I'm telling you. We're tradesmen, you and I: we've done our apprenticeship in a very special craft, so we can recognize other people's work, like tradesmen can. So I recognize—know—how you're thinking now. You're still trying to work out how I learned about Olga when Irena didn't know and how I discovered it was Olga who killed the wrong person. . . . I know you didn't have any alternative but you shouldn't have entrusted something like that to anyone but an expert, no matter what the Soviet training covers, incidentally . . . just as I know that within an hour of this conversation ending, you'll be evolving some way of recovering. Of surviving. Like I would do, if I were in your position. Which is why I'm not setting out all the demands, not yet. Because I don't want to give you the opportunity of anticipating and beating me. . . ." Charlie stopped, needing the breath. "Given you a lot to think about though, haven't I, Yuri? And there's one last thing, the most important thing to remember: I can do what I promise. To you . . ." The pause this time was for a different reason. ". . . Or to Olga."

"There must be something?"

"Of course there's *something*," agreed Charlie. "We're going to meet, you and I."

"Meet!"

"Of course," said Charlie, patronizing still. "I've got the address. Shinbashi, isn't it?"

"You know it is," said Kozlov. He felt entangled, like someone in the straitjackets of the mental hospitals in which the KGB put the Soviet dissidents, treating them as mad to make them mad.

"Wait for me there."

"You're in Tokyo?"

"No."

"When should I wait then?"

"Just wait, every night, until I come. Irena told me how it works." Kozlov had to be demeaned, in everything. Angry he would think less clearly and Charlie didn't want the tricky bastard coming up with anything he hadn't anticipated. "And, Yuri . . . ?"

"Yes?"

"Don't, whatever you do, think of something as stupid as killing me, when I get there," warned Charlie, always a believer in insurance. "That would automatically activate the source: watch what happens to Filiatov, won't you?"

"Irena's out?"

"Absolutely safe," exaggerated Charlie, who knew that at the moment the woman would only be in Canton. "Let's face it, Yuri. You're fucked, without so much as a kiss. You, of all people!"

"No disciplinary action whatsoever!" Harkness made no attempt to keep the outrage from his voice.

"How can there be any disciplinary action?" pointed out the Director, reasonably. "We sent the man to effect the defection of a KGB operative and that's exactly what he's done." Wilson paused and said, "Maybe he'll succeed in doing even more."

"He broke every regulation that exists!"

Wilson, who was anxious to get to the Chelsea Flower Show where he had a floribunda on exhibition, sighed and decided it was time to bring the matter to a head. He said, "Do you really think street operations can work to a strict set of rules?"

"They are laid down," insisted Harkness.

"By my predecessors," qualified the Director.

"A long and respected line of predecessors, all of whom considered them necessary," said Harkness, in unaccustomed and sustained opposition.

As irritating as Harkness was, the Director believed the man made a genuinely worthwhile contribution to the department, like being there to run it when he went to flower shows, and he had no intention of shifting him sideways. Gently Wilson said, "I think I'll make a new rule, to go with all the others of my respected predecessors."

Harkness looked at him in hopeful curiosity. "What?" he asked.

"Whatever works, works," said Wilson.

"I don't even believe that's original," dismissed Harkness, in continued, determined argument.

"Whatever works, works," repeated Wilson. "I like it. Let's add it to the list, wherever the hell that is. I don't care whether it's original or not."

Geographically positioned where it is—on a clear day literally within sight of Wakkanai on Japan's northernmost province of Hokkaido and literally again within flying minutes from the Chinese mainland—Sakhalin is one of the Soviet Union's most strategic islands, a top-secret concentration of listening posts and monitoring stations and rocket installations and front line defense units. One of the biggest concentrations of all is the KGB Rezidentura, and again because of its geographical positioning it was from here that the arrest group came to seize Boris Filiatov. There was no attempt at finesse or subterfuge. A group of five men arrived, unannounced, and while two held Filiatov—physically—in his office the remainder seized all his files for transportation to Moscow, rather than bothering to remain at the embassy to make any sort of investigation there.

"Come back," Kozlov said, when Olga made her now pointless telephone call, subdued but more controlled this time.

"You've found a way out?" asked the woman, the hope obvious.

"Just come back," said Kozlov.

28

There was a room booked at the Mandarin in Charlie's name— by coincidence on the same floor as the one Irena so briefly occupied—but the CIA group found Charlie sitting in the ground floor lobby lounge opposite the bar: there was a reserved tag on the table and six chairs arranged in a half-moon around a small circular table. Charlie sat with his back to the wall.

When Fredericks led the other three CIA men into the huge room Charlie indicated the prepared seats and said, "I wasn't sure if you would all be coming. . . ." He looked pointedly beyond them, to the reception area, and added, "Why not bring the others in?"

Fredericks remained standing, with Levine, Elliott, and Yamada grouped tightly behind him. The American said, "You surely don't think we're going to talk business here, out in the open!"

"We did in Tokyo," reminded Charlie. He looked past the supervisor to the fixed-face men. "Besides," he went on, "I feel more comfortable out in the open."

"Somewhere private," insisted Fredericks.

"You want Kozlov?" demanded Charlie.

Fredericks stared hurriedly around and the other men did the same.

Charlie indicated the adjoining empty table that also carried a reserved tag and said, "I booked that one too, so we're not going to be overheard. And if we were, it wouldn't mean much anyway. You want Kozlov, get your ass in a chair." It was ridiculous to think of friendship: any sort of professional compatibility even. So why bother?

Hesitantly, aware of losing face in front of the others, Fredericks sat in the space directly facing Charlie, who looked at the others, waiting. At a head jerk from Fredericks, they sat too.

Charlie nodded to Yamada and said, "See you still keep those shoes polished."

The Japanese-American looked at Charlie's footwear but didn't say anything.

"You got a hell of a nerve!" said Fredericks.

"I've also got Irena Kozlov and I know you haven't got him," said Charlie. "And I know why, too." He spoke studying the entire group, instinctively gauging the opposition. The two men alongside the one who had followed him on the underground had been those in the car, when he'd made contact with Irena. Levine and Elliott, he remembered, from her identification.

"Go on," encouraged Fredericks.

"Ground rules first," said Charlie. "Out at the airport you've got an army group and you plan to intercept and snatch Irena, right?"

"They were an escort group for Kozlov," said Fredericks.

"That's bullshit and you know it," rejected Charlie. "But it doesn't matter. . . ." He looked at his watch. It was an overly theatrical gesture but the conversation had purpose: it was important for them to believe him and this was a way. Charlie went on, "Irena Kozlov landed at London's Heathrow Airport thirty minutes ago. . . ." He smiled up. "Hardly likely I'd make any sort of meeting with you until she was safe, was it? It was a Pakistani Airways flight, out of Beijing. She traveled as Rose Adams. Our Resident in Tokyo, Richard Cartright, accompanied her. You can confirm the names off the flight manifest, to know I'm telling the truth. . . ." Charlie allowed another pause and said, "Why don't you?"

There was a hesitation from Fredericks, who nodded. Takeo Yamada was the one who got up and hurried out to the telephone bank.

"So your guys at the airport—and all of you, at the moment—are wasting your time, okay?" continued Charlie.

"Are we?" It was Elliott who spoke, ignoring Fredericks's instruction only to follow him.

Charlie was apprehensive of the man but knew it would be disastrous—maybe quite literally—to let the nervousness show. He said, "Elliott, isn't it? Picked you up in minutes that day you followed me to the airport. Irena identified you, too. Actually told me your name . . ." He watched satisfied as the flush spread across Elliott's face and wondered which was the greater, fury or embarrassment. "We're talking about ground rules, aren't we?" Charlie picked up. "So let's agree on a very important one. Let's not fuck around with any 'bang, bang, you're dead' routines because at the moment all you've got— every one of you—is a lot of finished careers and I'm the only one who can make it otherwise."

Charlie was probing when he threw in the suggestion of physical violence and from the darted looks that passed between the three men he guessed that was exactly what they had been planning. He supposed that it was only to be expected, after the business with their Director, but the virtual confirmation still gouged a hollow place in his stomach. He'd been wise to set up the meeting and not try to get past their airport armada. More important than ever not to give any indication of nervousness.

"How make it otherwise?" asked Fredericks.

By not arguing the point, Fredericks was agreeing that their careers were in the balance, Charlie recognized; and believing he was responsible was a further reason to cause him some pain. Once more Charlie refused a direct answer. Instead he said, "Kozlov never intended to defect. It was a trick."

"What for?"

"To get rid of Irena. That's why the plane blew up and Harry Lu got shot."

"You mean he pushed her across and then put his people in pursuit!" said Fredericks, incredulous.

"Yes," said Charlie, shortly. He intended telling them only what he had to and that didn't include anything about Olga: they might learn about her later, in the little time available to them, if they were lucky.

"That's ridiculous!" refused Fredericks.

"Did you blow up the plane in Tokyo?"

"Of course not."

"Or shoot Harry Lu?"

"No," said Fredericks, more quietly and with obvious growing acceptance.

"Well we certainly didn't destroy a squad of our own soldiers or kill our leading agent here, did we?" demanded Charlie. "So who the hell did?"

"Jesus!" said Fredericks. He looked sideways at Yamada's return. The man said, "Pakistan Airways confirms that a Rose Adams and a Richard Cartright were on the London flight. And it was scheduled to land at the time he said."

Charlie decided Yamada's reentry had come precisely at the right moment, one truth coming right on top of another accepted truth. He said, "I can make him come across to you."

Fredericks sat regarding him cautiously. "How?"

"How is my business," refused Charlie. "You want him or not?"

"Why?" said Fredericks, the suspicion more open now. "If you've got some way of making Kozlov cross over, why not keep him for yourself?"

The American had isolated the weakest part of the whole proposition, accepted Charlie: he hoped he'd prepared a strong enough reply. Greatly exaggerating but knowing there was no risk in being caught out, Charlie began, "He doesn't want England. We've got Irena."

"There'd be no reason for them ever to get together," persisted Fredericks.

The man wasn't stupid, Charlie decided. He was glad he'd started as he had. He said, "I told you about Bill Paul, one of your guys, when Kozlov was in England. And Valeri Solomatin?"

Fredericks nodded, remembering the reverberations the information had brought from Langley.

"That wasn't the only killing," said Charlie. "There was an anti-Soviet politician named Harold McFairlane, who was expected to become our Prime Minister. Kozlov knows we've the proof that it was him and thinks we'd charge him, once we'd debriefed him."

"What about Paul? And Solomatin?" questioned Fredericks, at once.

"He doesn't have any idea that you know," said Charlie, honestly.

"Would your people charge him?"

"Probably," said Charlie, the cynicism prepared like everything else. "Can you imagine the uproar in Parliament if they found out we were protecting someone who'd assassinated a government minister! And if we'd got all we wanted from Kozlov a public trial would be a hell of a propaganda coup, against the Russians, wouldn't it? Your people will arraign him, if there's a benefit in it. You know they will."

Fredericks was nodding, agreeing to the amoral logic of an amoral business, and Charlie wondered if the same argument would work when he used it later, but in reverse. Fredericks smiled, the briefest of insincere expressions, and said, "I think we've got a deal."

Directly regarding Elliott, Charlie said, "Straight play: no fucking about?"

"Straight play," agreed the CIA supervisor.

"I can make him cross. Or I can make him stay, by letting him know I've told you about the CIA magazine people," insisted Charlie, unhappy with the quick assurance. "If I pick up any surveillance . . . anything I don't like . . ." He gave himself the necessary pause. "If I get the slightest impression that I'm not safe, he stays. And you're all drawing welfare. Understood?"

"Understood," said Fredericks, with difficulty. "How are we going to play it?"

"Same as before," said Charlie. "Set up a room at the Imperial. I'll make him contact you there."

"You seem very sure," said Fredericks.

"Would I have openly met you here today, if I hadn't been?" said Charlie.

"How long is it going to take?" demanded Fredericks.

"Just days," promised Charlie. "He'll have to move quickly, now that he's lost Irena."

"I agree the ground rules: everything your way," conceded Fredericks. "Straight play, all the way . . ." He allowed himself the hesitation. ". . . This time."

"As long as we both understand each other," said Charlie. He wondered if Fredericks would remember and try to invoke the threat if everything worked as he intended. Something to worry about then, not now.

"You wouldn't believe how much I understand you!" said Fredericks. "You just wouldn't believe!"

Must be nice to be liked, just occasionally, thought Charlie. He wondered if his mother had liked him; she'd never said. "Everything's agreed then?"

"It had better be."

"I'm going back immediately," said Charlie. "Could you be in position at the Imperial by tonight?"

"Of course," said Fredericks, nodding to Yamada again to start making the arrangements immediately.

"You know what's going to happen?" said Charlie.

"What?"

"It's all going to work out like it was supposed to, from the beginning. You get him and I get the woman."

"We'd better," said Fredericks, another threat. "Believe me, we'd better."

Kozlov stood aside for Olga to enter the apartment, startled by her appearance. She was bedraggled, her hair lank and her clothes crumpled where she hadn't bothered to undress, to sleep. Closer, he didn't think she'd bothered to wash, either: there was a smell. He reached out for her, uncertainly, and just as uncertainly she regarded the gesture, unsure whether to accept it, and when she did, finally, she merely stood in his embrace, making no effort to respond and embrace him in return. Kozlov decided the smell was definitely from her.

"How are you?" he said, which he knew was a ridiculous question but all he could think of saying in his surprise.

"Do you know what you made me do!"

"You already told me."

"He just sat there, like he was asleep!"

Kozlov moved from the ridiculous way they were standing. He poured from what remained of their supposed celebration bottle of vodka—how many millions of years ago had they talked about their own private, secret party!—and offered it to her. Olga looked at the glass as if she had never seen one before and then took it but didn't drink. Kozlov swallowed half his glass in one gulp, topping it up at once. Because she appeared to have no motivation of her own, Kozlov led her to a seat by the window, pushing her down into it, and said, "I'm sorry. So very sorry. It was a mistake."

Olga snorted a laugh, cynical now. "That's what it was!" she said bitterly. "A mistake: one big, huge mistake."

Kozlov had been unsure how to tell her but decided now that it was the way to break Olga out of her crushed and beaten lethargy. He said, "She knows. Irena knows about us. I've no idea how she discovered it but she knows."

It worked. Olga blinked, as if she were coming awake, and said, "But how do you . . . !"

Kozlov gestured toward the telephone. "The Englishman, Charlie Muffin. He used the system: called me. Talked about everything."

"Oh my God!" said Olga, not even consciously aware of the invocation anymore.

"And then he said I was to see what happened to Filiatov because they had a disinformation source and could do whatever they wanted."

Olga's lassitude was completely gone. She was tensed forward, the glass in two hands before her. "And Filiatov . . ."

"They came for him. A squad. They got here quickly, from Sakhalin . . ." said Kozlov.

"They're still here!" she demanded, the fear immediate.

He shook his head. "Took everything with them . . . files, cable records, everything. Drugged Filiatov, of course. And had a closed-off section on an Aeroflot flight."

Olga brought her hand up against her mouth, to prevent the mew of despair, but didn't quite succeed. "What's going to happen to us?"

"He said—the Englishman said—I had to stay here. Wait for him to come," said Kozlov, practically as listless now as Olga had earlier been.

"What's going to happen to us?" she repeated, her mind blocked by only one thought.

"He's proved it," said Kozlov. "He can do anything to us he wants: we've got to wait, like he says."

Olga gulped at her drink, heavily. "I was right, wasn't I?" she said. "We *are* trapped."

"Yes," admitted Kozlov. "Absolutely trapped."

"You know what he did!" said Elliott. "He made us eat shit! Eat shit! That's what he made us do!"

"We don't have any alternative, not on this occasion," said

Fredericks. "But there'll be another time. I promise myself there'll be another time."

They were all in the Peninsula suite, even Harry Fish and Jim Dale, whom Fredericks had withdrawn from the Mandarin surveillance, strictly observing the agreement. Everyone was gripped with the feeling of impotence but only Elliott was openly expressing it.

"You sure Langley would agree with that?" demanded Elliott.

"Why don't you ask them!" demanded Fredericks. "Why don't you tell them how we were suckered by the Russian as well as the Englishman and how you think we should blow Charlie Muffin away just to get our rocks off and not go for Kozlov after all."

"You like the sound of all that crap he gave you!" said Elliott, shouting.

"I like the sound of it a damned sight better than I like the sound of the word *welfare*," said Fredericks. "How's welfare sound to you?"

29

The rainy season had literally descended on Tokyo when Charlie landed, as if the clouds had split at the seams to spill everything out at the same time. It was thick, impenetrable, at the airport, and the car crested more like a boat than something on wheels through water-cascading streets into the city, where the pavements were mushroom fields of umbrellas. So much for English weather, thought Charlie; compared to this, London and Manchester in November were positively tropical. Charlie came up in the military aircraft—enjoying again being called sir by Clarke, whose rank turned out to be a major and whose Christian name was Allan—and from the flight control exchanges he knew that the American C-130 was behind them. And while, as far as he could establish, Fredericks had kept the no-surveillance agreement, Charlie was still careful, knowing the CIA could have put people in ahead of his arrival, to pick him up when he got there. The weather made it easy. He got out at Nijubashimae, ducked off the Toei Shinjuku service after one stop, and emerged from the underground at Kamiyacho, deciding within yards of setting out for Shinbashi that while in theory the tradecraft was good, in practice it was bloody stupid. It was still pissing with rain and by the time he got to what Yuri Kozlov regarded as his safe house Charlie felt anything but safe: the rain had got through his topcoat and jacket and his shoulders were damp and he knew, from the sticky slip-slip when he moved his toes, that both his shoes were leaking. Maybe, with luck, they could be repaired.

Despite the discomfort, Charlie didn't enter at once. He went past the building, checking intently, and returned on the opposite side, looking not so much for American observation now but Russian: it still hurt when your balls got caught in the vise, irrespective of who manufactured the pincer machine, and he was not yet sure if Kozlov was sufficiently worried.

Satisfied at last, Charlie squelched into the foyer, shaking himself like a dog to get rid of the surface dampness, aware of the puddle forming around him where he stood. Charlie's irritation went beyond his physical discomfort: Charlie attached a lot of importance to psychological advantage in the sort of encounter he was about to have, and psychologically, arriving like someone emerging from a swamp, he was in the disadvantaged position. He took his coat and jacket off and shook them and then used his handkerchief to dry his face and hair.

Yuri Kozlov opened the door before Charlie got his hand down from the knock and Charlie decided the swamp-look wasn't quite the drawback he'd feared; Kozlov would have to have been waiting directly behind the door, to respond that quickly. The man *was* nervous, then. There was no greeting, from either of them: Kozlov simply stood back and Charlie entered.

Charlie was surprised by the Western-style appearance of the apartment and guessed the view was of the park and of the port beyond: the rain was too heavy to see anything now. It was the briefest of inspections—nothing more than to establish the siting of any doors so that he could avoid making himself vulnerable to anyone or anything behind them—and Charlie was back facing Kozlov when the Russian closed the door behind him.

"Well," said Kozlov. "I'm here."

Which tells me a lot, thought Charlie. "Quick to get Filiatov, weren't they?" he said, confidently. The arrest had already to have happened for Kozlov to have been frightened into keeping the appointment.

"You know then?" said Kozlov, in unthinking confirmation.

"Of course I know," said Charlie. "I told you how it would be, didn't I?" Kozlov had to believe he was practically omnipotent.

"What will they do to him?"

"You can guess that better than me. It's your country; your service."

"I meant what have you accused him of?"

"I didn't come here to talk about Boris Filiatov," dismissed Charlie. He thought the Russian was far smaller than the last time and then remembered he had never seen Kozlov standing, only in a car.

"You going to tell me now what you want?"

"It was a hell of a scheme you worked out, wasn't it?" said Charlie, avoiding the reply: nothing had to go as Kozlov wanted.

"Nobody knew, only Olga and I," said Kozlov, in sudden urgency. "How did you find out?"

This time the man could be answered, because it conveyed the impression of Charlie's complete control. Charlie said, "It's a big file, Yuri. You and Olga in London, before here. You weren't very discreet, you know: not very discreet at all."

"Nobody knew!" shouted Kozlov, in desperate defiance.

Charlie didn't reply. Instead he took from his bag the same photograph that had brought about Irena's collapse and offered it to the man. For several moments Kozlov made no effort to take it but at last he reached forward. Attentive, Charlie saw that the man's hands were shaking. Kozlov held the print for a much longer time and Charlie had the impression of the man becoming visibly smaller in front of him. Charlie said, with practiced carelessness, "There's a lot more."

Kozlov's reaction was not what Charlie expected. When the Russian looked up he appeared wet-eyed. He said, "I love her, you know. I love Olga."

"Like you loved Valentina?" There was a gain in continuing this conversation.

Kozlov winced, as if he had been struck. "Irena told you everything, didn't she?"

"A lot," said Charlie, wondering what else he could learn.

"I thought I loved Valentina, at the time. I don't know, not now. I only know about Olga."

This was like being a bloody Agony Aunt: Dear Charlie, I am humping three different women but can't make up my mind which one . . . Charlie said, "What about Irena?"

"Have you any idea what that woman's like!"

"Some."

"She's made me live in hell, for years."

"Bad enough to kill for?"

"I asked her for a divorce."

"She told me. For Valentina, not Olga."

"I don't care what you think: what you believe," said Kozlov.

Charlie was thinking and believing a lot. He believed that Kozlov did love Olga Balan and he thought that was going to make everything a lot easier than it might have been. Time to start wrapping it all up into neat little parcels. He said, "I made the right assessment, didn't I?"

Kozlov looked at him, uncomprehending.

"You *are* fucked, aren't you, Yuri? Every way you look. How much longer before Moscow will discover Irena's not around anymore? Filiatov is back there now, talking his head off to stop the pain. And any moment I want I can feed the information through. . . ."

"All right!" The yell this time was despair, not defiance.

"You didn't let me finish the option, Yuri."

"What do you want?"

"To help you," announced Charlie, simply. He stopped, intentionally, wanting the idea to register with the other man.

"Help me?"

"Well, you don't want to go back to an interrogation cell in Butyrki and then on to some gulag for the rest of your life, do you!"

"Help me how?"

"Get you safely out, to the West . . ." Charlie made another intentional hesitation. "And Olga, too," he finished.

"Olga!"

"You want to be with her, don't you?"

"Yes, but . . ."

"No buts. Both of you."

"Together?"

The training was emerging, through all the confusion, recognized Charlie. He said, "Not to begin with. You told me how the Americans wanted you and Irena, when we both thought it was a genuine defection. If I try to take you *and* Olga out, the same thing would happen: a pitched battle. My way you both get out and then you're reunited, very soon."

"How soon?" insisted the man.

"I'd even arrange a date," said Charlie. "That's part of the proposal."

"I want to hear it all," said Kozlov.

"I'll tell you and you can check," said Charlie. "Irena told me about Hayashi, at the airport. He'll confirm the Americans are there, with a military plane. So are we. I will take Olga, first. You follow, as soon as you know that we've cleared air space and can't be intercepted by the Americans. Fredericks is setting up the same contact procedure for you as before, at the Imperial. He expects to hear from you. . . ."

"You are working together?"

Charlie wasn't sure how to answer the question. He said, "Not together: we're keeping to the arrangement that we thought we had, originally."

"Are you sure it is necessary to cross separately?" asked Kozlov, doubtfully.

"Aren't you?" said Charlie.

Kozlov didn't reply and Charlie thought, I'm ahead of you, you crafty bastard. He said, "You're thinking, of course, why bother letting Olga come with me? Why don't the both of you go together to the Americans? That's what I'd be thinking, if I were you now. But you mustn't ever forget the file, Yuri . . . the file that's got more than McFairlane's name on it. Names like Bill Paul and Valeri Solomatin . . . and a very special name, a Senator William Bales . . ."

Kozlov was rigidly still and ashen, lips moving but without any intention of forming words.

". . . Fucked, Yuri, unless you do it all my way," insisted Charlie. "Hayashi will tell you about the military planes, like I said. We're watching them and they're watching us, so I'd know before the wheels went up if you ducked me, to take Olga along with you. And then I'd have London tell Washington all the names they don't know. Can you imagine the reception you'd get? I guess there'd be some debriefing: why waste an opportunity, after all? But then do you know what I think? I think you'd end up in some stockade and you'd be able to close your eyes and believe you were back in a Russian prison, after all. Maybe worse than a Russian prison: can you imagine that!"

The words came at last, a croaking, strained sound: "I understand . . . there's no need . . . no more . . ."

"Oh yes," contracted Charlie. "There's more. I haven't told you yet how you're getting to England."

Kozlov was looking at him dully, practically glazed-eyed, someone completely defeated, and Charlie said, "You hearing what I'm saying?"

"Yes," said Kozlov. "I'm hearing it all."

"We're using the Americans to get you out, without the sort of battle that would occur, probably getting everyone seized, including both of you," set out Charlie. "In Washington, there will be the debriefing. String it out; make them work for everything. And be difficult. Complain about the restrictions of the safe house and say you want to take trips out. They let it happen: they shouldn't but they do. Today's the sixteenth. Three months from today, the sixteenth, get taken into Georgetown: all the restaurants are there. And a particular hotel. It's called The Four Seasons and it's at the very beginning of the district. There's a large foyer bar and lounge: lots of plants. Break away from your escort on the sixteenth and come there. I shall be waiting from noon until four. . . ."

"But . . ." Kozlov started to protest.

"There could be a dozen reasons why you can't make it," anticipated Charlie. "I know that. So we'll run a fall-back precaution. If you can't make that first time, the sixteenth of every month from then on."

Kozlov nodded, assimilating the instructions. "And then I would be with Olga?"

"From that moment on," promised Charlie.

"Thank you," said Kozlov, in abrupt gratitude.

"It's not altruism," said Charlie. "We want you both."

"When?"

"At once: certainly in the next twenty-four hours."

"I'll have to talk to Olga."

"Do you have a way to contact her?"

"She is calling, to see if you came."

"Then tell her to come here."

"She's a good Russian . . . like I think I am a good Russian."

"It's too late," said Charlie, who'd heard it all before.

"For me, maybe. Not for her. There could be a defense."

"We want her, too," said Charlie, quietly.

Kozlov made an effort to straighten in front of Charlie and said, "I see."

"I told you it wasn't altruism."

"You'd really use your Moscow source against her?"

"Of course we would," said Charlie, brutally. "Don't be naïve."

"She can't be hurt . . . mustn't be hurt. . . ."

"Don't let her be."

"What's it feel like, not being able to lose?" asked Kozlov, in abrupt viciousness.

"What's it feel like to have someone in the cross-hairs of a gun sight seconds before you press the trigger and know there's not a damned thing the poor bastard can do, to avoid being killed!" came back Charlie, just as viciously. "Don't moralize to me! We're not in the business of morals."

"It must be her choice."

Charlie didn't know why the other man was playing games but he said, "Set out all the alternatives and let her make it."

Which was what Kozlov did.

First—while they were waiting for her to arrive—Kozlov checked with Hayashi at the airport and got the confirmation that the American and British military aircraft were there, officially in transit. And then reluctantly—once actually picking up the receiver and replacing it, before lifting it again—Kozlov called the Imperial Hotel and spoke to the Americans. Liaison was still Jim Dale, but the room this time was 202.

The knock was hesitant and Olga Balan's entry was uncertain, too, looking at Charlie with an expression difficult to define, a mixture of hostility and curiosity and fear. Kozlov said his name and she nodded and then he said her name and Charlie nodded back.

Kozlov said, "I think we should talk alone," and Charlie said, "Don't be stupid," intentionally reducing the man in front of his mistress. He was aware of the feeling registering on Kozlov's face and thought, I bet you'd like to, my son.

"And in English," he said. Would he have remembered the Russian he'd learned so well—and anxiously, in love after so long—from Natalia? Probably, unless there had been some dialect difference: still better self-protection to let them believe he did not have the language. Was there a similarity between this Russian woman and Natalia? Perhaps but then again perhaps he was trying too hard to find one. The other comparison, now that he could see Olga Balan other than in a photograph, obviously followed and Charlie thought again of Irena with a pimple on her strap-red but naked shoulder and decided as he had in Hong Kong that it was no contest. The rain had eased, but Olga was still wet and the strain of the previous days was clearly visible; despite all of which she was beautiful. Startling, in fact. She sat oblivious to him, near the window through which the lights of the port were becoming clearer, head forward to hear everything Kozlov said, the femininity—and the sex—radiating from her. How did Kozlov get a woman like that? thought Charlie; life was never fair. The reflections held part of his mind but he listened to the Russian's exposition as intently as Olga, alert for several things. He wanted to insure that Kozlov set out their earlier conversation but he was intent, too, to catch any small mistake or inflection to indicate that what was happening in front of him was a charade, an act put on to lull him into whatever false impression for them to try something that he hadn't anticipated. There wasn't anything.

"Defect!" she said, when Kozlov finally proposed it.

"You got a better idea?" said Charlie, coming into the conversation.

Olga made a don't-know shrug. "What would I do, in the West?"

"Cooperate," said Charlie, regretting the glibness.

"Be a traitor, you mean!" she came back at him.

"Yes!" said Charlie. "It's a hell of a lot more fun than being dead or shifting rocks with your bare hands for the rest of your life. Or becoming a gulag gang-bang hooker."

"Bastard!" shouted Kozlov. He used the Russian expression, which conveys greater obscenity, and Charlie came back in Russian, just as fluent and using the word the same way. "Try to see what a bastard!"

"We would be together, in the end?" said the woman. "Yuri and I?"

"Wasn't that how Yuri explained it?"

"Only three months?" she persisted.

"Providing Yuri gets away the first time."

She sat staring at him, not speaking for several moments. Then she said, "This is really ridiculous, isn't it? We haven't got any choice, have we?"

"No," said Charlie, bluntly.

"So what's the point?"

"You already asked that."

There was another protracted silence. Some tension seemed to go from her and she said, "Did you know him well?"

"Yes," said Charlie. "There was a wife and a little girl."

"He wasn't meant . . ." she tried, but Charlie came in sharply and said, "Does it matter, now?"

"I suppose not."

"Shall we go?" Charlie said to her.

Olga looked down at herself. "I didn't come . . . I haven't got anything. . . ."

Just like Irena, that day on the bus, thought Charlie. He said, "What is there?"

There was another don't-know shrug and this time a didn't-know outburst. "Oh God! Dear God!"

Not here or at the one walled church in Macao, thought Charlie. He said, "Ready?"

Kozlov and Olga both stood, looking at each other, restricted and embarrassed by the presence of Charlie, who remained neither restricted nor embarrassed, looking at them. They kissed, clumsily, as if they were coming together for the first time and parted the same way.

"Be careful," she said.

"And you," he said, matching the banality.

"No contact with the Americans until you know we are clear," reminded Charlie. He enjoyed the irony of invoking for his own protection the bullshit that Kozlov put forward to Irena, to get her into the firing line.

"I know what to do."

"The sixteenth, three months from now," insisted Charlie.

"I know that best of all."

"Just don't forget," said Charlie.

He alerted Clarke from the apartment and when they got out into the street they found the rain had stopped: in the heat that is always there during the season there was a rise of mist— more like a steam—and Charlie thought it really was like a swamp.

"What about passport?" she said, in the taxi.

"It's an entry, not departure, document. And you're going out under the aegis of the British government."

"What's going to happen to me? To Yuri and me?"

Kozlov certainly had a way of screwing up women, thought Charlie. Maybe it was literally that but surely it couldn't be just sex. He said, "It'll be fine, you'll see."

There was no difficulty with the diplomatic departure and within thirty minutes of their arrival at Haneda they were airborne: as the plane gained height Charlie had the impression of a great weight being lifted from him, at the release of knowing Fredericks was keeping to the agreement.

They sat separate from the army contingent, farther along the body of the plane. Major Clarke was plugged into the pilot communication and after about fifteen minutes he walked up to where they sat in their canvas webbing seats and said, "We've cleared, sir. We're on our way to England."

He seemed to expect some response from the woman and when it didn't come the soldier said, "Sorry about the seats. Not very comfortable, I'm afraid."

Charlie guessed it was the first time Clarke had been involved in an operation like this and that the man was enjoying it: material for a dozen dinner-table anecdotes—"Have I told you about the time I got a genuine KGB agent out from under the Russians' noses!"—but anyone who kept on calling him sir was welcome to whatever anecdote until it became threadbare. Answering for Olga, Charlie said, "The seats will be fine."

Clarke gave up on Olga. To Charlie he said, "It was really all remarkably easy, wasn't it?"

Charlie looked quizzically up at the man, deciding it was a genuinely innocent question. "Yes," he said. "I suppose you could say that. Easy as can be."

Winslow Elliott was with the Special Forces group who watched the British plane go and Elliott said, "She was there! It was all crap! He got her out tonight!"

Jamieson said, "So maybe we struck out." It had turned out to be a shitty assignment. You win some, you lose some, he thought: just follow the orders and think of the pension and the PX facilities. It was stupid to make it a personal thing.

"Know what I'm going to do! I'm going to turn in a report showing how Art Fredericks fucked this up, every step of the fucking way. That's what I'm going to do," Elliott promised himself.

The Special Forces colonel, more experienced in the way of buck-passing and report-filing than the CIA fieldman, said, "Wait awhile, buddy. See how the whole thing shakes down before you start throwing garbage into the wind."

At that moment Yuri Kozlov entered the enormous lobby of the Imperial Hotel, no longer concerned about security—no longer concerned about anything—and walked up to Fredericks, who was waiting for him at the steps leading into the sunken lounge.

"Thank you for being here," said Kozlov.

"I'm glad you finally made it," said Fredericks.

Fredericks didn't give a shit if the Russkie or any of the CIA guys watching were aware of how relieved he was. He'd just saved his ass.

30

The airport arrival in London went as smoothly as the departure from Tokyo. The aircraft went to the private, northern section of Heathrow, where the transportation was ready: a helicopter for Olga—and female as well as male escorts—to fly her undetected by any doubtful Soviet interception to the safe debriefing house in Surrey. And a surprising limousine for Charlie, with the sealed instruction carried by the security-cleared driver to go directly to Sir Alistair Wilson's house, in Hampshire.

"It's Sunday," reminded the driver.

Charlie lounged in the back of the vehicle, savoring the unaccustomed luxury. There was even a cocktail cabinet recessed into the seat in front and Charlie pulled the flap down and saw that the cut-glass bottles were full.

"Help yourself," invited the driver. "Comes off the Ministry of Work budget."

"It's been a long flight and it's early," refused Charlie. Guessing the reason behind the invitation, he added, "Bottles don't look full to me," and the driver smiled appreciatively at him through the rear-view mirror.

It *had* been a long flight and Charlie felt buggered. There hadn't been any proper washing facilities on the transport plane—the lavatory had been a hear-the-splash affair behind a canvas screen—and he felt sticky and he knew he was stubble chinned: he wondered if there was any gray in the growth. He was aware the suit looked even more than usual as if he had slept in it, which on this occasion he had but not well because the webbing seats he'd assured that cheery major would be fine had turned out to be damned uncomfortable: paratroopers weren't brave, just smart enough to know how to get out of the bloody things as quickly as possible.

A posh car with a driver in a uniform and a cubbyhole full of booze was a definite improvement. And indicative. If he were still in the shit he wouldn't be getting the welcome-home-little-hero treatment: well, maybe hero was a bit strong, but the rest was near enough. On a scale of ten, he was shooting at least eight. Charlie glanced again at the drinks cupboard, reconsidering a celebration. Better not: always the chance of the unexpected steel-shod boot and there had been too many of those in the past few days.

The driver turned off at a Micheldever sign and looped through lanes that hadn't been built for cars this size and certainly not at this speed and Charlie hoped the driver didn't go at the cocktail cabinet too hard before the journey back. He was grateful when they swept into an unmarked drive, past gate pillars surprisingly with no gate and a gatehouse even more surprisingly with no attendant. Charlie's unease was just forming when they came to the security, sensibly placed halfway up the drive where it was not visible from the road. Hidden though it was, the cordon was still discreet, the replacement gatehouse looking like its predecessor but less lavish, a boxlike guardhouse it really was but to unknowing visitors and tradesmen designed to look like a retraction forced upon a landowner whose fortunes were diminishing. It was, in fact, perfect protection, pitched upon an obvious elevation with a soldier's eye view of any approaching from the highway. The attendant was close cropped and upright and clearly ex-army and because he was looking hard Charlie managed to identify the concealed antennae which would be linked to the electronic surveillance of the place. Absence of any high wall was understandable: ground sensors and infrared television cameras were far more effective. The pass check was very thorough and when they went through Charlie saw there was a second man in the tiny building.

Sir Alistair Wilson's home was a square-built, weathered-red mansion with a parapet around the roof edge and matching, miniature parapets before all but the ground-floor facing windows. The front of the house was bearded with cut-close creepers buried in which—because he was looking and recognized them—Charlie picked out three surveillance cameras but guessed there were more.

The house was not, however, the focal point of the approach. It was the rose beds, laid out with the squared and rectangular perfection of the attack formations of Wellington's red-coated armies and with the same regimentation of colors, beyond the reds to oranges and pinks and whites and yellows and crimsons and peach. Everywhere was dominated by the varying smells when Charlie was let out of the car: the driver called him sir and Charlie decided it was becoming a habit.

Another man with a soldier's haircut opened the door but the Director was already clumping across the black-and-white-tiled entry hall, hand outstretched in greeting: "Charlie! Well done, Charlie! Good to see you back in one piece."

"There were times when I didn't think I would be," said Charlie. He rubbed his chin and looked down at himself. "Afraid I didn't have time to . . ."

"Didn't expect you to," said Wilson, dismissively. He said—an order, not an invitation—"You'll stay for lunch," and then, "Before drinks let's walk in the garden," and set off despite the stiff leg at a pace Charlie had trouble matching. The Director led him through a leather-furnished library, out through French windows, and directly on to the rear of the house. There were even more rose beds in military formations and Charlie thought, an army to the back and an army to the front. At the rear, ramblers replaced the creepers of the approach and the cameras here were placed again to be scarcely visible: if he hadn't been looking he wouldn't have seen them.

Wilson jerked his hand toward a pink species and said, "Displayed at Chelsea this year: got a commended."

Charlie was unsure what was expected, so he said, "Well done."

"Do better next year," said the Director. "Irena's singing her head off, incidentally; can't stop talking."

"Olga won't," said Charlie, positively. "There's still a lot of remorse at the killing—shock I suppose—but eventually she's going fully to realize what she's done by coming across. She's not a defector, not like they normally are."

Wilson pulled a branch of something yellow toward him and

said, "Smell that: isn't it wonderful? She's here though, isn't she? She'll have to cooperate, finally."

"I suppose so," said Charlie. He seemed to remember apologizing before but decided a repetition wouldn't hurt. "Sorry for any upsets."

"All forgotten," said Wilson, breezily. "Even got a congratulation at a session of the Intelligence Committee. Our estimation of Soviet technology espionage was about eighty percent too low: Irena's giving us names, dates, places . . . and everything about what her husband did. Names, dates, places, as well. She's very bitter."

"Got a bloody good reason to be."

"She's asked about you, incidentally."

"Asked what?"

"Seemed to think you would be her debriefing officer."

"What was she told?"

"Nothing positive: we'll have to put you in, of course, if we think there's something she's holding back, for you."

"I don't think we built up much reliance," said Charlie, wanting to avoid the chore.

"She seems to think you saved her life," disclosed the Director.

Reminded of someone's life which hadn't been safe, Charlie said, "Has Harry Lu's family arrived?"

"Yes," said Wilson.

"That's all going to be okay, isn't it?"

The Director stopped at the end of a walkway, did a smart about-turn without any apparent difficulty from his stiff leg, and announced, "Drinks and lunch."

Charlie followed, with foreboding, but didn't press because he knew it had to come as Wilson dictated. The Director poured the scotch, heavy handed, and Charlie dutifully expressed admiration at more roses displayed around the room and reminded the ex-soldier that Jun Hayashi was still in place in Haneda. Wilson said the decision had been made to do nothing about the man until Irena's debriefing had progressed to their uncovering the complete extent of Japan's witting or unwitting involvement in the high-tech smuggling chain, when Hayashi might be useful as a bargaining counter with Tokyo.

The meal was beef, thick carved, and there was a bottle of

Margaux on the table between them and another opened and breathing on a sideboard, for when the first was drunk.

"Don't like the officialdom of government service," started out Wilson. "Never have done."

"I have difficulty with it myself sometimes," said Charlie.

"Bloody forms and columns of figures."

"I'm not looking forward to getting back to that," said Charlie, anxious to keep an important conversation going.

"Think you should," said the Director. "Had a man in the regiment once, first-class soldier operationally but a lousy administrator. Got himself involved in some mess account and there was a discrepancy or two. Payments to tradesmen for which there were no receipts, that sort of thing. Forget the figures: eight hundred pounds comes to mind but I think the final audit was nearer eighteen hundred. Hell to pay: couldn't protect the poor bugger, although I didn't want to lose him as a soldier. Tragedy: an absolute tragedy."

"I can imagine it must have been," said Charlie. Christ, what a smashing bloke Wilson was! Charlie said, "Strange that we should be talking of accounts. Had a long conversation with Harry Lu, before he was killed. It was all a misunderstanding: just forgot to list those informants."

Wilson topped up their glasses and said, "Ah!" but there was a great deal of satisfaction in the expression. Then he added, "Glad you did that."

"I do like to keep the records straight, although I don't enjoy the form filling," said Charlie.

"Nuisance factor of the job."

"Nuisance factor of the job," agreed Charlie.

"We haven't talked about Yuri Kozlov yet," said the Director.

Charlie set out the meeting and the ultimatums of the previous day in Tokyo and Wilson sat nodding and adding to their glasses when it was necessary and when Charlie finished the Director said, "I like that. I like that a lot."

"I want to make it happen," said Charlie, a promise to himself.

"I don't think you can go, not the way the Americans feel," said the Director.

"I told him I would be the one."

"I suppose you could use a different passport but we've hammered that system a bit lately," said Wilson, doubtfully.

"We've got time to think it through," said Charlie.

"You're right," agreed the Director, reaching around for the second bottle. He said, "You must be bloody tired, what with the flight and everything."

Charlie recognized it wasn't a polite, social inquiry. Accepting the opening, he said, "Yes I am. Very tired."

"Why not spend a couple of days at home, resting up? No need to come into the department until, let's say, Wednesday at the earliest."

"That's extremely thoughtful," said Charlie.

"Never have been able to get over the tragedy, losing a first-class field soldier over a miserable eighteen hundred pounds," reflected the Director.

"Like you said," agreed Charlie, "a tragedy."

"An absolute tragedy."

When Charlie opened the cocktail cabinet on the return to London he found the whiskey decanter half-empty: the driver took the lanes back to the motorway with considerable care and Charlie decided that half a bottle for half the speed was a pretty good deal. He said, "Sorry I can't offer you one."

"Never drink and drive," assured the man. "Good meeting?"

"Couldn't have been better," said Charlie.

The memorandum from Harkness, demanding an immediate meeting, was uppermost in Charlie's in-tray when he arrived at the office on Wednesday, so he put it to the bottom and summoned a messenger instead of using the interoffice postal system, entrusting to the man his own expenses with an explanation of the addenda and in a separate envelope enclosed a list of informants with a second memorandum that they constituted the omissions from Harry Lu's accounts. Hubert Witherspoon was a blurred figure through the fluted glass. Charlie flickered his fingers but the man didn't respond and Charlie thought, fuck you then.

The telephoned summons did not come until after lunch, which was longer than Charlie had expected, and he guessed the deputy had been adding up the figures and he hoped he'd got them near enough right.

"You wanted to see me?" he said, ingenuously, as he entered Harkness's office. It was directly below the Director's, with a lowered view of the park.

"Do you believe in coincidence!" demanded Harkness.

"I've heard it said that life's full of them," replied Charlie.

The pink face became pinker. "You seem to have realized your previous expenses had a discrepancy of something like eighteen hundred pounds: and although you drew a thousand pounds before you went to Japan, you seem to have spent five hundred more than that."

"Lucky I had my American Express card," said Charlie. "I attached those little blue receipt things."

"You didn't use the card and retain the money!"

"Of course not," said Charlie. "That wouldn't be honest, would it?"

"No," said Harkness, sharply. "It wouldn't have been honest."

"I don't find accounts easy," said Charlie, apologetically. "You may even have thought that yourself. But I do try to keep a rough tally. According to my records, the department owes me five hundred pounds."

It seemed difficult for Harkness to talk. He said, "To be precise, it's five hundred two."

"See!" Charlie smiled. "I don't find it easy."

"I don't find some things easy, either," said Harkness. "Like coincidence, for example. I've checked the registers against the names you list for informants to whom you paid money and against the names that you've offered to whom Harry Lu paid money. And do you know what I found?"

"What!" said Charlie, his voice apparently excited at the thought of a revelation from Harkness.

"All the names on your list and all the names on Lu's list are of diplomats or staff who *were* serving at an East bloc consulate or installation but have since been withdrawn."

Charlie regarded the other man innocently. "If they were still serving in the West, you could hardly ask them if they were acting as spies for Britain, could you?"

"Were they?"

"But of course!" said Charlie. "In my case, I'd swear to it. I can only pass on the names that Harry gave me, naturally. He didn't feel it was safe, from a security point of view, to put them in those reports that you ordered."

There was a long silence from the man at the desk opposite. "Reports?"

"The case histories you asked for: a record, in fact, of what Harry did for us over a lot of years," said Charlie. "I know I can talk to you in the strictest confidence. . . ." He sniggered, as if he'd made a joke. "What else, considering what we are and what we do? But he told me he was very surprised and I must confess that I was, too, at assembling together in one document something that would cause so much troubling with Peking— sorry, they call it Beijing now, don't they?—if it ever became public. You know what?"

"What?" Harkness's face was crimson masked, like the makeup of those actors in the traditional Japanese theater that Charlie hadn't this time had the opportunity to see.

Charlie extended the moment, enjoying it. He said, "Harry was bloody good. Although I understand some people didn't think so. Harry actually thought there was something odd, in the request: maybe that there'd been some Chinese or maybe KGB infiltration into the department here. He took precautions, of course."

"Precautions?" Harkness was actually talking now with the strained, grunted delivery of that Japanese theater.

"Well, he didn't want to let us down, did he?" invited Charlie. "Maintained a copy, along with all the requests from London. From you. Just to be on the safe side."

"Does his wife have the copy?"

"She knows about the document but Harry was too professional to entrust it to her," said Charlie. "Said something about it being an insurance for her. A bank maybe . . ." Charlie smiled, brightly. "Talking of which, no objection to my drawing that five hundred two pounds, is there?"

"No," said Harkness. It was obviously difficult for him. Then, distantly, he said, "One day."

Charlie, who knew what the promise meant, thought, one day, asshole: but it would be a long time coming.

Epilogue

There is a narrow sliver of green where M Street leads into Georgetown and there are bench seats beneath the few trees. It was upon one of them that Charlie sat, on the sixteenth of the third month and not in the jungled interior of The Four Seasons lounge. So far, he thought, so good. In the end they had decided against overusing the passport-issuing facility but Charlie had been cautious, not attempting to enter America directly but flying first to Canada and then crossing the border from there. The check had been cursory but Charlie wasn't relaxing. Everyone else seemed to be. It was difficult to believe, watching the shorts-and-halter-topped promenade before him, that the tie and suit manufacturers of America could ever make a living: and why didn't jogging do what it was supposed to? It couldn't, judging from the wobbly-bodied wobbling of the Sony-Walkmanned runners. Charlie knew he wouldn't wobble, if he tried it: be more like an uncertain, plunging-everywhere-at-the-same-time landslide. Meat pies in pubs had all sorts of hidden dangers. Not that the size of his stomach was a consideration, anyway. He wondered if any of those funny laced or belted or buckled or even buttoned trainer shoes would be better than Hush Puppies. Maybe he'd try them out, if he had time: if everything resolved today. He still hadn't checked to see if the Hush Puppies he was wearing could be repaired against the sort of rain he'd suffered in Tokyo: there was always a reluctance against exposing old friends to terminal judgment. A braless woman in a T-shirt that read YES BUT NOT WITH YOU and shorts tight into her rear and who shouldn't have risked either went bounce-bounce by and Charlie thought automatically of Irena and then, naturally, of Olga. The demands, from both—Olga first, then Irena—had begun at least a month earlier and the debriefings had ground practically to a standstill. Charlie knew that if he could bottle and market the effect that Kozlov had on women—one way and another—he could make a fortune.

Even frightened and running again—almost literally—Kozlov was an expert professional. Charlie was late seeing him, because the Russian was so good at merging into his surroundings, a weaving little minnow of a man in a sea of bigger fish, coming from the direction of Wisconsin Avenue and cleverly on the same side of M Street as the hotel, so he wouldn't draw attention to himself even crossing the road. Closer, Charlie was conscious of how intent Kozlov was, head swiveling as he moved, alert to everything about him and with everything to be alert about. Charlie, who had chosen the hotel because Kozlov would have to approach this way if the restaurant ploy worked, had tested the same approach twice, the previous day, and was sure that where he sat was concealed by the larger of the trees on the tiny rest area.

Nearer the hotel, Kozlov slowed further, actually stopping at the bookshop at the very junction and feigning interest in the miniscule window, using its reflection and the opportunity to pause to ensure that it was safe.

Although he was still a comparatively long way away, Charlie thought he discerned a shoulder lift of relief, at Kozlov's decision. Certainly the man moved off, toward the final two hundred yards to the hotel, with more apparent confidence, a head-up stride of an ultimate winner.

The seizure was very good.

There were two cars, a boxed arrangement, one behind the other and stationary and a third actually moving, able because of the confluence of the streets to go in either direction if Kozlov succeeded in getting away from the first two. He didn't because they were stretch wheel-based, black-windowed American limousines that fitted so well outside of the premier hotel and Charlie admired the choice. Kozlov passed the first, unaware of its rear doors opening behind him, and when he jerked to a stop, at those of the leading car suddenly blocking his path, it was too late because the men behind were already encircling him, thrusting him into the open-mouthed vehicle.

The people in halter tops and shorts promenaded on and the joggers jogged, no one realizing what had happened virtually in front of their eyes.

Charlie decided he really would try a pair of those training shoes: Reebok seemed a popular make. Maybe black, so with a bit of luck he could get away with wearing them with a suit.

"All wrapped up," praised the Director. "Three out of three: we get the goodies and the Americans get the embarrassment."

Strike while the iron is making sizzling noises, thought Charlie. He said, "I've been a long time at this grade. Just one up would be another two thousand pounds a year." Maybe a bigger carpet, too: could sell that to Witherspoon to impress all the secretaries he was trying to get a leg over.

The Director breathed in, a sucking sound. "Permanently desk-bound administration, Charlie. Didn't think you liked that."

"Like it better than exploding airplanes," tried Charlie. This must be how King Canute felt telling the tide to come back tomorrow.

"Why don't I think about it? No rush, after all."

He'd tried, decided Charlie, resigned. He said, "Told either of the women yet?"

"The indications are that the Russians are going to give one of their press conferences: the admissions of a mistaken defector," said Wilson. "We'll wait. If it happens, we'll let them both watch the television coverage."

"That should unblock Irena," said Charlie.

"Olga, too, in a different way," said Wilson. "The realization that she's lost everything."

"What about Herbert Bell?"

"Too good to arrest, for a long time yet," said the Director. "Bell's established his credibility for years, providing the KGB with the time and date of Yuri Kozlov's double defection, from the Americans to the British. We can use him for all sorts of disinformation now. Of it all, settling things this way was your best idea, Charlie. Inspired!"

"Think they will put Kozlov in front of a press conference?"

"It seems to be the formula, at the moment," said Wilson.

"Difficult, despite everything he did, not to feel sorry for the poor bastard, isn't it?" said Charlie. "Knowing what they'll do to him, I mean."

"An innocent family on a motorway," Wilson listed. "A Permanent Under Secretary and his secretary. A crippled driver. Harold McFairlane. A television technician at Fylingdales. Harry Albert. Bill Paul. Valeri Solomatin. A group of British soldiers. And a friend of yours, Harry Lu."

"No," agreed Charlie, changing his mind. "It is difficult. Impossible, in fact."